PRAISE FOR THE SEVENTH AGE: DYSTOPIA

"Dystopia *explores what really happens when magic has returned to the world. It's like Cyberpunk and* Repo Men *meets* American Gods *and* Dresden Files."

—Kevin J. Anderson, *NY Times* bestselling author of *Dune: Duke of Caladan* and *Clockwork Angels*

"In The 7ᵗʰ Age: Dystopia, Rick Henz one-ups himself by dialing the action to 11. Monsters, conspiracy theories, snarky humor, and enough action to leave you breathless —this has it all. Way too much fun!"

—Jonathan Maberry, *NY Times* bestselling author of *Relentless* and *Bewilderness*

"The Seventh Age Dystopia Galley is a ride of ridiculous awesomeness! What would happen if the world vomited paranormal everything as it was almost ending? THIS!!! The writing and characters are addictive. Grab a drink (or six) because you will never want to put this down!"

—Erika Lance, Host of *Drinking With Authors*

The End is Nigh!

SEVENTH AGE: DYSTOPIA

BOOK 2

RICK HEINZ

Seventh Age: Dystopia

Copyright © 2021 Rick Heinz In Association with Prince of Cats Literary Productions

Tell Me A Story

Copyright © 2021 Courteney Penney

All rights reserved. No part of this book may be reproduced or transmitted in any form or by any electronic or mechanical means, including photocopying, recording or by any information storage and retrieval system, without the express written permission of the copyright holder, except where permitted by law. This novel is a work of fiction. Names, characters, places, and incidents are either the product of the author's imagination, or, if real, used fictitiously.

Trade Paperback ISBN: 978-1-952825-22-4
Ebook ISBN: 978-1-952825-23-1
Cover design by Kind Composition

Front Cover Art copyright © 2021 Vivian Lieu
Back Cover Art copyright © 2021 Katherine Bolan
Interior layout and design by Kind Composition

Prince of Cats Trade Paperback Edition 2021
Published by Rick Heinz In Association with
Prince of Cats Literary Productions
New Jersey, USA 2021

LUCY'S LEXICON

AND PHOEBE'S!

(With contributions by Doctor Daneka)
I WROTE SOME SHIT—AKIRA

The Second City Crew—The Sons and Daughters: democratization of power! Or revenge, revenge is good.

- [ ] AKA Boss—Patron for the Lady of Fate. I CALL HIM BIGGER BOSS—A.
- Lucy—Demon Hunter Helldiver. *She's currently lost in Purgatory.*—P. (Told her not to go alone—D.)
- Mike Auburn—Naïve idiot who actually pulled it off. Slayer of Golgoroth. Got killed. AWW ... BOSS ISN'T NAÏVE. HE WENT TO BAT FOR ALL OF US, PLUS LET US EAT DEMON HEARTS.—A. *Stop being mean Lucy.*—P. (Dead is a matter of perspective in this world. Jury is still out.—D.)
- Akira—Slayer of Marcus Danbury, archfiend plague demon, Boss's assassin. *AND* THE BEST DAMN VIDEO GAME PLAYER EVER IN THE HISTORY OF EVER.—A.

- Doc Daneka—Son of John C. Daneka, who is the acting head of the Unification. Mike's friend. Useful. (Hear that Phoebe. Lucy called me useful.—D.) *Of course she did.—P.*
- Phoebe—Prophet of the blood. Can drive anything. Mike had a crush on her while still alive. Useless in a fight. *Ugh, now she's just being a catty bitch.* (It's not untrue.—D.) DON'T WORRY LOVE—WE'VE GOT YOUR BACK WHEN SHIT GOES DOWN. SLICE!—A.
- The Captain—Sorcerer who betrayed the Society of Deus. Soul sucked into hell. YEAH, GREAT CHAP, BUT HE'S *ACTUALLY* FUCKED.—A.
- Kevin Thayer—New recruit. Pure human. *Tribune* reporter. *Uh ... hrm.—P.* (Stop vague-prophetic—D.) *Fine ... don't get ... um ... attached.*
- Jack—Akira's new hunting partner. Captured. WE LET HIM GET CAUGHT.—A.
- Edward Morris—Mind-Controlling Vampire—Runs Chicago now. *Good ol' Morris, holding down our fort.*
- Frankie—Edward's zombie friend. Unfortunately missing.

The Triumvirate States—Texas. "Bettering" the world through science, AKA bigger gun wins.

- Peter Culmen—CEO of Triumvirate Enterprises. ('Nother Warlock, we need his boss so study up, team—D.)
- Alex Kristov—Lead Scientist at Atlantis and Scientific Liaison to multiple companies. Peter's apprentice.
- Jane—Phoebe keeps looking for her. *It's important! Trust me!* LIKE THAT TIME YOU THOUGHT A PACK OF SMOKES WAS AN ANGELIC HERALD? *Tellin' ya. Third seal shit.*

The Twin Cities—AKA—The Society of Deus. Magical elitists and vampire enthusiasts. *Who the hell wants to live for a thousand years?*

- Warlock Vryce—Sorcerer turned Warlock ascended to Lichdom. Killer of Mike. Fractured the world. Luckily dead. (All accounts point to his son taking his spot.—D.)
- Gabriel D'Angelo—Sorcerer and current Primus of the Society of Deus. *I can't tell whose side he's on. Like ... the humans? Or ... the monsters?* WE KNOW IT AIN'T LAZARUS.
- Alexandria of Ur—Thousand-year-old vampire. Dangerous. *Fuck this bitch. She is playing some long-ass game.*
- The Gargoyles (Onyx, Jade, and Obsidian)—Stone creatures used to defend sorcerers of Deus. ARE YOU JUST GOING TO LEAVE OUT THAT THEY USED TO BE OUR FRIENDS? COLD—A.
- Slade and Cael—High Sorcerers who serve Vryce.
- Charles Walsh—Former Director of the Unification, administers logistics over the region.

The Archive—Denver. Keeping world-ending empires in check one spy game at a time.

- The Praenomen—Sorcerer who appeared after the incident. Unknown agenda. *Yeah, I can't see any future or scry, but it's bloody Delilah with supercharged powers. It's like its fate is hidden. Boss wants to work with it though.*
- Symon Vasyl—Former French Resistance member, vampire, specialty in sabotage. DID ANY OF US MEET HIM LAST TIME?—A.
- The Whisper—Master infiltrator. Faceless vampire. HUH, AGAIN, ANY OF US *ACTUALLY* FIND THEM ON THE FIELD OF BATTLE?—A.

The Unification AKA Church of Lazarus. THIS WOULD BE A LONG LIST. CUT TO THE CHASE.—A. (Bah, they want to have everyone believe in one person so that person becomes God. With a capital G.)

- Lazarus—The first Lich. Returned from the dead eighteen months ago.
- Death Lords—Thirteen Lords of Death that rule over various aspects of Purgatory.
- Bollard—A demon who imprisoned Lazarus and helped set him free. HE BETRAYED US. *He got his due. Shredded and shamed by Vryce. Cursed to wander with no allegiance.* (Let a demon of his power roam free? I doubt he is out for the count.)
- John C. Daneka—The thirteenth Lord, the seat of Heaven's Wrath. Seeks to unify the world under one banner and one religion to unlock humanity's full potential. (Gee thanks, Dad. Could have done this better than killing a few billion—D.) WAIT ... IS IT HIM OR THE SOCIETY THAT ARE THE BAD GUYS? *From where I sit ... They are* all *the bad guys.*

TELL ME A STORY

No, not one of romance, where the hero
rescues a damsel in distress locked away.
Where the two fall hopelessly in love,
get the happy ever after from childhood dreams.

Not one where the villain is caught,
and locked away in jail forever.
Punished for all they have done
against the laws that offer false safety.

And not one where people enter danger,
only to exit unscathed and alive.
To go on with their lives successful
and happy with the ones they love.

No. Tell me a story of woe and fear.
Where the antagonists win, and
the protagonists weep red pools,
unable to take a stand.

A story where all that is known
is challenged. Where the damsel
isn't rescued, but is left alone in
the tower that she resides.

One where at the end of it,
despite it being full of misery,
you want to pick it up again.
A story where darkness rules.

—Courteney Penney

CHAPTER ONE

Are you alive? Do you seek glory? If so, join the Knights of the Sky and the US Air Force. Win silver wings to a golden future for humanity on the Midwest battlefield. Contact your local recruiting office today!

I've got a big top! Seven orders of Barghest Burgers, two slabs of Unicorn Ribs, and a chopped salad with ground pixie dust," Jane shouted through the flimsy back doors of the Devil's Steakhouse. An old-fashioned steakhouse catering to rich businessfolk who disdained T-Cellular Arena's more public dine-ins. It was the Saturday rush before the live weapons tests began outside, and with the top brass in attendance today—everyone was here for the show. *You're costing me my tips! Where the hell are you guys ...* "Hey! I've got a big top, I need ..." she said again, cracking the door open to the kitchen, greeted only by the empty room of a kitchen staff cleverer than she. They had abandoned her for a smoke break and left the kitchen's auto-cooker running.

Hip checking the doors open, Jane walked up to the small black kiosk with a huff. She hated this evil little contraption.

Injustice made manifest, you little dictator of a robot. With narrowed eyes, she started keying in the orders she had. All the kitchen staff really had to do was load the machine with ingredients and verify freshness these days; the little robot arms took care of everything. Customers, however, still preferred the idea that humans were handcrafting each meal special for them, so the owners at least tried to pretend. Servers (it was always servers) got the short end of the stick.

"Why can't you invent a robot to go out there and smile," Jane lamented between frustrated pokes at the machine.

"How would you like the burgers prepared?" the black box demanded.

"Uhhh ... medium," Jane guessed while looking back at the table of seven executives. They looked like a medium crowd.

"Did you upsell for garlic fries?"

"*Mmm*, sure." She clicked yes, knowing full well they hadn't, but who doesn't like garlic? It's not like any of them were vampires.

"It's taken you fifteen seconds to enter an order, you are behind by three seconds. Please increase your efficiency or risk demerit. You must check with customers for refills. Remember to ask about an extra shot for only ..."

"You show your true colors at last." Jane bopped the top of the box, setting the kitchen arms whirring into motion over the griddle. Yanking a loaded Barghest hellhound from the meat rack, the machine arms sliced parts of it and proceeded to ensure any blood left in the creature was drained and safely contained. Jane supposed it did make *some* sense to use a robot for this kind of meat preparation. Sushi chefs that knew how to properly prepare toxic blowfish weren't exactly growing on trees after the world ended, and the blood of demons wasn't exactly safe to consume. *Just enough left to make the meat really hook you in for a return customer. Like cigarettes but for red meat, gotta love it!*

She shook her head at the absentee kitchen staff but smiled nonetheless; who would really want to stay in here with a time-keeping robot. *It's probably better this way; boss will think they are out getting more ingredients from the market.* Loading up a tray full of drinks, Jane bumped her rear into the double doors and back into the restaurant. She had a full section today with one large table and a few stragglers eating solo at the bar. A quick glance at the time put an extra bounce in her step. It wasn't even noon yet and she was set for a fantastic day of tips. Wiggling between customers while carrying a large tray of drinks she was an expert in, as if she was a world champion dodge ball player. Glass after glass was unloaded on full tables with nobody really noticing her presence. By bending over just right, Jane could pluck a glass and replace it deftly and without any of the rude excuses or apologies. No need to interrupt important conversation, and Jane always hated when waiters would ask how things were when their mouth was full.

"So how is everything?" Jane asked a table while they were in midbite and unable to respond. "I see everything is fantastic then!" She nodded with a smile and was gone before they had a chance to swallow. *I may hate it, but I bloody damn well see why waiters do it.*

The door nearly slammed open as a large man in an ill-fitted (but expensive) suit bellowed a salutation as he waltzed in. Ignoring the **Please Wait to Be Seated** sign, he strolled right up to the bar and sat down. Jane *tsked* at seeing this, because it caused a trend where three more people just ignored her sign and took seats all around. A man wearing a houndstooth jacket joined the bar, a couple just walked in and grabbed a table near those finishing their meals, and a third lady with a wide-brimmed hat grabbed a window seat. *Okay, what the fuck, assholes. I have a plan here, and you're messing up my rhythm.* Eyes closed and a deep breath later, her smile formed again ... even if it was more of a smirk. *Right, got an executive, a teacher, debutante, and some cute couple. Knock on wood, I've got this.*

"Hi, welcome to the Devil's Steakhouse, I'm Jane and I'll be your server today. Can I start you off with something to drink?" She saddled up to the bar and pulled out her tablet with stylus and looked over at the executive. *Ewww. His teeth are smoke-stained yellow, and he reeks of body spray.*

"My, my, I sure see why they hired you, Jane." His elevator eyes drank Jane in. "Well, how about this. You bounce your little self around to each table, and bring them a bottle of your *Screaming Eagle Cabernet* ... that's the most expensive wine you've got, yeah?" He puckered his lips at her cut with a hearty chuckle. "Tell them it's on me, along with their meals and dessert. They just won the lottery. As for me, I'll start off with some Jersey Devil wings and a glass of that brandy inside the glass skull there, whatever that is."

Jane blinked. Frozen like a deer staring down the oncoming honking horn of a full military brigade. *That bill will be so much money. Each of those bottles is easily worth a quarter Bitcoin and that could be a crap ton! Plus ... I'm going to earn a crap ton of tips!*

"Ma'am?" The houndstooth man politely gestured with a finger.

Ignoring him, Jane refocused on her new favorite executive. "Yes, sir, yes, sir. Would you like those Devil wings spicy or just mild?"

"Ma'am?" the houndstooth tried again.

"Whatever works for you, Jane," the businessman replied.

"Right! I'll get right on this!" Jane furiously began tapping on her tablet and started merging the checks together. Once you had a table of a certain size, gratuity was automatically applied and already this was going to make her week ... or even month. *I might even be able ...*

"Ma'am?" The houndstooth flailed his arms.

"Oh! Sorry. Yes, sir. Hi, I'm Jane, wel—"

"Yes, yes, Jane, I've heard." He pushed up thin wire-framed spectacles. "Listen, I'll regretfully need to decline the offer from our friend here. I'll just be having some tea, and could you pass me the remote for the screens? There is something I wish to peruse while we are waiting for the show to start. Separate check as well."

Jane slid over the remote with a nod, not caring in the

slightest about what he wished to display before racing into the back room. With a flurry of rattled orders at the automated kitchen dictator, she hunted down the requested drinks; most of which remained locked in a metallic wine cooler. Behind her, the automated kitchen arms pulled the slab of a Jersey Devil thigh and set about cooking the requested wings. Bottles on tray, glasses set, wine on the cart; she hip checked through the door like a boss and set about informing the guests of their newfound fortune. *Cha-ching.*

Upon hearing the news, patrons of the bar not only thanked the man, but decided they'd all order that extra chocolate mousse pie or some other variety of dessert. Even with the excitement over his generosity, a creeping feeling of worry tingled the back of Jane's neck. *I really hope this guy has the money. I should start up a bar tab.* Protecting her own job security wouldn't really be rude, she reasoned. Job security also meant security for all ten fingers and toes since she had a place to live in the quarantine zone. *At least I can bring him the Devil wings.*

"Hey, there," Jane asked, setting the plate down. "Can I get your ID and scan your wrist to open up the bar tab?" She flashed a small card scanner and gave a damn good smile. "I'm also ready to take your order. What can I getcha?"

The executive sneered at the wings. "You didn't bring me these first? You stopped by every other table. They're cold." He pushed the plate of wings back in her direction, the steam still coming off them. "I'll try ... the Bunyip burger. Is that shipped over from Australia? Or does that robot back there just use Chupacabra meat?"

"Umm. I ... I wouldn't know. I just bring it out, but I can ask!" Jane gave a quick bow and ran back into the kitchen with the wings. *Who bows? Uh, I'm not dumb servant, why did I do that?* "Hey, robot! Is the Bunyip burger really Bunyip? Also, the Devil wings are cold, return them."

"The Devil wings are still within acceptable tolerance. The Bunyip burgers ingredients are a kitchen secret owned by—"

"Yeah, just make me one. Medium. Comp the wings."

"The Devil wings are still within acceptable tolerance; a comp will be removed from your pay."

Jane growled in frustration. *This is why ... we need* human *managers who understand difficult customers.* "Fine. My tips will more than cover a plate of wings," she said, grabbing a bite of the spicy wing. *Pretty good, tastes like turkey.* "Be right back!" This time, Jane went right to the executive first, readying his preferred brandy.

"So, our Bunyip is indeed a true Devil," she lied. "I've already got the chef started on it. What else can I get for ya?" She leaned over the bar, chin on fist and smiled. "Oh! I still need to get your scan. Who you work for anyway, hon? Pretty big celebration you're having."

His eyes darted down her shirt and his cheeks became a shade redder. "Yeah ... you wanna know don'tcha?" Taking a sip, he looked around the bar, which had become emptier as people finished their plates. "I invented Angel-Be-Gone," he boasted.

No fucking way. "No fucking way! The little bug repellant that kept out the freaky shit?"

"Yeah, that's right. One-an-only. Sold it for the big bucks today, and now we celebrate. But I've decided ... I don't want the Bunyip Burger. Let's change my order to ... I'll take some angel filet, medium rare, hold the Devil wings, they won't mix. Oh, and do me favor, toots. Make sure that burger doesn't appear on my check. I'm spending more than enough money here today." He puckered his lips and blew her a kiss.

"Yeah." *Fuuuckkk youuuu ...* "Sure thing." *Fuck you and the cow you rode in on.* Jane checked her remaining tables, each of them in need of service in some way, but if she waited on them first—Mr. Angel-Be-Gone would continue to make her life hell. "I need to win the damn lottery ..." she mumbled as she got to work.

"Waitress!" He craned his neck back. "I changed my mind about those Devil wings. Bring them back out ... and get me a refill."

"For fuck's sake ..." she muttered under her breath and pushed her way into the back room with a heavy sigh. "Robot!

Cancel ... the Bunyip burger." She cringed as she said it ... noticing the complete burger ready to go. *Guess I'm going to eat that as well.* "Order me a fresh plate of Jersey Devil wings and angel filet, medium, hold the wings." Jane pinched the crux of her nose, unsure at this point if she even got it right. "God damnit, I forgot the tab ..."

"The burger shall be deduc—"

"I know."

"Jane?" the machine asked. "I sense you are frustrated. There are seventeen other people waiting for your shift today. Would you like me to call you a replacement?"

"No, no, I'm fine. We'll get through lunch." *I'm not passing this tip up no matter what. He's on TV and gotta be filthy rich. If I ask him to tab it now, he might get offended.*

"Very well. Query?"

"What is it?"

"Did you upsell for garlic fries?"

Jane eyed a sharp kitchen knife laying nearby and contemplated her more immediate future. "I'm going to take a smoke break ... I need a bloody pick-me-up." She grabbed the knife. *Everyone else is gone, leaving me with little robot and a growing asshole of a customer. I can sneak a journey in with nobody noticing, can't I?*

CHAPTER TWO

Brooke & Talbots is the premier apocalypse gear team, bringing you the ultimate in survival equipment. Featuring today's line of Iron Lanterns, as seen in use by the worlds most vetted helldivers. These specially made hooded lanterns will shine through any darkness for hours at a time and reveal things hidden by ghostly trickery. Each one is handcrafted, right here in America, and now available in chains that are still open. Today is the day you stop living in the dark and step into the light. Only with Brooke & Talbots.

A ngels. Fuck Angels," Jane said, peering through a crack in the kitchen door. "How the fuck did we end up here?"

Eighteen months ago, Jane's world ended. A terrorist group calling themselves the Sons and Daughters convinced the entire city of Chicago that eating the hearts of demons was an excellent plan. Sure, like most people stuck in a rut, Jane found their rants engaging and underdog style fun ... but on December 21st, the sun rose as a shadow of itself. Stuck in a grayish, blackish, purple eclipse—those trapped in the lands of the dead escaped.

Everyone lost their damn minds.

Stock markets collapsed, the homicide rate skyrocketed, and every government in the entire world received a devastating blow as both religious leaders and scientists gave the universal shrug of "we're screwed." Now, America was a shadow of its former self, divided to the core; which Jane had long rationalized as one tiny step up from the rest of the world. In the northern Midwest, sprawling out of the Twin Cities, a militant band of blood junkies called the Society of Deus used witchcraft to turn back the gates of hell and the dead. Chicago and New York threw in the towel and just accepted that their doubled population now included dear-old-dead grandmas. With nearly every ghost from the past century returning, the cities were a hotbed for vendettas and revenge. The rest did their best while bracing for impact. Meanwhile, every doomsday prepper, militia, and gun owner fought tooth and nail against the apocalypse.

In Europe, religious leaders took hold. Democracy was shredded and replaced with a theocracy under the rule of Lazarus and his Church of Unification. Even Jane had a tough time ignoring their teachings when you could walk out and see the black sun. Inch by inch, world leaders accepted the Unification advice and found their cities saved from the plague of ghosts. Inch by inch, everyone slowly started accepting the insanity of the world as it was. There were still holdouts, like the Republicans in the US government, or the Society of Deus, or the Nordic countries ... hell, Jane figured that there were tons of groups that stuck their noses up at the Unification.

Then a hillbilly discovered Angel-Be-Gone.

One lucky doomsday prepper with too much time in the Appalachian woods applied old folk lore, fallen angel dust, and a can of Raid ... and *poof*: mosquito repellant for angels, ghosts, demons, and other such oddities that were crawling back into reality.

That shit sold like hotcakes. Money was made hand over fist and production skyrocketed. It didn't even take till the end of the week until every single damn company had launched new apocalypse-based products. Most of them blended it with science or some other nuwave namaste bullshit—or were clever enough to just lie. That single can of aerosol sparked an international triumvirate of corporate buyouts and product launches like the world had never seen. All they needed was a climate that was pro-business, anti-regulation, and a consumer base that was hungry enough to try anything.

- Texas was a perfect fit for corporation ground zero.

As governments took a massive blow, international corporations got a foothold as the ultimate power. *Magic has returned. Companies branded it. Joy.* Which led Jane to her current ... more pressing problem than her musings over corporate conspiracies. Waitressing.

The venture capitalist who found the hillbilly and struck it rich? Was sitting at her bar. To say her day began with his harassment of her demeaned the definition of harassment. Since he walked in, she had practically become his personal gofer. *Rich folks get away with anything, even in the end of the damn world. Pfft ... it's not even noon yet and this day already sucks.* Survival of the most marketable and all hail the almighty God of Commerce. Losing a job in Austin was a one-way ticket to being kicked out, and Jane wasn't feeling keen on living in a wasteland where cryptids might suck out her bone marrow for brunch.

Throughout her entire life, she had always seen ghosts, and the world thought she was nuts. *Let's load up her up with Ativan! That didn't work? She's too costly to treat, kick her out!* Of all places to be deemed unstable, Texas is not where you want to be; without a job or a lottery ticket they put you right on the other side of the safe zone. *Service with a smile, Jane! Get out there and smile ... or pucker up and take the easy way out.*

She didn't.

Jane pressed the cool metallic steak knife to her jugular and pondered her fate. With a single slice her problems would be solved. It would take ten seconds before she bled out, she reasoned. A massive cow took around forty seconds before it stopped twitching on a meat hook. But her? She was a generous five feet eight inches tall and weighed in at one hundred and forty-three pounds. A kitchen door with a small, grease-stained window stood between her bloody escape or another shift of forced emotional labor. Blowing a lock of blonde hair out of the way, she looked closer at her face in a nearby mirror. Her green eyes were puffy, and an eternal sleep would do her wonders. Ten seconds and she would be free from the jackass sitting in her section.

All it takes is a little pain. How bad could it be? One little slice; bang my head on the counter, flop to that ugly-ass brown tile, and then become a ghost. Easy. The knife twirled in her hand as she took a fighting stance and growled into the mirror. "Come on girl, you've got this. There are tons of ghosts out there. Why work for a living when you can float around aimlessly. It's not like you've got a shot of winning the lottery and being famous ..."

Turning the point inward, she jerked the knife at the side of her throat to plunge it in and screamed as she braced for impact.

It never came.

Her heart raced; it was all she could hear as her shitty world faded from view. The stadium bar she worked at melted away before her eyes. Ash flew off the counter tops, the lights became sickly green, and the walls cracked and crumbled away. The stink of iron and rust filled the kitchen. She took a gulping breath and wore a toothy grin while moving the blade away from her throat. *Not ready to go all the way, yet, are we, Jane?* The heart-clenching rush of blood thumping through her chest and feelings of anticipation washed over her like a cold shower of ecstasy.

"Fuck, yes! This is what I'm talking about," she exclaimed. Purgatory was a sight to behold, and she loved every second she could get with death two-point-oh. "Not eternal sleep, but, *mmm*, sweet momma this feels like my private heaven."

By now she had figured out adrenaline and a brush with death would get her seeing Purgatory. She had spent her life haunted by dead people, and when the Black Sun rose on December 21st, she got drunk and laughed. Ever since then—whenever the living pissed her off—she tried to kill herself. Flipping the steak knife in her hand, she chuckled and threw it off to the side. *It never works, though.* Any time she got close, the world would become this ashen, gray hellscape. Jane had to admit she'd been creative in her attempts. Everything from attempted decapitation to trying to live on nothing but late-night burritos for seven months straight; in the end, she always backed out at the last second. Adrenaline was her real drug. *Suicide is not a thing I'm capable of; can't get over that I'd just be a nobody, forgotten like Tuesday's trash. It's why I'm stuck with the living.*

Not wasting her precious seconds of solitude, she looked out at her arrogant customer. His smoke-stained teeth were midbite into a rotten sandwich. He wiped his hands along his expensive suit and scarfed down the meal like he hadn't eaten in weeks. With an array of spittle and food, he shouted unintelligible words at her direction in the back room. That's when she saw it. Beneath the jowls of his neck, right around his tie, rope burn marks from being choked to death. *Probably by me if he keeps this shit up. Who knows when you'll die, but at least I'll rest easy knowing its suffocation. That's a bitch of a way to die.* Glancing back into the mirror, she saw herself bloody, beaten, and torn apart for her own death. "Yeesh, I need to leave a better lookin' corpse than this."

As quick as it came, Purgatory vanished. Jane was left panting in the kitchen, tracing her fingers along the flat of the knife blade. She dropped it before the short-order cook came through the doors. Even though the dead had returned, she still needed money to live. *That was enough brushes with death today, I don't feel like attempting suicide via Texas gun enthusiasts trying out the latest in anti-freak hardware just yet. That shit is noisy.* Grabbing a pot of coffee, she bumped hip first out through the swinging double doors and put on her best customer service smile.

Her customer's face mutated from annoyed concerned over her scream in the back to unspoken sexual desire as she hip checked through with a smile. "Ah, aren't you rarin' to go with them legs and that smile? See, I told ya to smile for me, and consider how pretty you are now," the thick suit said. He had that annoying air of confidence, swagger, and money that dangerously combined with assholery. "Listen, babe, a young girl like you ... what are you ... twenty-four? World's gotta get repopulated, ya know? Why's a hottie like you workin' in an arena diner? You should find a man who can—"

"I have cats," Jane said. She recapped his coffee and did her best to hold snickers in. There were two customers in the diner, him, and a balding man in a houndstooth jacket. Mr. Houndstooth had been nothing but polite. "Hey, you know this will be your last meal?"

"The fuck you finding funny, bitch? I'm trying to help you out here. How you know I will die, anyway? You one of those blood junkies?" A fry vanished in his mouth hole. "Why say a thing like that for?" His eyes darted to the array of expensive dishes and drinks he'd stacked up.

Jane leaned in on the counter, planting her elbows over each side of his plate and gave him a kiss on the forehead. "Sorry, this is Austin, Texas, all the blood-freaks are up north. I can just tell. You've got the face of someone who won't make it in this city."

She sauntered down to the other customer and refilled his coffee with a victorious grin on her face. "What do you say? Think he will make it?"

The man in houndstooth pushed up his thin golden-framed glasses over his longer hawkish nose. Pale skin that begged for more sunlight, a condition more people suffered every day, somehow made him oafishly distinguished with his dirty blond hair and a receding hairline. "Well, on an infinite timeline we are all going to die ..."

"So not helpful," Jane replied. She operated under the continued assumption she was a living sack of meat. It was a shitty attitude to have and didn't do much to win her many friends. She had her reasons, though. When your entire family dies in a freak series of accidents when you are three, you get the distinct pleasure of being raised in the United States' award-winning foster-care system.

Her case left social workers speechless. Mother was killed by slipping on water near an open dishwasher loaded with knives, while Father met his end via airborne fire hydrant shortly after. While strapping her twin brother and her into car seats, her aunt was crushed to death by a *Taco Bell* sign. A superstitious foster-dad loaded her in a cab one night and shipped her out of state for her (or their) own safety. He fell off a crane in Chicago three days later.

Thus, she had become *really* adept at survival by any means needed. *And that survival hinges upon a daily paycheck from the safest job in town.* "You think for an adrenaline junkie ... I would pick a more exciting profession ..." she said aloud while cleaning tables.

"I'll give you a shot of—" the suit began.

"Here's your check. I hope everything was to your liking, please come again," she cut him off and set the check down while taking a tray of dishes to the back. *You better leave a tip. That was some magnificent poise on my end.*

A long whistle came from the Mr. Houndstooth. "You, sir, have been shot down."

Jane popped back into the dingy kitchen and let out an exasperated sigh. It was only noon, and she already had to retreat to Purgatory once.

The first day the black sun rose and *everyone* got their first encounter seeing millions of dead people got an appropriately apocalyptic reaction from everyone. She figured that out about ten minutes after she crawled out of bed on the first day of the Black Sun. She tried jumping out of her apartment window and ran right into the lands of the dead instead! Jane chuckled as she remembered it fondly while precariously balancing more dishes at the wash station. *I spent two whole days thinking I had become an actual ghost. Ha! Oh, black sun ... my gateway into Purgatory. I love ya to bits.* The cheers from the stadium outside bled through the windows in the restaurant. "Well, so much for letting a lady slack off proper ..."

She plopped up and sat down on the slimy prep counter and fished a smoke out of her apron, letting her feet dangle. "Fuck it." Screw stepping outside, she figured, and lit up with a shaky hand. Any brush with self-inflicted death screwed with her perceptions. Spiking up her adrenaline and bam; one-way trip to the reaper's waiting room. So, any time she needed the ultimate pick-me-up, an escape from the dismal realities of her current life, she brought herself close. *Annnd that's why I can provide service with a smile as a waitress. Look at me excel.*

Hearing the slight jingle of two bells placed on the door, she twisted out her smoke on a half-eaten burger. *Break's over; let's make some coin.* One skirt adjustment, bra strap fix, and a toothy smile later—Jane slid out of the back doors.

"Hi, welcome to the Devil's Steakhouse ..." There was nobody inside. Red wooden booths sat empty with leftover dishes, and the once-spotless bar was now littered with ashtrays and upside-down shot glasses. The TVs still highlighted a variety of talking heads and provided extra light for the otherwise dimly lit joint. But Jane's eyes only focused on one, particularly out of place, object.

The bills.

Out of the customers she had, one had left her a stack of free drink coupons for another bar in downtown Austin, and the asshole left her a note.

Get a real job bitch

"Oh, hell, no. I am *not* paying for you." Jane panicked inside. That suit had racked up a tab equal to a pack of drunk girls on Mardi Gras. Demon steak was also expensive as hell (even if it was just bison meat with a fake name), and at the end of her shift, she had to settle. With the deficit leftover—rent, food, her own booze, and smokes were off the table for the month. Living behind the quarantine zone was a privilege and one missed payment meant being homeless. *Fuck ... no, no, no. I can't ... I will not end up a crazy bag lady eating worms in Louisiana.* She ripped off her apron and bolted out the front door.

T-Cellular Arena was a major source of entertainment in the Triumvirate quarantine zone. At one point, it served as the perfect place for rabid sports fans getting drunk and having brawls while covered in body paint. Now, its wide, concrete reinforced corridors and open seating served as the showcase grounds for unimaginable weapon advances. Often by engaging in colosseum style battles with demons, fairies, and other mutated blood junkies from the north. Blood sports were a common occurrence. The joint she worked at sold fake Demon meat (and everyone knew) but unchecked capitalism reigned supreme. A giant blue banner dangled over the crowds.

Welcome to Utopia!

Jane knew she was a terrible waitress, her only gift being a damn good smile and an otherwise pretty demeanor, but that did not mean she was without talent in other areas. Even though the crowds were packed hip to shoulder waiting for the gates to open, she slipped and slid between them with ease. *The trick is not caring where their hands go while you lift what you need.* She doubted that her mark, the bastard who stiffed her, had the same talent. Cutting through the crowds was always a fun pastime for her. Ducking, weaving, a polite tap and a pretty smile, and making the right call to put your bum forward or your front was an element she excelled at. If she was a six-foot-tall lumbering dude, she would just shoulder check everyone.

One well-lit gate after another, and another, and another, Jane slipped through the crowds. Each time taking a moment to hoist herself on old metal radiators that lined the arena walls; a boost in height to scout ahead. *Shit. No mark in sight.* She picked up the pace, and half pondered doubling back after five minutes of searching. That feeling of self-doubt had taken hold, like a crippling panic attack pulling her lungs apart from the inside. *Do I go back? Make a run for it? Maybe I can just sell my liver for money?* It hurt her cause that every inch of the arena was covered in bright neon ads. Their constant barrage of marketing new security products or hawking some new alternative drug made the corridors look like a rainbow of desperation. With every color in the spectrum. Looking for a rich, cocky, arrogant—

The idea cemented in her head; she saw where he would be. His overly nice suit for a day like today, an expensive bar tab, and ordering every single thing he could. Even if he ate a nibble. *He's up for the trials. He's going* into *the arena.* Realizing her error, she gave a short elbow jab and cut crossways through the crowd to the nearest set of stairs. Two by three she bounded up a flight of stairs. She felt pleased that even being a smoker, she wasn't out of breath or feeling any burn yet. The fifth floor was where the entrants stood in line. Desperate suckers willing to try any new drug or gun, and put it to the test, live, for sponsorship. *He's loaded, why is he going there? The lottery is for those who've lost everything. Like me.* Once you won the lottery (or stole someone else's ticket) you could be an arena lifer. Everyone applied for the free tickets, more worked dangerous-labor jobs, a minority bought extra, and the rare hunted monsters for even more chances. Fewer still won the chance to peddle a company's products until you died, or the crowd hated you. *Least they're famous.*

The fifth floor was less crowded; more people came to watch the show than end up a lab rat for some untested drug. Small company kiosks lined the hallways with their products and samples on full display. Often with some scantily clad babe trying to convince others that angel dust mixed with almond paste would rejuvenate your skin. *Hey, whatever pays the bills, right? I'd do it if I could. I'd rather have their jobs than the wait for a lottery ticket every day.* Such posh gigs weren't easy to come by, though—you needed connections.

She didn't see him among the day's lucky lottery victors past the red velvet ropes, so her eyes flitted from one nervous, nail-biting applicant to another hopeful holding a lottery ticket, praying for their corporate salvation. *If I don't find this bloke, I'll be the one here praying.* Just down a tad, next to a Pelican Pharmaceuticals' booth, she heard a familiar sound. Luck, it seemed, was a little on her side.

"Don't you know who I am?" he shouted down at the technician.

Jackpot.

17

"I've got an alpha pass," he continued. "Vice president of—"

"Sorry, sir." The doctor stepped in to intervene, rescuing his intern. "You were stripped of board privileges last night. You're out. So, I can't let you in." The doctor leaned in closer.

People congregated around the Pelican kiosk. Its awkwardly poised Pelican mascot had a set of binoculars and little cupid angel wings. Besides the doctor and former exec, everyone else looked like they needed a little lottery in their life. Crutches, ragged clothes, a missing eye, and even a former suburban housewife in mom jeans with a wild look of murder in her eyes. Jane took this chance to creep closer and slip into the crowd. *People love watching someone successful fail hard. Heh. If he wasn't such an arrogant douchebag, I'd almost feel sorry.*

"Look, I'm sure we can work a deal out," the exec said. "I sold my company for millions and was given plenty on my way out. Let me in the trials. I'll sell millions of what you're peddling. You know I've seen the company footnotes so we both see what you've got on the horizon. Let me in. It wouldn't be the first time I've discovered a breakthrough."

Jane was close enough to smell the body spray on him now. Thick pungent spray that smelled of peaches and aerosol. *Angel-Be-Gone. He must've doused up before he came up here.* With a steady hand, she set the stage to steal his wallet. First was giving a crass smile and a knowing wink to the housewife in the crowd while making an ass slap gesture at the exec's rear. It warranted a chuckle from the housewife, and a mouthed silent "no way." Jane nodded and did it again. A few more chuckles. *Now!*

With a loud slap, Jane cracked the exec. Raucous laughter exploded among the crowd, and Jane quickly used her other hand to pry an oversized wallet out of his suit coat. Ducking back through the crowd, Jane giggled to herself. The crowd would protect her identity and keep her safe from retaliation as she slipped off with her prize. *Heh … sucker.*

Bounding back down the stairs with a little spring in her step. Jane flipped open the fat, worn leather wallet. Thumbing through a stack of Franklins the size of her hand, she discarded the hundreds on the floor like toilet paper. *Five hundred ... seven hundred ... one thousand five hundred ... no, no, no.* Her stomach turned knots ... *don't tell me.* The spring in her step faded, and she came to a complete halt in the concrete stairwell. Leaning on the rusted metal rail, Jane let out a cry.

"This fucker is broke ..." she moaned. *He sold his dumbass company for US bills ... there isn't a damn Bitcoin chip in here. Corps don't care about DC money anymore.* "I'm totally fired and even more in debt." Jane threw the wallet to the side and sulked down the remaining stairs. "I hope you get strangled by a chain demon in the arena, you bastard," she whispered under her breath. She was not looking forward to becoming homeless.

CHAPTER THREE

*You woke up tomorrow, the Republicans were still in control, what then?
Does their government provide you with food? Do they have the
weapons to keep us safe from the dead? End the welfare state. Science
paves our future with unprecedented technological innovation. Let
science be your light in these dark times. Vote for freedom. (Ad paid for by
the Technocratic party.)*

M aybe I can beg for my life?" Jane stood outside the
Devil's Steakhouse. Soft orange lights bathed the inside
of the steakhouse and stood in contrast to the oppressive fluo-
rescent arena lighting. She had to admit, for a bar tucked away in
an arena, it had a nice atmosphere—even if dated. It wasn't her
coworkers that scared her, they were semi-regular staff like her,
or her absentee supervisor. They were human. She could plead
her case and have discourse with them, perhaps finding a helping
dose of sympathy. No. It was the small digital kiosk tucked away
in the staff closet. That brickish little box logged every employee's second, every Bitcoin and every morsel of calorie that left its
little empire. *The Skynet of restaurant chains everywhere ...*

Running her fingers along the back of her left hand, she caressed the small black dot of an RFID tag that was implanted nineteen months earlier. A new medical procedure meant to store all your personal information for the budding corporate campus in Texas. Social Security number, clinical trial availability, special certifications, and even your credit score. *One month before shit goes haywire, they tag us like cows. Yay, patriotism. Go 'Murica.* What pathetically tried to stop illegal immigrants, now marked who could hold a job. Citizenship and border controls were stricter than ever now, and any crime, no matter how small, put you on the watch list. *They should put the asshole who didn't pay on the bloody watch list. Why do I have to take responsibility?*

She shook her head and walked in, the soft jingle of bells heralding her arrival to the empty bar. Thoughts of robbing the place and making a run for it crossed her mind. As did the grimmer thought of setting the place ablaze. *Blame it on a kitchen fire, destroy the kiosk overlord, it could work ... right?* Out of sheer habit, Jane wiped down tables. With the weapons showcase starting in the stadium soon, there wouldn't be any customers.

"Can I trouble you for more tea?" a polite voice said.

Jane jumped like a cat. "Holy shit!" She fell backwards into a table, knocking over salt shakers and spilling a glass of water.

"Careful now, salt is offensive to some customers. Old folk-lores and all ..." The man from earlier, in the houndstooth jacket, was sitting at his spot in the bar with a deadpan face.

"What the hell? When did you get back in here?" she said, pulling herself back up, her apron now a granular mix of salt-water and grease. *Gross.* "Also, how about some courtesy? You knew that would make my hair stand on end. Jerk." She threw the towel down and picked up the table.

"You remind me of a cat," he said, closing his eyes and sniffing the air. He stood up and walked over to pick up the towel and dried off a wooden chair.

The moment he came within arm's reach, her fear was sucked away. One second, she was on edge and jittery. Not just about his rudeness, but about getting fired, about getting eaten, about ...

everything. Watching the man calmly clean the chair, wiping it down in a circular pattern, calmed her. Thin wire-framed golden glasses and a receding hairline made him seem less threatening. With each hypnotic flip of a towel, her fears became lessened, and floated away. She was so enthralled, she convinced herself that he didn't have fangs after all. He clearly wasn't a vampire, sniffing and licking white fangs protruding down from ruby red lips. No, he was just a harmless chap in the bar.

It was the rhythmic shaking of the ground from the crowd chanting outside that brought her back to reality. Her customer was already back at the bar, sipping tea out of the only glass he could find, a beer stein.

"Bottoms up," he smiled.

Jane definitely saw fangs.

Okay me. Let's take stock of the situation. You are alone in the bar, a customer ripped you off earlier, there is a vampire drinking tea out of a beer glass, and five hundred feet outside they are testing heavy weapons. No one would hear me scream. But ... I don't even feel like I want to? An odd sensation to be sure. Her emotions told her she was fine, but every ounce of brainpower screamed for her to run to the door. *I've lost some time ... but not much. Did he already drink my blood? Is he some perv?*

"Welcome to the Devil's Steakhouse," she said reflexively. *Why say that? Stupid. Stupid.* Now more embarrassed than anything, she stood up and fidgeted with her apron.

"You can call me Doc," he said, gesturing to the bar. "You ran out earlier when I was in the bathroom, what happened?"

"Vampires don't use the bathroom; you're an undead," she snarked while heading behind the bar. "You know damn well what happened, that jerk stiffed me." She crossed her arms and leaned on the back counter.

"Knowledgeable about the undead, you think? Well, I won't say you are wrong. This might go easier than last time ..." Doc furrowed his brow with his gaze fixated to the ground. "So, did you kill him? The jerk, I mean?"

"What?" Jane grabbed a bottle of whiskey and poured herself

a shot. *Fuck it, Skynet will fire me anyway.* The fiery burn of black-barrel bourbon snapped her wits back into place. "Kill him? I'm not a blood-sucking northerner. What do you want here, leech? Your kind isn't wanted here. You know they are literally blowing up"—she flailed her arms at him—"whatever type freak you are ... right outside?" She slammed the shot glass down and poured another.

"Wow, so she was right about you." Doc held out his hands in a peace gesture. "Relax, I'm here to talk, not eat. I've been shooing customers out of this place ever since I arrived this morning. That last one wouldn't friggin' leave, however ..." He waved dismissively. "Regardless, I've already had a meal; I don't suck blood. I'm the world's laziest psychotherapist and I'm here for three things." He held up three fingers. "One. I want to watch the arena events from a safe spot. Two. I'm recruiting you as the next champion for the Sons and Daughters to fight a war against ancient creatures and demons. Three. I will buy that swordfish your owner has hanging off that wall."

Confused, Jane looked up at the taxidermized giant swordfish on the wall, its turquoise blue fin and silver body twisted as if it was still on a live fishing line. *The hell?* She took another shot—it helped. "So, let me get this right ... you want a dead, stuffed, swordfish?"

"It's interesting, that of the three options, you focus on that one. Says a lot about you," he said, taking a sip. "The matches should start soon; why don't you turn on the TV?"

"But ... wait ... I wanna ..."

The high-pitched sound of an energy rifle discharging outside preceded the loud roar from the crowd. The ground shook again. Jane fished out the controller, pressed her RFID tag to the sensor, and after being verified, flipped on several TVs in the restaurant at once. Each screen showed a different scene of the experimental corporate violence below.

Seven hellhounds, or Barghests, pulled against wrought iron chains near the thirty yard line, their blackened and reddish skin flayed open by protruding bones that formed spines along their backs. Despite the thickness of their chains, they stretched them taut as their jaws snapped at lottery winners across the field. Only a few patches of Astroturf remained behind them, blasted away by the demonstration. At the opposite end stood a handful of scientists in perfect white lab coats, monitoring the experiment while lucky winners got their fifteen minutes. Each winner held a new experimental rifle hooked into generators behind them. Banners with their company logo, MAGA Arms, fluttered in the wind while an MC announced the effectiveness of their railguns.

Another gun test. Booorrrriinnng ... it's just a shooting gallery. Jane hopped up on the counter and sat cross-legged. She remembered to grab the rare bourbon and took a swig out straight from the bottle. "Ahh, that hits the spot. I'm screwed anyway, so might as well enjoy this. Want some?"

"No, thanks, I'm dead," Doc replied.

"Why would you ever get yourself killed? And if you're dead, why are you sipping tea? Doesn't that like, rot in your belly or some shit?"

"The powers of Englishmen transcend life and death, my dear. That, and I prefer the fine taste of emotions or a demon's blood. Bourbon kills the flavor of both."

"So, what did you want to see? It's the same old boring gun matches week after week. Nobody cares about the guns, everyone wants to see the demons get *esssplooded ... kerrrchooww.*" Jane followed her sound effect up with her hands arcing wide.

"Don't you find it strange, that when these creatures crawl back into the world, they aren't a threat? That after the initial shock of it all, companies and militaries already had equipment on hand to deal with them?"

"Who cares, right? It's why we have a military. To blow things up. If we can nuke a country, what's a handful of creatures going to do? The bigger threat are people like you. I mean, I know you will kill me when you're done here. Eat my heart or whatever it is you do."

Doc sighed and pinched fingers on his nose while shaking his head. "They really have you guys living in a news bubble, don't they? This will be harder than we thought." He stood up and watched each monitor for a minute.

I could sneak out now ... Jane felt conflicted to her core. She was the calmest she had ever been, but she knew it was stupid to stay here. Ultimately, it reminded her, of ... well ... her. Always working or staying in places she shouldn't because it *felt* okay. For years, it was her gut she trusted, not her logic. This was no different.

"There," Doc said finally, pointing to the third screen. "That's them. That's what I came to see."

Jane followed his finger and saw the VIP section of the stadium. The square-cut jaw, sharp suit, long braided dreadlocks, and striking blue eyes—a trait rare among black men. It only made him even more striking. Peter Stein Culmen. CEO of Triumvirate Enterprises. Savior of Texas. Famous for preventing a massive outbreak of demons and magic by having his company mobilize to quarantine Mexico from the US last year. Mexico City was one of the ten cities in the world categorized as ground zero. A nexus point where the barriers between Purgatory and here first opened. Along with the Twin Cities, Jerusalem, Tokyo, most of the Nordic countries and so on.

"You came to see Mr. Culmen?" Jane laughed. "You know he's like ... on every news outlet ... *all* the time. He's famous. I mean, he's the reason you are standing in a safe quarantine zone."

"Jane, I'm going to tell you advice that will make your future easier. *Power* is a double-edged sword. It always has a price. Power itself calls out to those who are desperate, and many succumb to its siren's call." Doc pulled at his neck skin without taking his eyes off the monitor. "But it's not power you have to fear. It's those who wield it."

"I'll need another shot," Jane replied.

"It's true, Peter Stein Culmen saved Texas, but that's because he was the one responsible for ground zero in Mexico. He's only a puppet to larger masters. Masters whose conquest of the world, heaven, and hell, is still underway. This"—he gestured wildly at the screen in anger—"*this* is a charade! Nothing more than a lie to placate pretty blonde waitresses into subservience. Bloody oligarchy bastards ..."

Jane felt his anger radiating off him. She retreated off her post behind the safety of the bar and inched closer to the door. Fear was returning to her. "Chill man. Just ... chill. I'm screwed here anyway, you can have whatever you want." *Run, Jane. Get out of here.*

"You don't believe me. I know. But look. Open your damn eyes and look. Who is your savior sitting next to? Who else is in that booth?"

"You're one of those terrorist freaks, aren't you? You weren't kidding about recruiting me to the Sons and Daughters. You here to blow up the arena? Unleash a demon plague? Start a war? Please ... just let me go. I—" Flashes of her dance with Purgatory earlier flitted around her vision. "I lie to myself!" She formed tiny fists as the ball of self-truth escaped her gut. "I'm not ready yet; I'm just a nobody. Nobody knows who I am."

Doc slammed his fist on the table and glared at her with fangs bared. His former calm demeanor was now a twisted scowl. "Look, or I will rip out every ounce of emotion that makes you human." The vampire lurched forward, long white canines curled over his thin ruby red lips, kicking over a chair with a loud crack. Jane jittered like a skittery deer, eyes darting between anything that moved, and even caught the calculated calmness glinting in Doc's eyes as if he knew exactly what he was doing. *Predator.*

Her hands trembled, so she placed them on the cool wooden bar for something familiar, and backed up to the door. The smooth polish barely put her at ease. Looking up at the screen, she saw a green-robed figure with a golden mask on. The mask curled around his blackened eyes, with feathered wings that jutted out above the hood. His pale skin seemed taped to his face, or rather, stitched on in surgery to hide his real face. The gold trim on the robes all led to a single red clasp that held his outfit together—a deep crimson pendant with the roman numeral II.

"Who? Who is that?" She tried not to tremble in her voice.

"That, my friend, is the Lord of Suicide. A loyal supplicant to Lazarus himself and one of the high priests in the Church of Unification, and they own more stock in these corporations than any other organization," Doc said as his fangs snapped back into his mouth. As he took measure of Jane, he straightened his posture and tried to compose himself. "I ... ah ... sorry about that. I know you need fear to activate your second sight, so nothing personal."

As he took a step closer to the bar, Jane stepped back, refusing to let any distance close between them.

"Listen, I ... there is no easy way to put this news, but the world you know is a lie. You've been living in a propaganda bubble. The rest of this globe is dying, and many cities like this, that still stand, have the Church of Lazarus pulling all the strings. They engineered the end. They are pulling the strings of your city now, mining it for weapons to win the war over any in opposition. Like Chicago or Iceland." He ran his fingers through thin strands of hair and chuckled. "Man, you aren't the only one nervous here. I'm the one tasked with convincing people like you to join a war ..." He let out a long sigh. "Mikey was always better at recruitment."

"Just ... please leave," Jane said, wanting nothing more than to escape.

"This is awkward, but ... I still need to buy that swordfish. If anyone asks, I caught it on a fishing trip off the coast, okay? Here." Doc laid out a series of more free drink coupons on the table. "I don't have any Bitcoin, so, just accept these." As he walked around behind the bar, Jane circled around, keeping plenty of distance between them, but her eyes glanced to the coupons. Even fear couldn't suppress the slight glimmer of greed-induced hope. *The Jungle? That place is riiichh. Lottery winners get in there.* Despite his skinny arms, he plucked the swordfish off the wall and held it with ease.

A gangly, tea-sipping, teacher-jacket-wearing, balding, English, swordfish-hunting vampire ... this is it. This is how I get eaten. Jane looked up to the hellhounds on the screen being eviscerated by gunfire. *Cornered animals as well ... maybe we aren't so different.*

Doc straightened his suit jacket and gave a small cough. "Listen, it's only natural you will have an onslaught of feelings after this. They will come back harder than usual. You'll ask questions like 'Why me?' or 'What could I have done?' and until you decide your path forward I can't give you all the answers. It's important that you take personal time ... and ... quit working here. It's bad for your health. Too many freaks eat here." He smiled.

Jane kept her jaw clenched and only nodded. *Oh, you can bet I'm not coming back here. Fuck this place.*

Doc opened the door, the soft jingle of the bells rang throughout, and he took one last look back. "As for why you ... well, Jane ... not everyone can see Purgatory when panicked. Most people can't even see the Lord of Suicide sitting up there." Doc nodded back to the monitor, raising a single eyebrow. "Think there is a connection?" He left, the door slowly closing behind him.

"Thank you, please come again ..." Jane mumbled to herself before peering out of the corner of her eyes at the ghastly figure with blackened eyes sitting next to Mr. Culmen, who was more soulless than she'd ever imagined. Culmen's soul had been ripped out.

Jane shivered.

CHAPTER FOUR

"Safe. Purified. Refined. Why eat the entire heart when a simple injection will do? Pelican Pharmaceuticals now offers the latest in magical enhancements for lucky winners in Austin. Enter the lottery today and be the first to enjoy our limited clinical trials. Imagine yourself soaring with your newly-grown wings."

Daneka proudly marched through the connecting skyway. The stuffed swordfish tucked neatly under his arm drew several confused and wary looks. He had plenty of room to walk. Jutting over into a nearby parking garage with a scurry, he held the door open for a few strangers before popping up the stairs. Then down three flights. Then he cut over between four more downtown buildings using a mix of walkways, back-alleys, and at least one jaywalking attempt (he failed at the jaywalking due to fear and instead waited at the crosswalk like a normally sane person). It wasn't until he counted seventeen-and-a-half buildings later, when Daneka found himself strolling through a construction site, that two others had begun marching alongside him.

On his left, strolled a small gutter-punk girl with a bouquet of colors for hair. Despite her small, skinny, or, as he often thought, malnourished frame, Akira was part of his murderous family. On his right, dressed in the latest Austin fashion and wearing black shades that hid any hangover, Phoebe was danger waiting to happen. *She was out again, which means we'll have three broken hearts and maybe one new recruit.*

"Don't give me that look," Phoebe instantly protested while eying the swordfish. "I've brought in more recruits than either of you."

"I mean, technically, I'm the reason Mike Auburn joined... " Daneka, holding up a finger, was about to lecture before Akira daintily stepped in and grasped his hand, folding his finger nicely back into a balled fist.

"Shush. Mike's not dead, he's just lost. Let's ... let's just keep focused until the others find him."

All three fell silent as Mike's passing came to memory again. Daneka had been the first to start calling Mike lost rather than dead. To him, it seemed to make more sense. After all, they live in a world where in some parts of the country the dead literally walk around. Clearly, their bullheaded construction worker friend was just lost somewhere in Purgatory. It was a lot easier to swallow than him being obliterated by an ancient, spell-wielding psychopath.

Akira craned her neck and kept eyeing nooks and crannies. "I don't see any cameras ..."

Cameras. Peter. Right. Daneka refocused his attention. "Oh, it won't matter if the warlock has any. Let's ... let's get this over with. I hate this part of business."

Plywood planks nailed together gave the three vampires a temporary floor to stand on several stories up. Whistling wind cut through the shallow iron frame of a new pharmaceutical headquarters. Akira pulled out a small, handwritten notebook with a long list of names, the majority of which had already been crossed out. Jane's name was the most recent.

Akira held her pen over Jane's name and looked up. "Did it go well? Do you think she's got the eyesight?"

Daneka recalled the taste of her delicious fear as she saw the Death Lord on screen. Even some time after, it still filled his stomach. "Yeah ... yeah. Absolutely. She's remarkably on point, but also an adrenaline addict."

Akira crossed off her name. "Great. Well, hopefully this one can help. I still like our odds with Jack better. He at least *knew* better."

Phoebe grabbed Akira and rustled her hair with a chuckle. "Trust me on this stuff! Visions are my thing. If we are going to rebalance the power, she'll be damn helpful. Killing Death Lords is a hell of a lot easier when you can find their souls in Purgatory."

"You know," Daneka pondered aloud. "Just over a year ago, I was a *very* well-off psychologist. I had my own office. Chinese food on demand. Now we lead our own band of anarchist freedom fighters that fight the Unification, Society of Deus, and the very forces of Heaven and Hell. Have you guys ever missed ... you know"—he waved his free hand frantically—"Chinese food."

"No," they both said in unison and made puckered faces. "That shit is terrible."

"Heathens," Daneka sighed.

"Look, hoss." Akira lit up a smoke and practiced pretending to breathe. "Before you ever showed up, I was already killin' people for the bartender. Sure, not *all* of them were bad people, but a few eggs had to be broken. Yet *nobody* ..." Akira flayed her arms out as the wind almost carried her off a plank. "Nobody is as bad as these Unification fuckers. Left unchecked, they will have the world worshipping them as gods and reprogram us all to be like—" Akira's eyes went wide, and she marched around in a circle like she had no joints in her legs. "Immmootep. Immotep!"

"Yeah, but Chinese food." Doc chuckled at Akira's mummy impression.

"Pfft." Phoebe elbowed him. "You know this ain't about

31

Chinese food. You can still get that a few blocks over. This is about the long journey we've got ahead of us, isn't it? Much easier to sit back at home than fight a war ..." She counted several fingers. "That might take us a century or more to win."

"Uh, yeah!" Daneka nodded furiously. "Look. That kid Jane? She's not ready for this. She's just a waitress. Why don't we leave the war killing up to those sociopaths like the Praenomen and her crew? Or the Society of Deus seems strong enough to take a fight. Fuck it, I say we recruit her and then run off back to St. Louis to rendezvous with everyone else."

"No can do, hot potato," Akira shrugged. "The bartender says this is where we need to be to hit our goals. We been working our butts off to set this up for a while now."

Phoebe gave a small catlike growl and crossed her arms.

"Phoebe," Akira corrected. "Come here, group hug, pep talk time, guys." She twirled a finger ... and failed at getting the group huddle. "*Tsk.* This is it, man. Corporations unbound. No restrictions. What do you think happens if the Church of Unification gets *all* of them on their side? There won't even *be* a century-long war if we can't take him down."

Daneka tipped his head back, letting his thin blond hair get tussled in the wind. *This is why I always hate this part. Changing the world is bloody hard. A century-long war ... I'll be over a hundred by then and I still wouldn't have my own fishing boat. There is no way my father will let me escape this.* "I suppose I can't let my father escape. He is the bloody head of the Unification after all. Hell of an upgrade from being Senator McCarthy's psychologist."

Akira pounced on the opportunity. "You never mention him! Dude, your dad is one step away from being a world-controlling demagogue. How did you even make it through high school? When he fucked your mom, were they into kinky shit? He was into kinky shit, wasn't he?"

"Freud indeed had plenty to say," Daneka growled as his cheeks turned red. "... and now you know why I never mention him."

"Do you know how hard it is to be around you and not ask that question every day?"

Daneka put his palm over Akira's face and calmly turned his attention back to Phoebe. "So anyway, I get it. We need to be here. New recruits, special recruits, and this is where the big fight is. Despite my reluctance, I've been on board. The sooner we finish here, the sooner we can go back to looking for Mike."

Phoebe nodded. "... and recruiting that waitress will make that much easier. Look, Doc. I know the bartender keeps secrets from us. You know I keep secrets from you. I can't tell my friends everything I see in my visions or"—her shoulders slumped—"yeah, you know how I feel. You know how *everyone* feels. That's your gift."

Akira continued to ask questions into Doc's palm.

Daneka let out a deep breath and adjusted his fishy companion. "Yeah, I know there is no stopping the tide. People always revolt against their oppressors. Even if they take the form of a tech giant, a church, or a cult. Least we can do is point them in the right direction."

"Didn't they have a bunch of crazy sex parties in the Jet Propulsion Lab?"

Both Phoebe and Daneka just glared at Akira.

"What?" she shrugged.

"None of us have ever figured out if you are into guys or girls, Akira," Daneka began.

"Eternal mystery, my friends. Eternal mystery." Akira shot finger guns at both. "Just like several others here."

"Oh, really. What other mysteries are there?" Daneka said as he awkwardly popped to another set of planks and began heading out.

"Yeah." Akira bounded after. "First is ... if cameras don't matter, why the hell did we meet here?"

Daneka pointed to a billboard advertising the lottery outside. "Cameras don't matter because the bartender can make people forget him, and us if needed. Including Peter. That doesn't mean I like standing around under them ... or by all the spam."

"What's your other mystery, Akira?" Phoebe gave a cheeky grin and a wink.

Akira paused. Both arms raised slowly and pointed at Daneka's swordfish. "How have we not addressed the broadbill in the room?"

CHAPTER FIVE

Since 1940, Burger Lord has provided basic shit food wrapped in crappy advertisement. Not anymore. With our new Freakmeat, our burgers have never been better. Harvested here in the US, this medley of flavors will satiate your hunger and cure color blindness. Don't just survive. Eat. Consume.

Jane hit the streets of her concrete metropolis the moment she felt safe. Rubbing her hands for warmth around her visible breath, she took stock of the abomination in the sky. The black sun peeked through new skyscrapers on the western horizon, beginning its descent. Climate change and global warming had been the apocalyptic talk for the past few decades and hot shit were they wrong. She flipped the bird at the sun. A customary ritual she performed every time she saw it. Jane had enjoyed her Texan winters, but forty degree year-round weather was not something she approved of.

Buttoning up her brown wool peacoat, she wandered around the neon blue streets of Austin. Ducking in and out of crowds staring at giant monitors blasting the news, her duct-taped well-worn boots prevented most of the water from the terror of soggy socks as she splashed in puddles that ran along the gutters. It had been a smaller city before. Downtown Austin was downtown, central had the culture, the deep south was no-man's-land, and the east side was where most people lived. Now, thanks to advancements in technology and twenty-four seven construction—everywhere was up. Cranes loomed thirty stories up hoisting prefabbed apartment floors; extra roadways loomed over 15th Street to make way for automated vehicles. Companies in the Triumvirate were keen on trying to capitalize on the hordes of people outside the quarantine zone waiting to get in. This, Jane reasoned, was the reason those bloody advertisement screens were everywhere. *More customers!* She plodded through wet gutters trying to avoid hucksters and refugees. It wasn't working.

A scrawny man with sunken eyes spied a quick glance at her and took a few steps behind her. As she plodded through cool, wet gutters, he moved casually on the sidewalk. *Maybe he's just going this way?* Out of habit, she turned back, and unfortunately for her, made direct eye contact by accident.

"Hey, girlie, smile for me," he said, before spinning around himself and backpedaling in front of her with relaxed shoulders and a bobbing head.

This refugee construction worker standing in her way as rain-water seeped through a hole in her shoe was just a bother. Tilting her head to the side, she studied his neck. *You know, being a vampire wouldn't be so bad. At least you would have the power to stop this kinda shit. Bah, who am I kidding, this one will die by blunt force trauma.* In one second, he was grinning ear to ear with those coffee-stained teeth. In a flicker of her vision, his head was crushed in and his left eyeball dangled out, his mouth twisted in agony.

She smiled. All things considered, it was the least she could do with the fate that lay ahead of him and the reason she loved her Purgatory dance. Until the adrenaline finally left her, she had a near-death-induced leg up on these interactions.

"Oh, hell, you're a pretty lass, aren't you? What's your name?" He'd clearly misunderstood the smile as a semblance of interest.

"Listen, pal, I've had a shit day. I get it. I've been bounced from more towns and places than you can count, and guess who lost her job? Had the shit scared out of me, and, overall, I want to murder the ever-living shit out of a demon." Jane kept her smile and talked in a higher-pitched voice than usual. She hated that about herself. A survival instinct to put on a show for strangers was ingrained deep within her, like some sort of over-sized stuffed peacock.

"Well, if you're looking for a time ..." He held his arms out wide. She noticed the blackened skin around his elbows. The marker of using those new arc bolters to construct the skyscrapers. Dangerous work with no regulations or safety precautions, but one of the few jobs that paid decent money to refugees with no training.

"I mean ..." Jane blushed a little and looked down. In no way was she seriously considering it, but having to let down a person (even an offensive, ugly one) when you could see their demise was hard. "Look, I've got a battery-powered lover at home you wouldn't be able to keep up with. I need to feed my cats, and I'm not even sure why I'm wasting my time here anymore. Do you ask your daughter these things when you see her on the street?"

Her words struck a chord, and as he struggled to find a response, she stepped out into traffic and cut around him, breaking into a jog. *That was so stupid. Come on, Jane, get it together.* She zigged and zagged through pedestrians and vehicles alike as she ran home. Street harassment was common as hell before, but when you throw the end at people, they act like animals. *If it wasn't for the Technocratic party down here, we would've eaten each other already. Just like those northerners.*

Even though her place was five miles away, Jane kept her pace. She loved running. Once she hit a rhythm, she could run for hours. In a few short blocks, the urban landscape around her became nothing more than a track for her to zip through. Every neon ad, automated car, and pedestrian (well-dressed citizen or hodgepodge refugee) became secondary to the sound of her footsteps. Numb from the day, she zoned out to her breathing, letting the cold air turn her cheeks rosy red while working up a cleansing sweat underneath. The runner's high hit her so well that she was still bouncing on her feet when she ran up flights of stairs to her fifth-floor apartment.

"Ah, phew ... heh, that hit the spot," she said, putting her hand on the plastered wall outside her door. A small package sat in a box for her on the floor. *Oh, cat toys arrived!* She grabbed the package as she swiped her left wrist across the door scanner. A mechanical latch clanked as it released, and the reinforced metallic door slid open sideways, summoning forth the welcome smell of old furniture.

"Hey, kids, I'm home, I've got a new present for ya!" Jane shouted as she came in, kicked off her boots, and wiped cold sweat off her forehead. A quick glance in the mirror showed her nose was beet red and her ponytail was barely in place. Tossing her coat on a hamper filled with unfolded laundry, Jane plopped down on her orange hand-me-down sofa and set the box on her cheap IKEA table. Soft lights turned on and every electronic in her house buzzed to life.

"Your carrots," a synthetic female voice came from Jane's fridge, "only have 13 hours left before spoiling. Would you like me to order more from the Devil's Steakhouse?"

"No, thanks, but Siri, how long until I run out of groceries?" Jane replied as she unpacked the cats' latest contraption. A small, lifelike imp filled with catnip. *Heh, perfect. Cats are the natural enemies of imps, gotta teach 'em young.*

"13 hours," Siri responded.

"Wait, are you telling me I only have carrots left?"

"That is correct; would you like me to order more?"

"Siri, remember when I told you that if you ever let me starve, I'd rip out your programming and feed you to Alexa in the TV?" Jane said with a smile as her two tabby cats meowed and nuzzled up against her legs. Alexa heard her name, and a saucy purple-haired avatar inquired if it was time to put the refrigerator in the grave. She, after all, knew the perfect replacement from Atlantis, the machine makers!

Jane ignored her synthetic friends and focused on the stray tabbies she had rescued. Maru and Paru, she named them. Their purrs vibrated through their bodies as they rubbed the top of their heads against her chin. Clawed paws batted at the imp as Jane nestled her face into the cats' bodies. *Snuggling is the best medicine ever.* "Hey, guys, so what did you do today? Kill any shadow imps? Break into mommy's closet again and get your fur all over my black clothes?"

They meowed in response.

"Yeah, you didn't choo ... you've ..." Her thought trailed off. Just a few hours earlier she was standing face-to-face with a vampire terrorist from the Sons and Daughters. An hour before that she was trying to kill herself again. *And yet here I am talking to my furry children and my house robots. Could life get any stranger?*

"Alexa," Jane asked. "Tell me about the Sons and Daughters." She stood and emptied her waitress apron and pockets, tossing the free drink coupons on the table. *Don't think I've forgotten about you, Mr. Houndstooth. Tonight, you're buying the rounds.*

"The Sons and Daughters," Alexa responded, as the TV filled itself with multiple videos of Chicago and the Twin Cities, "are a domestic terrorist organization based out of the Second City. One year ago, their founder, a twenty-eight-year-old ironworker named Mike Auburn, fought the first demon that appeared outside the United Center. In his speech, Auburn decried the US government and many corporations, calling them responsible for the events at hand ..."

Jane slipped into her bathroom and grabbed her toothbrush before returning while brushing.

"Afterwards, Auburn convinced the citizens of Chicago to join his anarchist ways. To start eating and drinking the blood of demons for power, which caused a widespread outbreak that went viral. In multiple cities, members of the Sons and Daughters summoned creatures from beyond and caused global devastation. Try as they might, the United Nations could only contain the initial impact so much but could identify that ground zero for the *event* was centralized in the Great Lakes region. This gave rise to apolitical militias like the Society of Deus that embraced vampirism and the consumption of highly addictive blood without regard to the consequences."

"Hey," Jane said, pulling the toothbrush out of her mouth. "I get it, the world jumped the shark, the Society of Deus and Sons and Daughters took over the Midwest. It's magic as fuck up there now with unicorns, demons, and vampires walking around. Tell me about the Sons and Daughters leadership. Is there anyone with the nickname Doc?"

"Not on record. The only known structure of the Sons and Daughters is Mike Auburn and his companion Akira, the 'praying mantis bug demon thing' as often shown in viral videos where they assaulted the Society of Deus in the Twin Cities before the sun rose black. Status of the two terrorists is unknown, although they occupy the number one spot on all international crime lists with the highest bounties in history."

Jane got undressed and ready for a shower. "Bounties; tell me more and turn up the volume." She listened as she booted up her shower. Electricity was cheap. Water was rationed. Way too many people were dying from tainted water these days thanks to a quadfucktrillion plants dying without a proper sun. So the companies in Austin purified all water for its citizens. Expensive ... but safe. *Ahhh, I could be rich* ... She dreamed as the fresh water melted her stress away. The amount of bounties on the Sons and Daughters' members was insane. The United Nations, and the Church of Lazarus, were paying high coin for their capture.

Squeaky-clean, refreshed, and with skin begging for the nearest lotion to relieve the dry burn, Jane attacked her getting ready routine with all the righteous indignation she could muster. There was no way she would pass up free drinks at the Jungle, one of the richest nightclubs in town. Makeup then lip balm and lotion were slathered on her face in her own magic ritual of beautification, but for her hair ... she only found odd-colored scrunchies.

"Where the fuck is my hair tie? Maru! Paru! Did you eat them again! Where are they! I am *not* wearing a scrunchie." She raced out of the bathroom. Sure enough, Paru had the small black band in his mouth, completely ignoring the expensive imp toy. *You son of a bitch. Your sister is way better than you; I'll remember this betrayal.* After five minutes of corralling a hyper cat, Jane reclaimed her last hair tie. *In my life, I've put my hair up like four thousand times. Why the hell am I always on my last band?*

"Why does it always feel like it's our last day together?" she asked the entire room as a tear slipped its way through her façade and made a wet spot on Paru. "I don't know if things will be okay ... I saw them, Maru ... he had no soul, and the priest from the Church ..." Jane felt herself lurch at the memory of the flayed skin and crazy mask. *I can't.* She raced to the bathroom, eternally grateful she had her hair tie before unceremoniously giving a sacrifice to the porcelain throne. *The Church of Lazarus, why should I be surprised that their priest or whatever is something crazy?* All the Church has ever done is shake hands with companies here and give them ancient Vatican texts about the nature of monsters. It suited the needs of everyone if you knew where to put the bullets.

The Church hated the Society of Deus, the Society of Deus hated the Church, the Technocrats hated the monsters, and the Sons and Daughters seemed to hate everyone ... *least in the Triumvirate, I have a toilet to puke in. What can I do about rich people running the world? Win the bloody lottery and get powers?*

Jane heaved another bout of dry heave and wiped the spittle from her mouth. *I feel like shit.* Maru meowed while Paru knocked a curling iron off the counter.

"You're right, just jump off and get out there, girl. Ain't shit I can do about it. I'll just be another hysterical crazy if I go ranting ... so which dress has less cat hair? The green dress or blue dress?"

CHAPTER SIX

Looking for a new lease on life? Migrate to the Triumvirate Cities of Austin, Dallas, and Houston, Texas. At the hub of the newly formed Technocratic party, our companies are forging our future with new products, services, and research. Just because magic has returned doesn't mean you need to live in the dark ages.

The Jungle perched in between two skyscrapers via skyways. A giant, neon blue, glass nightclub filled with rare plants from every country. Ferns, flowers, and oversized genetically grown vines wrapped their way across every surface. Jane heard many stories about everything inside being an artificial creation, cultured to grow in hostile environments—the people were no exception. Cut from soldiers and recruits that fought the supernatural, enhanced humans inside tried to shake off the PTSD with a heavy cocktail of drugs, booze, and dancing. They always said every aspect of Peter Stein Culmen's utopia was on display, where humans with bionic eyes saw the world in infrared while others, high on pixie dust, changed their skin color based on their mood.

For a normie like Jane, entry was possible, but difficult. Only those fortunate enough to win the arena lottery or who signed their life away in corporate sponsorships made it through the gates of fame. She held the small stack of plastic coupons that the vampire had gifted her with while she stood in line—wondering just how an undead like him made it in. Between the scanners, the guards dressed in body armor and white gas masks, and all the enhanced humans, it seemed unlikely. *He probably ambushed a poor sap on their way out of the club. Oh, well, entertainment for the fittest ... mine now.* She slinked forward in line, cautiously tapping and asking for each person she cut in front of. A lie whispered from her lips for each foot of progress made, ranging from the classic friends are waiting to I'm on the guest list. After a half hour of progress through the nighttime crowd, she was standing at the bouncer's door, which looked tiny compared to the hulking 'roided out man.

"Hey, listen," she said, holding out one of the small drink cards. "I totally won these off the radio, so like, that means I can come in, right?" Bouncing on the balls of her feet, she tried to look naïve and excited.

The bouncer raised an eyebrow and sized her up before scanning her left wrist with a wand. "ID JK-47, foster child, three counts of larceny, termination from Devil's Steakhouse pending, and no enhancements." He paused. His green eyes weren't those of a dumb 'roid junkie; he was paying attention to every detail on her. "You didn't win those tickets off the radio; those are VIP passes, and you need to go grocery shopping. Your fridge is low on carrots. So, no, you don't get in. Now go hit up a different joint."

Before he waved the next person up, Jane scrambled to get his view again. "Wait, wait, okay, don't you think the VIP *wants* me to come meet him, then? I got fired from Devil's for these. The damn bastard paid me in them. And can you believe it ... another one tried to pay me in cash." She thrust out the tickets one more time. "And I'll promise to get more carrots. I know they help in a low-sun environment. I need a night, man ... a chance," she whispered.

He laid his giant mitt on the smooth metallic handle and bared her way further, leaning back slightly. The metallic green door creaked open an inch, enough to let the thumping sounds of the Jungle wash over her. With a knowing look and a slight nod, the bouncer averted his gaze. *Success! Hell, yeah!* Jane bolted in before he could change his mind. The lush fragrance of plants was everywhere. Taking a deep breath, Jane enjoyed the smell of a greenhouse; it reminded her of a forest after a rain. The music's vibration rattled her bones as she walked further into the club. Overgrown violet lilacs and deep red chrysanthemums the size of basketballs decorated the initial catwalk. *Huzzah, the heroine made it to the saucy nightclub! Now my adventure begins with the sweet release of chemical intoxication.* She laughed, recalling countless movies that used the trope, and made a beeline to the bar.

Water poured down from sprinklers onto patrons on the dance floor. Above them, the glass dome encompassing the joint filled the space with 3-D projections of other dancers, creating a packed dance floor. Even if it was just an illusion. The black sun had set hours ago; in nightclub time that was nothing, so Jane couldn't fault the owners for fake intensity. Only one bartender was on shift; a tall old man with a black vest, rolled-up sleeves, and a towel around his arm. She landed a seat at the bar and realized just how empty it was. A man drinking alone in one corner, a soldier team fiddling with cybernetics in another, and a handful of business executives snorting powder off a table were only a handful of patrons. *Perfect! I'm in early! I've got until dawn ... now, how many drinks can I get from these?* She squinted her eyes at the fine print on the back of one coupon.

"What can I getcha lass?" the bartender said as he cleaned off a glass.

"Amaretto stone sour?" Jane asked, more curious about how long this VIP time lasted, or if it was a roped off area, or was there a cool secret area. "When does this place get busy?"

With a flip of a glass, the bartender mixed the drink. "That depends on your definition of busy. Tonight is VIP night, so who knows. A booze baron from North Carolina booked the entire joint. In theory, she, and her entire party, should be here by now ... but ..." He slid the drink over.

"They haven't showed," Jane finished his sentence.

"Bingo. But what do I care? I just work here. They paid, and so less work for me."

"What about all the people outside, the anti-freak units and soldiers?" she asked, taking a sip of the sweet drink.

"Too bad for them," he shrugged.

"Don't you think that's a tad unfair? Some rich bitch rents out one of the best nightclubs in town, and everyone else is just stuck waiting, thinking they can get in? Are you even going to tell them?"

The bartender slid his hands into his pockets and rocked back and forth for a moment, sizing her up. "Care about people you don't even know, eh? That's not how the world works anymore, sweetie. If some out-of-towner wants to kill a joint and pay enough bits to keep the illusion, that's on them. Hell, free market at work, they say. Since people can't get in, and we sell out a full house, everyone thinks this is the best joint in town. Even you."

A thought crossed Jane's mind as she lifted the glass to her lips; a pervasive earworm, the thought bounced along the walls of her skull before finding form along her lips, preventing her attempt at free booze. "Wait a hot minute, how long has this lie been going on?"

"Since we opened," he chuckled.

She spat her drink all over the bar. "What!" As the bartender looked down at his now wet white shirt, Jane sunk back on her barstool. "Uh, sorry, sorry, I'll help clean ... I get it, I do."

"New girl giving you trouble, boss?" A voice came from Jane's left followed by the sound of bubblegum popping.

A leather-clad girl sidled up into Jane's personal space. Her purple hair peeked out from behind a white hood, drawing all attention to her eyes ... and a plunging open zipper on the skintight leather.

"Name's Phoebe, pleasure to meet ya." She held out a hand.

Jane touched the ice-cold hand and watched Phoebe's eyes turn solid white. *Oh, fuck! Another freak!* Before true panic set in, she felt another hand rest on her shoulder.

"Easy there," the bartender said, patting her on the back. "Phoebe's just got a few bio-mods from Ronin Insurance. I know you normies aren't used to seeing tech like that up close. You're stuck in the nosebleed of the arena."

It made sense to Jane, and her heartbeat relaxed a beat. *Phew, okay, that makes sense.* "So ... um ... is that what everyone in here is?" She pointed to the other patrons. *When they said rare and exclusive, they weren't kidding.* "... and what are you doing with that white eye thing? Checking how fast my heart jumps?"

Phoebe leaned in. "Learning what your body likes ..." She popped another bubble with a wink.

"Coming on a little strong, there, aren't you?" Jane said, and gestured for another drink. "At least some dinner and dancing first ..."

Phoebe smiled. "Relax, beautiful, checkin' you out for mods. She could be a winner, boss. Finally found a keeper, I did. This means I win the pot?"

"It was rigged from the start with your tricks." He smiled, reached below the bar, pulled out a dusty brown bottle with a corkscrew top, and poured Phoebe a thick, viscous shot before sliding both the bottle and glass over.

"So, adrenaline junkie, what's your story?" she said, taking a shot.

"Uh, adrenaline junkie? Me? What about your story? Tell me about this club, first ..." Jane looked out on the dance floor at the holograms.

"Yeah, adrenaline junkie; your body craves it. So that makes you a winner. I"—Phoebe patted her chest—"am a talent scout. You've got what it takes to win the lottery ... and I have a *very lucky* lottery ticket." She pulled out an arena ticket and bit the corner with her lips.

To Jane, she looked like a cat up to mischief. Something was off, but try as she might, she couldn't put her finger on it. It reminded her of having a song stuck in her head but not recalling its name. *But a lottery ticket to the arena? Magic powers in a needle or one big damn gun and my own TV show. Everything I could ever want without all the debt. If I can survive ...*

"What's the catch?" Jane asked, pushing her drink to the side.

"No catch, but I want a date," Phoebe said, looking at her with eyes that appeared red in the nightclub setting.

"Bull-fuuuckiing-shit." Jane cackled out loud and slapped her legs. *No fucking way ... no way ... I ... I can't.* "You think I was born yesterday? What the fuck is the hook?" she asked while still laughing at them.

"Fine." Phoebe tucked away the ticket. "You can pass, that's all you. Don't save the world and rise to great heights."

"Yeah, no thanks, I'm out. I see this game. You get a creepy asshole to give out VIP tickets to girls in need and then sell them with the classic talent scout trick. Next thing I know, I'll be sold into some sex slavery and shipped off to another state." *Heckin' sex slave traders. I need to get out before they jump my ass. Okay, make a shock then split ... maybe grab the ticket.* Jane stood up and slapped Phoebe hard enough to knock the bubblegum out of her mouth.

The bartender's eyes gaped open and he held a finger up as if trying to find the right words to say. Jane slapped hard enough that her hand both hurt and tingled at once, but Phoebe's cheeks didn't turn red like a normal human; instead, she sat there, shocked, with her mouth open.

Jane jammed her finger into the chick's shoulder. "You're real fucking sick, you know that. You sit here as some hot bitch to disarm other girls who get in. How long have you been doing this? Since it opened?"

"I did not see that coming ..." Phoebe mumbled.

"Yeah, no shit, Sherlock. All I wanted was a nice fucking night out, and instead you come at me with this rapey-ass bullshit. Man, this country is sick. Think ya pick some low-hanging fruit, eh? All the fucked-up shit blood junkies do to each other, and ... and ..." Jane waved a middle finger inches from Phoebe's face. "Now, are you going to let me live and walk out of here or did I drink something I don't know about?"

"We have a misunderstanding." The bartender put his hands back into his pockets and began rocking. "I get it. Take the ticket. It's worth a fortune, you know that. Leave and get the hell out. No strings, we don't want the trouble."

Phoebe held out the lucky ticket and placed it on the wooden bar.

Jane snatched it. *Creepers. Well, now that those people have moved in, this town's going to shit and bringing its seedy, flea-ridden underbelly with it.* She marched through the holograms on the floor, ripping off her heels and storming back out the plant-filled entrance. *This was such a waste of time.* A thick layer of rage caused her shoulders to visibly shake as she burst through the exit door, and the terror and sadness welled up in her eyes as she scurried past the bouncer.

An oddly pear-shaped woman with olive skin and a short faux-hawk impatiently picked at her long acrylic nails. Even in the dim lighting, Jane could see they were filled with glitter, charms, rhinestones, and who knows what else, but they were slowly starting to shed off her fingers.

"It's all a lie, guys," Jane said to the crowded line, trying to avert her eyes. "They will not let you in, ever. Nobody is inside. Some rich CEO chick bought it out and keeps it as her own private drug joint."

"Hey, guys, check it, normie got chucked out. Who's your sponsor, girlie?" The girl quirked an eyebrow up and wrinkled her nose at the cat hair on her blue dress. In the neon light, it stood out in clear white, and there were just some things no technology ever got rid of—cat hair was eternal.

"Oh, I'm sorry." Jane clapped her hands together. "I forgot

you're an all-important lottery winner. Just how exactly is L'Oréal Cosmetics going to save the world, little girlie?"

She hissed back at Jane, revealing two long, needlelike fangs that unfolded at the side of her jaw and stretching her body in a snakelike fashion.

"Really." Jane remained skeptical. "You *hiss* at me? Are we twelve? Get in line, you aren't the first person baring fucking fangs at me. Why the hell would you get implanted fangs?"

"You're just a sad normie with no abilities." She sniffed the air. "Is that ... is that desperation or cat piss I smell on you? Get enhanced or get out. Just remember Jessica Montoya when you see my face on TV."

She was constantly met with nothing but vitriol and disdain from people like her. *Fine ... fine ... screw you. At least Maru and Paru are at home.* The night was a sullen reminder of why she was alone.

Life never went Jane's way.

Sitting in the Jungle only a few empty bar stools away, Delilah Dumont ran her fingers along the cracked porcelain mask she wore as the Praenomen and watched the entire encounter. *I had to stay invisible for all of that?* She questioned why the bartender wanted her to see this exchange. *Was it to watch his Phoebe's failure? Or is the failure going to set everything up?* A small crystal with gold-trimmed spheres around it dangled in front of her, and on the bar napkin she had drawn an inverted triangle with a circle interlacing around it. A martini olive representing her little pocket of invisibility soaked the napkin, a simple spell. *That was painful to watch.*

Going bottoms up on what remained of her drink, she slipped on the mask, letting its unholy power seep into her bones yet again as she waited for the right moment to end her hiding spell. The Archive was her organization, and, tenuously, the bartender asked them to play kingmaker with rising factions while his group, the Sons and Daughters, worked at killing Lazarus's Death Lords. Kingmaking was a job which Delilah thrived at, even if she despised the tedious machinations of immortals and their outdated reliance on single heroes. *A single man does not build a nation, nor their armies; it's the women and laborers who build the bullets.*

Phoebe sat at the bar and took another shot from the rare vintage of demon's blood, and Delilah watched her face become more vibrant and her skin naturally blush as the demon's blood rejuvenated her. "Ahhh, that hit the spot," she said with her fangs bared. "How dare she? I mean, really, how dare she!" Phoebe slapped the bar, wearing a twisted smile of indignation.

"You are really going to ask that?" the bartender said with a smile as he lit up a cigar. "She's just like her older brother."

"Yeah, and he was a pain in the ass. But sex trade? Really? The Sons and Daughters aren't a bunch of cyberstalks. Who knew picking up mortals and goading them to kill undead gods would be such a bother?" She pulled out a stick of gum and let the stress from her shoulders relax.

"So, tell me, little miss prophet, this going to work out for us?" the bartender asked.

"Well, she took the ticket, didn't she?"

"She did."

"Who knows, then?" Phoebe shrugged. "There are too many players and not enough cards so it's getting difficult to see the future, anyway. All I know right now is that I don't think I'm getting that date …"

The bartender took a long drag from the cigar and let the smoke hang. "You need not be a prophet to see that …"

Right, time for prophecy is over. The Praenomen flicked the olive off the napkin, becoming visible once again with a muted sigh. They didn't flinch. *By Balor's blessing, let this work.*

"How your little ragtag organization helped end the world last time is beyond me," the Praenomen said, its voice both male and female, alternating in and out as several souls spoke at once. "Is this how your lot recruited that Mike bloke? Pathetic." *My lord, it is a bloody wonder I engineered the Society of Deus's rise to power with this lot as instigators.*

The Praenomen rose and snapped her fingers, summoning her two soldiers waiting nearby to her side. True undead vampires, Symon and Whisper, who would die for her without a second thought.

"I think it's time that my team take over. While you fret over insignificant worms, we aim to convert the Warlock Peter himself. Lazarus cannot be allowed to have his grubby burnt hands on the weapons being designed here or your little ragtag squad, us in the Archive, and the Society of Deus are proper fucked." *Even together we couldn't stop the growing armies of Lazarus's Unification if the Triumvirate arms the lot of them.* "Let's not forget, either, that the current consensus among you"—she narrowed her eyes at the lot of them—"is that you morons think every devil or angel will sit idly by and allow themselves to become cheeseburgers," the Praenomen said as her arms crossed. *"Face them. Kill them. Eat them," Mr. Auburn said. If only it were that easy.*

Whether she was the Praenomen or Delilah Dumont, this dance with other people seemed the same to her. Ancient idiots with power and knowledge just assumed that events would fall their way without sacrifice. *I had to cut out my own tongue, bleed, and be forced to drink the blood of that damn demon-king Bollard in order to win.* The thought sent shivers down her spine. Here she was, working with tenuous bedfellows to stop a Vatican madman from getting access to militarized magic, and every night that passed Bollard became a higher-ranked devil. She sighed. For all their faults, at least the bartender knew *everyone* and that made it ... worth the headache of his incompetent crew.

"Well, they are rather delicious cheeseburgers," the bartender chimed in. "Yet how, pray tell, do you intend to convert the likes of Peter? Day by day, the entire nation looks up to him more. Seems he's holding the right hand of cards, if you ask me."

Delilah smirked underneath her mask. "Simple, to break his growing nation, you've got to give them hope first. Just don't come crying when I kill your pretty blonde recruit." She paused.

"Jane, right? She will do great on camera, and I'll even help make her a star. But when she can't hack it and I kill her, let's just say ... you knew what this was when you proposed this joint venture. The Archive will finish what the Society of Deus set out to do—prevent Lazarus's Unification from making a singular god. It's what I want. It's what the Society should want. It's what the world needs. Maybe one of these days you little Sons and Daughters will stop fussing over underdog heroines and recruit those with enough power to end worlds." She spun on her boots, with a long coat twirling behind her as she blitzed to the double doors in the back. *You want Peter to back out of the Unification, bartender? We'll get it done. You just keep doing your job of information gathering.*

"Ya can't kill a Death Lord without her!" Phoebe yelled. "Good luck!"

"How many have actually tried?" Symon asked with a wink and a quick elbow jab into Whisper. The pair of soldiers both gave a bow to the Sons and Daughters. "Maybe she needs to die, eh? In order to kill that which is dead, no? At least this dance shall be fun. Kill a Death Lord ... I want to eat his heart." They started to walk out after Delilah. "Think it tastes good, Whisper?"

"I would imagine ... not," the silent soldier replied.

CHAPTER SEVEN

Pelican Pharmaceuticals now offers its groundbreaking medication, TrueSight, over the counter. Never live in fear of a freak masquerading as a human again. TrueSight is clinically proven to identify blood junkies for what they are. Consult your local company to see if this medication is for you. (May cause hallucinations, paranoia, and mild cases of neurodegeneration.)

D espite the events of the prior night, which ended in a not-so-terrible evening of social documentaries, cats, and apple pie moonshine, Jane made damn sure she was up bright and early. The black sun shone its obsidian rays from high above the horizon as she took her place in front of the arena gates. *Bright and early, my ass. Maru wanted to snuggle, and it was comfy.* Jane made a tsk noise as she surveyed the length of the line. Huge concrete pillars flanked the wrought iron gates, illuminated by the dim LED blue lights, which were but a temporary obstacle to fame and fortune. Jane waited with a hundred citizens and refugees (a number that was growing by the minute) for the lot-draw while she shivered her ass off. *Jesus, no wonder crazy people always win this; you've gotta be insane to stand out here in this cold.*

As one of the largest areas in the continental United States that kept their shit together, the fast-growing cities of Austin, Dallas, and Houston had a logistics problem. Dozens of corporations launched new technology in the past year and provided safe haven for those fortunate souls who lived near corporate campuses—each day that went by, more survivors flooded in. A lottery system, conceived under the guise of fairness, launched early on. Work hard enough, and a golden ticket was in your horizon. Jane rubbed her hands together and blew on her ticket in between the chattering of her teeth. *It's like some Charlie's chocolate bullshit for poor people.* She gave the side-eye to those standing around her. Northerners, former TV producers, and a larger group of militiamen ready to showcase their years of combat training for fame and glory.

"Sorry, cats, getting a ticket is one thing, getting a *winning* ticket is another matter," Jane whispered to herself. A citizen could win everything from better living quarters, new refrigerators, or a full-ride ticket into a suit of monster-slaying weapons. Everyone dreamed of becoming another gladiator, but even if Jane won a refrigerator—she could at least scrap her old one.

Right as the sun's gray rays reflected off the reinforced glass of the city, the wrought iron gates clanked upwards. Loudspeakers blared on, relaying the message Jane had heard day in and day out for the past three months, in a metallic, sterile message.

"Attention citizens," Jane mimicked. "Welcome to the daily draw, please make your way inside for registration and tagging. For those citizens already registered, you may proceed to the fifth floor. All our shops and businesses will be open for you after the drawing. Thank you for helping us build a new utopia— where life begins anew."

Just like clockwork, Jane made her way in. While everyone else made nervous jokes about the *Hunger Games,* Jane saw the arena in a different light. Rather than the narrow white concrete hallways and sterile industrial corridors that filled service tunnels for employees—the first level glittered with wonder. Company holographs showcased great arena battles of the past while spokesmen extolled the virtues of science versus magic. Before today, all this glamour and fame seemed out of reach for Jane. Working endlessly for lottery credits wasn't what she desired, and she wasn't making enough to enter daily draws. For a long while now, it was just easier to keep her dreams in check.

Parents and kids alike stopped by each of the booths with a look of awe on their face, their first time standing at the feet of legends. Jane smiled. Somehow, looking at the arena in this newfound light of hope made her happy. The cynical illusion Jane held for the arena, her tomb of workplace imprisonment, melted away as her hopes rose. *You can't go from being a barista to demon-slaying bad ass without a little help. Despite what they said.*

She made her way to a military recruitment table and grabbed a complimentary cup of coffee in a small Styrofoam cup. It was toxic swill, with powdered creamer, but at least the steam coming off warmed her cheeks as she sipped. *Besides, dairy is a dying industry ... hashtag thanks black sun.*

"You think you've got a winning shot today? Have you given any thought about your future if you don't? We offer full sponsorship and extra lottery credits here in the city if you sign up for weekend service," the recruiter said.

"I'm not a fighter, thanks," she lied. The truth was something closer to a set of crazy gun-toting foster parents that taught her more survivalism than school work. She recalled hating it then but wore a smirk as she took the stairs to her old work out of habit. *Evangelism, guns, and the American way. World sure thought they were crazy when they used snake venom to fight a flu, but who's laughing now. Well, not them. They're dead. Idiots.*

Lost in reverie, before Jane knew it she was standing outside the oaken door to the Devil's Steakhouse. Closed and quiet with nobody on the floor yet except a few cleaning robots that roamed around in repetitive circles.

"You see this?" Jane held the ticket up to the automatic door lock. "I don't need you anymore. I'm getting the good stuff." Out of curiosity, she swiped her left hand in front of the lock. To no one's surprise, it made an ugly beep and pulsed red. "Oh, don't worry, I'm breaking up with you, not you with me."

As she walked up to the fourth floor, a deep-seated, terrible thought crept into her mind. By the time she walked to the lottery booth, nestled among countless kiosks, the mindworm had spread to icy fear in her gut.

What happens if I lose?

She waited behind the velvet rope, looking at the empty stage. Scientists, spokesmodels, and stagehands hurried about putting final preparations while getting ready for another day of games and sign ups. Lottery applicants would beg for entry or extra chances. Meanwhile, company reps prayed for attention by a big fish like a former famous movie star or social media models new to the Triumvirate. Snagging a rich or famous person that came in with refugees was surprisingly common, and the companies hoped their invention proved successful enough to propel them both to glory. The fact CEOs and other famous people got *extra* lucky is probably what kept Jane so disillusioned about the whole process. Even famous video game players and E-sports pros sometimes got snagged in if they were lucky to survive outside long enough.

One by one, more ticket holders took their place by her side. Within a half hour, crowded summed it up, and in an hour, Jane was fighting for elbow room and got real familiar with those next to her.

A Mexican family with a seven-year-old kid; the mom had crow's feet under her eyes, and the dad with an old postal service hat. An overly tall man with a crooked nose, his cheek scarred, and sunken eyes, in a tattered doctor's robe. A young teenager with a bugout bag and combat boots, prepped for any eventuality. The tickets in their hands clutched to their chest, cradling their hopes for a return to a normal life which would never come.

Do I even deserve to win? I lucked out. Hell, I didn't even work for this ticket ... what if I'm arrested? Am I just like that asshole yesterday buying my way in?

"Welcome!" came the voice from the stage. As red and green lights kicked on, the MC skipped out onto the stage. "Are we ready for another day!"

The crowd cheered.

"Remember, here at T-Cellular Arena, everyone's a winner. You've all worked hard for your tickets and none of you are going home empty-handed. This is our thanks to you, for all the hard labor you've given us. Every ticket grants a year's supply of supplements and nutrients. Others will win a host of prizes from new living quarters to fantastic body upgrades. But for one of you ... For one of you today, the chance of a lifetime. You'll be given a full ride to the most advanced upgrades we offer! Fame, riches, and glory will be yours. Are you ready?"

The crowd cheered.

"I'm sorry, I can't hear you ..."

Jane joined the screams. Feet pounded the pavement. The rhythmic chanting began.

The MC waved his hand and leaned over the edge of the stage. Silence followed. "Then let the games begin." With a flourish of his hand, a message from today's sponsor, Pelican Pharmaceuticals, played over the loudspeakers as the lottery machine churned behind him. The gateway out of poverty tumbled multicolored balls in an ever-spinning wheel, while the masses dreamed of greatness.

Several blue balls tumbled out and down the silver track to the MC. The grand prize winner. Even the MC raised his eyebrow, covered his mic, and asked the voluptuous assistant if that was correct.

"Aren't we in for a surprise today," he said. "Normally, we save the best for last, but Lady Fate wants to get right into the action. They say she's fickle; the grand prize winner is up first, but don't leave after this drawing. Fantastic prizes from our beloved sponsors await each of you ..." Picking up the ball he held it around for the cameras and the viewers at home to witness. The perfectly polished blue ball reminded Jane of a pool table two ball.

Clearing his throat, he read the first number. "Six." The crowd was full of whispers and swears.

Jane's heart jumped in her chest. "I'm a six. I'm a six!" she said to those next to her.

"Thirteen," he spoke louder and deeper into the mic.

Oh man, oh man, oh man ... Jane felt her heart race from the frenzy of excitement. Those around her threw up their hands in frustration, but she bounced.

"Eigggghhhtt," he said while waving his hand out into the crowd. More moans and sadness from the masses, but for the few that still matched, their screams cut through the rest.

Jane was one.

"Six," he said.

It's happening! I can't believe it! Instead of frustration from those next to her, they joined in her excitement, her friendly neighbors getting intoxicated from the jubilee of victory.

"Our final number ... Six. Six-thirteen-eight-six-six," he let his voice echo.

Jane's lottery neighbors were ecstatic, winners by proximity and happy to touch the next star or hope to ride her coattails. Jane stared at the ticket, stunned. Her body moved of its own accord as they pushed her past the velvet ropes and up on the stage. She looked out at the crowd. As they cheered for her, the realization set in. She wasn't just the winner; she was their hopes projected.

"Miss, what's your name?" the MC asked for the third time before Jane snapped back to reality.

"Uhhh ..." was all that came out.

"She's stunned, folks!" The crowd laughed as the MC took her hand and scanned it. "T-Cellular Arena is pleased to present you with Austin native Jane Kilburn-Auburn, ID JK-47!"

My bum is hanging out. Jane tried her best to cover her rear with the white hospital robe. No matter which way she tied the blasted thing, it was always drafty, so she elected to sit on the thin paper that covered the medical table. The cozy room had leather sofas, all the drinks she could want, a full-service bar, and plenty of informative pamphlets about winning the lottery. Jane poked a massive mechanical contraption dangling from the ceiling, filled with scanners.

"Life certainly has taken a rapid turn, eh?" she said to the empty room. Before dawn she was freezing her tail off outside, and by noon she was practically naked in a medical office below the arena. *They don't give you much time to process this, do they?*

A skinny, pale doctor came in flanked by a team of staffers and one suit with a binder.

"Greetings, Jane, I'm Dr. Alex Kristov, nice to meet you," he said holding out his hand. "Let's get started, shall we? Do you know what happens now?" he said through his thick eastern European accent.

Jane shook his hand and nodded. "Yeah. What's next?"

Dr. Alex smiled. "Well, there is legal stuff we have to process. Everything we do here is cutting edge and experimental, so we'll need signatures. But before that, let me tell you what you've won." He pulled out a solid-silver tablet and waved his hand; its form morphed into a 3-D screen that showed Jane's vitals and posture as she slumped on the edge of the table.

She looked up at everyone, and straightened her posture; the silhouette followed.

"I've done a lot of work with Peter Stein Culmen, and, even though my Atlantis robotics series are my specialty, thanks to the team at Pelican Pharmaceuticals you will be our first attempt at a concentrated drug cocktail called ElcollMax. It will increase your speed, agility, and stamina to superhuman levels. Congrats, Jane, you've won a full body upgrade," he said.

"That"—Jane raised an eyebrow—"doesn't sound promising ... the first attempt? I'm a guinea pig? Will I die?"

Dr. Alex chuckled while those in the room held awkward

smiles. "Oh, nothing of the sort. Well, I should say, you won't be invincible, so don't go losing your head in the arena. I mean, you are the first commercial rollout of the cocktail. You'll be debuting along some other first-run military applications." He pulled out a small light and shined it into Jane's eyes.

"Will I get to meet him?" Jane asked.

"Meet who?" Dr. Alex said as he looked into her eyes and checked several blinking screens. "Yes, superb, and your vitals show an exceptional release of endorphins during stress."

"Mr. Culmen," Jane said, blinking. "I've always ..." Brief flashes of her Peter vision yesterday caused goosebumps along her arms.

"If you accept," Dr. Alex said with a pinch on the back of her arm.

"Ow," she said, rubbing her arm. "Well, I mean, yeah, I will accept. What are the details?"

"Excellent!" Dr. Alex spun around on the chair and made the image on his silver tablet grow larger. "We will be issuing a series of injections that will override the body's natural response system and limiters ..." As he talked, the mechanical arm in the ceiling came to life and rotated around Jane, scanning her. "If successful, then we will take a young, athletic girl and allow you to go toe-to-toe with some of the worst freaks the divine host has prepared. It will be a triumph of science! After that, we'll put you through hair and makeup."

"Sounds great!" Jane said with a smile, but she wavered with enthusiasm and self-doubt. *Purgatory, undead, fired from a job, and almost sold into slavery.* She rolled her eyes. *I'm still alive, so this won't kill me either. Right? Is something wrong with my hair?* She blew a stray strand away in a puff.

The door opened and the striking blue eyes of Peter Stein Culmen were the first thing Jane noticed. Her heart skipped a beat, and she quickly checked her hospital robe. *I meet him now of all times, half naked and stressed to the nines.*

"Kristov!" Peter said. Up close, Jane marveled at his smooth black skin and long dreadlocks tied neatly into an elaborate knot. The sleeves of his red dress shirt were folded over his elbows and his bright blue framed glasses played a video that only his left eye could see. "How are the patients? Are we ready to begin the launch? What is the status of the MK-2? You have calibrated everything based off their synapse response time?"

Dr. Alex nodded with each question as his hands split apart into two cybernetic claws and typed. False panels in the room slid back, revealing the vitals of multiple patients with different names. Jane noticed she was one of four. "Sir. Everything is to your specifications, we need your final blessing on the Adramelech equation. The Qliphoth spheres all hold well past the predicted sanity thresholds."

"Fantastic, Kristov! I've high hopes for our work today. Nobody knows what the future holds, so our potential is infinite. Let us begin!" Peter thrust out his arm and pointed right at Jane. "You there!"

Jane jumped up off the table and tried to salute. "Yes sir! Thank you for—"

"Have you accepted your fate yet?" he asked while reaching up and taking control of the mechanical arm, concentrating more on the room around Jane, than on her.

The suit with the binder stepped forward, trying his best to keep his eyes down and avoid contact with Peter's. "Ah, sir," he murmured.

Jane reached out and grabbed the binder. "I sign here and here, right?" The lawyer nodded while Peter looked her up and down. She blushed. Jane perused the papers while Peter Culmen himself readied the surgery bed. Truly, she was too excited watching everyone dance about as they prepped the experiment that she mostly skimmed the entire contract and just signed on the dotted line. Clamps on the table were fastened into position; as Peter slipped on gloves, he twirled his fingers for Jane to get naked and on the table.

"I didn't think you'd be a pervert ..." she whispered under her breath, regretting it, but complying.

"I would say," Peter said with his glasses turning mirror

white, "that the person with perverted thoughts is the pervert. Kristov!" He tipped Jane back horizontally, not even noticing in the slightest that she was nude.

"Yes, sir." Dr. Alex slid back over, putting on a surgery mask himself as people moved out of the room. The mechanical arm split into multiple arms and the two doctors moved them down over Jane's body. Small cold clamps locked into her at ten different locations.

"I can't ... breathe," Jane whispered. "What are you guys doing?" *Can't I have a moment?* The world around her faded into the ashen gray. As each white metallic clamp latched around her arms and legs, she watched the world decay around her. The informative pamphlets decayed into ash that fluttered around the room, Dr. Alex faded away, the sofa rotted, and the medical gear looked abandoned.

But Peter's eyes grew brighter as he stared into her. His hair was a mix of fiber-optic cables and his frame made of synthetic muscle. While the world decayed around Jane, he looked stronger, more machine, and most importantly—aware.

"Only your consent can make this work, Jane," Peter's synthesized voice echoed inside her skull. "We are taking nothing from you, only giving you potential. Will you step forward in the name of science, or will you let the folly of humanity keep you at the gates of oblivion? I can only give you a tool. It is upon you to wield it."

Jane recalled her abandonment as a child, her bouncing between homes for years, all the shitty jobs, the end of the damn world. She focused on his glasses and her ashen world faded back to reality. *I'm not turning back.*

She nodded.

"Then let us begin," both said in unison.

The soft sting of injections began and the rush of power flowing through her as they did. Jane felt as if she would never be more alive than in this second. *It's really happening. I have a future.*

Jane grinned.

CHAPTER EIGHT

With our country in peril, safety from terrorism and immigrants is our utmost priority. Don't let murderers, rapists, and demons into your town. America has the best walls, with the biggest guns. They are huge. So this November, vote Republican. Or say goodbye to the Department of Homeland Security, and your life.

"Kristov," Peter said as he leaned back in the four-wheeled chair. Jane's heart rate was at a new resting heart rate of 160 bpm. "Her glycogen and glucose levels are holding within threshold. Patient is stable." *Another victim, another attempt, and one more chance. Sorry, girl, progress races forward without hesitation.* "How long is her predicted cellular structure going to last?"

Alex Kristov pulled off his mask and slid the mechanical arms back up into the ceiling. He looked at Peter but didn't want to answer.

"I asked you a question, and lest you forget who I am or think me some meek medical student, let's not forget the work we have to do," Peter said, standing up and throwing his blazer back on while fixing his watch.

"She has one year at normal activity before the drugs will cause total organ degradation. Based on how far or how fast she pushes herself, less time than that."

Peter pushed his glasses up with a single finger and glimpsed himself in the mirror. Rich. Powerful. Conceited. *I am not who I set out to be.* "I keep telling the Church of Lazarus that biomedical drugs are not the way to go. Advancements in cyber prosthetics will be far more reliable. Oh, that reminds me ..."

"Yes, sir?" Alex asked.

"I'm concerned about the quality of candidates you and the board of directors are feeding me. I've sponsored Atlantis Enterprises since the 1980s and the best volunteers you can throw my way are lottery winners? This Jane, while agreeable, is not a peak human specimen. What good will my Singularity do us when your cohorts stymie my progress at every turn?" Peter leaned into Alex, placing one hand on each of the arm rests and getting close the Doctor's face. Kristov had been vital to Peter's team— once magic became public; once the profits became crystal clear. Peter smiled a toothy grin with his fangs bared. "I may be on the side of Humanity, dear Kristov, but let us not forget who is gifting your companies with your 'tricks.'" He held up two fingers in quotation marks.

"The lottery is twofold ... Peter," Kristov snarled back. "Citizen morale and free labor. Don't feign empathy for a dumb meatsack like her when you could easily make her a proper vampire. You know, feed her one of those demonic hearts like the Northerners. But no, you've distilled ..."

"A world," Peter snapped back as he opened the door, "filled with undead vampiric bloodsuckers will tear itself apart. The blood addiction alone is enough to get us eating ourselves." He looked at Jane lying on the table. *Perhaps a short life will allow you to burn brightly.* "Technology must destroy us before it can build us anew. Onward and upward, Alex! We've an important guest to entertain and more work ahead of us. The day is young and waits for no beast."

Peter ducked into the hallway at a brisk pace, flanked by assistants as he reviewed their projects. An experimental fertilizer that turned corpses into electricity, and a sterilization virus for the rampant pet outbreak were on his plate today. Ever the multitasker, he maintained engaged conversations with the CEO of Encom, a South American subsidiary, and cracked jokes about his golf game. A Russian oligarch from Rasputin's neck of the woods called to inquire about investment opportunities and the latest in designer drugs to combat a small wyvern nest that cropped up.

Despite all of this, Peter still had time for self-reflection and stopped to admire the progress of construction at every intersection. Kristov, meanwhile, clumsily followed in the hallway behind him, cursing at the pace while scrambling to follow security protocols. Sealing each room they passed before racing ahead of the pack yet another time and swiping his wrist to open the next.

This, my fellow warlocks, is how you save the world. Peter worked for the Unification. Deep down, he knew he didn't have the raw power of the late Warlock Vryce in the Twin Cities. Nor would he ever have a litany of True Names like Rasputin or the backing of an entire Royal nation like the Jade Warlock. *But with a little more research, I will revolutionize the world.* His technomagic was nothing more than Hermetic principles, applied in new ways, that other warlocks were too old to see. As he rounded the corner in the white-walled medical rooms, with assistants and rogue scientists struggling to keep up with him, Peter knew he only had to convince one creature—the Lord of Suicide—that the world would survive through tech, and not going back to the dark ages. *He gave me the power and all he asked for was compliance. I gave it. Now I'm ready to show my mentor what his faith has wrought.*

The Death Lord stood with an amused smirk on his face and his hands thrust through his gold-trimmed robe as he waited just outside the sealed lab of Peter's latest experiment. His golden mask, crested with wings that poked out of his hood like demon horns, represented the flight one takes when leaping off a building. Beneath the trappings of the Church, however, was the famed leader for the Ordre du Temple Solaire, a suicide cult that came to prominence in the early 90s. Layers of skin from suicide victims were stitched over his entire body, a macabre paper-mache abomination with robes, and he was the Church of Lazarus's champion here in North America. *And my boss, of all things.*

Peter kept his face straight as he reached out to shake the thing's hand. Peter had grown used to his boss's real appearance over the past decades; everyone else just saw an old man. How Death Lords came to power was a mystery to Peter, but he knew it involved the Masks, secret societies, and rulership over a portion of Purgatory. Each Death Lord could recruit one warlock in a messed-up master-apprentice fashion that reminded Peter far too much of the Sith. For the most part, if he did his job in the great ritual to revive Lazarus ... the Death Lords stayed out of his way. All they wanted was their God returned, he supposed, but to Peter—it seemed they didn't have a plan for what came next. That meant the Death Lords sudden arrival in Peter's territory was either very good ... or very bad. *Anxiety is just another form of excitement. This is our chance.*

Peter went to make introductions, only to find his assistants making themselves scarce through a variety of excuses. Even Kristov ducked into the nearest room to keep his hands busy. *Not ready to reveal yourself, are you, Lord? Keeping yourself hidden still?* When the Death Lord wanted to talk alone—anyone unwanted found themselves subtly influenced to be elsewhere. On a few occasions, Peter wondered to himself if that's the reason he rarely contacted the council.

It shook Peter's hand, sending a warm, calm touch through his body. "That's correct, child. The world is not ready for my peace yet, and we place our hopes in you to avoid such a fate," he said with a calm French accent. No matter how many times they met, the outward appearance of the Lord, and his inner kindness, always surprised Peter.

"I hope the past few days in your city have illuminated the luxuries of transhumanism to you, my Lord," Peter said, bowing, beads in his hair rattling as they broke the silence.

"*Our* city, child. How many times must I remind you? It was you who saved it from the traitors to the north. Without your fast action, the outbreak of Mexico would've spread." He placed a hand on Peter's shoulder, and through the use of his magic changed his appearance back to that of an old French Canadian with gray hair, glasses, and a surprisingly oversized set of bushy eyebrows. A simple spell, that burnt the edges of his skin off and left small flecks of ash in the air, but altered every aspect of the hideous lord. "Without my teachings, these cities would be ruled by demons instead of men."

Peter broke eye contact briefly. Mexico City was his act of compliance that stained his soul. Peter unleashed a magical prototype. Ravenous shapechanging lifeforms based off silicone rather than carbon that spread like a virus, ending demon and human alike. A small sacrifice in order to save billions more. *Hideous, mindless creatures, but, as they say, the ends justify the means.* "Why do you always wait until you see me before you change?" Peter asked, rising.

"To remind you of Lichdom. The glorious fate of those who drink from both heaven and hell, and reclaim their souls," he said as they began strolling. "To be shackled with divine purpose for eternity in a universe that has long since been broken. The dead need guidance, and we are forever chained to offer it."

"As a Warlock, I'm aware." Peter paused and prayed. He had already consumed the heart of both Angel and Demon years ago and had his soul shredded seven ways by the unholy process. A cost warlocks paid in order to save the world, for without Lazarus's return—the afterlife was eternal. Despite being of shattered soul, Peter was still free to pursue his own agenda. Fixing his soul could get him imprisoned in Purgatory for thousands of years like Lazarus or bound as a Death Lord, hearing the petitions of those who died. Bound to govern over those who committed suicide wasn't exactly a morale-boosting job description and freedom served as a damn good reminder of why he should let that matter lie. After all, locked away in a crypt or shackled in a form of eternal community service like the Death Lords would severely hamper his personal drive. Even Warlock Vryce died when he broke rank to become a Lich. Even if he was free for a bit, it was still too risky. *Instead I've come up with a Plan B.* "So, I think the final touches are being put on everything. Are you ready to see what we can do for the Unification?"

"You still believe this is a material war fought with guns and bullets, don't you?" The Lord's posture deflated as sadness took root. "Yes, the Unification needs an army for its crusades. The fate of reality is at stake. Belief and propaganda shape minds, child. It will take more than your mechanical contraptions to unify the afterlife and the living under one banner."

"Kristov," Peter leaned into a microphone outside a reflective mirror. "Fire up the Terror Twins, Tyler and Taylor." He wiggled his eyebrows and smiled at his Lord. "Oh, these are not mere mechanical contraptions. Divine will, magic of the universe, now bent and broken at our command. Talk of souls, flesh, and faith may win hearts, but when a thirty-foot-tall demon of war is raging through your city, you'll need these two." Peter pointed inside the oversized lab that resembled a hangar.

Two twin pilots of clear relation—both had the same pointed ridge on their nose and stick-straight black hair—stood on suspended platforms. They climbed into two sets of mechanized power armor. Tubes, clamps, and wires set themselves into place as the suits sealed themselves skin tight around each. With nothing but their thoughts, the twins moved the mechanized creations and cycled through the weapons chambers in a deafening display of firepower.

"The secret is," Peter shouted over sounds of heavy footsteps, "its core power system. A hermetically sealed antechamber of a still living angel heart! Why turn everyone into something they aren't meant to be, when you can build a suit around them! And, as I told you, I didn't make these! Regular humans did all the construction by following our blueprints for years. All they needed was the fuel!"

The Lord of Suicide waited with his weathered hands folded in front of him until the showcase subsided. His poker face was unflappable. "So, you are saying regular non-blooded humans harvested, built, and trained in the contraption with the heart of a Seraphim? Careful, Peter; like Prometheus, you may be burned by your own fire. Still, I'm interested in seeing what the will of man has wrought; now, show me the one I ordered for your debut to the council."

Peter nodded. *Yes! Debut is good. We can work with a debut. It's not a no.* He led the Lord back to Jane's room. Passersby in the hallway now saw Peter walking with a kind old man and correctly assumed he was an important figure. Opening the door to Jane's room, Peter heard the Lord let out a slight gasp.

"What happened to this child?" he said as he took to her bedside and placed his hand on her forehead. "She is near the precipice of death, and in my domain of suicide, nonetheless. She consented to her own demise?"

"I'm afraid the latest batch of refined Elcoll is still unstable," Peter said, keeping his voice low. *Suicide? Science could advance to save her tomorrow. When a clinical trial fails ... it will count as suicide? Because she ...* Peter bit his bottom lip and recalled Jane skimming the contract. Peter knew damn well there was a clause against liability from side effects within, but that was no assurance it would *kill* her by her own hand. *He sees something I don't, and if that's the result ... we've got better options.* "While it will no doubt produce great physical enhancements, it will burn her life out in the months to come. Like Icarus, we flew to close to the sun with this project. I think we should move on from future study. The cost is too high."

"No, no, no, this is perfect," the Lord whispered under his breath.

"What, what?" Peter dropped his phone in surprise and, in his hurry to catch it, whacked his elbow on Jane's bedside in the soft spot. *You've gotta be kidding me!* Peter wasn't sure if it was the pain or the Lord that surprised him more.

"The Unification's goal is to prevent fractures and divisions of belief from tearing creation apart, and what a beautiful flower to burn brightly in life, before carrying that battle to the edge of Purgatory in death. A warrior who will fight our material enemies in this world, and then those eternals beyond." The Lord stood up from Jane's bedside and pulled out a small model airplane from his robes. Handcrafted from wood, it was something the Lord put great care in, and he placed it on Jane's chest before uttering a prayer.

"My Lord, I understand my place as your Warlock, but I must object. You cannot rebuild the world with an army of the dead," Peter said, not taking his eyes off the figurine.

"That is correct, and I don't want you to make any more like her. I want you to refine the formula more. Create one which will placate their minds, ease the burden of facing a black sun each morning, and prepare their souls for a journey beyond. Dial back its potency for combat if you must, but don't worry about accelerating the side effects of death; most humans die at some point. Everyone knows that isn't the end."

"I mean, I can just order up some Prozac if you want a happy pill ..." Peter smirked.

Even the Lord allowed himself a small smile.

Poker face busted. I'll deliver what you seek, even if it is beneath my abilities. Generic, barely effective combat supplement from a pill, easy to distribute to all countries in the world? Another antidepressant for the black sun with nasty side effects? Fine. I'll put Kristov on it later.

"I believe it's your turn?" The Lord glared at Peter as he gently closed the door, to not disturb the sleeping patient.

"That is correct, but I want you to watch this live. Demons, Angels, these are enemies, yes. But other sorcerers like the Society of Deus or the freaks in Sons and Daughters? They've got mind control nearly perfected. Not only have I hacked their system, I can improve on it! With this breakthrough, it's the first step in preserving our minds. In time, we can even defeat death!

I will build the ultimate weapon out of an anarch blood junkie conditioned to follow orders, and you'll get to watch." Peter spun on his heels and practically sprinted out of the room. His enthusiasm taking him faster than his companion. "Onward to progress!" *Let us make flesh into steel* ...

CHAPTER NINE

Get to T-Cellular Arena this Sunday for riveting action! Watch your new Texan hometown favorites, the Terror Twins, as they crush the demonic scum for your amusement! Witness the first basilisk get peppered with lead! Fun for all ages! 124 oz. dead-drinks are buy one get one half off!

Jack was certain he tasted peanut butter. He couldn't feel his legs, or his arms, or anything else for that matter. But the sweetness of peanut butter, he was sure of. As he worked his tongue around in his mouth, or at least as he tried to, the room came into as clear of a focus as possible. A light blue light had mimicked a lens flare from a bad action flick right above him, causing him to squint his eyes. Only he couldn't. It was around now that the realization dawned on him. *Oh ... I must be dead or something. At least heaven has peanut butter, right? Better not be that cheap non-organic shit. Shouldn't I be asking how I died?* As he thought about it more, he glimpsed Peter Culmen looming over him.

Hey, it's that famous guy from TV, is he dead as well?

Jack saw the clear plastic that surrounded him and the smooth alabaster medical arms that slowly moved around him. At the edge of his vision, mirrored windows reflected the contents of the room, including himself. With no arms, legs, or much of a torso left—the sight of his lungs breathing artificially felt surreal. *Hey ... it's me.* His eyes met his own in the mirror, and the top of his skull was wide open with wires sticking out where hair should be. *It's not real!* He couldn't move anything but his eyes, and they darted around the room in ever-increasing panic, anything to avoid seeing his own reflection.

"Gentlemen and fellow transhumanists, technocrats, and war profiteers," Peter addressed a crowd outside Jack's vision. "We gather here today because the world as we know it has shattered. Scientific reason crushed under the heels of folklore and magic. Just over a year ago, there were over seven billion humans on this planet. Today, we stand strong at an estimated number of five billion. Life continues for those of means, wealth, or determination. Should we be willing to accept such a massive loss of human life? Ask yourselves, deep down, if you really think we can survive."

Am I watching a video? No, no, I'm pretty sure this is real. Why can't I blink? Last thing I remember was getting caught up in a protest. There was this crazy bug mantis vampire bitch cutting down police officers in the Twin Cities ... or was it St. Louis? I was arrested, in the back of the cop car for a prison transfer, when ... Ah, yes, Akira, her name was. She cut me out of the cuffs and set me loose, that's for sure. Akira. I robbed three banks when everyone else was losing their minds over demons from Doom crawling out. Jack certainly wasn't sure of his current situation, and the memories of fighting in a riot, robbing banks, and drinking demon's blood seemed impossible. *It's not real! Don't be an idiot. I'm a fucking shitbag who got arrested for muggin' people and have spent the past year playing virtual reality games in prison. Playing soldier and capturing cities, blasting monsters with rockets. I lost on the last level and got captured. Do I still have a lawyer?*

"The sun"—Peter paused and put a finger to his lips—"is under a permanent eclipse, despite satellites showing us that no object blocks the sun. Inexplicable phenomena happen daily. The ghosts of the dead walk among us. Demons from the pits of hell have poured forth into the world. Beasts of myth and legend roost in the vast unoccupied landscape that makes up our country, let alone the world. This was just the first day."

What the fuck did they do! Assholes! I only robbed a few people. Everyone looted! Viva la revolution! I need a fix. I need a fix. Just a dash of demon's blood! Where is my trial? Even though Jack wept internally, his body did not twitch in the slightest, not even a dilation of pupils. He didn't live the best life, and he knew it. A former Blackwater mercenary, he engaged in military actions that were detestable, and when he was washed up he fell into local violent crime and murdered an ATF Agent. That part of his past was clear, but when the riots started, and the sun turned black, his memory felt like a fog. On his tongue he could feel the sweet taste of peaches and recalled the intoxicating rush of power from drinking demon blood. Since Akira busted him out of that cop car, he lived for that rush. *It wasn't real, right? All that fighting with Akira? The plan to get arrested ... to get here ... one prison to the next? I can't think straight. I'm here to kill someone, aren't I? Because my shit life is worth nothing and I can redeem myself.* He craved blood. *Even Peter's if he could get his teeth around his neck.*

"A single day is all it took for social order to break down," Peter said as he spun Jack around and propped him up. Jack could see the room of doctors and suits ahead of him, all of them staring on with a wide-eyed intense gaze. "Murder, looting, rioting ... cannibalism. These things devastated the civilized world. Dare I say, it may have outright destroyed the third world. To this day, many places remain dark. Who knows what happens in Montana or Tunisia? But hope was not lost. Thanks to the Church of Lazarus's intervention, backed by the global body of the Unification, control was forced upon those willing to listen. Yet this control was based on a fallacy ..." Peter gazed at a kind old man with bushy eyebrows.

All right, man, you know torture. This isn't it. I'm still alive and this motherfucker is nuts. He's been affected by chemtrails. None of that stuff happened. Akira wasn't some vampire revolutionary, she was part of a movie. I remember when that black sun rose. The shadows started talking to me in the transport. That was fucked up. Become your own god, they said. Called on us to take up arms against the soldiers attacking the Twin Cities. I ... I don't remember what happened next. It was like I was possessed by a demon. Jack recalled a series of flashes, him fighting soldiers, or crammed between Akira and other undead as they ripped the National Guard limb from limb. They were fighting to escape the chaos. Escape the undead, escape the guard, escape the cops, escape the end.

Amidst the gasps of the crowd, Peter stood in front of the old man. "That fallacy was that Science was defeated. That its principals were tested and found wanting. Its measuring cup, unfilled. Just because magic hath returned to the world does not mean the tools that make mankind divine are any less!" Peter flung his arms out wide as small blue rings of light appeared around his hands. The medical equipment burst into life around Jack and worked in concert with Peter's gestures. "Science had many questions about our universe. Dark matter, the Higgs Boson, the nature of consciousness, and the quest for immortality eluded us because we only had one part of the equation. Gaps that we now have answers to. With science as our shield, we have applied tried and true methods of reason to magic and bent it to our will."

Jack watched in the mirrors as neon green fibers grew from mechanical arms like tentacles from a jellyfish and dug their way into his shoulders. Searing white pain shot through what remained of his body. He screamed in silent terror.

"Marketable." Peter orchestrated with his hands as machines danced to his whim behind him.

Jack perceived his past get eaten away, memory by memory. Thousands of minutes erased in a flash. Akira training him to fight hellhounds, deleted. A delicious grin from a girl while making love, deleted. The terror of being possessed, deleted. The cold, vomit-inducing sweat after he took his first life by gun, deleted. A top-secret plan to infiltrate the Triumvirate, deleted. His daughters, deleted.

"Reproducible." Monitors flickered to life, each filled with images of a human body merging with silicon fibers. Pumps pushed oxygen through artificial lungs and black blood flowed through a centrifuge before flowing into Jack.

Jack fought to hold on to memories. Few were worth keeping, so he focused on his training. Fighting, killing, and survival took hold over sorrow. Sorrow over the news of his daughter's death at the hands of humans high on demons' blood. Sorrow over his own failure as a father, as a man. Survival, however, he was good at. Killing for country, survival for money, fighting for drugs, and most importantly—running from the pain.

"Controllable." Peter pulled his arms together and inhaled deeply. By will alone Peter weaved thousands of neon green silicon fibers through every inch of Jack.

I am Jack. I am Jack.

"We need not fear the darkness, the undead, the sorcerers who tried to bring this world to its knees to forge their empires of chaos. Science will destroy us. Science will build us anew. Today you each witness the evolution of humanity. The first functioning prototype of a full-body cyborg. A living brain, spinal cord, and nervous system merged with a machine built right here in what remains of the United States of America. Each component bought and built from one of your companies with my silicon fibers as the glue. Now we assemble them into an advanced creation to defend us for generations to come, all by turning the Society of Deus's soldiers against them. Or any military on this planet that uses monster blood to strengthen its army. Can't we, Jack?" Peter leaned over Jack, holding his chin with two fingers, and gazing into Jack's eyes.

Jack focused on Peter's bright blue eyes and blinked. It felt like heaven. Most of his body tickled and squeezed upon itself, as if he was wearing a giant metal shell that lit his nerves on fire with the gift of sensation. A hard coating to the normal sensation of touch—but he could twitch his finger. A wide grin crept over his face, visible to him through his own reflection in Peter's eyes. His short brown hair spiked off in every direction and a fresh goatee poked out over a metallic chin strap. Dark gray mechanical arms jutted out of his shoulders with plates merging and covering up his internal systems. His legs looked powerful as the pistons within itched for exercise. In the upper right corner of his vision, a green overlay showed his health and vital statistics. Deep within himself, Jack accepted the coding dancing in his thoughts taking hold as systems came online. With each passing second as each system came online, the world appeared more digital to him as an AR Overlay wove together with normal sight.

I'm a player in a game. This makes a lot more sense. He tried his best to ignore the occasional flicker that showed a strange gutter-punk-looking girl with brightly colored hair standing in the audience, tipping her head slightly. She seemed to study his current plight with emotionless disdain. He tried his best to ignore the constant palate of peanut butter in his mouth. He even tried to ignore that he couldn't remember any concrete events before yesterday, just ... things, places, and a healthy fog of instincts that felt elusively out of reach. *I'm a player named Jack in some techno-virtual reality game, I suppose. Cyborg, did he say?*

"What do I get if I win?" Jack asked. Not surprised his voice sounded nothing like what he imagined he sounded like.

The audience cheered and erupted into applause. *Hey, I did something right!* Everyone except the girl with purple-and-green hair and emotionless eyes applauded. In a flicker, Jack knew she was a friend, a killer, like him. *Kinsmen or even his teacher,* he wondered. *She's a player. Different power set, I bet.*

"Well," Peter said as latches unbuckled themselves and the table stood upright, releasing its mechanical prisoner. "If you win, you'll be a legend within history. Like the gladiators of Rome, you'll prove that even criminals and terrorists can be redeemed among the living in this glorious new age. Fame, money, and the keys to mankind's evolution rest within you." As Peter turned, Jack saw his neatly braided dreadlocks cascade down as the man spoke with greater pride to the assembled crowd. "With Jack, we've taken an enemy soldier who's murdered and fallen to pure demon's blood addiction and reformed him. At his lowest point, his own family was cannibalized by those junkies who sought to extract the slightest ounce of power. The addiction to raw divine blood ... angelic or demonic ... is real and deadly. Few have the power and determination to devour a heart of such creatures and shed their humanity."

Jack hobbled forward like a newborn calf before gyroscopes balanced him out. *Wait ... what?* Clanking rang through the chamber as the crowd watched him take his first steps. It felt like controlled falling more than walking. With a sense of vertigo, he stumbled to the right quickly, legs peddling underneath him of their own volition as he came crashing into a wall to the right, shattering the mirror.

"Even Rome wasn't built in a day," the old man with fuzzy eyebrows said inches from where Jack crashed into, wiping a tear from a tired cheek and averting his gaze from the embarrassing display.

There was an emotion there that Jack couldn't seem to process. Humans make faces with sunken eyes and water when ... the words just weren't in his language anymore. Everyone else was happy and applauding or staring into the room with murderous intent. Those he understood. His balance regained, Jack stood upright and took more controlled falls back to the center of the room. This time, without fault.

"I beg to differ, my Lord. With an army of Jacks, we could rebuild any empire we wanted. Without sleep. Without injury. Without remorse." Peter spun around on his heels and held his finger up. "The world is devouring itself for magic!" Peter's voice boomed. "We now have the ability to take any blood addict and keep them human. Pry ghouls away from masters, turn witches to our side, and repurpose lost men safely thanks to science."

The crowd gave a soft, yet uneasy, applause. Jack saw many eyes darting to the old man.

Peter smirked, as if he had more tricks up the sleeves of his bespoke suit. "I may be a true believer, but you are motivated by profit. So thus, I will play by the rules of the arena." Peter took a huge bow and waited for the crowd to silence before rising. "Jack and three others will showcase their talents with no training. Thrust into the fires of combat so that only the sheer effectiveness of their corporate enhancements is on display—not inherent skill. Let the free market decide." Peter put his arms out wide and gestured to most of the crowd. "Will you at least allow the masses to decide their future?"

Jack watched the old man give a nod and a sly grin appear on the young face of Akira. Why doesn't anyone else seem to notice this awesome killer chick in the room? I mean, she looks about ready to separate heads from shoulders. He watched her mouth a message to him: "You've got this, cupcake. You're the big gun now."

"Huh?" Jack said aloud.

"Sorry, sorry," Peter said, hurrying over to his creation. "We detract from the wonder at hand! Let's get you some weapon systems on this magnificent frame of ours." As Peter put his arm around Jack and escorted him out of the room, he waved to the audience. "So, tell me, any special thoughts about rocket launchers?"

Jack smiled, as he recalled holding a rocket launcher. Not in any specific moment of time. No memory before, or after. Just an edited video clip of his life, shot in the first person. A memory pulled up from a digital file in his own brain ... he was pulling a trigger.

"Rockets are fun. Who doesn't like explosions?"

CHAPTER TEN

Tune in tonight for an in-depth look at the horrors happening in Minnesota where the terrorist group Society of Deus continues its expansion. Our reporters are live on the scene as we witness these savages herd the dead and harvest the divine. Did the liberal north, led by Anarchist Mike Auburn, bring the downfall of America? Find out more. Only on CNB.

L egends never die," Dr. Alex Kristov said as he bolted supplemental armored plating onto Jack. "It will take time to synchronize with all of your new body's features, but as long as that brain of yours stays intact"—he tapped on Jack's forehead —"you're immortal."

As they sat in a modified skybox looking over the arena, Jack ran through his possibilities. Either he could remain a stubborn bastard and resist this game they wanted them to play. Or he could march down to the Astroturf below and let the small hellhounds rip him limb from limb and win the entire bloody game. It was an obvious choice. *Whoever I was before, fuck 'em. This is way cooler. I've literally got an arm cannon.* No matter how many times he said it to himself, though, it still never rang true. The conversion from flesh to machine was too fast and the numbers didn't add up. Even if memories played back in snipped cuts, there were still lingering feelings—remorse, bitterness, desire, and indignation—that yearned for definition in his heart.

In a year, technology had advanced to where full cybernetic conversion of a human body was possible. *Bullshit.* The secrets were obvious. They were at this for decades behind closed doors and judging from the serial numbers printed at the base of his components—he wasn't the first. *Nor will I be the last.* He fidgeted with his matte black right hand, opening and closing it and trying to feel each servo activate. It moved at his command like instructed, but to Jack it felt like someone else's arm. As if he was picking up the phone, calling his right arm, and telling it to move. *Man, I better not have to call a damn eight hundred number for tech support. Just shoot me now if that's the case.*

"Don't worry, you're still you," Kristov said with a pause, looking up at him with an oddly shaped headpiece filled with lenses and microscopes. "The silicon project can't transfer a soul or a conscience yet, even though Peter is working on it. For now, the best we can do is control a body through your squishy brain housed in a mechanical shell. You'll notice a lack of memory and the inability to comprehend emotions for a time, but it's temporary. We think."

"Why?" Jack asked.

"Why what?"

"Why not just build a mindless killing machine, a robot, or use someone who signed up for this?" Jack shrugged and looked out through the window. Fans and citizens were filing in and filling up the rows. Many of them shirtless with black and blue body paint on, in the triangle-shaped logo of Triumvirate Enterprises. Cheerleaders and merchandise cannons fired off during the pre-show to rile up the crowd.

Alex looked back down and resumed soldering the armor plates. "The uncanny valley effect."

Jack grunted.

"You have no clue what that is. I know. Even now the world grapples to accept magic and the supernatural. It was the same with robots. When something is close to a human, that isn't human, it provokes a strange revulsion from people. They can just ... tell. It's stupid, I know. But nobody ever said the unwashed masses were intelligent. After all, people still believe the earth is flat."

"So. Let 'em die. If they aren't smart enough to survive, fuck 'em. In this game, it's survival of the fittest." Jack heard the words come out of his mouth, but as he spoke them, he couldn't quite pick where he had picked them up.

Kristov grinned. "Annnd there's your answer. That's why we picked you. You are America's new weapon, along with a few other side projects. The big fucking gun. Metallic Jack. Patriotism personified. Guns, engines, consumerism, and walking, shooting billboard of progress. When you crush the competition out there, you'll be a legend. Our legend. Rather than flocking to the north and sipping on demon's blood for power, people will line up outside the gates to have their arms replaced." Sparks flew as Kristov finished his final touches. "Perfecto."

Jack stood up, towering over the doctor, and tried to crack his neck from side to side. Rather than the satisfying pop of spinal fluid being released, his only reward was the slight hum of servos. With measured footfalls forward to the reinforced glass, he opened the skybox door and stepped out onto the balcony. Only on his face did he feel the refreshing cool air as he looked over the assembled crowd. An advertisement broadcasting a pixie-driven lost item service was playing throughout as people loaded up on calorie-laden refreshments. *They all look gray.* None of the people looked in full color; instead, facial features blended together, their colors didn't stand out, as if they were part of a backdrop in an artificial world. Jack looked back at Dr. Alex, who stood out in full color, and recalled that Peter looked the same.

Shaking his head, Jack looked back into the arena. The hellhounds looked vile, slimy and red with burnt, black flesh as they snapped and tugged on their iron chains. *Barghests. Hounds of Tindalos, messengers of the seventh layer.* The information flowed into his brain as his visual recognition snapped into place. Thoughts that were his, but again, pulled from some distant memory bank. *It's like I'm downloading myself. Where the hell is the porn?* He whacked the side of his head and grunted when none came.

Even with the black sun in the sky, the Astroturf looked fresh. Across the way in another skybox, Jack saw a pretty blonde girl with electric blue tubes coming out of her arms and neck. She was in full detail. His vision zoomed in automatically and he could see every stray hair that was out of her ponytail. She smiled and talked to her handler as she jittered and bounced on her feet. *Jane AKA JK-47. Bioprogram Initiative.* To his left, he brought his eyes on two pilots in skintight jumpsuits with olive, tanned skin and jet black hair. Each of them was eating a nutrient bar (a nasty-tasting one from the looks on their faces) and leaning on giant metal boxes. *Taylor and Tyler AKA the Terror Twins. Hardsuit Initiative.*

"I think something's messed up with my vision," Jack said, gazing out the arena window.

"Ehhh, don't worry about that," Kristov said with an annoyed tick. "We've jacked you into a database with a combat protocol. Allies and enemies will appear sharper and give you what information we have. It helps with the mental stress. It only activates when violence is just around the corner."

So how can I be sure I'm really me? Which thoughts are mine and which is the combat feed? Wait. Got it. If I sound like a talking toaster, it's the combat feed. For someone who was meant to be emotionless, Jack couldn't help but laugh at the idea of his body making toast.

"Hey, big guy," Kristov said as he opened the door to the hallway. "It's time to make your big debut and live interview. Chin up. Smile on. Not everyone gets to conduct a live interview side by side with Peter and a legion of press."

Jack lumbered over to Dr. Alex and stared at the small,

skinny man who froze while clutching his headset. It was easy for Jack to imagine his cybernetic hand crushing the little bastard's head like an orange. Something about the doctor just rubbed Jack the wrong way, even though he couldn't put a finger on it. Like a forgotten song, it sat there in his mind, eating away at him. He settled with jamming his finger into the doctor's chest. "I'm part of some trial program. I get that. Hell, I'm probably still on a table and this is all a simulation. I get that. You screw me, I'll find a way to—"

Kristov's eyes widened for a brief second and his pupils dilated. *Terror.* He took a step back and looked at a diagnosis sheet written in a language Jack couldn't understand.

"It's unwise to threaten the person who will put you back together." Kristov cracked his knuckles and kept himself three paces away. "Once assembled, you can just as easily be disassembled. I'm your only hope for survival. After all, survival of the fittest ..." He held his arms out wide with a cocked eyebrow.

"See." Jack walked out. "I knew you were lying. I'm only immortal as long as you wish it."

The flash and flicker of bulbs, cameras, and cellphones shuttered so quickly the world moved in slow motion to Jack. With each heavy footfall of his as he lumbered out to the shark tank, a hundred photos were snapped, with many appearing live on billboards and screens nearby in real time. Peter Culmen held his crystal blue eyes wide open with an ear-to-ear. Jack wondered how a man could be so vibrant and imposing at once. *It's gotta be the dreadlocks. Everyone looks better with dreadlocks. He's thrilled about this, isn't he? Do these people think the Earth is flat?* He shook his head, brushing the worry off with his metallic hand, and tried to walk up the steps.

It didn't work.

Falling forward as a means of walking was fine, but stairs were a whole new challenge. His ankle twisted and tried to bend inward. Off-balance and top-heavy from extra armor, Jack spiraled down right shoulder first into the ground. Flecks of concrete flew off from the impact as the ground shook, and he instinctively rolled forward. Left hand over right knee, a few gears twisting to the left, a small boost from a piston in his right arm, and a shock wave thundered out as he slid to the nearest rusted pillar in a three-point landing. Small calibrations in his body adjusted themselves as he rose. The dead silence of the room was broken by small clicks and servos whirring as Jack stood. *Why are they impressed that I can fall? Also, who the fuck debuts this shit so quickly?*

Claps echoed off walls as Peter's loud thunderous applause picked up steam from his followers who apprehensively followed suit. The reporters and those beyond the red tape were less enthused. Jack couldn't help but feel they were seeing him for what he was—another failed science experiment.

"Ladies and gentlemen," Peter said. "Hunting monsters is suicidal. Our military has been devastated. Conventional tactics simply Do. Not. Work. Those who are born from the abyss, the fiends who have crawled out of Purgatory, and the vengeful who have descended from above, do not acknowledge fortifications, structures, lines of combat, or any rules of war. We need the ability to take a regular man ..." Peter paused and paced around the platform.

"What is the cost to build that?" A cacophony of reporter's questions filled the void. "Is that thing street legal? Do we need a payment plan? What's its power source? Is there any truth to the rumor you intend to deploy nuclear weapons against other states?"

Jack's vision shifted. The reporters went from being grayed-out nobodies to crystal clear in an instant. Every object became high-resolution and quantified: their weights, heights, estimated speed, and strength. *These blokes need to lay off the booze and find a treadmill.* Even though their questions were aimed at Peter, Jack took deliberate steps forward and marched up to the podium. This time without the showmanship of a fall. The questions tapered off. His hairs stood on edge, though. Somewhere in the crowd was a threat, a hunter or a spy, stalking them. He couldn't explain the feeling any better than a glitchy security camera in his heart; it picked up something, but you couldn't make it out. *I know, I know this feeling ...?*

"Not just regular men," Peter continued. "We as a nation have paid zero attention to the plight of our elderly, our infirm, those born with defects, or injured in the early days. The malnourished and starving. While *we* here within the walls, have the *privilege* of advanced life, the rest of this country suffers." Peter spat the words out and slammed his fist on the podium.

Jack could feel power radiate off him, and by the looks of the reporters, so could they. *There in the back.* He saw mixed into the crowd a soldier in a brown trench coat, leaning with one knee up on a rack of vertical conduits—smirking at Peter. Jack noticed the green duffle bag at his feet, and his sandy blond hair. Just as Jack zeroed in on the suspect, it became a two-way street. The soldier was looking right at him with his piercing red eyes. Jack ran through data fluttering before his eyes. *No vitals. No heartbeat. No pulse. No estimated speed or strength. Soldier Symon Vasyl died during the Second World War. He's either a ghost or a vampire, either way ...*

Symon pointed at Jack, his hands wearing tattered, fingerless gloves, and faked a gunshot. "Kapow," he mouthed. Then he was gone. After shaking his head, Jack looked again. It wasn't a case of him running away. He was there. Then vanished into thin air. *Am I hallucinating?*

"So that's why," Peter's voice rang out, "we will debut Metallic Jack in the arena with no prior training at the same time as our other debut products."

Jack had missed something important.

"You can handle it, right, Jack?" Peter asked.

"Ummmmm ..." Jack looked around at the crowd. "Yup." *It couldn't have been that important.*

"Why don't you show them your technomancy, Jack, while we answer questions?" Peter nodded and patted him on the back before whispering to him, "Did you think you wouldn't attract a little attention from our enemies? Unlike them, we won't risk the collateral damage. So just relax and show off."

It was entirely important. Technomancy. What the fuck is that? How long was I locked eyes with that Symon soldier?

"All right, Kevin Thayer, I know you will hit me with some real questions. Let's get 'em out," Peter said.

A tall man with wire-framed glasses cracked his neck and chucked a cup of coffee to the side, oblivious to the burning effect it had on those nearby. "Mr. Culmen."

"Ow! That hurt!" The nearby reporter protested getting a cup of scalding joe to his right ear.

"Quiet, the parents are talking," Kevin Thayer said, and wrestled free from the crowd closer to the podium. "Mr. Culmen, you've opened a can of worms with this project, and I think many will agree that you've gone too far."

"Stick to the questions, Kevin, not the bias," Peter's deep voice carried over.

"Well. If there's a human inside, does it get to retire? What is the life expectancy of those biological components? Are you committed to performing maintenance on this unit as long as it desires this? How long until that affects profits as units like this one become obsolete?" Kevin's questions cut through the air.

Peter raised an eyebrow and looked to Jack with a nod. *He's enjoying this.*

"The reality is," Peter said leaning in, "retirement is not a luxury anymore, and I've spoken with countless elderly who have been fortunate enough to survive who are itching to get back in the fight. With proper maintenance, those biological components can be refreshed until brain damage sets in. So, no, we aren't making immortals yet, but we predict a longer than normal lifespan. Lastly, profits aren't the concern of Triumvirate Enterprises. Evolution is. Units like Jack will never be obsolete as we can upgrade them at any time."

Kevin nodded before firing back. "Given the poor history of psychological health in both the military and police, how do we know that these units won't snap and become a danger? You've also done nothing to present this unit as a human, simply a weapon for police and military application. Have humans just become another component for your products? How does this make Triumvirate Enterprises any different from—"

Peter cut him off. "Why don't you give him a little show, Jack?"

Jack stared at Peter and silently worked his mouth open and shut. He did not understand what Peter wanted him to do. On a whim he held his right arm out to the side and mentally activated its weapon mode. He knew that much. Red proteins mixed with green silicon as the plasma spiraled around and charged up, distorting the air around his arm from the heat. Peter ran next to Jack and slapped his hand on his back before he fired.

"Sorry for the lack of briefing, or instruction manual. We weren't intending to put this show on yet. Someone has been forcing our hands to move early ... but don't worry about that. They don't know just how ready we really are," Jack heard inside his brain. He tried to move but couldn't. When his arms raised above his head, and his vision turned blue, Jack had nothing to do with it. He watched, a prisoner in his own shell, as Peter's magic moved his arms to fire off safe electrical discharges instead.

"Activate your technomancy protocol and command the televisions. Here. I'll show you how."

With a flick of his wrist and a foreign mental thought, Jack saw the power cells and batteries in every device. He saw energy flowing through conduits in walls up to dingy yellow light fixtures dangling in the arena. Among the camera lights, he saw their power packs. Anything that was mechanical and powered, like the motorized shades and arm-mounted TV screens, had an interface. Jack's arm reached out at Peter's command and gestured, a small quick code for each one. Even though he was pressing on air, to Jack, it felt as satisfying as typing on a mechanical keyboard. With a whir, all the mechanical devices he activated and power switches came on and danced at his command. TVs rearranged themselves, steel doors clamped down, and a small cart drove up next to them.

"See. Like that. Don't worry. It would've been a miracle if you could do that in a day ... but just wait till you get to drive a VTOL jet fighter with that little trick."

Peter removed his hand and Jack lurched forward, back in control. "This is America and, yes, magic has returned. Now we've branded it and made it safe for consumption. We've used it to defend us. Advance us. And now save us. But enough of turning my creation into a glorified TV remote and Uber App. Let's get to the show you are all here to see—arena combat."

"Does it come with Bluetooth? Where do I sign up? You didn't connect that thing to the internet, did you? Have you ever heard of *Skynet?*"

A million more questions raced past as Peter, Dr. Alex, and Jack headed to their private elevator. As the doors closed, everyone remained silent for a few seconds.

"Glorified TV remote, eh?" Jack laughed. "Tell me I get the skin-e-max channel? Even robots have needs."

Even though Peter looked worried, Jack saw a small smile creep out.

Doc Daneka tapped his foot outside the arena impatiently as he, Phoebe, and a gutter-punk named Akira smoked cigarettes like they were a gang of vampires from the '80s. In a way, they were. Thanks to Akira's neat trick of hunting, they could hide in plain sight. Akira had consumed the heart of a plague demon a while back and taken a liking to predatory insects. Cigarette smoke was one of her hunter's camouflage tricks—it had nothing to do with the plague demon. She was just crafty. Doc's eyes fell to a duffle bag of outlandishly colored clothes at their feet. *Except when it came to taste.*

"He should be out by now," Doc fretted. "It doesn't take that long to ask a few questions at a press conference. We've gotta tell the boss."

"Calm your tits," Phoebe retorted. "You know Peter is a warlock, it's like their weakness that they can't shut up. Just go on ... and on ... and on ..."

"They screw with my recruit and I'm going to kill 'em," Akira said matter-of-factly as she perched on top of the bench.

Kevin Thayer jogged up, putting away his notepad and sliding the reporter credentials in his satchel. He held up his finger and took a moment to catch his breath. "Sorry," he panted. "Man, that was a lot of stairs."

"You were running *down* the stairs," Phoebe quipped. "We've gotta get you on some satyr blood."

"He would get spotted right away," Doc said. "Would be a baaaad infiltrator then."

Akira didn't wait. She prowled right up to Kevin, leaning her head sideways and looking at him from an odd angle as her purple eyes blinked sideways. "What of Jack, is he okay? Did he survive?"

Kevin shook his head. "I'm sorry, guys, I don't think you can trust him anymore. They've rewired him from scratch. If he's still in there, I can't tell. You'll have to focus on the other recruit, Jane. They didn't even debut the twins. All focus was on that mechanical failure."

Phoebe popped a bubble from her gum. "Shit."

"Why shit?" Kevin asked, finally standing back up.

"She basically ran out on us." Phoebe sat down. "Maybe my vision was wrong? It gets a little tricky these days. We tried all three major companies by rigging the odds for Jane, Jack, and the Twins to be the arena fighters. Pulled every string the boss had to get timelines rushed and matched with the Death Lord's arrival, and took a really big fucking gamble on this." She hugged herself and began to rock in a panic. "In the upcoming war we need someone who can get close to the Death Lord or Peter for the kill shot, otherwise we are totally ..." She trailed off into panicked mumbles as she lost her handle on the situation.

"I'm gunna kill 'em. I'm gunna kill 'em." Akira walked off as Doc grabbed the back of her hoodie.

"Hold yer horses, killer." Doc pushed up his glasses, his telltale sign of scheming. "Boss still wants us on the sidelines until the war begins. He wants to let that psycho Praenomen and her boys have a shot. We've got those disguises, yeah? Let's go watch this charade of an arena fight. When in Rome, they say ..."

"Kevin," Phoebe said. "You're newish around here. Tell Akira again why we aren't leapin' into the fray."

He nodded. "Someone has to keep their integrity, I suppose ..." he said, chuckling at the bag of outlandish outfits. "Akira, each of these test candidates can get close enough to the Lord of Suicide for us to kill him. The rich and the elite still own this world, even more so than before, and someone has to start chopping the heads off the hydra."

Akira ran a long-clawed finger over her throat and tipped her head. "The boss isn't always right. Look what we did last time with Mikey. Let's just go, right now—with no plan, and fucking cut their heads off." As her head craned practically horizonal, several joints cracked. She tried to shoo the party along inside. "Come come, kill kill, happy happy."

Phoebe hung her head down and sighed before holding up a bag filled with sports jerseys and plastic hats with beer coolers on the side. "Akira, you need the boss as much as us. He got his name magically stripped from history so no *other* fortune teller or prophet could see our movements. Without following his plan, some Wall Street bros at Insight Investments might be in a drug haze and witness our assault, turning the whole thing to shit. It's a hellishly complicated game now when scrying, spy cameras, tech, and magic wards can protect someone these days." She held up a jersey. "We will seriously wear this shit? Crampin' my style, Akira. Crampin' my style."

"Fiiiine," Akira relented. "But just for a bit. Let's see what spooky crazy Praenomen and her peeps can do. Put some shoes on and gear up. I'll even let you win at the video game of your

choice tonight. Did you know that I won an E-sports tournament to get us these seats?"

"Yes, Akira." Everyone rolled their eyes. They had all heard
the story of her bloody foray into fighting games.

The Sons and Daughters donned their gaudy gear and
strolled toward the stadium.

CHAPTER ELEVEN

After Hurricane Sandy, we saw the hellish world that the gun prohibitionists see as their utopia. Looters ran wild in south Brooklyn. There was no food, water, or electricity. If you wanted to walk several miles to get supplies, return before dark or you might not get home at all. You think the Black Sun is any different? Donate now to the NRA, lest the monsters in the north unleash their fangs and fury upon you.

J ack fidgeted with his right arm while sitting in a violet-lit staging chamber. *Plasma arm on. Plasma arm off.* Each thought clicked open hidden chambers that heated before shutting off. Smoke hung low in the room, a purple haze reflecting the dim lights from above. Massive iron doors with a horizontal split barred the four occupants inside from the shooting gallery outside. Jack didn't care that Taylor and Tyler were both smoking massive stogies—he cared that they didn't offer him one. *Plasma arm on. Plasma arm off.*

"Do we need to get you some lotion for your self-masturbation, tinman?" Tyler asked. Taylor delivered a swift elbow and a stern glance at her brother. Tyler flicked shades resting on top of his head over his eyes and gave a toothy grin.

Both sat on the oversized knees of their mechs, bathed in the deep crimson red light that glowed from the machine's cores. Jack flicked his plasma cannon open and closed at them again. *Atlantis Corporation, Dr. Alex Kristov's pet project.* With a cocked eyebrow, he looked over at the little girl who had her feet up on black weapon crates. Her boots looked mechanical and custom, with the branding of Angelius Flight Company. The rest of her was nothing special. No enhancements, no custom armor, and no special weaponry. *Jane Auburn, JK-47, Elcoll Corp. Bio weapon.* Jack watched her open and close her hand around a small model airplane just like he was doing, with a stoned look on her face.

"Don't look at me," she quipped, more aware than he had given her credit for. "I won the damn lottery. It's easy sailing from here on out. No risk of refugee status, sweet-ass penthouses, and all I've gotta do is put a bullet in a chained-up hellhound. Things are coming up Jane." She flashed a thumbs up at him.

Taylor cackled, slapping her knee and choking on cigar smoke at the same time. "Wait, wait … it's your first time in the arena? What about you there?" She hopped off the mech's leg, producing a wrench from one of her thousand pockets and clanged her machine.

"Yeah," Jack replied. "Guess I won the lottery as well. Go me."

"Ya think he's gonna break down, Sis?" Tyler said.

"Not before she overdoses of a heart attack." Taylor walked and placed a small flask on a nearby table. "Let us vets give you a bit of advice. No matter which equipment or gun they have us showcasing … the two of us? We keep our duty to the corporations that made us. Call it our way to pay our great saviors back." Taylor spun the flask around and watched it wobble back into place. "The enemy isn't the chained-up hellhounds; it's something far more sinister."

"Wait, no, I've got it." Jane leaned forward with her hands out. "There is totally a super secretive council that watches us and judges our every movement. Secret fifth column Nazi forces are recruiting us with experimental robot science. The moon base is on the dark side. Tinfoil hats are the only protection we need." Jane walked up and grabbed the flask and took a swig without hesitation. "Listen, clearly you two haven't been in danger of starvation, homelessness, or had fucking creepy-ass vampires invite you to some dumb cult. Sinister, my pasty-white ass."

Jack chuckled. "Ever wake up to a crowd of doctors gazing at your naked body whilst a CEO operates on your brain? Does that count as an enemy? I'm not even convinced you bastards are real."

"Don't waste your tiiiimmmme ..." Everyone could *feel* Tyler's eye roll behind his shades. "You always do this, Sis, try to offer advice to the newbies, and they think they are hard-asses. Let their new gear blow up in their face. Stop trying to get attached."

"Is he always such cock holster?" Jane said.

Taylor blinked in surprise. "With good reason. We've been experimenting with magic-tech hybrids for a decade—er, since the black sun." She wiped her palms on her cargo pants and climbed into her mech. "You know what, you'll see, it's probably the only way to explain it, anyway. Many hunters died to bring these beasts here for execution. This is justice, don't disrespect it or you won't last. The crowd has a type." She hopped in her pilot seat and closed the surrounding compartment. Green liquid gelled up around her inside as she fastened on a headset and the breather before it filled in around her.

Silent alarms, red lights fastened to the ceiling, alerted Jack that the time was now. Massive doors swung upon, steel grating on concrete as heavy chains dragged the doors into position.

"Thumbs up, chaps, good fucking luck," Tyler said as he hopped in his smaller, more mobile suit than Taylor's, and went through the same containment process. Both marched out through the doors first with the sound of pneumatics moving their suits forward.

"What kind of patriotic bullshit was that?" Jane said before finishing the flask. She stared down at a handful of weapon crates trying to figure out how to carry seven crates with two arms. She settled on stacking them and dragging them out. "You coming?"

Jack shook his head at the comical sight. "Do I have a choice?"

"Yeah, you can sit in here and rust until they dismantle you." She rebalanced her sixth crate before it toppled. "Or you hit a payday."

"Fair enough." Jack flicked his plasma arm one more time before following her out. *Hardsuits that need trained pilots, a bio weapon that still needs weapons, and me ... the all-in-one package. I've got this.*

"What the fuck are those?" Jack said as he looked out into a jam-packed stadium and straight at the chained fiends at the far end of the stadium.

"Yeah, this place looks way different from inside, way fucking cooler as well ..." Jane said as she looked around at the Astroturf in amazement. Jack briefly considered the possibility that someone operated on her brain.

The Terror Twins hardsuits already marched through the field, waving their hands to rile the crowd as they closed the distance. Before them stood seven Hounds of Tindalos. Motorcycle-sized hellhounds without skin, charred and blackened. Spikes made of thin bone jutted out of their backs along their spines like a porcupine as they bared their fangs and struggled against the chains. In the center of the pack stood three naked humanoid creatures with massively oversized heads. Their skin was hairless and bright pink, wrinkled and ugly like a hairless cat, with a nose larger than the head of a tall man. Unlike the hounds, who appeared as mindless beasts, raging against their inevitable fate, these demons judged the upcoming machines with disdain.

An overdressed, squat gatekeeper who was missing his neck put his hands up before the two of them strolled onto the field and shook his head. "You guys aren't up yet. One at a time. Don't need the goods being hit with collateral damage," he said, putting out a cigarette on the fence post.

Jack wasn't sure how he felt about most of the arena citizens being nameless and grayed out in his vision. He could see them waving banners and oversized decorative fists, but the blurring effect made him feel detached from the crowd. Peter Culmen, sitting at the center yard line, flanked by a dozen other executives and an old man with bushy eyebrows, was bright as day. Even Jane to his right stood out, same with the Terror Twins, and absolutely the demons. *So, Jack, how do you feel about having your brain not-so-subtly controlled.* "Why Jack, not so great at all if I say so myself. I've got programming for whose cock I'm supposed to suck and whose I'm supposed to bite off. Now just to put them in order." He laughed, clutching the metal plates over his ribcage out of sheer habit, before wondering why Jane and the gatekeeper were looking at him.

"You know you said that out loud, right?" Jane said.

"Sorry, loose circuit." He shook his head. "So, what are those?" he asked while pointing at the tall creatures, ignoring the digital display in his retina that gave him the exact information. Asking a question at least had the side effect of feeling more human.

The gatekeeper shuddered and lit up another smoke. Jane grabbed one from his pack with a wink. "Those, buddy, are the Ukobach. Since the Church of Lazarus is in town, they've brought some extra legends in from the field. Low-ranking demons, but they stoke the fires of hell themselves. Legend has it, they are the inventors of fried food and fireworks. Which if you ask me, is pretty darn messed up."

The Terror Twins made it to the first Hounds of Tindalos and stood inches away from their snarling jaws and spun into action.

Taylor's voice boomed from speakers around her suit. "Hounds of Tindalos, here to test our loyalty and cause us to betray another ... often by eating your family and dragging them to hell!" She chucked an iron rod to the nearest hound and let the crowd witness its bite power as the hound ripped it into several chunks. "This particular hound was caught in New Mexico, preying on survivors huddling near Roswell. Each day, its pack would pull a new victim back into Purgatory ... at least fifteen humans have died by its pack's jaws. Now the alpha dies for its sins." Taylor hit the ground, swinging her suit's legs out with bone-crushing impact while Tyler leapt an easy ten feet in the air and came down with his fist. With a yelp and a crunch, the killing was over as fast as it begun. The crowd quieted down as the opening executions had begun, anticipating the next "glorious" death.

"Jack-o'-lanterns." Jane snapped her fingers several times. "Uh, uh, what's it called, the, uh, Ukobach! They make the oil that goes into jack-o'-lanterns. I know these big demons ... so, buddy, what's going on? Why them?"

The gatekeeper grunted. "Why not them? People get tired without variety, and if the Church of Lazarus is going to have their own hunters catch fine kills, so be it. Take advantage while you can. Besides, those three were caught in Waco starting bonfires with people they killed and stole their souls for fuel. Fuck 'em."

Jack watched as the Terror Twins went from Hound to Hound, each time opening with some gizmo or new feature of their suit to showcase its ability. Seconds before each execution and the inevitable shower of splattered demon blood, one of the two twins read off a list of crimes committed by each hound. Even though Jack saw the crowd as hordes of the same, he could tell portions of them were crying or distraught as the Terror Twins meted out retribution on their behalf. With each killing, the old man next to Peter nodded his head in prayer. For Peter's part, he cared less about the killing, and more about making sure the machines performed as expected. *This isn't really an entertaining affair, is it? It's all business and tradition. I think that's what Taylor meant about respect.*

Soon, only the three Ukobach's remained. Their giant eyes looking at each other, then down upon the two metallic suits standing before them. Jack thought they looked like cross-eyed frogs. Right when Taylor recited their crimes in Waco, and their decimation of that town, they let out a blood-chilling scream. Jack threw his hands to his ears as they burst into neon orange flames of their own making. The gatekeeper and Jane both clutched their heads, slower in reaction; the crowd reacted the same.

The Twins rushed forward, oil-coated blades from Tyler's elbows shot out and Taylor's suit had gray-silver spikes around her knuckles. Punch by punch they pounded into the stationary demons as they screeched—glass skyboxes shattering and stadium lights popping despite the incoming damage. With each cut, their blood spilt on the field and ignited into a small flame of its own, producing its own tiny little scream. With a spinning cut, the first head detached, crashing into the ground as Tyler sliced into the next, and finally the third. Taylor kept embedding silver spikes into the headless bodies until their rib cages imploded. Silence soon followed. The crowd erupted into chants and cheers of jubilee after.

The executives offered a small applause before holding up signs with numbers on them as ticket takers took down orders.

"Owww ... motherfuckers," Jack said, shaking it off. "So, what the hell are we supposed to do now? Everything is dead?"

"That's just round one, man," Jane said. "I've seen these before, each company gets its own little showcase, and those guys up there bid on the leftover parts. Give it a week and you'll see Ukobach-branded whiskey shots."

"Waste of time," Jack said. *They upgrade us so we can go into a dry arena like this? No, fuck that. I'm not playing their way.* "There are way more efficient ways to handle this. It's disgusting that they harvest the parts. I'm going next."

The gatekeeper nodded and let him in. The Terror Twins were waving goodbye to the crowds as they exited out the other side of the arena, ducking their suits to clear the entryway. A crew of stagehands and a single priest of Lazarus cleared the remains and dragged the corpses off while a second crew brought out six more creatures. Jack didn't know, or care, what they were. They were already dead to him. He positioned himself where the fifteen yard line once was and stood at attention facing Peter and the other executives, waiting his turn.

The six creatures were female of varying ages, from what Jack could only assume was a teenager to an old, wrinkled hag— but they all had similar features. Jet black, wide eyes, olive and pale white skin with a face that drew itself into a beak, and feathered hair. The older ones had a full beak and wings out of their back, and their arms were scaled like a bird's foot. *Plasma cannon on* ... He felt the whir of heat rise as the plasma charged and built up. He held it while he waited for the announcer to tell the crowd he was Metallic Jack. He waited for them to announce the Lechuza Owl Witches that had been plaguing the border town of Del Rio with their curses.

The crowd applauded. Once.

He released his charge, bracing himself for the kickback as the bolt slammed through the air. *Right on target.* The explosion melted flesh off bone before turning bone into powder before his eyes. The witches didn't even have time to react to his assault or scream. Astroturf showered fans in the distance. *Plasma cannon off.* The crowd hung on the edge of their seats, wondering how they should react.

Jack turned and gave a salute to Peter. "Don't waste our time," he said before marching out of the exit. *Harvest that, you idiots. If you can make me out of science, you don't need that trash.* He smirked as he realized that most of the crowd hadn't even taken a single bite out of their hotdogs before he was done.

And even though they didn't know it yet, they loved him for it.

"America. Booyah," he said plainly to the stunned stage crew as he entered the dark tunnel.

CHAPTER TWELVE

Friends don't let friends order coffee. Friends get their friends the newest in caffeinated crack. Midwinter Black. This special brew, infused with the purest ingredients and grown from the rays of the Black Sun, will awaken you from a thousand deaths. Literally. A cup of blackened blood is the perfect way to start off your morning AND add a dose of minor immortality to your routine. Get ready for ultimate flavor. Get ready to say goodbye to death by a heart attack. Get ready to sip Midwinter Black. Only available in some locations. May cause heart attacks. Not responsible for any side effects.

W ell ... that's a thing," Jane said, leaning forward on the gate watching the fans comment on Jack's abrupt performance. Awe and regret hung in the air like a dense fog. On one hand, Peter's prize was certainly combat ready out of the box. *He will make one hell of a poseable action figure.* On the other, he was a damn shitty entertainer. The packed arena, *no ... colosseum,* perceived themselves robbed of revenge. With a cocked eyebrow, she side-eyed her stack of matte black weapon crates and knew she could do better. *But first ... I see something none of them do.* As the thought danced in her brain, she was wiggling her boots in the gravel like a cat ready to pounce.

"So, what kind of monster are you?" Jane wiggled her brow and smiled at the gatekeeper. She could see right through the fake appearance he was putting on to everyone else. Much like the Death Lord sitting next to Peter, the gatekeeper looked like he was wearing someone else's skin. In one world, he looked like a normal unhealthy American, but in her ash-covered and decaying world of Purgatory, he was as inhuman as they came. His face was no face at all, and his body was pale, gaunt, with porcelain-smooth skin. No nose, barely a slit for a mouth, and if his eyes closed, his face was as featureless as a blank sheet of paper.

Thanks to the drugs flowing through her, his reaction seemed in slow motion. A sideways look, jaw creeping open, leaning backwards while hands inched up in a defensive posture. Before he even spoke, his body's microlanguage told her his response. *What are you talking about? I'm not a monster; you can't see the real me; I'm just a drunk who likes whiskey ...*

"What are you talking about?" he said as she let her perception return to normal speed. "I'm not a monster, other than the kind who enjoys too much fine scotch," it said.

Hmm. Was off on the drink of choice. Tsk, tsk, Jane. "Aww, aren't you a cute little liar? All faceless and shit, pretending to be someone you're not." She leaned in and put her hands behind her back and touched his nonexistent nose with hers. "Wanna know how I can spot a liar? Because I'm one. Unpaid emotional labor is a specialty of mine, cutie, and I've been smiling for years. No point in hidin' it. Catch is, you aren't important like that emaciated corpse up in the bleachers." She patted him on the head thrice and watched the pain of realization set in as his pupils dilated in microsecond reactions.

He looked down and to the right while taking a step with a formal bow, flourishing out his right hand. "Very well, my lady, it seems you're gifted with the sight ... how unfortunately unexpected this is," he said with a rise. Despite his momentary defeat, his poise remained impeccable and infinitely more British. "They call me the Whisper. Agent provocateur at your service. Proper undead I am, not the blood junkie swine you find feasting on the tattered remains of garbage demons. My identity, and thus the fate of my mission, now hinges upon your desire, for you hold the cards." He rose and placed both hands behind his back, reminding Jane of a soldier standing at ease. "So, what will you do with me moments before your big debut?"

Jane let out a low whistle and fidgeted with an old model airplane she woke up with, flipping it between her fingers like a coin while she pondered. "Right. Agent provocateur ... that sounds *fun*," she said with a wink. "Just because you, that stage-hand scraping up owl lady ashes, and the Death Lord are all dead-looking things doesn't mean you're all on the same side. Based on my luck—I'd say the two of you are part of those idiot Sons and Daughters trying to put a hit on the priest of Lazarus up there."

Both of the Whisper's forms smiled, the real one with a row of pointed teeth like a shark and an impossibly wide smile. "And you can see my companion, the tinker-tailor-soldier-spy Symon Vasyl. You've told me so much about you now. By many names, but all the same; a descendent of Lazarus, a walker of Purgatory, or a clear-sighted soul—but a naïve one. But you haven't answered what you want. An assassination of the Death Lord, preposterous, a nigh-immortal creature sitting higher than all warlocks in power is a fool's errand. But you ... that's another matter entirely."

A descendent? Walker? Bah, fuck it. I'm me regardless and this world is so messed up who cares if I'm a descendent of Buddha himself. Still, Jane leaned back and looked at her face plastered on screens all around announcing the next match. She was ready to go, and if the little old Whisper wanted to tango with her, Jane felt she could pull out each of his teeth before he even took his first step. On the field, she saw two large crates being forklifted in and readied by Whisper's companion. Through the planks, she saw one creature glowing a bright azure blue and the other a pale alabaster white. Thick chains covered in runes, bound to each crate, fell to the ground before being dragged and clamped to the same posts as every other gift-wrapped monster. *Legends never die, girl.* She flipped the airplane one more time as an idea blossomed from within her.

"You aren't after me any more than you are after a late-night ramen bowl while drunk. At least, you didn't start off that way. If you want me dead for knowing your identity, you must make it a show. This"—she twirled her finger, referencing all the fans—"is my damn origin story. You want me to keep my trap shut, you and your stagehand boy will make it a motherfucking show. I don't care what voodoo you bastards do, but whatever is in those crates isn't staying chained up. I'm tired of living in squalor; I *will* win those sponsorships."

"Your tragic fate is looking so clear," Whisper said. "Well, I suppose this will further our own goals. You're lucky that Symon over there is a master of sabotage. We'll give you your fight. If you die, it's a win for us, and we'll get to see dear Peter's defenses when he must step in. If you win, then our debt vanishes and you'll keep this secret until your dying day." He held out his hand. Jane noticed that his fingers were longer, with more joints than normal.

"It's on." She shook.

"Excellent. Well, if you'll excuse me," he said with a shorter bow and left.

Even with her enhanced senses, she noticed that his steps and movements were now soundless. *He's letting me know he can sneak up on me. I doubt I'll have this encounter with him again.* "No matter. Time for the big show." Jane grabbed several crates, one under each arm, one strapped to her back, and two more in each hand by their handles as she wobbled out into the arena and threw them on the ground. *All right, scientists, you wanted me to lug these cases out here for show, but which sweet-ass toy should I use.*

Jane unlatched crate after crate to reveal the contents within while a camera drone plastered the video all over. Behind her, thick timber crashed into the ground as a crane lifted the last shackles on the beast's cages. The crowd gasped. Two wolves, each the size of a large SUV, growled and tried to stand, lifting their glowing chains. Their fur was already bloodied and singed (the azure one already missing an eye) but each of the creatures looked no less aware. Jane chucked aside the empty case that once held the jaw-droppingly gorgeous Angelius rocket boots, plucking only the instruction manual.

"As a gift to all of you," a female announcer's voice rang over the loudspeakers. "The high priest of Lazarus has brought us spoils from the war in Europe. We present to you Odin's wolves, Geri and Freki!" She waited for the crowd to erupt in a cacophony of cheers before continuing. "Taken from the war happening right now in Norway, as UN Peacekeepers and Knights of Lazarus win battle after battle versus the traitor warlock known as Verkonis, Odin's High Priest; on this day, we give you the gift of revenge with the death of legends!"

Oh, fuck. Well ... couldn't ask for anything better. Jane quickly tightened up her violet combat suit, provided by Midwinter Black Coffee. Smooth and squishy to the touch, Jane likened it a ski suit with a gel coating beneath for impact absorption. *Or a superhero's uniform.* Snugger than she liked, leaving little to the imagination, but it worked for her newfound speed. A speed she was eager to put to the test. Ultimately, she tossed the complex instruction manual to the side with an overly animated shrug. While the announcer went over her background as a waitress and a recent lottery winner, she cracked open her weapon crates and winked. *It's all part of the show. Poor wolves though, looks like I get the only non-demons today. I'll have to work extra hard at winning fans just in case anyone out there likes dogs. Maybe I could be a little clumsy?*

"Guns, guns, and ... let me guess ... more guns. Yup, more guns," she laughed. Just like all the shooting galleries prior, they loaded up the lottery winners with more firepower than needed. Like most Texans, Jane knew how to shoot a gun, but it wasn't her forte. Still, she settled on an assault rifle with a grenade launcher underneath. *How the hell do people mess up shooting? Death comes out the pokey end.* She latched the clip into place, readied the weapon, and took her place on the bright green Astroturf. Seeing her face on every screen set her heart racing. *Anxiety is also excitement. Anxiety is also excitement.* She struck a quick pose, flashing her pearly whites and inwardly thanking her makeup artist. Downwind from the legendary wolves, a cheering crowd all around her, and the rhythmic sounds of bleacher cheers—Jane held up two fingers, one for each beast. *Okay. Now don't fuck this up. Come on, Whisper, gimmie a show.*

A series of white lights flickered across the locks of the chains holding the wolves, followed by the rat-a-tat of targeted detonations. With each pop and clang, the runic chains flew off the azure wolf, Freki, who grinned like a shark. The chains shrunk in size and clattered to the ground; the runes still glowed, but now only a fraction of size. Greki howled and shook as her chains flew off in the same fashion, leaping forward away from the crates with her hair on edge. Jane watched the wolves' lips quiver in the rage of a ravenous hunger as it circled. Freki walked backwards, a low rumble of a growl as it checked in on its former handlers. The crowd couldn't just hear the growl, it rumbled through their chests, as the wolves moved closer to the only prey in sight.

As the world around her slowed, Jane saw Peter Culmen move to leap from his seat while the Death Lord demanded he stay. *Come on, Mr. Culmen, you made me, have faith.*

Freki leaned back on his legs. Jane fired three shots. Pop, pop, popping sounds echoed off the walls in quick succession as she flanked to the left. In her vision, the bullets moved in slow motion; she half-wondered if she could outrun them. She felt every vibration in the gun, the reverberation up her elbow, the impact into her shoulder, and the wind blowing from behind her. Two bullets missed their mark, imbedding themselves in the concrete thirty yards behind the wolves in a small cloud of cement dust. The third grazed through Freki's azure ear.

They now knew their enemy. Their lips curled over drooling fangs in a wicked snarl before vaulting into a sprint.

Muscles tightened underneath their shaggy fur coats as they

raced toward Jane, Freki on her left, Greki ripping up Astroturf on her right. *Eeny, meeny, miny, moe.* Greki. Jane fired off three more shots at the white wolf with the missing eye and started sidewinding to the right. First two bullets missed again, but Jane had her eyes on the third, beelining right into the wolf's side. Before her eyes, it was there, and then it was ten feet closer— leaving a trail of white cloud behind it. *Fuck, it teleports!* She dug her right foot into the ground and tried to change directions. It leapt through the void again. Ten feet closer, its jaws wide open as it launched itself into the air for a tackle. Jane threw her shoulder into the ground and rolled under, close enough she wrinkled her nose from the rotten-meat odor and terrible breath as iron jaws snapped furiously to eat her.

The roll got away from her and she tumbled faster than she planned, seeing the world spin once, twice, three times as the ground and stadium zipped past her. Bone-shattering impacts took the wind out of her, and briefly her gut clenched in fear response, yet after the third tumble she realized her suit gelled like a freeze-pop around any impact, protecting the precious sanctity of her bones. She tossed her left hand out for balance, righting herself, and now sliding backwards in a three-point slide. *Where am I? Ten yard line? My spleen is still intact, yes?* She checked. It was. Greki finished landing and Freki was already changing course. Around the combative trio, Jane heard the crowd go wild; she permitted herself a wry grin. Balance restored and spleen intact, Jane unloaded three more rounds at Greki as it raced back to her left. *They are keeping me between the two.* She missed once but watched the wolf phase out for the other two shots. Jane paid close attention to its eyes; she may be faster, but the wolf could read her all the same.

Freki came in from her right. She cocked the metal handle and planted the grenade launcher right into the beast's face. *Dodge this.* Jane rolled to the left as heat and shrapnel filled the air. Much like before, the tumble turned into one, then two and more. She slid on her side into the wall at the edge of the stadium. Freki was unphased and still on her heels, a blue streak of lightning with jaws chasing her as Greki was rushing in from upfront. *The fuck, weapons don't work?* Jane ran. Three steps up onto the wall and then three more ... and then three more as Greki closed in and before gravity took its hold. Tossing caution aside, she took the gamble and pressed the on button near her wrist and promptly had her head jerked down as the rocket boots activated, catapulting her through the air.

It was a strange sensation as she seemed to float thirty feet in the air upside down. Jane knew she wasn't floating, rather, the middle of a sideways flip (or frantic flailing with jet-fueled propulsion) thanks to her time-dilated perception. *Drugs were a beautiful thing. Thanks, Elcoll.* The blue wolf was already jumping off the wall to keep chase, and the white one crashed into the wall at full speed. She had a millisecond to look in awe at the shock wave rippling out from the wolf's impact before it phased out of existence again. That millisecond felt like a minute. With Freki in midair, Jane fired her boots again to change direction, along with three more shots right into its chest. Each bullet found its mark but passed right through the wolf like it wasn't even there. Freki continued through his arc and landed next to Greki. Jane backflipped again and struck a gymnasts landing as she backpedaled to keep her footing. She couldn't help but smile.

Whatever drugs they had given her were working. Between panted breaths she marveled at how tingly her entire body was. It felt great. She had never been more alive. The wolves and Jane had taken each other's measure, and they resumed their circling pattern, and Jane fired off shot after shot in their direction to little effect. "It's a wonder they ever captured you guys ..." Jane said before breaking into a sprint up the middle. She had chosen her weapon poorly and raced to her stack of weapon crates. Throwing her assault rifle up into the air she grabbed two bright green pistols and unloaded into Freki who at this point, Jane decided, was a bloody bastard as he crashed into her. Airborne yet again, Jane tried not to panic as she flew back even further, spiraling out of control. She tasted dirt and landed face first and buried her right shoulder in the ground. Jane spat out the plastic taste of fake green grass and stood up, white flecks of stars sprinkled around the edge of her vision, but Jane already knew—guns would have no effect. In that brief sortie with the azure wolf, she watched every shot from the semiautomatic pistols rip right through him like he was a ghost.

Greki wasn't giving her any time to plan as it blinked into existence right in front of her. She leapt up in reaction, firing her boots, and flipped through the air as if she was jumping off the air itself one boot after another. For what seemed like an eternity to Jane, she raced around the arena, ducking, dodging, and deftly maneuvering out of the creature's jaws. As long as she stayed on the defensive, they couldn't touch her. *This can't go on forever, but it's a hell of a show.*

Adrenaline raced through her, the world of Purgatory clear as day came into focus, as the blackened sun hung in the decaying sky. The wolves glowed as brightly as ever as they paced majestically around her, waiting for the next chance to pounce. Standing entirely out of place in the grim world lay the coiled-up glowing runic chains. Bright electric blue, greens, reds, and a cacophony of pulsing colors in a sea of miserable grey emanated from the artifacts. *The chains!* She didn't have a clue how to fight with chains, but figured if something bound the wolves in them, then the chains could hurt them. The second Jane bolted to the chains, the wolves followed. She slid into the end zone and grabbed two broken, glowing chains as the wolves landed right behind her. The chains felt cold, more than physically icy, they sent a chill right to the bone, in stark contrast to the hot breathing from a wolf's maw right behind her. Over her shoulder, she could see the awareness in the beast's eyes—they knew fear.

The prey quickly became the hunter. Jane kicked up the chains and watched their links spiral around her. A shoulder twist here, a flick of the wrist there, even without knowledge of chain fighting her speed allowed her to control them as easily as a jump rope. Greki and Freki backed up, their tails dipping down in a defensive posture. Jane vaulted forward. Wrapping the chain around the neck of Freki before he could bolt away, tumbling over his matted fur and firing her rocket boots, Jane launched herself at Greki, who returned the attack. While Freki yanked at the neck to a sickening crunch, Greki sunk her jaws into Jane's left arm with rabid abandon.

"Fuck you!" Jane screamed, and punched with the chain. Each hit welted the creature. Jane poured everything into the assault. Bloody punch after bloody punch was met with the meaty sound of Greki's skull being crushed as red blood covered her fur since the wolf refused to let go. Spinning the loose chain around, Jane latched it around the wolf's oversized neck and locked in her knee. Rocket boots provided the momentum as Jane and the two wolves spun counterclockwise in the air, with a searing pain in her left arm and choking force around their necks, they crashed to the ground ten yards away. Free at last, she wasted no time; ignoring the pain, she brought the chains down like whips into the spirit wolves at full impact. It worked.

The wolves, resilient creatures, tried to hobble to their feet, but the fight was already over as Jane wound up Greki by the neck again and used the other for leverage before hitting the rocket boots. She jerked back briefly midair before feeling the tension of the chains release, separating the alabaster wolf's head from its body and coating the field in a fountain of blood—most of which sprayed on her as Greki gave its final death throes. Freki was panting on the ground, its neck already snapped from earlier, as Jane planted her boot on its neck; hunched over with an elbow on her knee, she took the second to catch her own breath. Sweat was pouring down her face, hair tousled, and her blue suit glistened for the cameras as she watched drops of Greki's blood form pools underneath them, and she finally looked at the crowd.

"Are you not entertained?" She couldn't help it, Jane *felt* like a gladiator. The movie reference flowed out of her naturally as she held her arms out wide, basking in the glory of victory to the crowd's cheers. The Lord of Suicide was on his feet with applause, and in Jane's dual vision, she saw a great smile on both his forms, one vastly more horrid and skin-stretched than the other. Even Peter was at the edge of his seat, still biting his fist with a grin. The crowd's chant slowly but surely turned to cries for execution. They wanted blood. Jane obliged.

"Fuck ... I'm ... hungry," she panted to herself after the deed was done. Like a runner who had just won the Olympics, Jane wore a smile of victory and marveled at her arm. It was already stitching itself back together, and the pain gave way to an intense itch as scabs formed before her eyes. *I'm fucking immortal?!* Jane laughed before collapsing backwards onto the field with her heart pounding at a thousand beats per minute. It felt like her body was on fire, every synapse firing, every nerve aware, and an insatiable hunger raging at her core.

"I am going to eat an entire Chinese restaurant. Like ... the whole fucking thing," she said to the clouds above.

CHAPTER THIRTEEN

::Begin Transmission:: No airwave is safe. No computer unhackable. No consciousness ... uncontrollable. Und3rGround Dr3ams has a message for you. The Peter Culmen, CEO of Triumvirate Enterprises, offers you safety and enhancement. At the cost of what makes you human. His company sucked Mexico City dry, leaving poverty and death in its wake. Wake up, sheeple. It's only a matter of time before he steals your mind.

Peter leapt forward from his seat and joined the standing ovation. Deep, heavy-handed claps echoed with power, drowning out the marketing executives chattering around him, and he basked in the crowd's enthusiasm. He'd done it. Decades of research, blasphemy, and betrayal, and he'd finally done it. He turned magic into a marketable, reusable, and manufactured commodity. In his joy, he allowed his true eyesight over his rather mundane disguise, eyes changing colors to a translucent neon blue. The arena filled itself with the dancing electrons of the digital world all around him, the province of the techno-mancer. Every wire, every text message, and every screen was on display for him to see—the fans loved her. But not just Jane, the entire day. The wolves' escape was unplanned, but that was another matter; to those in his expanding kingdom, today would go down forever in their dreams.

The display laid bare before him brought Peter to tears. Long ago, he was nothing more than a kid tinkering with disk drives and assembler code by night and forced family church by day. By his teenage years he struggled with depression—brought on by the obvious problems of being a black kid in the south who mastered the art of binary. It wasn't long before he found himself in a pool of his own blood. In his state of near death, the Unification discovered him, or, more accurately, the Lord of Suicide. Seeing the potential in Peter, it offered a second life. The best schools, fraternities, job openings, and true wealth unlocked like the gates to a vineyard for suburban white women. *Oh, Vryce, Verkonis, and Rasputin, you outdated fools with your selfish visions. I wish you warlocks could see me today.* The irony of his success, based off a centuries old society that wielded magic, didn't escape him. But this display today proved his theories about the modernization of magic were right.

Peter kept the ovation going while every CEO seated around him spoke of acquisitions and mergers. When the world shattered, they panicked. Terrified the kingdom of man would crumble under the weight of magic gone awry, in eighteen months corporations bled steel, profits, and concrete for Peter. The nation may be fractured, but he had transformed three cities into one evolving paradise.

"Why fear magic," Peter said to nobody in particular, "when we have the tools of reason to shape our world?" The bankers and financiers all nodded like toadies and agreed. Peter smirked. A decade ago each of them would've smiled through their teeth at him. While they put planned obsolescence into smartphones, each year—Peter was leading teams of Unification scientists in new applications of divine blood. The showcase below was impractical two years ago when there wasn't enough divine blood for mass production. Everyone who knew about magic, hoarded it. Secrecy and elitism were rife in all societies. Moreover, when the Unification's timetable to revive Lazarus was put into motion, even Peter believed magic would be put back behind the curtain. The Unification planned on Lazarus *fixing* everything with his return. *Then came the black sun incident, and now I will forge us a new destiny.*

"You fear magic," the Lord of Suicide spoke softly to Peter alone. "You may lie to these sycophants and fools you surround yourself with. But I remember when I gifted you with the angel heart. You, still bleeding out from your own wrists, begging for life, and the terror in your eyes as you took your first bite." The Lord placed his cold hand on top of Peter's, like a father comforting a child. "I watched you master new gifts of perception, before you hungered for more, and when you pleaded for an archdemon's heart—I warned you of the risks. 'If I shred my soul to gain power, I'll just build a new one' you said." The Lord's fingers dug into Peter's shoulder. "So we gave you that heart, ripping your soul piece by piece, and making you into the warlock you are now. You fear magic because you know you are nothing without it."

"No." Peter swallowed his inner fear and indignation. *You are always here to "remind" me of my place aren't you?* "You think I fear magic?" He flicked his shoulder free, hoping nobody saw him wince. "There's no going back. You expect people to get on with warding circles, golden bowls, and drinking blood? This world is all we have. I fear obsolescence. Bringing back Lazarus was just the first step. Shit went south, obviously." He waffled his hand to-and-fro with a smirk. "Now if you will, sir, we have to make the world work. For kids who just discovered the wonder of dinosaurs. You didn't recruit me to bring back a dead god; you recruited me to lead us into a new age."

"Careful," the Death Lord tsked. "Lazarus is our God, now, and his divine hand stitches together the world. As for your children ... they wouldn't be so stricken with awe if they knew gods a Utahraptor paid tribute to."

Jane, Jack, and the Twins dominated every news station, feed, and channel. Peter could hear the world through their broadcasters in dozens of languages, and they all shared something in common. Hope.

"Put down your cell phone," the Lord sighed.

"Relax, old man, I can multitask." Regardless, Peter internally lowered the volume of his streams. "Right. Magic, I don't fear it, it's just in serious need of upgrading. Do you think the thirteen Death Lords and the power of the Unification alone is enough to rebuke sixty-four million years of dream and myth crashing back in?" Peter gestured out into the arena at the cheering fans and the dead wolves of legend. "It takes decades to train a single sorcerer, vampires and shapeshifters need to eat hearts, which don't grow on trees. Let's not get started with Warlocks. Those aren't exactly popular given how many broke rank—and have the power to form their own kingdoms. Through my technomagic, we can give a waitress drugs in the morning, and have her be a killer by nighttime, and a champion in a week."

The Lord of Suicide let out a low, raspy, mocking laugh. "A single sorcerer can bring a kingdom to its knees, a lone vampire can rule an empire for a millennium, and I assure you—we Death Lords have killed more than our fair share of Gods." He patted Peter on the back. "But I'm not here to diminish your achievement. I see the potential. Our legions swell because of your city, and this display was divine. You should be proud. The Unification and the Church of Lazarus need heroes. The demons are getting smarter, banding together, and the heathens draw the faithless to their banners. You've birthed new champions to lead our war efforts. Enjoy your victory, son."

"War?" Peter stepped back and looked confused. He let his digital vision disappear and focused entirely on the Lord. "I wouldn't call it war, exactly, my Lord. Let them eat themselves. We are just getting started here. As long as we can defend our perimeter, the creatures of heaven and hell will learn to fear us. In time, I expect the attacks to stop entirely, and we will continue with advancement after advancement. Don't tell me that Lazarus will fall into the same trap as all humans. We should focus on progress, not war."

"Now you're becoming naïve. Why do you think I am here?"

"Don't do this." Peter ran his hand down his face. "You want a crusade, don't you ... a bloody, expensive, pointless crusade."

"Your dreams are important, but we live in a world where heretics cracked open the heavens and hells, ushering in a thousand terrors and blotting out our sky. Those heretics deserve death for their crimes. A message must be sent that will be heard on every continent and in every shadow of the world. Dance with devils at your own peril; only the Church of Lazarus can bring back the light, and *only* after these other"—he spat in the direction of the wolves—"distractions ... are obliterated."

"At your behest, I was *there*. You put me in the same ritual." Peter grew impatient. He remembered when the Unification demanded all the warlocks work together in an absurd ritual to return a soul from the afterlife. They meant it to bring back Lazarus, to prove that resurrection—a strictly divine act—was possible for mortals. It not only was, but so much more. Whoever thought those with power would settle was a short-sighted fool. *Or had never seen a corporate take-over.* "I've done my part and stayed silent about our involvement. Hell, you've had my newscasters broadcasting the lie about the anarchs causing everything for months. You *owe* me the chance to rebuild and undo the damage we caused in Mexico."

The Lord of Suicide closed his eyes in reflection and crossed his hands. Peter watched the arena reset itself for more displays, this time on new forms of water filtration, and knew deep down that the citizens couldn't care less. The CEOs in the surrounding boxes already had their agents and marketing reps on board, splitting up which spin-offs they could make. *Don't do this, Lord. I know it's tempting to wage war. It's so easy to destroy. So much harder to forge ahead. Please, Lazarus, hear me now. If you truly want to unite the world—save them. Use weapons for defense and build a paradise. Draw people into you, not obliterate your enemies. Yes, there are monsters we shall obliterate but ...*

"You are anything but a pacifist," the Lord said. "You've eaten the fruit of the heavens and devoured the soul of hell. You will serve when called to war. But"—the Lord held his arms out wide and smiled—"there is a time to cast away stones, and a time to gather stones together. A time to build up and to tear down, a time to kill and a time to heal. In time, we shall discipline the nations that are evil, but Lazarus has heard your prayer and will grant you time to build and gather your stones. You have been among the faithful, and we shall reward that faith."

Oh, thank Lazarus. Peter turned and clasped his hands together with his head down, shocked and confounded that Lazarus heard his prayer, even as a soulless Warlock. "Thank you. You won't regret giving us time to build further. We can build a bulwark that will stand in defense to the atrocities beyond our walls."

"There is enough war in the world already. The council agrees that we need at least one spot on this blackened rock where hope can flourish. You should keep praying, however, that evil does not find its way within your walls. Even the smallest maggot can prevent a wound from healing." The Lord folded his hands and strolled away. It had made his point.

Peter leaned on the railing, chuckling to himself as he gazed on the arena. He would not correct the Lord about how helpful maggots were to healing wounds. In fact, it was only the developed nations that were facing their own apocalypse. Peter smothered any news story about how the Pacific Islanders were flourishing with the return of magic. *They are self-sufficient and not bound by the creature comforts, but that's not a narrative which helps the Church put the genies back in the bottle.* There was one lingering truth that bothered him even more after the Lord's comment about maggots, however.

How the fuck did those wolves get free?

CHAPTER FOURTEEN

Sleep on Heaven's Cloud with our new Angel Feather mattress. Made from the finest feathers of the celestial host, Heaven's Cloud makes your dreams a reality. From the moment you lay your head down on our feathered mattresses, they whisk you away to a personal dream state to live out your most inner desires. Why suffer back pain, a stiff neck, or a snoring partner when you could dream of flying through the fields of Elysium. Don't suffer another minute. Order your own personal Heaven's Cloud today. Financing is available. Only at Ascension Mattresses.

Y ou have thirteen thousand new followers," Jane's apartment informed her as she slammed the door shut. "And twelve thousand swipe rights on Tinder. Would you like to respond?"

Jane plopped down face first on her couch, comforted by the smell of old fabric, and let out a satisfied sigh. Metal clanked on her new boots as she wiggled her feet up in the air, and she let out a scream into a pillow that turned into laughter. Maru and Paru, oblivious to her victories today, stood nearby and cried for food. Even though their dishes were half full, in cat terms that clearly meant they would starve to death. She reached out and petted her feline children just behind the ears, and received a mix of purring and friendly bitings. She didn't just feel good tonight; she felt *validated*.

Putting her life on the line paid off.

It wasn't the first time, nor, she figured, would it be the last. Gazing into Purgatory always made her feel alive, and this time was no different. Only now she would get paid for it. No more crappy dead-end jobs. No more robotic impartial timecard-punching bosses. No more wondering what she must do to scrounge up a few more Bitcoin for rent. It didn't matter to her how she came into it, much like most people didn't care where their iPhones were made. She got a winning lottery ticket and made the most of it.

"What do you say, kids? Should we hit the town tonight?"

They ran to their imp-shaped food bowls.

A quick change of clothes later, Jane was bounding down to the back alley. Amidst the first snow of the season, people dressed in heavy Carhartt construction jackets packed the rusted stairwell. Jane ducked, weaved, and took a shot of whiskey from the seventh-floor house party. Huddled amongst each other, they shot the shit while scratching off the day's lottery tickets; one won a few Bitcoin. *Good luck is contagious today!* At the bottom, a few workers surrounded a trashcan where they burned old trash for warmth. Peeking over the side, and emboldened by several cheers, she winked and let impulse take over. Jane landed with a flip from three stories up and smiled at their surprise. Soon after their recognition set in, they posed for a selfie and a few fist bumps before Jane sprinted off into the night—exploring the ever-growing, ever-crowded city.

First stop was food. She had already eaten right after the arena, a pack of NutrientGoo that Dr. Kristov made her eat, or, rather, an entire box. It sufficed. But like a hunter, she wandered the streets in search of her real prey this evening. Ducking in and out of crowds with ease and grace while making every impulse purchase she fucking felt like. Street musicians playing drums in the cold got tips, various meats on sticks made it to her, a new hat (it had Jack's grumpy face), and a resold chintzy Katana. *Hi-yah!* Jane sliced the air, and quickly remembered she was in public. "Sorry!"

More fliers for local watering holes filled her satchel as she explored the newly vertical East Austin. Gone were most of the eclectic businesses that gave it flavor years ago, now replaced with a veritable bazaar, refugees, and block by block of one-bedroom smart homes—and tonight she loved it, but her prey eluded her yet.

Somehow the neon purple and green Thai food truck that haunted the area took a bit for her to find. Parked out front of some mattress store that sold angel feathers, the ugly van sat. A stubborn and gaudy business, the kind that propped open the back door with a vat of stewing meats marinating in sauce and violated every type of code imaginable. Jane ordered the menu. It took a moment for the restaurant to realize what she was asking. Not just number four, or the dinner special, but the entire menu. Her stomach had become its own magical black hole, metabolizing everything she ate almost as soon as she swallowed. After her sixth bowl a sudden realization hit her.

What goes in must come out.

Twenty minutes later Jane scurried out of the mattress store. *I can never come here again.* She blamed it on the NutrientGoo from earlier. Surely the holy grail of eastern cuisine would never betray her so. Jane made sure she was at least seven blocks over before she let her night continue. Bouncing and dancing from one bar to the next, drinking as many shots as the patrons bought her and listening to just as many heartfelt tales about an encounter people had outside the walls. It was at 3:30 AM in the morning that Jane made two more discoveries—she never got tired and couldn't get drunk. The vast cocktail of chemicals racing through her veins made every moment more real, however. Every touch, every music beat, the sights, the smells, and even the burning cinnamon taste of Ukobach whiskey were heightened.

Bars in this town never closed anymore, and any regulation on getting shit-faced had been thrown out the window months ago, so when Jane wandered out at sunrise she was still bouncing and ready to go. Surely the party was continuing elsewhere, she figured. Establishment after establishment met her with more disappointment, though, as the only people drinking at 7:00 AM in the morning—were the people who *really* wanted to drink at 7:00 AM in the morning.

They weren't much for conversation.

In the afternoon, Kristov gave her an examination, checking her vitals and monitoring her charts. Along with another box of NutrientGoo to choke down. By early evening, Jane was in the arena again, going toe-to-toe with a Rage Demon. They didn't bother with the shooting gallery this time, instead letting her get to work with the runic chains. Limb by limb, she dismantled the creature like a matador. Which wasn't very many limbs ... Rage Demons were common, and lived half in this world with one foot, and half still trapped in hell. So she really only had one leg and one arm to pluck off. The video footage showed her cutting loose and getting *really* bloody, but she didn't remember the fine details. *Just caught up in the moment. Am I becoming a killer?* It was a thought she buried down in the box where all terrible emotions are locked up in your brain.

By night, she petted and played with her cats and hit the city again.

Day after day, week after week, this routine continued. The dancing partners changed, who she let in her bedroom fluctuated, and she crossed more restaurants off her "can never patronize again" list. With each creature she slew in the arena, more of the city opened to her. Soon she had real estate on the tenth floor in Downtown, then the seventeenth, then the thirty-second. The bars went from seedy dive bars filled with refugees to high-end cocktail bars with other augmented citizens.

Companies, admirers, or a mix of both sent new clothes, mattresses filled with angel wings, and strange booze made from the blood of faeries to her in crates.

Jane found new routines to add to the mix as the days went on. Soon she was standing in front of cameras holding up new brand models of Rocket Boots, praising new lines of instant ramen noodles, and attending overly ignorant political talk shows. All they asked about was who she was dating and how much Elcoll Corp had helped her.

Her fighting routine became more serious by the third week. It wasn't the difficulty of new opponents, but her desire to put on a better show. More acrobatics, more speed. Better. Faster. Harder. Once Jane raced forward, she never stopped. No sleep, no fear—and no mirrors.

She didn't need to look at Kristov's charts to know the truth as she slipped on her hospital robe after a daily checkup. A sideways glance, one she couldn't help but take as she saw herself in the mirror, told her all she needed to know. Jane looked healthy and vibrant on the outside, but in her ashen world she could see the poison flowing through her veins. *Everyone dies. At least I get to live before my time.* It was a lie she told herself every time she put her head down to avoid her reflection.

One she wasn't ready to pay just yet.

On an early spring evening, Jane found herself back by her old crappy apartment in East Austin, looking up at the crowded fire escape. The same workers stood outside, drinking and burning more trash, and cheering her return. Inside the veins of a younger refugee, easily still a teenager with oil smears on his face, Jane saw the same burning poison flowing through him.

"What are you on?" Jane marched straight up to him and looked him in the eyes.

He stammered for a moment, utterly in shock that his new idol just showed up at his dumpster fire. "I ... uh ... it's you! Can ... wait ..." He fumbled for his phone.

"Listen kid, what ... drugs ... are you on?"

"Elcoll-D. It's ballz amazing, JK-47. I got the first commercial batch! Stores already sold out across the country. But you've still probably got the best shit, eh? They give you stars all the good stuff. Still—"

"You paid for this?" Jane asked, shocked that this kid could afford a chemical cocktail so extravagant. *I guess Kristov worked out some bugs?*

"Well ..." He rubbed his head sheepishly. "I kinda took out a loan. Got chipped with this RFID tag. It's not a problem though; I can pay it all back since I can join the anti-freak squads now and get paid to capture stuff. Oh, hey! If I capture something and let you know ... will you kill it hastily?"

She blinked. *Who am I to crush this kid's dreams? I did the same thing, right?* She muscled up a smile and put on a pretend perky face.

"Of course! Here." She handed over a keychain with a black cat on it. "Tag it with this so I know it's yours. I'll return it to you after I flip kick its arm off."

She walked up the stairs to her now foreign apartment, which had surprisingly kept up with fresh groceries. Jane never got rid of it. *No reason to, and I'm glad I didn't, this is where I'm needed most.* With her new routine, Maru and Paru have had more free time as outdoor cats and ... recruited several friends. Whenever Jane popped in, the cats were starved for attention. *You guys miss me, don't you? You ... you can smell the death in me?* She fought back a tear as she gave kitty scritches to a new friend. *That kid down there would not die from the drugs in his veins but burned alive in some hellfire.* It was just a matter of time.

CHAPTER FIFTEEN

Safe travel at the speed of your fax machine ... is that even possible?! Zip around the country in your own helicopter, complete with a licensed anti-freak armed pilot and hors d'oeuvres to keep you on top of your game. Get from point A to point B within minutes! Visit our website online to find out more about how you can beat the traffic, on land or in the air. Need to book that flight right now? Call us at 555-6482. Show up in style (and on time). Fly to your meetings today with Direlife VTOL.

Jack poked the small metal box on the counter. He felt awkward, standing in a chef's robe, with an array of cameras and lights shining on him. The overzealous young director was leaning forward, silently gesturing for Jack to continue with the teleprompters text.

"It ... shall ... make the best toast ... with the fury of hell's ... kitchen," Jack said. He poked the metal box again. "Now ... you, too, can own your very own. Toaster. It makes toast. Just ... like me, when I make the toast of bad things in the arena every day."

"Cut! That's perfect, Jack! Don't worry about a second take, our special effects team will CG in all the action shots and explosions," the director said as the crew prepped for the next commercial.

With each mind-numbing commercial after another, Jack helped fill in the backbone of a new, growing economy. For several months, he'd followed the same pattern. By day, he sold common household items rebranded, by night he slew creatures by the dozens in the arena. He wasn't sure which was more tedious anymore. *Jane gets all the fun commercials and arena fights. Gotta hand it to her, she's a showman for sure. But seriously, who the hell will buy a toaster with actual hellfire? Who the fuck comes up with this shit?* His chef's robe was replaced with a maid's uniform and before he could question a vacuum cleaner was thrust into his hands.

"Roll!"

"Nobody sucks up more ash than ..." Inwardly, Jack was sure he had died.

Hours later, Jack lumbered into the back of his blackened SUV, envious of the security team having a smoke break. *Can't they give me a nicotine injection?* Freedom, Jack learned in the past weeks, wasn't something that Peter or Kristov had ever intended. His every action had been monitored, and each movement escorted. Not that he blamed him, he supposed, he wouldn't let a multi-million Bitcoin demon-slaying machine walk around freely either.

"You could stand to put more *oomph* into it," Dr. Alex Kristov squawked from the back seat. His small frame rocked back and forth as Jack got settled.

"And you could stand to quit wasting my time," Jack retorted. "Let the damn creatures off their chains. You do it for, Jane— why not me?"

Kristov rolled his eyes. "Not this again. Look here, buddy," he said, leaning in closer. "You're a commodity. If I had my way, I'd rewrite that brain of yours. Well ... if Peter didn't take a liking to you, or those *idiot* reporters always babbling about your awareness. Fucking dolts." Kristov mocked them with his motions. "I think they loaded you up with too much hardware for your own good. But don't worry, you serve as a good starter to the Terror Twins, a nice little warm-up to sell the dream."

Jack placed his head on the cool window as they drove up through ramps. *Didn't you already rewrite me enough?* With each ramp, aspects of the city got visibly more refined. With each month, any memories that leaked through always lacked context of their predecessors. Giant stone statues of Prometheus lifted even more roads. As one of the safest places in North America, the growing cities had an unlimited amount of near-free labor. The higher Jack went in the city, the more he saw the builders enhanced with cybernetics like him—and the more fantastic their buildings.

"What dream am I selling?" Jack asked, breaking the silence.

"Redemption and recovery," Kristov said while looking out the other window. "That we can make anyone overcome their handicaps, be they disease, ideology, injury—and still find pride in their trade. The Terror Twins showcase skill for our budding military, which lets everyone know we can stand toe-to-toe with the armies of the world. Then JK-47 gifts them with the tasty dessert of awe." Kristov hit Jack's shoulder like an old friend. "Don't worry about it, though, she won't be around long!" He laughed. "Speaking of being around long, however, how are the headaches?"

Jack thudded his head on the window in a vain attempt to forget his real problem. Every single night at 3:00 AM in the morning he was foaming at the mouth from pain. At first, the migraine only lasted a minute, but recently they had been pushing upwards of four hundred and eighty excruciating seconds. He dreaded coming home, no matter how automated and nice they made his penthouse. One they were pulling into now.

"Getting worse."

"Well, progress has his flaws. Peter is looking into it, I assure you. The science used to make you ... is even beyond my abilities."

Jack perked up at the mention of Peter. "Is ... is he coming by tonight?"

"Looks like it's on his schedule. He's giving a tour to our visitor, so I don't know how much one-on-one time you'll have. But we're here. Time for me to pick up the Twins. They are doing a podcast tonight."

"Right." Jack got out into the filled parking garage where LED lights illuminated the decorative concrete columns with a soft blue light. The powers that be reserved most of the building for him and the technicians that worked on him, but they only occupied a quarter of the spaces at best. Unknown cars filled several other spots illegally throughout the restricted garage. Raising an eyebrow, Jack turned around. "What's going on?" he asked.

"Fan meet and greet. Plus, Peter will be here later," Kristov said, already dialing his cell phone for his next appointment. "Remember, Jack, give it some ... oomph. Smile a little. We aren't going to get rich with you scowling all over." Kristov leaned over to close the door. "Yeah, Taylor, honey, I'm swinging by—"

You've gotta be shitting me. Jack watched the door slam and the armored car pull away. "That little worm is getting way too big," Jack said aloud.

"Well, of course, chap," a voice echoed through the garage. "His creations, those Terror Twins, are the only ones that aren't suffering from malfunction."

With a whir, Jack's arm heated, cascading the ebbing light of charging plasma.

"Woah, woah, woah!" A small girl with cut-off jeans, wallet chains, and short hair dyed purple stepped out from behind a column with a smoke still in her hands. "I'm a fan, just out here on a smoke break," she smiled.

"This part of the garage is off—"

"Off-limits, yeah, how else you think I will get that prized photo op with you?" She walked up and held out her hand. "Akira, charmed, I'm sure."

Jack's arrayed vision picked up a few traits about his new fan, and he was rather sure she wouldn't like what he saw. For starters, she was dead as doornails. Not like his crazy theory he was secretly playing a video game and everyone was dead, but a complete, computer-verified infrared registration she was an undead. The second was that she was crawling with insects under her clothes and probably rotting from the inside. *How she's not scratching and clawing at her stomach I do not understand.* But most importantly, she was familiar to him. In that foggy way when you see an old high school friend after a few years and cringe at how badly they aged.

He leveled his plasma gun at its face. "Give me a reason."

"How those headaches treating you?" She didn't even flinch at the charged arm inches away from her nose. "Don't you remember me, chief?"

"Those are questions, not a reason." Just seeing her caused a sharp pain to start behind his right eye. A headache was encroaching. He remembered her. *It was her who gave me ...*

"Oooh ... they are getting bad. Dem headaches. You got pale, which is funny, considering I'm not sure you have any blood left in you." She took a drag and produced a small vial from one of her many pockets. "Let's go to your room. I can make that go away."

"Demon's blood. In the Twin Cities. I got caught up in your riots ..." Jack let the charge die down. Even the thought of a demon's blood sent his brain into a full-fledged migraine. He fell to his knee.

"There weeee goooo." Akira reached out and gently lowered his arm. "That's right, buddy. That and more. You're a full-fledged member of the Sons and Daughters. I knew we erased some of your memories, but these guys must've taken it a step further. Here." She uncorked the bottle.

The sweet smell of peaches and spice were intoxicating. As his eyes were rolling back into his head, Akira put a drop on his lips. The hit was instant. Every synapse lit up on fire, and the blood filled every living nerve he had left with ecstasy as his headache receded.

"Come on, buddy, let's get you in." Akira lifted him up with one arm around her shoulder and helped him lumber inside.

One elevator ride, a stumble through white hallways, and a retinal scan later, Jack was seated on a giant metal swivel chair.

"Well, isn't this place festive," Akira said, looking around the room.

Giant black monitors filled his entire east wall, each of them with a different TV station on, babbling about some news in the world. A single chair, or throne, rather, sat in the middle of an otherwise sparse room, with bamboo wood floors. There was no bed, no bathing products, and most of his clothes comprised of trench coats and sunglasses. Akira strolled over to the window and looked out at the vast cities below them and let out a whistle.

"Man, they've really got you set up here, eh?" she said, looking out and tapping on the glass.

Jack shook his head. Not only was his headache gone, but he felt fantastic, albeit already craving more. *Wonder if I can get that vial off her.* "So, what do you want?" he asked, leaning forward and swiveling around.

"Our reporter friend, Kevin," she trailed off as she traced her fingers on the glass. "He thinks you are gone for good. I don't believe him. I figured by now security around you would be a little lighter, so I came to pay a visit. Besides, these cities are a shitty-ass place to feed. It's not exactly demon-hunting territory, and they won't let you drink human blood, either."

"Is that why they keep the demons chained up?"

"You got it, buddy; you're a blood addict." She shrugged. "Well, at least you are now. You *weren't* before the infiltration. Do you really think a regular human would've survived the surgery you underwent?"

Jack chuckled while running his fingers through black hair. "So, I was a monster?"

"Woah, hell, no. Just damn good in a fight. You ate a demon heart like most of us and ... well ... you did just fine." She looked off to the side. "More than fine, really. But some special forces caught up with us in St. Louis and you went down. We had a choice, let you die or get you treatment. Since we wanted to get in here anyway, you told us to muddle up your memory and let you get captured. None of us thought they would chop you up and put you in a new body. Which sucks because that's why you're getting headaches." She slinked over and tapped his metal chest. "You've lost your heart."

I get it ... I'm dreaming again. This is one of those I'm asleep and it all seems so real. Fuck man, could they at least give me a liver so I could drink again?

"So." Jack leaned back in his chair, folding his arms. "Why the hell would I want to come here and let them do this?"

"Well ..." Akira's eyes fluttered around the monitors. "Someone has to rid the world of Warlocks and Death Lords, and in this case ..." She pointed to a few monitors in the corner. They showed an atrium filled with people in plastic cosplay of Jack. Another showed Peter Stein Culmen, an old man with red and black robes, and a small security detail moving through a white hallway.

Jack's white hallway.

"We're going to kill 'em," she said with a nod.

"Sure thing," Jack smirked. *All right, dream bug lady. Let's have fun.* Without standing up, Jack fired up his plasma cannon, to Akira's insect-like surprise. She froze. Swinging his arm out to the right and pointing at his closet, Jack unleashed supercharged fury through three walls.

On the monitor, Jack saw the bodies of two security guards pop like balloons as their skins boiled over. Frame by frame he watched the old man's face turn into a snarl as the flames melted off his disguise, and threw him back through another wall, ripping off legs and arms. Peter cast an electric net out to shield himself, but even he flew back and slammed into a wall.

Jack reloaded.

"Well ... I did not see that coming." Fangs popped out of Akira's mouth as she started shape-shifting. She seemed torn between racing to the Death Lord and keeping an eye on Jack. "They say it's best to lie in wait ..." Bones snapped and clothes shredded onto the floor. "Apologies, Jack, that trigger was pulled too soon, by me, it appears. Without knowing their powers, it's suicide. Pardon the pun." Thousands of small voices chuckled in unison. "Know thy enemy and jazz."

"Wait, what?" Jack turned and looked at the looming green insect rising over him. He had faced all kinds of creatures in the arena, but a giant undead praying mantis was not one of them. A sensor flashed in his vision, informing him that his right arm had malfunctioned. *Peter's override.* He heard the clatter of his arm hitting wood floors and registered a second later that Akira cut it off. *Oh, fuck me sideways.* A flurry of strikes impacted him, the insect's raptorial arms dented and sliced through his steel, pulling him to shreds.

He screamed and tried to fight off his nightmare. A left hook grabbed onto an iridescent wing and ripped it off, showering the room into ash. Mandibles clamped around his shoulder, worming their way under armored plates and tearing off his other arm. Akira body checked him and sent him through the gaping hole in the wall.

Jack's vision tunneled as his head slammed into the hallway wall. Peter, with a look of unchecked fury, raced in his direction chanting incantations, digitizing a rifle from thin air. As Peter slid in front of Jack, shielding his creation with his own body, the hellish insect creature shattered through the windows and took erratic flight. More of a controlled fall thanks to a missing wing. Peter's bolts lit up the sky, each round emitting smoke as the chambers fell to the ground. *Silver bullets, eh, Peter? Cute.* With a dissatisfied grunt, Peter let his customized rifle dematerialize, and turned his attention back to Jack.

"From the look on your face, I take it it's pretty bad," Jack said, letting his head thud back onto the bamboo floor.

Peter nodded.

"Well, there is an upside to this." Jack coughed up a slimy oil.

"And what, do tell, is that?" Peter turned his back to him, and marched into the room, unafraid of any other assailants.

"I don't have to do fan night." Jack gave an oily grin.

CHAPTER SIXTEEN

Truth is a match. It can bear light or set your world ablaze. Wouldn't you rather wield the flames than be charred by them? Numen is a proven pyrokinesis technique that will unlock all your chakras and reveal the truth in your world. For one regular monthly payment, these techniques can be yours. Each month will reveal new secrets about the lost art of pyrokinesis and the supplements required to practice it. Don't stay in the dark any longer.

D elilah Dumont allowed herself a single drop of Rakshasa blood from a small amber vial that was getting frustratingly emptier as the months marched on. *All the powers of the Praenomen and the one thing that yet eludes me on this blasted continent is a single demon king. I'll find you yet, Mr. Bollard ... just you wait.* Out of habit, she cleaned her wire-framed glasses with a small purple cloth and looked out the second-story window of St. Mary's Cathedral into the ever-increasing snowfall. It was already May, and many needed to face reality about what a permanent black sun really entailed. Even if the current snowfall was her doing. *I wonder how long it will take southerners to get used to snow. Probably never.*

Even though she didn't need glasses anymore, the act of cleaning them brought enjoyment while she admired her latest spell. Weather witching was still relatively new to her—a recent addition to her arsenal. Warlock Vryce, her mentor and six-hundred-year-old grandfather, preferred flashier methods of lightning, tornados, even the occasional firestorm. Delilah felt fresh snowfall would calm and cripple a city at once; it was more her speed. *After all, if you're going to kill someone, at least have the courtesy to dress up the scenery. We aren't savages.*

That last thought was partly in question, she realized as soon as it crossed her mind. Her gaze refocused to her reflection first. Her left eye was a sharp golden color with scarring around the socket. A gift from Mr. Bollard when he carved out her natural, green-colored eye. *I hate how I'm addicted to his blood, yet love his cunning. I will flay his skin from his body and devour his heart in revenge. Keep your enemies close, they say.* Stick-straight blonde hair fell to her shoulders, framing her angular face and giving her a professional look she had catered for decades.

The rest of her wardrobe was anything but: a black duster trench coat, long enough to touch the floor and filled with hermetic runes on the inside that clearly indicated her witchcraft, cold iron nails strapped to a bandolier over her body armor, three pistols, seven stakes, an ax blessed with holy water, and white leather gloves with the seal of Solomon marked her as ready for war. But most importantly, the cracked porcelain mask of the Praenomen and an inverted wooden Rosary hung around her neck. Feeling a tad sentimental, she ran her gloved finger over Vryce's phylacteries. They gave her knowledge beyond her years, but power was never without cost. *All the power of a Lich, no, my mentor. Bending reality to your will and spellcraft the likes of which the world has never seen, at the small cost of self-inflicted possession by him.*

Several pleas for help passed in the room around her, but it was the licking and smacking sound of two vampires slurping up blood that broke her reverie.

She slammed the wooden table. Symon and Whisper jumped up from their prey and stood at attention. The anti-freak unit soldier gripped for life while flayed out, blood dripping out over the wooden table. His dying cries echoing off arched ceilings.

"Can you ..." Delilah pinched the bridge of her nose. "Can you two *not* feed so loudly? I get it. You haven't had a meal in days. But couldn't you go for the femoral artery and finish this quickly? I would much rather ..." She looked away and shook her head.

"Eh, come on, 'ave a bite to eat with us, eh?" Symon said with his broken French accent. "What's the worst that can happen? You're already scary enough as is. Get it while it's fresh, we say. Don't we say that, Whisper?"

It animated the gray vampire in response, gesturing that he in no way agreed with the statement. Whisper tipped the soldier's broken neck to the side and confirmed his camera feed was still live. He gave the signal. Authorities were officially monitoring them.

"How many times must I tell you, Symon, I'm not a vampire." She pulled out an iron nail and slammed it into the dying man's shadow. He instantly went silent. "I'm a bloody witch, a daughter of darkness, Satan's slut, a hag, a sorcerer, a blooded human, a cauldron crony, occultist, or my personal favorite—conjurer. The only blood I'll ever drink is that of Bollard when I rip his heart out and devour it myself."

"I do think she's still properly pissed," Whisper said at last.

Symon threw a napkin on top of his now-dead meal. Once humans had died, the blood soured. "Just pissed? I'd say that's a glass half full statement." He paced to the far side of the room and leaned back along the wall. "So, is that why you have us scavenging inside these walls? For a damn demon prince?"

"Insubordination is ill becoming of you, Symon," Delilah intoned.

The Frenchman bowed and held his head low. "If you wanted

mindless slaves, you could've turned us into gargoyles long ago. I apologize for zee offense."

"Whisper, what's the status report from our agents elsewhere?" She changed tone and pace and left Symon in his bowed position.

"Madam, Washington is still in chaos. President Drummel probably cut a deal with a demon lord for power, and in an election year, *tsk*. While the Secret Service remains exceptionally difficult to infiltrate, we have seeded one agent in their ranks. The Pentagon was far easier, mostly because they were already corrupted by the Unification long ago. As of right now, the US military stands at a mere twenty-five percent of its former strength. Mostly due to troop abandonment to return home for their families. Although, I suppose that's still enough armed forces to wipe most other countries off this planet."

"Symon, is the Archive's new base of operations in Colorado finished yet?" Delilah strolled back to her window. *Tell a little truth, put on a little show. I know you're out there listening, Peter.*

"No, madam. Many of your Unification-enhanced construction crews 'ave been delayed because they are here. You've been helping build this city for some time now, and you've kept all of us in the dark about your plans. Or why you are even working with those anarchists. What the fuck is up with us organizing fan clubs for these weak arena people. The Twins? Jane? They be strong enough to beat an army of demons?" Symon let out a good laugh and darted over to Whisper, patting him on the head. "We aren't much of a terrorist cell if all we do is build the things and make parties, no?"

Delilah slid on the mask of the Praenomen and relinquished part of her mind to the vast power within. Cold tendrils of shadow inched their way into her skull and grasped onto her brain, causing shivers from head to toe. The secrets of the world opened to her, along with the fragmented thoughts of the presumed dead warlock. Vryce wasn't dead by even the furthest measure. She could feel him—a single fragment of him —possessing a teenager somewhere in the Second City, practicing his own newly discovered magic. Another fragment walked around the great occult libraries buried beneath the Twin Cities, watching Gabriel D'Angelo's every move. Vryce was part of her, now, and also nothing more than an object on a shelf in a dark closet. Each of his phylacteries carried his power and his soul. A gift he granted to his acolytes to further on his wishes while he hid from greater threats like Lazarus or other warlocks until the time was right. *Don't worry about your precious Society of Deus, sire. You brought magic back in the world. Now I'll ensure that no singular god controls it all and let all the blame fall elsewhere.*

"The time to strike," the Praenomen spoke, its voice now both masculine and feminine, both one and several voices at once, "is now. This city has had enough hope. We've let Lazarus's descendant take the show, helped the Sons and Daughters watch their mechanical friend, and seen the best weapons and pilots that Peter could conjure up. For a warlock, we say Peter's creations disappoint us. Paltry, ineffective weapons when he could build a nation. Now he's just a choir boy to a priest of Lazarus, when the man was a genius as a Warlock."

The powers of lichdom were rather intoxicating. With a snap of its fingers, the Praenomen summoned its shadowy soldiers by its side as they marched down the stairs. Near identical clones made of liquid shadow given form. Symon and Whisper both geared up, but also shadowy versions of them took by their sides, two by two, three by three, an ever-growing army of illusion and shadow. Unlike Gabriel, Delilah enjoyed the power of Vryce flowing through her. With his strength, *willpower* alone was enough for grand magical effects. Her body's fingers cracked, and she felt her lips curl over her teeth by another's command, but her steps were her own. Being partially possessed felt like driving a car but with some else controlling the brakes.

"He wasted all his time, precious time, building a kingdom that would best keep things at bay and turn a profit. Not even once paying attention to the world outside his little glass house. Never questioning why armies of demons were congregating in

Michigan. Or why the Death Lord fawned over Jane like a doting grandfather, and why he's here now."

"Yeah, what's up with that?" Symon asked while signing to Whisper a countdown to open the doors.

The Praenomen readied several arcane instruments and iron needles for battle. "Within the blood lies the True Name of a myth, personified by drought and blight, a sunless legend. Lazarus and Purgatory go hand in hand, and like her brother, Jane's a distant descendent. Jane isn't the first, nor the only. Just like every other kid born who tells mommy she sees ghosts." She pinched her fingers a tad. "Maybe a tit-bit more. And like most gods, maybe Lazarus got jealous, and doesn't like it when other gods like Odin, or even Hades, start coming back. Thus, the new corporate policy for gods. Eliminate *or* buy out the competition before they get a foothold. Hell, don't even ask how many people were related to Bacchus, the Roman God of Wine. Remember, it's popular belief that makes a God, so it's no surprise the Church of Lazarus wants their own to be megastars. It's a shame, because whatever Peter is up to with Jack is promethean in nature—and the Church of Lazarus is never going to allow it."

The Praenomen gave a small chant in an ancient demonic tongue, a whisper of old, long forgotten myths and fairy folk. "Maybe a secretary forgot to email everyone in the boardroom that demons have their own gods." *That should do.*

Whisper yanked the church's double doors open while Symon chucked the soldier out onto the street. Several bullets instantly landed in the doorframe in response.

They burst out onto the snow-covered streets. The screams quickly followed as the shadows raced in every direction, killing anti-freak snipers and local militia that surrounded the church.

The Praenomen flung his gloved hands out and swirled them into a circle motion before pushing forward, sending a raging vortex of wind flying down the corridors of downtown Austin, shattering glass and ripping off freshly constructed building facades.

Symon and Whisper went to town, unloading crossbow bolt

after crossbow bolt into anything that moved. Only a few citizens braved the cold, but the vampires didn't seem to care. Each shot found hit its bullseye regardless of distance as their eyes glowed red, using their enhanced undead sight to shoot the earliest reinforcements.

Police cars raced in from side streets before telekinetic force crumpled them like sardine cans while their drivers had their souls sucked out by shadows. The Praenomen struggled with this. On one hand, the regular police helped them on many occasions. On the other hand, to make omelets, eggs needed breaking. "Whisper?" The Praenomen repositioned closer. "As a fellow espionage expert, you see that our dear Warlock Peter has his own agenda that he's not showing, right?"

The grey vampire walked along the side of the building at an impossible angle, occasionally darting down to stick a fresh dagger in the throat of someone still trying to run, or stupid enough to stick their head outside a door. "A warlock with a secret agenda? Why, you don't say? It seems as if this playbook writes itself."

As more anti-freak units rolled in, now armored with the best in corporate equipment, silvered and blessed rounds, and every armament possible to deal with creatures like her—it didn't matter. Be it the Army, the Marines, Air Force, or even new anti-freak squads, most mortal armies were still relying on one fatal flaw. *Their soldiers were alive.* The Praenomen commanded the weather yet again, sucking the air out of the area and into a massive cloudburst above. They fired bullets, of course, which Symon valiantly shielded her from with his own armored body, but the living need oxygen. Instead of firing, even soldiers in armored vehicles were scrambling for their tanks. In those precious seconds, the shadows claimed their lives.

"Symon, I do wager that Warlock Peter isn't the least bit concerned about the name of the God which gets whispered on the lips of creatures recently returned. I think, and correct me if I'm wrong, that he's up to something with JK-47, Jack, or the Terror Twins ... and the key to figure out which one he cares about most is simply to take one away." The Praenomen called down lightning from above, crashing into anti-freak units and dancing to the next as they screamed. The latter was more Vryce than Delilah, but she didn't have much of a choice in that matter.

Symon picked himself up and cringed as he yanked out a silver round from his withered left kidney. "Ah. Ehhh ... I'd say Lazarus will wipe out all our gods, Madam. Even Peter's."

The ground shook beneath the Praenomen as she heard the high-pitched sounds of jet engines echo through the city walls. Her target was en route.

"Indeed, Symon. Indeed. After all, who will help the god of destruction, the deadly one, the god of plagues, king of the Fomorians—Balor of the Piercing Eye—return. If not for us." Behind her mask, Delilah winked. She knew the entire show was on display, feeding through some camera to the technowizard's brain directly. Every act of destruction, every death, every word uttered, was a careful act of espionage. A mix of truth and misdirection. *Espionage is a tricky business.*

Around the corner on Congress and Eleventh Street, the Terror Twins flew into position. Each took up post to defend the Texas Capitol building, a white, nineteenth-century, beautiful display of architecture. Yet with a gaudy sign for *Stubbs BBQ* within eyesight that killed the ambience. Snow instantly melted around them as their hardsuits landed and readied themselves.

The Praenomen dismissed Symon and Whisper, sending them off to get in position, without a word. This next part was on her. *Time to bait and switch.* She scanned the now-deserted street. Paramount Theater behind her, the Cathedral to her right, and countless structures crawling vertically to the heavens beyond them.

"Surrender!" Taylor shouted out.

The Praenomen waited.

Tyler was less vocal. He opened fire, sending round after round her way, each one firing right through, like the Praenomen wasn't there. Delilah rolled her eyes behind the mask. *This is a child's play trick. Every witch learns this as a beginner spell. Come now, Peter, you couldn't even teach your toys how to spot an illusion?*

"Hail Fulmen!" the Praenomen shouted from the left of her shadow double while rapidly producing a series of gestures and pointing at Tyler. A blinding flash of white-hot light streaked down from the heavens and contacted the mech. A second later, the sound erupted into a shock wave as the explosion turned the mech into molten slag at over ten thousand degrees. The pilot inside his armored liquid capsule barely clung to life, even as shadows crept in behind him.

"No Jack and no Jane, eh, Peter?" the Praenomen asked aloud in several voices and a few languages at once. "I guess we know which of your toys are expendable, then ..." As the Praenomen stepped forward, she pulled one of her cold iron nails out and slammed it through her foot. Even behind her mask she winced from the sharp pain as her blood colored the snow red. Falling to her knee, she let her mind go free and race along the ground at Taylor. All the armor and mechanical claptraps in the world wouldn't save her from a possession spell.

Delilah blinked. No matter how many times she practiced Vryce's art of possession, it always felt ... off. She looked out through the orange-tinted window at herself—kneeling on the ground with an iron nail in her foot, a scene of devastation behind her body from their assault. Symon and Whisper both long gone, doing their best to take the battle elsewhere. She turned her new body's head from side to side, curious about the peculiar liquid that infused the cabin, even more curious about how this body didn't breathe. While searching for a control panel, among the myriad of lights and sensors, a realization came over her.

She did not understand how to pilot this thing. *Well ... that was a slight miscalculation on my part. No matter, let's just eject.* Yet no matter where her eyes fell, there was no sign of *any* control or motor. Only a rather foul-tasting liquid and plugs in places that made her feel uncomfortably vulnerable. Out of the corner of her eye, she watched a white VTOL helicopter descend near her real body. Five armored soldiers zip-lined down ahead of the craft and quickly secured her body.

Maybe more than a slight miscalculation. Okay, there has to be an eject button. No matter how much she tried, though, the arms would not move. Or rather, she could feel the pilot's arm move inside its mechanical gel-filled shell. But the arm itself was as stationary as a giant boulder.

"Neural signatures," a voice rang out across the field.

Delilah snapped her vision up, and saw Peter Stein Culmen, his dreadlocks glowing a slight blue, wearing a set of black wraparound sunglasses. Despite the surrounding carnage, his fine black and blue suit was as pristine as ever, complete with an ornate pocket square. She let her shoulders lurch. *Well, shit. I had this whole grand plan about making him kill his own soldier and now it's all jazzed up because these damn suits don't have buttons. This is why we stick to checklists, and no evil plans. Evil plans never work right.*

"Make sure you bind each finger on that sorcerer. Whatever you do, don't remove that nail. I'm not ready for our prey to leave just yet." Shouldering a rifle, he strolled forward, but not before kneeling before her body and touching something to her neck. "After all, if you are going to kill someone, you might as well dress it up."

Can't we just skip to the part where you throw me into the arena after I surrender? This, ladies and gentlemen, is why you always bring a sniper when you need to die. I'm so proud of you for not snapping and killing Taylor, Peter. Shame about what comes next.

"Weather control, shadow magic, possession, and even telekinesis." He whistled as he knocked on the hardsuit's visor. "You are quite the accomplished apprentice, aren't you? I'd recognize these trappings anywhere. Hell, most Unification members would assume you were the great warlock Vryce—but the cold iron nail is a dead giveaway. You aren't a master of possession, are you? Trapped inside this coffin, eh?"

Delilah couldn't see what he did, but suddenly the hatch around her face opened, spilling gel like liquid out around her.

"Coffin is a matter of perspective," she coughed. "This is still your pilot."

He raised an eyebrow. "According to you, these are the expendable ones. But you're already wrong about so, so much, dear Delilah Dumont." He held up a small, clear piece of glass with a small DNA helix spinning on it. "Oh, this? I'm not even going to take off that mask over there. A simple blood prick and I've got your entire history. We were friends once. What happened?"

"Oh, you know, when the Church of Lazarus campaigns for a crusade, sorcerers get ... jealous when locked into servitude."

Peter shook his head. "You've got quite the history of putting yourself in the middle of terrible situations and spinning them to your advantage. Every society heard about your little spat with Bollard last year. But you seriously are wrong about me." Peter saw the soldiers moving to pick up the body, and pull the nail out of her foot in order to do so. "I *told* you not to touch that nail."

"Which part?" Delilah forced Taylor to say. "That you're being a willfully ignorant sap?"

"I don't care about what happens outside these walls, because what I'm doing *inside* of them will bring a utopia for all humans. Even if that includes the Church of Lazarus. The project I'm working on will revolutionize the world and erase any need for any man to be dependent on any higher power."

"Oh, I've heard this before. Gone will be disease, aging, death, poverty, and so forth. Wasn't that the same line the Unification told everyone on why we were to bring back Lazarus?"

"You mean you aren't a believer?" Peter feigned shock. "Guys, she's not a believer!" He leaned in close and whispered, "All warlocks have secret projects."

Delilah made Taylor give the biggest teenage eye roll she could muster. "Then you should've just joined us, then." She was growing more impatient with how long it was taking Symon to get into position.

"There are very stark ideological differences between us. I'm not willing to murder the world to bring back magic when technology can march us forward."

"We aren't murdering millions," she said. "We are letting the ignorant get eaten. It's not much of a difference, but it's there. Now are you going to lock me up in prison or what?"

"I think ..." Peter shook his head no. "I think Taylor might like to take out her revenge on you for killing her brother."

Delilah saw a trail of smoke rise from a nearby office building. *Finally.*

Death was instant. Delilah's mind flowed back to her body, now bound up and shackled, but it was still more comfortable. She looked up at splats of blood oozing out of where Taylor's head was. Peter was furious.

"So," the Praenomen spoke. "How's she going to get revenge on me now that she's dead?"

Peter paced for a moment as he ran calculations and replayed video. "You know, you were right. The Church would want to root for their own. Putting you in the arena will be plenty of revenge. For everyone." He gestured widely to the carnage she had caused. "And ... and when my *ineffective* toys break you, then people will believe in us even more. Isn't that what this is all about? Marketing a myth? So, when whatever demon god you backwater Deus witches are sipping on loses its champion ... *Poof* ..." The warlock flicked her forehead before signaling a rollout to his security detail. "Oh," he snapped. "Before I forget, two can play at misinformation. Let's see how Deus likes it when I blame them for you, and whatever aces you are still holding onto."

If I were him, I would've just killed me. It is delightful to play this dance with competent opponents. Nice pivot, Peter. The Praenomen shrugged, looking around at the five soldiers with guns pointed at her. "You heard your boss. Let's go." She felt fragments of Vryce chuckle in several places. *Sometimes plans need a minor edit, but this dance is just beginning.*

CHAPTER SEVENTEEN

You. Deserve. Peace. Nobody should have to watch the world fall as it has today. To watch the dead rise or listen to companies hawk you products. Elcoll will provide you with the peace you deserve and the ability to rest secure with the knowledge You. Were. Here.

The purple light from the Lilith moon shone down on the packed arena. Not a cloud remained in the sky after the earlier blizzards. Someone pushed snow to every side of the field, packed against the high concrete walls in preparatory haste. To Jack, it felt like the entire city hit the brakes for this emergency execution; anyone who wasn't at the arena was tuning in from the comfort of their home. He fingered a hole in between his armored plating where Kristov slagged on metal plates with a welding torch an hour ago and took a deep breath. *It's one thing getting ripped to shreds by a giant mantis, but it's a whole new method of horror to watch your doctor jury-rig you back together.*

"It's fucking cold," Jack said aloud as he manually loaded ammunition into his right arm. As each bullet clacked into the chambers, it echoed throughout the corridor. Thanks to his earlier "misfire," the powers that be determined that the plasma rifle was too dangerous for casual use. So Magladon Arms outfitted him with a semiautomatic machine gun and grenade launcher in the name of safety. "Like this shit is any less deadly, am I right?"

"Huh?" Jane said while bouncing up and down to keep warm. Her cheeks were rosy red and her nose equally bright. Even though she had her now-famous rocket boots on, Jane wrapped herself up in so many coats and gloves she was an unrecognizable poofball. "Yeah, the cold is deadly, no shit, Sherlock," she chattered.

Jack's scanner picked up her body temperature, and he shook his head in response. "You know the cold doesn't affect you, right? You've got a metabolism of like ... forty humans or something. That shit's all in your mind."

"Screw you, northerner, a single snowflake used to be enough to shut down our entire state. This?" She waved a mittened hand. "Is the fucking apocalypse to us ... and I'll chatter my damn teef if I want to."

With the final round loaded, Jack rose from his bench and limped down the corridor to the entrance and leaned out. Huge monitors showcased the capture of a rogue sorcerer, the first non-creature to enter the arena since its launch. In between video cuts, the talking heads would showcase footage from the leader in the Society of Deus, Gabriel D'Angelo, each cut a heavily propagandized sound bite.

"So that's him, huh?" Jack pointed the barrel up at the screen as Jane bounced over and looked up.

"Gabriel, eh? That's a face I haven't seen since the early riots ... in ... forever."

For an insurgent leader, Jack didn't think too much of him. In the captured footage, he was an overly tall blond man who looked rather lanky, with scraggy unkempt hair and an eternal scowl. Gabriel never seemed to smile, and his piercing green eyes didn't make him seem any less intense. Instead, he wore pristine white gym shoes, hoodies, and carried a cavalry saber strapped to his back, clamped in place by a golden ouroboros buckle around his chest. *Take that off and he looks just like a regular guy.*

"How many times has the US military tried to kill him now?" Jack asked rhetorically. "We should've just dropped a nuke on that whole mess up north and called it a day."

"Dude, what the fuck?" Jane shot him a sideways glance. "Don't be a bigot; we aren't at the point where we are bombing our own country yet. Work a restaurant long enough and you'll hear all kinds of stories."

"Like ones about where the Society of Deus sends down magical assassins to tear through our streets and kill our comrades?"

As they poked their heads out through the gate, they watched the assailant get wheeled in by anti-freak soldiers and chained to a familiar post. The rogue sorcerer was shorter than Jack expected and easily a few inches shorter than Jane. It held its head low, and it obscured its face with a white porcelain mask, one that matched the color of the snow under the moonlight. The crowd threw insults, jars of piss, and other obscenities down at the defeated creature as handlers worked to secure the prisoner. Massive spotlights clicked on from around the top of the stadium and shone down on the target. Curious, Jack adjusted his vision to block out the light and see beyond them. *Snipers? This thing is that deadly?*

Jack recalled the myriad of executions he had performed and couldn't recall a single time that SWAT team members or anti-freak units took a position around the field. Nor had he seen so many news outlets, or military craft, hovering in the distance. Given how easily he had "accidently" shot the Lord of Suicide earlier, he rolled his eyes. *Just wait a day and let me get some better hardware and I'll shove a volcano up this blood junkie's ...*

"Don't forget, you ain't any better there, Jack." He shook the memory of drinking demon's blood away. Ever since Akira had visited him, his migraines vanished, and he felt a shit ton better. "Hey, Jane?"

The announcer started with the opening ceremonies.

"Yeah?"

"Looks like this show will be in my wheelhouse rather than yours. Standard execution. I don't think they'll let it off the chains. Might as well get yourself some peppermint Pegasus mocha or something. They completely defanged this one, look at it."

Jane stepped out further, causing some nearby fans to lose their minds, and she squinted through the spotlights at the chained-up victim as blood left her face.

"No ... no ... Jack! They defanged nothing; Whisper is her damn handler!" She hit the side of her head a few times, cursing herself for being stupid.

"Whisper? Who the fuck is Whisper?" Jack focused in and saw the regular handler wearing Carhartt's and an orange safety vest walk back to the prisoner and double-check all the locks. *Jane's ... never lied to me, so ...* on her hunch, he refocused his vision and zoomed in. With near-impeccable sleight of hand, the handler produced a dagger-shaped object and jabbed it under the sorcerer's shirt. Jack couldn't tell if he was stabbing it or putting it on her. "Hey—"

Jane sprinted out into the arena, ripping off her winter possessions and screaming at the top of her lungs.

"Get out! It's a trap! Get out! Evacuate!" She tried to shout over the announcer but received only confused looks or oblivious crowd cheers, mistaking her warning for enthusiasm.

The lights exploded, one by one in quick succession, followed by return gunfire from the snipers at a fast-moving shadow. Jack saw someone he recognized running along the edges with a spear, impaling SWAT officers as he slid past them on his knees. *Symon Vasyl. All right, you little shit stain. It's on.* Jack cocked his grenade launcher and hobbled out into the arena. At last, he would see action.

The targeting reticle locked onto the vampiric soldier that was racing along the catwalks. Symon's eyes glowed unholy red, doubtless some supernatural power, and leapt between pillars to the next officer who struggled to get his sidearm out in time before the spear found purchase. Without hesitation, Symon ripped through the neck with his fangs and sprinted to the next.

Jack waited for him to get midair before he unloaded. Each round fired left a trail of hot orange light as the tracers zipped and found their mark, riddling the spear-wielding psychopath. Like a sack of bricks being thrown into a pool, Symon did an ugly tumble down between the metal framing—hitting each bar with a satisfying crunch that bent bones in impossible angles before landing on a fifty yard bench. *Now we are talking.* Jack hobbled over as the crowd erupted into cheers. "Even if I'm still half-assembled ..."

Out of the corner of his vision, Jack saw a blur zip close, heralded by the sound of rattling electric blue chains. Jane planted her left foot on his back and vaulted up into a flip. "Don't mind me!" Out of the corner of his eye, he saw the locks binding the Praenomen shatter. The distraction from the gunfire must have been all the sorcerer needed to break free. Jane's aerial flips increased the force behind her chains and brought them down hard on where the prisoner was, a second too late. *I gotta admit, she's getting better at this,* Jack thought as he scanned for targets. Symon was slowly pulling himself off a hard-plastic stadium bench and popping his shoulder back in place. The Praenomen, for its part, seemed to duplicate itself with illusions and be putting as much distance between JK-47 and itself as it could.

Jack laughed and lobbed a grenade at Symon, whose eyes went wide before the explosion ripped through him. *Jane can handle the Praenomen; I trust her. The snipers should have just shot this creature at the first sign of trouble.* He sighed. *Advertising. Least I get to play now.* With the satisfying clacking of a gun cock, a sound the audience knew well, Jack unloaded another grenade as he lumbered up to the vampire's position. When the flames died down, all that hung in the air was a thick red mist. No sign of the creature at all. *Blown to smithereens, the best kind.* He raised his gun high and tried his best smile for the cameras on the large screen.

To his chagrin, the crowd only cared for the battle down field. *Ahh, come on.*

JK-47 was a mix of flurries, flips, and chains as she raced through an ever-increasing number of shadow illusions. Every time she got close to the Praenomen, however, she was thrown back by an invisible force like a rag doll and crashed into a snow-bank. The remaining snipers above took shots at any target in their sight, unsure of which to kill. Each of the masked doubles seemed intent on making gestures with their fingers to cast a spell. A spell delayed every few seconds when the real one had to bat away Jane again.

Looking up at the snipers, Jack kicked in his tech-control program and hijacked into their communications network.

"Hey, idiots. Shoot the one that Jane is going after," he relayed. "She's not dancing around for your pleasure down there, you know."

This doesn't feel right. Jack loaded another chamber and stormed back, leveling his cannon at the one Jane beelined for, when a sharp pain struck him in his right shoulder. He looked down at the crossbow bolt sticking out between the spotty armor plating and his actual self. A small M80 firework wick was burning down, duct-taped to the bolt.

"Boom," Symon said from behind.

Jack raced to rip the bolt out, but his arms just didn't bend the way he needed. Metal and steel appendages locked, just inches away from the bolt, when the makeshift explosion went off. He panicked and jumped with a twist. A swift kick greeted him right in the chest, throwing his top-heavy self completely off-balance and tumbling over the wall into the stands. The explosive did nothing more than char his plates, but it distracted him.

"Bet you wish you had zat plasma cannon, eh?" Symon taunted. His body was a mixture of mist and real, the real part still riddled with bullets. He loaded up another crossbow bolt and fired it with his left hand above Jack into the field. "I think dat's enough for me today. Good luck, boss ..."

As the vampire receded back into a red mist, Jack craned his head to watch where he shot. Jane raced at the Praenomen, oblivious to the incoming firework-bolt, and leapt into the air. It sent ripples of smoke through the air, along with a giant heart-shaped firework display at ground level. Jane fired her boots to dodge the flares and looked like a confused jackrabbit as she zigged and zagged around them.

Free of distraction at last, the Praenomen finished the spell.

"Fuck," Jack groaned as he pushed himself up. *Sigh, here we go.*

Blood dripped from the dagger as the Praenomen sliced its hand and flung forth droplets as reality itself bent to its will. The air coalesced into a gel-like substance, and Jack watched the crimson droplets skip along its surface like a stone on water. With a tilt of its head, the sorcerer snapped its fingers, and the entire stadium became a raging inferno. Jack fell onto the cold field as the heat washed over his back; looking behind him, he saw the grayed and muted faces of the crowd scream as it melted flesh off bone. Parents tried to shield children to no avail; others flung themselves off railings to a sickening wet thunk as they hit the ground. Anything to end their pain. The world moved in slow motion.

The Praenomen's assault was far from finished as streaks of lightning crawled along the thickened air. Even Jane appeared slow as she twirled in a dodge, her knees bent in and her hand tracing along the bolt—her face a visceral rage. The sorcerer completed a series of tai chi movements, pushing forward with its spell and coming back to rest with folded hands, when reality sped back up. Jane screamed as her arm pulsed and exploded. A spiderweb of electricity danced between the craft overhead, frying snipers and news crafts alike. The ground shook as a VTOL craft fell into the nosebleed section, an array of sparks and more panic—at least among those who still lived.

"We brought magic back into the world." The voices rang out from every shadow, danced along every edge, and echoed throughout the entire field. Both male and female, the Praenomen addressed the entire city. "To awaken all of humanity and allow each of you to become as Gods yourselves. Even if you purchased it with a low monthly installment of nineteen ninety-nine. Not"—it mimicked a disgusted spit—"to slaughter every myth and legend that doesn't meet some church's approval."

Jack raced to Jane, who despite injury was lifting a chain with her teeth and getting back into the fight. *Damn girl, remind me not to piss you off.* He leveled his grenade launcher at the Praenomen and took a half-ass aim. *Close counts in horseshoes and grenades ... annnd ... boom.*

There was no click.

Confused. Jack looked down to see a blue wire dangling loose from where Symon had fired earlier. *Oh, you son of a ...*

"He's rather exceptional, you know." The Praenomen focused its attention on the two. A gaze he would much rather was elsewhere. "Always keep a saboteur on hand. But you two ... just look at you." With a flick of its wrist Jack and Jane flew off the ground and levitated helplessly.

"I swear to god I will put your face in my garbage disposal," Jane hissed.

Jack was more curious about why small metal bits and bolts were forming a small debris cloud around him.

"You are free to hate us, my dear, but I need sacrifices for the greater good. Kill ten thousand, to save five billion. It's elementary. If we didn't act now, your little science experiment would be the rank and file of Lazarus's army. One by itself is fine, but an army?" The sorcerer twirled its fingers and moved closer. "But I must say, I'm unimpressed with the prototype."

Bolt after bolt unscrewed itself as armor plating clattered to the ground. Jack looked to Jane in panic as he saw sensors and vital systems go offline in his vision.

"Hey, Jane. Please help."

Bit by bit it dismantled him while Jane struggled to break free. His arms released from shoulder sockets, it twisted out ribs that popped like candy when released from his spine, before finally he felt light as a feather. He knew that nothing more remained than a set of lungs, a spine, and a head, without looking down. Kept alive by freak science or Peter's techno-magic, he didn't care.

With a flick, the Praenomen threw Jack into Jane's arms and let her fall to the ground.

"As for you," the shadows around whispered. "You would've rotted from the inside out and died here while selling drugs to kids. What a waste of your talents. So, let's give you a new start. Ignis. Vitae." Jack watched the Praenomen saunter closer and grab Jane's throat, and watched as blood burned through her veins and burst through her skin as a fine red mist flew out of her body. The hissing was louder than her scream as her blood boiled until she slumped over onto him.

"We won't meet again." It pulled forth flame and electricity to scorch the earth as it painted a symbol. Jack saw the words paint the sky. Amo-A-Deus.

Stuck where he was, his panicked eyes flickered over to the Jumbotron and saw the drone footage. On the field where Jane and he lay, occult symbols burned themselves into the concrete and field, desecrating the arena. Subtitles informed viewers of their Sephirot and Tree of Life significance. *Apparently Amo-A-Deus means like a God. A wrathful god indeed.*

And with a final drop of blood hitting the ground, a deep red glowing door rose from the ground, and through it, Jack could see a military hangar, with undead soldiers scurrying about in the distance. Helpless, he watched his new, spiteful god walk through the door and take one last look at the pair. Just as it was pulling off its mask, the door slammed shut and shattered into a thousand rose-colored glass pieces.

The Praenomen was gone.

"Jane?" Jack cried. "Jane, are you alive?"

As the sirens and muffled sounds of emergency personnel raced into the arena, Jack kept repeating the question, again and again.

CHAPTER EIGHTEEN

Blood! Glory! Victory! Come see the new riveting star JK-47 as she rat-a-tat-tats into your heart at T-Cellular Arena! And who's that man that's on our list? Metallic Jack zapped into the dreams of every red-blooded American girl. T-Cellular Arena now offers insurance policies for all attendees, so bring the whole family on down.

C lear!"
       She was ripped out of a cold swimming pool and gasped for air.

"Hit her again. Clear."

Jane jolted awake, instantly crying out in pain, as the gurney raced through the private hospital. Dark green lights covered in ash flew past her as the emergency room technicians spoke in muffled voices around her, as if they were underwater. In hospital hallways she saw burn victims climbing out of bed and peeling off flecks of charred skin while doctors stood next to their bodies and nervously explained their plight. Jane wondered if the doctors just wished the dead would disappear behind the veil sooner.

They're dead ... I'm ... dead.

With the next jolt, her head flopped to the left where she saw her arm was significantly shorter. A line of people, clothing melted to their skin, kept leaning in to look at her, with curious looks on their faces. Jane could hear them whisper as the gurney moved into an operating room. They kept asking if she was alive or dead, and none seemed to know the answer.

"Do we have the blood? Good. Begin the transfusion," a doctor's voice rang out.

"Blood?" Jane said in a weakened state, slipping between reality and Purgatory. "What's ... what's going on?"

"She's awake?"

"Anesthesia won't work on her; she has to deal. Elcoll Corporation will not lose this asset."

"My daughter will be fine. Tell the board that the Church of Lazarus is taking direct action, and our investments will double in the next quarter," the warm voice said.

Her eyes rolling in and out, Jane caught a glimpse at her side. A warm-looking old man with white bushy eyebrows, chewing on caramel corn, sat in a wheelchair hooked up to IVs of his own. He reached out and patted Jane's hand with the skeletal claw of his own. As she slipped back into Purgatory, she saw him as he truly was—an emaciated mummy with skins stretched over his face. Golden wings formed a mask around his face, leaving only his lipless, toothy grin, dripping with bloody fangs while it carved a small wooden figure. Half of its body was nothing more than exposed ribs and melted robes from an earlier assault. In the tubes connected, however, Jane watched the glowing red vitae flow from the creature's heart into tubes that a doctor was holding.

"Left arm isn't savable. We must amputate and move to prosthetics. Begin the injections."

"Huh, fuck this," Jane whispered. When the high-pitched sound of a saw started up, Jane elected to slip back into unconsciousness. Rather, she calmly, logically, and with not a hint of terror emerging, decided passing out from internal terror was preferential to whatever medical act that bone saw was intended for.

"Let your Grandpappy Fredrick tell you a story," the warm voice rang out.

Jane fluttered her eyes open in the beige hospital room. It was dimly lit, with a soft orange lamp in the corner as the only source of light peeking over flower vases from concerned fans. Several carved wooden figurines lay beside her. Model airplanes, Taylor's and Tyler's mechs, and even a train.

"It smells like a hospital in here," Jane remarked, too numb to move, much less give any fucks. "What does something like you want with me ... I know you are really some dead thing, so just spit it out." Jane didn't even bother to look at the figure sitting to her right, who would no doubt appear nice, but secretly be monstrous in the lands of the dead. *Well, maybe just a peek.* She looked. *Yup. He's fucking horrible under that mask. Did he really say his name was Fredrick?* She tried not to imagine young Fredrick telling a third grade class he wanted to become the Lord of Suicide when he grew up. She failed.

"Once upon a time, there was a little shit of a kid known as Adam. He was a conceited little bastard. Thought the *entire world* was his. He didn't notice, or seem to care, that there were plants, animals, and angels all around him. He took a shit on the bones of bygone legends every morning and pissed on the memory of dead gods each night while he scratched his balls. Until one day, he saw her." The Lord of Suicide paused as he took a sip of water.

"Oh, a love story," Jane remarked. "This is surely going to end well."

"Lilith grew up in her own garden, far away from the little bastard Adam. Unlike Adam, she worked with the angels that made the grass grow and danced with the angels that made the wind sing songs. She knew how their divinity made the world turn, how the magic in their blood was potent. And, as you already pointed out, they fell in love, taught each other many secrets, and had a few children of their own,"

"And then," Jane interrupted, "she came along and brought an apple? Look, man, I know most of us agnostics were slapped in the face with a supernatural reality recently ... but like ... spare me the church shit?"

To her surprise, the Lord only frowned and sunk back into his chair. Slowly whittling away on the next figurine. Each scrape with the knife timed perfectly against the soft click of a digital clock nearby. Click. Scratch. Click. Scratch. This went on for a solid minute before Jane snapped.

"Okay! You can tell your story."

"Eventually, Adam's god became a jealous one, and ripped the spirited child back to his garden and made him Eve. Most of us know the story from here. But even old flames can sputter back to life, and our little bastard snuck out one night to go visit Lilith and his old children—now fully grown. Ever the creative type, the children were collectively called the Lilim."

"Like ... when celebrity couples date? Lilith and Adam?" Jane cut in.

"Exactly. Prehistory tabloids were clearly trendsetters. As it were, the children didn't just work with angels, but could command the very blood in their veins. With a secret from their mother, and the birthright from their father, angels danced at their commands. Storms, hurricanes, and even great floods were possible by commanding the right angels. Adam thought his first children had grown wicked with power and bloodlust. So, he pleaded to Lilith for an answer as to why, and she gave him one —go home and fuck his new wife. Eve was there to bear children, so he better get on that."

"Well," Jane said. "I mean, I don't blame her. He kinda left her out in the cold with a bunch of kids. I mean, there were probably saber-toothed cats and shit back then."

The Lord chuckled. "Something like that." The creature shuffled out of the hospital chair and used the wheeling IV unit for support as it hobbled over to a floral bouquet and smelled. "What Lilith didn't tell Adam was that each child he had would slowly weaken his own god. And have children they did ... let me tell you ... billions. Hell, at some point, they had sucked up all the energy of that god and split it among more babies than possible. So many that some of those poor kids had to go without souls—but that part is a different story." He held up a long, skeletal finger at that.

The Lord paused for a moment before continuing. "It turns out that Adam's God wasn't that infinite after all. In one fell swoop, Lilith paved three ways to kill a God for the world. Those in the know have been using her playbook since. Kill all the god's followers ... you've seen that one a lot. Steal all the followers, like the Christians did, and, far more subtle, bleed the god's power dry. Maybe Adam should've paid attention to those bygone bones he was shitting on every night. Who knows how many times Lilith had lured gods to their death?"

"You're seriously putting a story about soulless children on the table then backing off ... pfft." Jane struggled to pull herself up and settled on using the bed controls to get vertical. Her left arm was still missing right where the bicep used to be. A small metal plate sat there, awaiting some sort of mechanical limb, no doubt.

"Oh, don't worry, it gets good," the Lord said as he came and sat down at the foot of her bed, grimacing in pain as he did. "From time to time, Lilith's children would sneak into Adam's garden and play around. Unlike Eve's weak kids, they walked around as gods, drunk on the blood of angels ... and, by this time, demons. The world turned, gardens expanded and faded, but the children always remained. They'd pose as gods, or pharaohs, or other great rulers, and it wasn't until a *whole* lot of Eve's children got real angry that they'd have the strength to run one out of town. But one time, well after Adam had died of old age, one of Lilith's grandkids thought it would be a neat trick to bring back Lazarus from the dead. And oh boy, let me tell you."

The Lord patted her knee. "In the history of great ideas, this takes the cake."

"A bucket of fifty Chicken McNuggets after a box of Franzia wine is also a great idea," Jane smiled. She had to admit, even though this creature's true appearance was the stuff of night-mares, the way he spoke and his calmness was warming. She was even enjoying the fairy tale.

"When Lazarus was on the other side, he realized that God was dead. Or rather, that all of God was hidden among the living humans. Lazarus knew that ... *all* the dead knew that, only the living weren't listening. Necromancy was a thing that only those pesky children of Lilith did, and they sure weren't spilling the secret that Adam's God died ages ago by their mother's cunning. Somehow, Lazarus convinced a few other Children of Lilith that this was wrong ... and trust me, we are all curious about how that happened."

"Easy," Jane quipped. "A fruit basket and a fifty-dollar gift card to Target. Everyone loves new bedsheets."

"Lazarus and the children of Lilith unified under a front and bore their own children, keeping it hidden before the angels and demons caught wind of their plan to resurrect a God. Secret plans eventually worm their way out. The 'heavenly' host dragged Lazarus back to Purgatory before they could recruit enough followers and unite all of humanity under that banner. The"—he waved his hand flippantly—"number of followers someone has is part of the plan. Don't sweat the details. Anyway, without a leader, the order fractured into a thousand pieces and cults, prac-tically tearing the world apart again over the next millennia. Those remaining Lilim and descendants of Lazarus largely prac-ticed their magic in secret but in different ways. For each had a gift. The Lilim were true sorcerers, able to command the blood of angels and devils alike through incantation and will alone—they didn't need to drink it. The get of Lazarus and Lilith could see into the lands of the dead, how people would die, and many ... many ... other talents related to the dead. Sound familiar?"

Jane lowered her eyes and looked to the side. *Well, he clearly knows.* "Yeah, something like that." Jane's high school version of the Crusades would have been more riveting with Fredrick as her teacher. *Didn't one fracture happen because some king wanted to murder his wives?*

"For years," his dry voice cracked, "the fractured cult tried to search for Lazarus, or any dead legend they could find, by diving into Purgatory together. One to open the gateway and one to be the eyes and ears. An uneasy truce between forces deemed unholy, and a race against time. You see ... Adam's children with Eve were pretty numerous, to say the least. They had pushed all the demons and angels out of the world by now, and the divine blood was drying up. In a matter of centuries, there would be no more magic. No more diving into hell. And more children born without souls until eventually ..." The Lord held out a single yellow flower, that wilted and decayed into ash and spiraled into the air.

"So, what happened then? Because I'm not sure if you looked outside recently." Jane waved her left arm even though the stump ached.

The Lord reached out and tousled her hair with skeletal hands. "A demon king and an Archangel got involved." He bobbed his head in contemplation. "And mostly, Adam's shit-for-brains soulless children got wide-eyed with power. The moment someone offered them immortality and the return of magic," he scoffed, "governments leapt at our command. Of course, Warlocks, I mean ... Lilim, didn't help the matter any. Plus, it seems no two people agreed on anything ... I think the victors will write this history." The Lord stood up and hobbled out of the room.

"Wait, that's it? Why are you telling me this?" Jane asked, leaning forward.

"Because when you die in a few months by your own hand ..." The Lord looked back at her with a grin. It was at that moment that Jane realized, as she saw him in both worlds, he saw her in both as well. "I want you to know when that time comes and you work for me, that I am friend and relative. And don't worry, I won't sell you off to some vampire of Lilith for mating or any of that mumbo jumbo bullshit." Fredrick the Death Lord continued shuffling out of the room. "They don't call me the Lord of Suicide for nothing, you know? Peace comes to us all."

Jane reached down and held up the last figure he left on her bed, a small, crudely carved kitty cat. Her eyes darted between the figure and a calendar that hung to the left of the door. She stared at it, shook her head, and looked again.

July.

The Praenomen's attack had been weeks ago. Weeks since she's seen her cats.

She broke into tears among the dozens of figures and empty flower vases.

CHAPTER NINETEEN

Join the morning cast of CNB for a glance back at the events of December 21st. The day the innocence fell and the black sun rose. We welcome special guests from militias around the country that helped us survive the attack and weather the storm. Join us as guests from the NRA show us new firepower on the horizon. Followed by a special prayer for those souls who were lost by the ideological corruption of Mike Auburn—the lead terrorist who sparked the riots. Only on CNB.

Jack dangled, legless as it were, on the rack in his penthouse apartment while slowly flipping through TV channels and grumbling about the size of the remote. It was one of those complicated universal remotes with more bells and whistles than any person could ever possibly need. Floor-to-ceiling TVs covered every surface off his living room—and the magic remote was supposed to control them all. He had never really used it before; instead, he controlled everything in his apartment with but a thought. Instead, Jack was going through a cruel form of motor therapy—forced to calibrate fine motor control of his prosthetic arms with the lure of entertainment. *Why the hell does a remote need a tilde button? Who the hell makes this?* He butterfingered his way into pressing the button, hitting countless others along the way. It did nothing.

"Jack, you have another toaster," Dr. Alex Kristov said as he walked into the room, flanked by a small flying drone that set the small package on top of an ever-growing mountain. A group of technicians followed, pushing carts that contained a series of arms and legs from different manufacturers. Kristov posed and raised an eyebrow at the TV. "I did not strike you for a fan of home shopping networks. A bit of a narcissist, aren't you?"

With a jerky motion, Jack swiveled his rack to face Kristov and grimaced. "What kind of cruel bastard hooks a man up with over fifty TVs but only gives them basic cable? They could classify this as a war crime ..."

"On the bright side. You *get* to watch TV while we repair you. JK-47 spent most of her time in a coma." He gestured to the mountain of goods purchased for nineteen ninety-five. "See all the fun gifts your fans have been sending you. A ... lifetime supply of vacuum bags designed to pick up faerie dust. Super useful! You know how hard it is to keep that off blacks."

"Most people get things like flowers ... or maybe even extra vacation time?" Jack rolled the rack over to the limbs, driving and cursing while he did so. After a series of jerks, stops, recalibrations, and slow three sixties, he finally made it over to the cards. *I hate the way Kristov is looking at me. I get it; I'm handicapped. Put me back together, you dolt.*

"Most people aren't the equivalent of company-owned car," Kristov replied, throwing the box behind him with a crash. "Buuuut luckily for you, you are under warranty, yes?" Thin lips stretched over his perfectly white and aligned teeth.

"Is Culmen visiting me today? Why are you here?"

"Yes, you'll get your wish, little puppy, but you'll have to deal with me first. My company, Atlantis, is the one who makes your parts. You should be nicer, considering your origins and the risk of this project being involved with a blood addict. Yet what Peter want, Peter gets. Still, he only deals with your nervous system. You should be happy ... you and Jane now have something in common."

"Wait ... no." Jack shook his head in denial. "She's not like me, now, is she?"

Alex held up a left arm and inspected it while technicians flanked Jack and overrode his rig. The bed whirred as he raised up in the air, preparing him for an operation. "Only a part ... only a part ..." he mused as he caressed the arm. "It's amazing what we can do with science these days. Just over a year ago, your body would reject cybernetics and implants; now, with the right *power*, upgrades can be done in the comfort of—"

"Unless," Jack cut in, "it's the kind of power that can stop whatever the fuck was in that arena, I don't care. Just get me back on my feet."

Kristov smiled. "Cute. Hey, team, look at Jack, he's finally enthusiastic about pulling his weight. Which is good considering the little stunt he pulled firing the weapons on Peter. And all it took was him being ripped apart bolt by bolt." He leaned forward, gazing at Jack dead in the eyes, searching for something inside. "Just imagine if those were your bones, your tendons, or ligaments that held a human body together. Now if only I could remove that brain of yours and replace it with code ..."

"Such a thing will not be happening, my apprentice." Peter Culmen strolled into the room, already rolling up his sleeves and removing thick rings off his weathered hands. "An identity is important to any sentient creature. Metallic Jack, here, deserves every bit of his handle, just as I did mine."

Jack beamed at the sight of Peter. Whenever he was around, he worked *better.* It was hard to explain, but being close to him, Jack felt more in control. Like he had someone to relate to. "Wait, what was your nickname? I've only ever heard you referred to as the CEO Peter Culmen."

Holding up his hands as technicians outfitted him with anti-static gloves, tied his dreads back, prepped the grounding mats for operation, Peter wore a devious smile. "People like me don't become CEOs by playing fair, Jack. The Man had it pretty well stacked against us. Honestly, I had been so focused with my research of late, I haven't had a chance to go play myself." A silver briefcase unlatched, and a technician handed Peter a white Guy Fawkes mask. Only rather than being simple plastic, it was made of silicon with small bits of circuitry etched along the corners. He donned the mask and sat on a small stool as he pulled himself up to Jack. "I used to go by the simple handle of Mr. Anonymous back in the day. I was everywhere in the world, and nowhere, simultaneously. No system was safe, no secret secure, and the legion of us made the powerful shit themselves with a simple video."

Kristov tried to hide it, but Jack saw him roll his eyes. *I'm going to kill that man.*

"What is it with you nutjobs and masks?" Jack asked. Kristov coughed in laughter.

"Masks hold incredible potential my friend," Peter, or, rather, Mr. Anonymous said as he rolled back behind Jack. He felt his skin open like a zipper as the warlock opened Jack's spinal column. "They hide your humanity, allowing you to do what must be done. They allow you to put forth the identity *you* wish the world to see rather than the one you were born with. But they are the best arcane focus for a warlock who needs to work with his hands to cast spells."

"Wait ... what?" Jack said with wide eyes as he tasted peanut butter, a taste that only came the first horrifying day he woke up here. *Honestly, if I never think of a peanut butter sandwich again, that would be heaven.*

"You want more power, right? The Praenomen ripped you apart bolt by bolt ... but not again. Truthfully, it was a hasty hypothesis to think we could use a combat cyborg against wizards. Telekinesis is a very common trait and one of the earliest psychic phenomena. A spell most used. Psychics and wizards fill the Society of Deus. We need to make sure your defeat doesn't happen again. I will lace some specially developed silicon nerves along your base installation today. It will prevent that." Peter swung around facing Jack, while tapping a finger on his anonymous mask.

In Jack's vision, he could see electrons crawling along the mask and entering right into Peter's eyes, which only made them more vibrant. *Demons, vampires, and technomagic. No escape, is there? A long nightmare I'm eternally trapped in. I must've fallen asleep watching the home shopping network on my couch.*

"Ready to begin when you are, sir," Kristov said as he flicked beams of light off his tablet into the surrounding air, highlighting every aspect of Jack's systems. The screens floated in the air and informed the technicians of what tool was needed and when. While not as powerful as Peter, Jack wondered just how strong of a technomancer Kristov really was.

"Now, Jack, I want you to keep talking while we work, okay?" Mr. Anonymous said. "Ask questions that have been plaguing you. Do you understand?"

"Uh ... yeah," he nodded. The two doctors set about into him, working on a level that Jack could never understand. It felt like being tattooed, he figured, a slight burning, tingling, with the occasional bout of cringing pain as they connected a nerve back online.

"You're not talking," Mr. Anonymous commented, his voice coming from speakers in the room instead of his own mouth.

"Yeah, sorry. It's kind of like when a doctor tells you to keep talking ... it scares the fuck out of you. So, the last thing you do is talk. Because you don't want to mess up the doctor."

"You will not mess us up," Kristov's voice rang through speakers. "Go ahead. Ask questions. Your thoughts and motor controls let us know if we accidently crossed a wire," he laughed.

"All right," Jack said, watching his stress levels rise on a monitor nearby. Cortisol, heart rate, adrenaline, all began to spike. "For starters, what do you know about that person who assaulted us?"

"Superb question," Mr. Anonymous said. "That would be the Praenomen, or, at least, that's what it probably wants one to believe. I've every suspicion Warlock Vryce is not as dead as the world, or the Society of Deus, makes him out to be. The powers the Praenomen wielded in the arena were well beyond what any normal sorcerer is capable of. Not that I begrudge Vryce for possessing his most capable assistant Delilah Dumont after being killed in public by Mike Auburn."

"Who the hell are these people, then? Why don't you guys just blow them all up? And I mean, wasn't I part of that killing? Is that why it took such revenge? Why you picked me?"

"The questions are flowing freely now, I see," Kristov said.

"I picked you, Metallic Jack," Mr. Anonymous said, "because I wanted to send a message to my former colleague. That anything he could do, we could refine it and make it available to everyone. Even your first form will help countless people with enhanced prosthetics. Warlock Vryce had a tendency of capturing people, brainwashing them, and stitching them together into hideous gargoyles. We've taken that terrible process and magic, and refined it to create you. Sleek, powerful, and acceptable."

"Without all the mind control bits," Kristov added in. It didn't sound like he was as happy about that.

"So, I'm basically an enhanced gargoyle, then? I mean, at least I'm alive, right?"

"That's a fantastic opinion, Jack!" Mr. Anonymous said cheerily through the speakers. "You are very much alive. The Society of Deus is focused entirely on training regular people on how to wield magic and use it in their everyday lives. Their leader, Gabriel D'Angelo, appears dedicated to spreading the occult to as many people as they can. Sorcery takes years to learn and is only viable for those with a strong will. You—you knew nothing!"

"He did indeed know nothing, sir," Kristov said.

"Hey, hey," Jack chimed in. "I knew things. Just not that magic shit."

There was a pause before both agreed that Jack knew nothing.

"But that's okay," Mr. Anonymous said. "You prove that our

science can turn magic into something for everyone. Not just the strong. They may have an army of undead vampires or sorcerers at their command ... which I suppose has its merits. But we offer something for the rest of America, and soon the world. Never lose hope, Metallic Jack; you are the wave of the future."

"Why do you insist on calling me Metallic Jack?"

Everyone fell silent.

"Well ... your name is Jack and you're Metallic. I'm Mr. Anonymous, and he's ..."

"Don't you say it," Kristov's voice chimed in.

On the screen above Jack, he saw Dr. Alex's online handle appear. GhettoBootySmsh37.

"Ghetto Booty Smash Thirty-seven?" Jack burst out into mechanical laughter.

"Smasher. Ghetto Booty Smasher. I ... messed up the leet speak on my AOL profile back in the nineties and it stuck," Kristov's voice said over the speakers. Even the technicians let out a snicker.

Jack saw Mr. Anonymous's mask lurch over into his vision. "All done," he said. "Jack, if you could just look up and to the left, I can activate you. This will hurt."

"Oh, wow, that was fast ... uh, okay?" Jack looked up and off to the left. He saw Kristov standing there biting on his glove while trying to avoid looking at back. Jack saw Mr. Anonymous pull out a giant metal spike and open his left eye; he wound it in. *Wait, what, what are you doing?* A horrific icepick pain shot through his entire nervous system and the vision in his left side blurred.

"Eeeaassssyyy, Jack ... Shhhh," he reassured. "I need to punch through the interhemispheric fissure with the orbitoclast and make a connection."

Jack felt the pressure in his sinus as they slid in the metal rod; he tried his best to avert his gaze, but it was near impossible with the closeness of the instrument.

"Hey, Jack, who's Akira?" Kristov asked out of the blue.

A flood of memories raced to the surface of Akira and his conversation with her. Here, in this very apartment. *Cameras?* Right then he felt his head jolt back as Mr. Anonymous broke through into the brain and Jack's frontal lobe with three chilling taps.

Tap. Tap. Tap.

The seizures started immediately as Jack lost control of his faculties. Shaking and trembling on the rig, Jack struggled to remember anything about Akira, or even who he was again. His tongue rolled out of his mouth, and the taste of peanut butter came to focus. In the distance he heard Peter reassure him. A metal rod was in his brain. Cold, medical sterile cold, rod shoved through his skull, and the only part that hurt was by his eye. A flash of children zipped in his mind. A desire for blood welled up from the center of his soul. Yet no thought made his body work or move, just twitch and seizure.

"Don't worry, the tremors will only last about forty, maybe fifty, minutes as the synapses land into place. You'll be right as rain then, Metallic Jack, and with a lot less stress wearing you down."

Jack felt trapped behind his eyes.

CHAPTER TWENTY

They use their media to assassinate real news. They use their schools to teach children that their President is another Hitler. They use their movie stars and singers and comedy shows and award shows to repeat their narrative over and over again. That the rich are vile. To make them march. Make them protest. Make them scream racism and sexism and demonism and vampire phobia. Smash windows, burn cars, and rip out your hearts. The only way we stop this, the only way we save our country and our freedom, is to fight this violence of lies and death with the clenched fist of Unity. We are the NRA, and we are the Unification's safest place.

*Y*ou won't *understand my actions, Jack, but it was either this or we dismantle you.* Peter washed his hands, letting the cool water flow over them as he stared at his own mask on the black marble countertop next to him. *Mr. Anonymous. A mask I wear when I can't face myself in the mirror. Or perhaps it's who I really am but just can't admit it.* Before his meteoric rise to CEO and the far more palatable face and name as Peter Culmen, he'd enjoyed his anonymity in the digital world. Loved every second of arcane training under the Lord of Suicide. But most of all, he craved every secret he pried from the other warlocks. *Well played, Delilah, you truly have dragged me back into the trenches of these insidious power wars.* He twisted their magic and refined it into something more useful. *I've been working on a way to free us all, just a little more.*

"Rasputin binds demons, Verkonis commands spirits, Vryce possessed children, Montague plays with fortunes ... and so on and so forth. Well, bitches." Peter straightened his deep purple tie that added to his blue eyes. "I make shit useful." With a smile to himself in the mirror, he held a small blood injector up to his neck and released a dose of angel vitae straight into him with a smooth hiss. *After all, even Warlocks need to feed, but who said it had to be messy.* The rush of power flowed through him, and, for a brief second, the physical world faded around him. A landscape of electrons flowed along wires, tracing the entire horizon from his private bathroom.

Every building in Austin, Dallas, and Houston were all connected to him, and him to them. His empire was growing each day as crews worked overtime on the installation. Beneath his vision of electrons dancing through pathways and conduits, a central hub of servers ebbed and flowed with his life force. Unlike the other selfish warlocks, he had turned his attention to something that could benefit everyone. *At least, if I can perfect it in time. Everything looks on schedule. Now let's see how the old men are doing.* Old men didn't understand the digital world, and with their trust he was able to move in secret. Nobody in the Unification truly questioned how his technomancy worked, or why he had built the world's largest server farm in ritualistic fashion beneath the three cities. *Information overload makes it easy to hide right in plain sight.*

It had been weeks since the Praenomen assaulted the city. Sensationalized news ran twenty-four hours regarding the terrorist attacks, what happened, who died, and what the US government would do about it. Earlier this morning, the Republicans declared official war on the Society of Deus, the first official declaration of war since the sun rose black. *Even though we know about the Archive and Delilah, everyone still blames the Society. Given the way it was at ground zero, I can't blame any of them.* And with the influence of the Death Lords, Peter figured they would give his private military their marching orders soon enough. *And that is the dumbest thing they can do. Old liches have no vision. No foresight.* He stormed through long executive suite corridors with his destination in mind as he grumbled under his breath.

Two ancient wooden and iron doors, from a Moroccan palace, framed Peter's opulent CEO office on the top level of Triumvirate Enterprises. They added eccentric flair that every executive needed to display from time to time. They swung open as he approached, already keyed to his neural signature. Inside lay his second home, only second to his private sanctuary and server farm below the city. The only real furniture in the sparsely furnished office was a monolithic-sized desk, adding an intimidating imposition to visitors. Obsidian black ceilings, etched with a spiraling Fibonacci sequence which began at the doors and twirled throughout. From his desk, deep burgundy wood crawled out in uneven patterns through the floor, creating a work of art on the floor. To most of Peter's guests, they thought nothing. To a few, they saw the human genome in binary format.

He grabbed an old office chair with tattered red cloth, worn and used for countless hours, and dragged it to the center of the room. It didn't match the rest of the place, but Peter preferred it, and it was with him since his teenage years. Through the skyscraper's windows he watched the black sun set and the purplish hue of the Lilith moon rise. Peter killed the office lights and waited. Unlike most Warlocks or ancient liches—he was always first to his meetings.

As the hour went on, the horizon grew darker, with his city remaining a beacon of light standing defiant in the night sky. One by one the astral images appeared in the room. The Lord of Pestilence, the Lord of Murder, Lady of Fate, and even the Lord of Suicide, came in astral form. Thirteen Lords of Death who ruled the world, even if the world hadn't realized it yet, took their places in Peter's vast office. The council of Unification, the Church of Lazarus, the Children of the Stars, or whatever nickname people gave them, Peter knew them as a bunch of soul-sucking humans who stole the power of Gods. He willingly joined them and stood for the opening prayer to convene the meeting. "The powerless have no power to change the world. What must be done shall be done."

"You summoned me for this meeting, my Lords?" Peter bowed and held low after the opening ceremony was complete. For this month's meeting, it appeared to only be the Lords of Death, and none of their warlocks. Either they truly intended a meeting just for him, or the betrayal rate among warlocks is greater than Peter had known. *I don't really believe Lazarus is a true God more than the next God over, but power is power.*

The Lord of Suicide stepped forth, raising an emaciated hand to silence the others.

Come on, Fredrick, you are seriously in a hospital down the street. You could at least wheel your dead ass into my office yourself.

"We have given you enough time without war, my child," the Lord of Suicide began. "The time has come to put your projects to the test. Just as the time has come for the Unification army to march by your side. A show of unity between the global companies of your council and the Church of Lazarus. The people of the world need hope in these dark times, and the Lord of Heaven's Wrath has seen fit to grant them this aspiration."

Yeah, saw this one coming a mile away. Anybody else see this? Jack, did you? Kristov? Fellow CEOs? Even though he was only thinking it, Peter saw through his digital world other CEOs nod at their computers as they listened in. A meeting of old, and new. Ancient liches astrally projecting into his office, and the Triumvirate Board of Directors telecommuting in. Peter straddled both worlds that were more similar than they realized.

Peter lifted himself from the bow. "What of the US government, are they not already mobilizing?"

"They are indeed. Yet we are not sending them our aid. Only your armies will stand side by side with ours as a symbol of endorsement for your loyalty. The Republicans will take umbrage to our foreign, and unnatural, army that is already mobilizing into your region. Even with our influence, President Drummel can be ... *headstrong*," the Lord of Suicide remarked.

"I will," Peter said, "officially lobby my protest against attacking the Society of Deus like the US military. Despite what they are or what they have done, our resources could be best spent on expansion and restoration of twenty-first century lives. Much of the world has gone dark, and even though we've most first world cities operational—who knows what magic has taken hold where we cannot see."

"We know your opinion well, warlock," the Lord spoke softly. "But the council has cast their votes, with a tie broken by the Lord of Heaven's Wrath, in what everyone knows is a terrible choice. We are not blind to the devastation that this war will cause. We are not blind to the lives that will be lost in shunting your city's progress. We are not blind to the toll this will take on those who still breathe. But we draw our power from death. The more that is reaped upon the world, the stronger we grow, and thus, the council has voted."

Peter hadn't heard the Lords be so ... frank about an obvious power grab like this in decades. *Something must have them spooked. Is it the power of the Warlocks? Vryce? Or that they aren't the only game in town? Still, I won't idly sit by and let them reap the world for their power. I stand for greater things.* The astral images argued with each other. *Fear.* Amidst their screaming accusations of treason, betrayer, consumer, and so forth, Peter understood they were lost. None of this was planned. The black sun. The Society of Deus. Magic being free. Even the Triumvirate was a band-aid solution to them. *They are afraid of the future.* Until the Lord of Heaven's Wrath silenced them. *Well, that's pretty typical.*

The Lord of Heaven's Wrath, the voice of Lazarus himself, spoke in a clear and powerful voice, though. Unlike all other Death Lords, he was unmasked, so that all may look upon him. Something melted the grave clothes of Lazarus into his singed face and third-degree burns covered his entire body. He spoke not only as Dr. John C. Daneka but also as Lazarus himself. He was but a vessel, with hollowed-out eyes, fangs, and the devoured hearts of countless assailants that have tried to kill him. For lack of a better term—he was the world's new god.

"Through faith and deed the dying will find the gates of paradise open to them and the pain of the flesh removed. I hear your opposition, Peter Culmen. We shall allow the kingdom of man to liberate the world. Only the Lord of Suicide will assist you and the US government together. If we reveal too much, we risk what goodwill and public opinion we've garnered. Men, not the dead, shall lead this charge. We shall remain neutral and let you grow—for now. Show us your science, warlock."

It stunned even the council. *I mean ... it's not my main request of no war, but ... I'll take it.*

Peter quickly bowed, noticing that the Lord of Suicide was the only Lord who wore an arrogant grin. "Thank you, my lord. You won't regret this choice." *Smile all you want, Fredrick, but when I'm done with my project, the world won't need armies anymore.*

"You'd best deliver your speech to your city quickly, my child," the Lord of Suicide spoke.

Each of them closed their eyes in prayer, as their astral forms faded back out, leaving Peter alone in his office yet again. "What the fuck just happened, again?" he said aloud to himself. Even he was having a hard time following the confusing orders of the Unification Council. They started off declaring war, threatening to murder everyone, fought amongst each other, and then the Lord of Heaven's Wrath said he could work with the government and only one Death Lord?

He ran through the mental gymnastics at a frightening pace, calculating all the odds and probabilities that seventy-seven supercomputers could compute and came to only one conclusion.

It was a farce. A show of power that the Church of Lazarus did not really wield anymore. None of the remaining warlocks appeared, so Peter must be one of the last semi-loyal ones left. They're goal is to unite the world under one banner in order to fix the afterlife—but that is tenuous, Peter reasoned. Other Gods and myths were already rising and the Unification's home-field advantage of being first was starting to run out. Even if they wanted to send everyone after the Society of Deus, they could spare only the one Lord of Death that was already here. *The rest are probably putting down rising Gods before they amass as many follow-ers.* Which meant that it was on Peter, *no, Mr. Anonymous,* to bring order back to the world. If he could win, then the world wouldn't even need Lazarus.

Peter smiled as he pulled up an override for the cities' communication network and sent a memo to every press corps in the world. *Alright world. My turn.*

"May I have your attention, please?"

Peter's visage appeared on every active monitor across the globe. His voice rang through every radio or speaker still connected to a satellite or form of internet.

"I know each of us have had varying fates over the past year. All of us have felt the tragedy as the world has changed, but we have grown stronger for it. Come together as a species, standing strong against the eternal night. Tonight, here in the state of Texas of the United States, we have chosen to be passive no longer. Tonight, world leaders, diplomats, and corporations have come together with a vision of solidarity. To pave a new way forward for our children and ensure that the return of magic to this world is a boon to all, rather than an elite few.

"Inequality has plagued humanity since the dawn of commerce, and with that comes power concentrated into the hands of a few, upending the democratic process that has made many nations great. In the past, it was the concentration of wealth, slavery, and military might that led to this inequality. Tonight, however, it is knowledge of the arcane. Knowledge hoarded about the myths and demons that have returned to the world or why the dead have risen and walk among us. Even we here, my company, Triumvirate Enterprises, has been guilty of this. Along with those at Google, Amazon, Apple, Atlantis, Lockheed, and many more. But none so much as the Society of Deus.

"The United States government, at 8:45 AM this morning, declared an official act of counterterrorism against the Society for their assault three weeks ago in Austin. Today, we stand in unity—not in war, but in action. Triumvirate Enterprises will take to the battlefield not out of revenge, but out of aspiration. Hope. Equality.

"I know all of you are familiar with a viral video featuring one Mike Auburn months ago, telling you to consume and eat the hearts of demons for power. Many of you have, often at great cost to those around you, yourself, or your very humanity. Yet it's how you survived the world that has crumbled around you. You did what you had to do. But no longer does the world need to crumble. The truth is our companies can turn this magic into a safe, reusable, and uplifting service for all.

"Not only can our world be whole again, we can be better for it. The Society of Deus has put forth the show that they are hunting demons for your benefit. That they are at war with armies of angels and creatures of legend for your sake. This is not true. Instead, they steal the blood and hearts of these creatures to train more sorcerers and vampires to grow their ranks. Today. That ends. The council of corporations and business leaders will engage in sanctions to cut off the supply of blood into the Society by attacking the largest known supernatural body on US soil in northern Michigan. The demons and cryptids there speak the name of their god, whom they pray will annihilate us off this planet. Should we stand idly by and let the Society hunt them down and claim their power? Or should we bring this power to your doorstep. Safely.

"Leading this charge will be examples of our products, to show you what will come your way, to a store near you, once we can fully engage in mass production. Metallic Jack and JK-47, two of your very own reality stars, are both alive after the Society's assault. One could say they've been champing at the bit for revenge. Today, why don't we all give them the best form of revenge? Success! Rather than war with the Society of Deus directly, we will show the world a better path! A path that benefits us all. JK-47 will be a beacon of morale and Metallic Jack will lead the charge to both eliminate the supernaturals in Michigan and provide the world with a much needed boost in safe, reliable, magical products.

"To Gabriel D'Angelo and others within the Society of Deus, I know you are watching this, and I have but one message for you. If your crusade to enlighten people is as noble as you claim, then stand aside and let us fight these vile creatures instead. In the interest of treaties, I extend an offer to you, Gabriel, to meet with us to discuss a better path forward. A path even the government is not affording you. If you are truly after the slaughter of demonic or supernatural armies that plague the territories around you and the north, then let us step in. Show the world you are better than mere power-hungry sorcerers."

Peter paused and wiped a fake tear from his eye.

"To those who miss this message because the world around you is hell itself. To those locked in countries forgotten by the developing world. If you hear this message, hold out longer. Make your way to us. We welcome you in our Triumvirate cities any time. Our lottery system is fair to all. You work, you have a chance, and with your help we can expand even more. To those still living a quiet life in rural America or Europe watching the world change around you. Huddled in your family's arms as you try to live a normal life ... know this: if you can't make it to us, we will bring our products to you. They can make a difference. They can save your life." He smiled and showed Jane's footage with her rocket boots. "Hell, they can make you fly. Thank you."

Peter killed his camera feeds and went dark. He could already see the council of CEOs cheering his speech. *Of course. They are going to make a fortune.* Even more, there were already requests from other companies to join the growing corporate empire filing in. He watched sponsorship requests go through the roof and, most importantly, he saw a world come alive online with zeal. Even he was excited, but also nervous beyond belief. His entire project was still months away, years potentially if there was a failure. Yet even among that nervous apprehension, there was *excitement*.

"And not even over the war itself, just a promise of more new technology. See that, Lazarus, you need not slaughter your enemies to build hope. You need to offer them a new TV with a low down payment. But just wait until the world sees what I've really got in store."

CHAPTER TWENTY-ONE

Now every family can enjoy the fun and excitement of owning your very own Sparkles the Hairless Squirrel Demon Cat Thingy. Petcare, Inc. is now stocking this lovable line of hairless imps in every store. Far easier to take care of than cats, and twice as fun, these imps are family safe for all ages. Pizza, beer, and garbage is all you need for food and care. Plus, they serve as the ultimate in freak watchdogs, alerting you to potential intruders you can't even see. So, don't hesitate, give a loving imp the life it deserves today.

I'm going to do what!" Jane screamed at the TV as she shot out of bed. "Fuck going to Michigan! I wanna go find that cunt's face and rip it off!" A controller smashed into several pieces as it shattered against the hospital wall. *Ugh, what a bitch move, Culmen. Thought you had a pair of mechanical balls or some shit that clanked when you walked.* "Pffft." Jane ripped out the IVs on her right arm, watching the small pinprick close up the instant she yanked the needle. They had replaced her left arm with a bright green-and-ivory cybernetic arm. Thanks to whatever drugs she was on now, *or whatever blood they threw in my veins,* she didn't have much physical therapy with it. The doctors prattled on about how they built Jack's for strength, but hers kept up with her unique biology and feminine physique. *Alright, it's kinda cute, I'll admit. Their marketing team did a good job with this. Plus, I can still feel things ... which makes it easier to cope with—*Jane pushed down the morose thought of her loss and permanent injury. She never expected that she would lose a limb. *Who really expects to lose any part of themselves?*

Truth be told, there were plenty of events Jane wasn't expecting. Like being in a coma, visits from strangers, having her fucking arm blown off, or the blood boiled out of her. "Ah, let's go get wasted and party the world away, eh, guys?" she said to a nightstand filled with wooden figurines of trains, airplanes, and cats in various poses.

"I'm afraid that would only heighten your latent escapism, Miss Auburn," a voice rang from an alcove out of view. Jane heard the door close, and the doctor stepped into view. His blasted houndstooth coat, balding head, and picking at the loose skin on his neck while he read her notes, Doc scrolled through the tablet and flashed her a nervous smile. "It's okay, don't panic, I'm not here for anything creepy."

"You're the one who should panic," Jane said as she adjusted her hospital robes.

He froze in his tracks and looked at her with a raised eyebrow. "Oh, that's a reaction I didn't expect, considering our first two encounters."

"A lot's changed since then, buttercup. I could remove that head of yours with a pillowcase from Room 307 and tuck myself back in this bed before you even blinked. So, yeah. I'm not going to panic. Didn't you hear? I'm leading the army now." She stood up and went through drawers looking for any change of clothes. *Seriously, they give me like, eighty thousand Bitcoin worth of flowers, but not one motherfucking fan can buy me an outfit? There should be at least one creeper out there ...*

"I suppose that has merit. So, you would say that as your

power has increased, you"—he chewed on his pen—"*feel* more at home in uncomfortable situations, yes?"

"What do you want, dude?" she sighed, finally finding a set of Elcoll Corp sweatpants and a Rocket Boots orange hoodie. "Like, didn't I give you guys the finger last time? I've got shit to do. I'm not joining your little anarchist movement. Besides, how dumb are you? You've gotta know they bug this whole place or something."

"I swear you Auburns must have a genetic trait for being flippant arrogant bastards with an extra coat of bastardish." He laughed at his own joke before getting serious. "I'm the shit you've gotta do."

Oh my god, would somebody please get this pervy bastard a nondescript white van to complete his ensemble. Jane threw on the hoodie and shuffled off the hospital robe underneath. "You really need a PR rep, mate. I'm not doing you or any of"—she dressed him down—"whatever this is."

"I'm assigned to do your psych evaluation for release. You know I am an actual doctor, right? Did you really think I'm just some stalker or hopeless fanboy? Hospitals are a great place to get blood, and one member of our gang is in charge of food. And, yeah, we know you're bugged. Are you stupid enough to think this whole thing is"—he waved his arms wildly to the sides —"even remotely legit and legal? I mean, you had a bloody *Lord of Suicide* visiting you in a wheelchair for weeks. What kind of hospital did you *think* you were at?"

Jane fidgeted with her left arm and looked around like an annoyed cat. "A ... normal hospital ..." *Alright, fine. I didn't put that together.*

"Now, we are getting somewhere." Doc pointed at her with the pencil and swung a chair around before plopping into it. His giddy excitement only made him seem like an undead muppet as he grinned openly with his fangs. "So, I imagine you have a lot to process and let's get right into it. Who do you want to kill?" Doc pushed up his thin wire spectacles.

Kill? Well, that porcelain mask bitch, of course. Should I say that?

Does it count as murder if the target is not human? Without answering, Jane made a variety of faces as she worked out a series of events in her head and shaking it with each internal conclusion. *I mean ... the justice system really needs a full overhaul ...*

Doc snapped to bring her back to reality. "Hey, over here. The question? Who do you want to kill? If it makes you feel any better"—he put his hand on his chest—"I want to kill the person responsible for the black sun. My father taught the Death Lords the power of radio and television to focus belief. But I also want to kill every warlock, Death Lord, and demon king I can get my hands on. After that stunt a few weeks ago, even I want to rip the face off the Praenomen and her agents."

"Oh, okay. Yes, that. What you said," Jane said with a nod. *Well ... that really does about sum it all up. Alright, creeper, what else you got? But ... they seriously let him work here? Why?*

"You would kill Peter Culmen even though he fostered the think tank that got you your fancy arm and drugs?" Doc said.

Ah ... there we go. Trick question. "Oh, no, duh, I mean, I work for him in a way."

"What about the Lord of Suicide?"

Sheeesshhh that's ... complicated ... I dunno, man, his story was messed up and ... Jane struggled with the awkward question and scanned the room for cameras before giving an affirming nod. "No," she lied.

Doc mumbled under his breath as he filled out paperwork. "Yes, yes, I see, *mmmhrm,* a typical response. Okay. We're done here." He stood up and put the chair back and dusted off his coat.

"Wait, that's it?" Despite wanting to get rid of him moments ago, Jane now found herself worrying she had done something wrong.

"Yeah, I mean, you'll be a good little puppet for the last few months of your life. You've clearly come to terms with that, and have a *lot* of fun selling products." He rolled his eyes hard. "Oh, you and Jack are both reporting to Culmen's office at Triumvirate Enterprises. Your clothes, weapons, and gear will be brought in shortly. They'll escort you to a helicopter on the roof when you're dressed. Chop, chop, little dolly. Bring the world to war with your pearly whites front and center." Doc clapped his hands and bounced as he stepped out of the room.

Ohhh, fuck you, buddy, I hate you so much right now. Jane stood there with her mouth open as attendees wheeled in black cases with various locks and unlatched them. She wasn't concerned with the crates, the weapons, her boots, or her chains. Hell, she was never even bothered by the skintight impact resistant gel suits she wore. It was the inclusion of cameras on *everything.* Jane knew exactly what that meant. Staged shots and props. She elbowed attendees out of the room and furiously got dressed. *I am nobody's fucking doll, and that won't be on my bloody tombstone.* She hated to admit it, but Doc was right; so far all Jane did was what someone told her. *It took him only three questions to convince me to join. Fine, you undead shrink. I'll see you soon.*

To say Jack was unhappy was an understatement. In the vaulted hallways of Triumvirate Enterprises, Jack loomed over a small vampire in Church of Lazarus robes, his mirrored shades reflecting the creature's uneasiness. They filled the hallway with these scum. Different contest winners, each brought in by different companies, but mostly the Church of Lazarus scum. Both were proving to be equally bristling to Jack. An annoying one who didn't wear shoes and had bright green-pink hair had won a fighting game tournament. She wouldn't shut up about it. Even worse, for the past hour, she kept trying to buddy up to him like she knew him or something. Every time he turned his back on the shoeless freak, she got even more nervous and talked louder. Which is why he was scaring the shit out of some undead priest in robes. *To avoid her.*

This hallway is filled with disgusting swine. Peter and Kristov would be better served if I incinerated the entire lot. He had heard the news feeds, and he knew what his assignment was. Jack was more than content to blast demons for Peter, but this church shit they were bringing in just seemed like a bad idea.

As the next wave of occultists made their way around the corner, Jack saw Jane strolling behind them with a cigarette dangling out of her lips. She was in a new bright purple combat suit with her neon blue chains slung over her shoulder like usual. Jack's vision picked up multiple body cameras on her. Out of all the people in the room, she was the only one flagged as green instead of a dull grey. Her face lit up as she saw him.

"Hey, hey, stranger, looking snazzy!" she said running up to him. "Who are all these clowns?"

"Not looking too bad yourself," Jack said as he tapped her arm. "See you are packing some new upgrades there, eh? Finally figured out that Metallic is the way to go, eh?"

The giant wooden doors opened, revealing a massive sparse office inside, where a masked Peter, *no, Mr. Anonymous,* sat behind a small desk, flanked by the Lord of Suicide himself in full Lazarus regalia. Jack found it disgustingly ironic how much influence the old man seemed to have in a world of companies. *Money buys you everything apparently. Even a seat at this table.*

"Lords and Ladies of the night, helldivers, and members of the Unification, please enter. Let's get this started," the Lord commanded.

People filed into the room, including the annoying green-haired arena girl, who was growing paler with each step. JK and Metallic Jack exchanged increasingly confused glances. "Talk later?" they each said with a nod, and they followed in.

Jack folded his arms and took up a spot next to Jane as far away from the other creatures as possible. Unlike prior meetings, there was no pretense of science on display here short of the massive city-scrawl skyline outside. He sneered at the boldness of one vampire who had the gall to drink a glass of blood out of a wine glass like it was socialite meeting. *At this point, I would honestly welcome Kristov's presence here.* When a nearby sorcerer in Church of Lazarus robes uttered a prayer, and three ghosts wielding helldiving equipment materialized behind him, Jack couldn't hold it in anymore.

"Okay, I'm sorry, what the fuck is going on with this?" he asked Peter, pointing at the litany of freaks.

The Lord of Suicide's eyes filled with black flames and his face twisted into a horrid monstrosity of seething rage. "Silence your windup toy," he fumed.

Oh shit, that's the fucker I shot, right? Jack shot up in soldier's pose so fast that Jane snickered. A needlelike pain lanced through his mind, and Jack quickly discarded any thought of trying to recall that memory.

"Man, they shoved that stick up real far, eh?" she teased.

With a flippant wave of his hand, Mr. Anonymous summoned a holographic grid of the United States with border lines drawn as the room's lights dimmed. The green and luminary blues generated by the map only made most of the room look further dead and pale.

"The Society of Deus," the Lord continued, the flames never leaving his eyes, "had one of the worst demonic outbreaks one year and six months ago. Occupying the regions of Minnesota, Iowa, Wisconsin, and Illinois, all the regions hit hard; this is one of the eight critical zones. Thanks to a group of experienced helldivers in the Second City, most of the demonic forces were pushed out across the lake into Michigan by putting the legions of ghostly recruits to war. Because of this, the dead walk openly within their cities and magic has become a way of life in a short time up there. They have Michigan as surrounded as any could have, and their coalition is continuing to grow south. The cutoff point for their control is here." He reached out and pointed to St. Louis. The map highlighted Michigan, surrounded by water, and the rest of the land around it as occupied by the Society of Deus and Second City forces. There were smaller dots of several "cults" and militias that littered the hostile zone which had all joined up to push the demons out together.

Mr. Anonymous stood up and looked around the room. "Many of you are from the Unification, helldivers, or even from the Society of Deus or the Second City itself. Some of you hold allegiance to the terrorist group the Sons and Daughters." He looked right at Akira. "I know who each of you are, and I've even allowed you to help with this mission because I will prove to you—we are not your enemy. Some of you are the best, and some just lucky enough to sneak past a quarantine. Yet all of you chose to answer our recruitment calls for this mission. Our mission is simple. I will break you down into teams and lead a small strike force north out of Texas, stopping in each town along the way to offer general help as professional helldivers or demon hunters."

"While doing so," the Lord of Suicide added, "my followers and personal sorcerers will march up behind each team to swell our ranks with recruitment, offer medical assistance, and take care of larger threats. You"—he points to everyone—"are to find a way through into Michigan, where the demon hordes have taken refuge, with your squads."

Jack smirked. *Easy enough, just fly a damn plane over and land. Duh.*

"The bulk of the US Army," Mr. Anonymous continued, "will mobilize from the east coast and be moving against the Society of Deus. As we expect, the primary battlefield between those two will be in the skies, and we don't have the capabilities to match. So, we are looking for a ground route and we have a plan." The map refocused on St. Louis, and Louisville, Kentucky. "Caught on the edge of the border between the magical bleed from eighteen months ago, a crumbling civilization, and devastated economies, these communities are barely holding on for life. It is the edge of the Society's forces, and they are trying to tame the region by controlling the St. Louis archway. The Lord's armies will move in and set up within those cities. Once claimed, your squads can blitz into Michigan. The archway can be used as a gate, apparently, allowing the Church's forces to march from there to your position in Michigan when ready. Questions?"

The room buzzed as creatures who knew each other talked about the operation. The second an opportunity presented itself,

Jack raised his hand. "Yeah, I'll ask again, why are you letting our squads be comprised by things like this? Much less, why not just fly in from Canada? I mean, there are a million tactical holes here. Who the hell planned it?"

Jane leaned in. "You've got as much tact as a Molotov cocktail, ya know that, right?"

"Metallic Jack, a star of this show, and I'm glad you asked," Mr. Anonymous said before the Lord could respond. "The simple answer is this—it's not a military mission for you. Sure, it has all the trappings, toys, special aircraft with guns, and some occasional ground fighting. But in truth, your squads are an aid task force, carving the path forward for the real army, our Lord of Suicide. You'll be bringing new toys, wind generators, UV generators, and more to places along the way. Think of Michigan like an oil field. If we are able to claim all those demons, we'll have the ability to bring our products far beyond our own borders. You both market them on the way, and the Church of Lazarus will do the bulk of the fighting."

"Maybe we kill a monster or two?" Jane cut in.

"Absolutely kill a monster or two," the warlock clarified. "Save a town, be a hero. Everyone here, even if they are undead or a dangerous threat to society, is here because of the drama they bring to the screen. We've been holding contests in the stadium, and many of the people will want to join your fight since you are a known commodity." He marched forward, pulling off his custom mask, and grabbed Jack by the shoulder. "Jack, you can't just go scream *science* at a crowd full of people when magic and demons have crawled out of the earth and the sun is black. It's literally the dawn of the next dark ages, and we need you to put on a show to keep people like *us* in the game. Can you give me a reason we shouldn't be marketing to everyone? Why we shouldn't offer special abilities and prepackaged immortality or a cure for cancer through a combination of the two? We've failed the nation by not producing enough and being able to distribute it, my friend. Sending one aircraft every now and then means stores sell out, but what about everyone in the middle? What about the millions who can't make it to a safe zone?"

Well, I mean ... this is just ... but you've got me? Jack felt like he was wearing a tinfoil hat in a room filled with crazies. *If everyone becomes supernatural, then why would they need to maintain what I am now?* "I mean, Peter, this just seems like a change of pace from where you were headed before ..." Jack asked.

"It is indeed!" He spun around and sauntered back to his chair. "We started simple with guns, enhanced drugs, boots that can fly, mechanized infantry. Things to hold back the tide and earn early adoption." He interlaced his hands as he spoke and his gaze levied upon the entire room. "If you want to forge a new world ... well, you've gotta invite some different people to the table. Even if they will churn a profit," Peter said while sinking back into his chair.

The Lord of Suicide clapped his hands thrice. "Alright, that is enough for now. You will each have your assignments and directions given to you as you leave. May Lazarus's gaze fall upon your soul."

Jack lumbered up behind Jane and leaned down. "So what are the odds this ends badly?"

Without looking back, Jack could tell she had a shadowed face as she wore a wicked grin—it showed in her voice. "Two hundred percent, buddy ... two hundred percent. Peter is playing tennis, the Lord is playing chess, the Society is playing *Hogwarts*, and the US Army is playing thermonuclear wargames."

CHAPTER TWENTY-TWO

Gentlemen: Devil's Dick does more than help guys with ED get and keep an erection. Over 23 million men have already tried the V and come up ... short. Now, it's nighttime all the time. Give your partner the night they deserve. More POWAH! Double your size with one regular daily dosage of this safe, effective, and treated Devil power. Cock push-ups! Now a thing. So be sure to tell your doctor about your medical conditions and give your dose of Devil's Dick a try.

Jane blew a kiss for the cameras while striking a picture-perfect pose with one leg bent at the knee behind her. The roar of new VTOL Boeing CV-23 Special operations gearing up right behind her at high noon. It was larger than the smaller ones that flitted around the city, big enough to carry JK-47's squadron, camera crews, and other gear. A fresh spring breeze rolling through kept everyone in bright spirits despite the black sun feebly shining its light down on them. While they loaded everything up behind her, Jane kept posing with different weapons for advertisements and did interviews. *Service with a smile ... Yaaaayyy.*

A whistle cut through the air. "Hey, twinkletits, let's roll!" a hired gun in Culmen's corporate army shouted at Jane from the cargo bay.

Jane ended the conversation with the reporter abruptly, jogged up into the plane and tapped her weapon crates for good luck before strapping herself in. Among her assigned squad, Jane didn't recognize a single face. *I could probably kick all their asses, so that's cool, I guess.* After getting their mission assignments, her sponsors forced Jane to fulfill her press obligations. Out of all the people on the plane, she and the journalist assigned to cover her, Kevin Thayer, were the only ones still alive. The rest tried to hide their paleness, fangs, or other deformities under balaclavas, helmets, and other mercenary gear for public palatability. They probably don't poll well, Jane figured. Of course, Jane naturally cut through the obfuscation, but it was the journalist she cringed for—she side-eyed the tendrils of Purgatory slowly seeping off him. *Ripped apart in ... Purgatory? That's going to hurt when he dies. Yikes.*

"This is your captain speaking; we've got a short flight ahead of us, expect plenty of turbulence and nobody touches the growler, or I'll chop your hands off." The female voice over the radio sounded familiar, but just out of instant memory.

"Hey, Kevin," Jane shouted as the craft lurched into the air.

He looked up from his laptop. "You don't have to pretend to like me, you know."

"What's a growler?" Jane asked.

Kevin pointed to the light jeep near the back of the cargo bay with a large, mounted machine gun fixed to the top and resumed ignoring her.

The hell? This guy is my journalist? Is he still obsessing over Jack? Pfft. "Hey, Kevin," Jane shouted again.

"I already know I'm dying, Jane," he said without looking back up. "I've gotta finish work before that happens."

"How do ya know you're dyin'?" Jane asked.

"The pilot told me."

The craft was shifting from vertical to horizontal and lurched forward. Jane unbuckled herself and strode over to the cockpit, unbuckling the door. *Who do you think you are telling people they will die?*

She hid behind her arm and snickered at the sight in the cockpit, where Phoebe wore an oversized aviator's helmet and was flying the craft while Doc Daneka was in a fetal position with his legs on the chair. *Maybe they aren't so bad.* She was stuck between two opposing conflicts in her heart. On one hand, the Lord of Suicide and Peter had changed her life. On the other, she was starting to understand that the Sons and Daughters targeted people like them for a reason—world-ending power. Like militarized environmental activists and nuclear weapons: both shape the world. At the moment, though, they just reminded Jane of people.

"Hey, Jane," Phoebe said casually as she flipped switches and leveled the craft.

"It shouldn't surprise me, should it?" Jane asked.

"Nope. Welcome to the Sons and Daughters Squad." She moved a mic down. "Alright guys, you can ditch the masks; we've got the golden unicorn and are passing the quarantine walls now."

Jane looked out the front window at the massive concrete walls towering over nearby buildings. Covered in construction scaffolding, the walls were a source of constant skilled labor, as crews worked to shore up defenses. Jane had never actually *left* Austin or the three cities since the Black Sun. *I mean, why would you? The place is a ...* the craft flew between two watchtowers and revealed the blasted landscape on the outside. It wasn't barren by any measure, but rather filled with camps of refugees that littered the mossy and muddy ground. The stark contrast in colors, between a place like the Jungle inside, and the withering landscape outside, really took her aback.

"How?" she uttered.

"The same way most Americans," Phoebe replied, "ignored conditions in Africa for—well, ever, really. Those that have it good need not pay attention to those that don't. I mean, think about it, a booze baron is reserving a top-end nightclub right inside Austin for weeks on end, never showing up, while people sleep on the street. Those who can work a power-welder get work, the rest rot outside with business degrees. Think of the old economy with a full fifty states, and then instantly take that away. Capitalism doesn't care if you can't adapt." The craft picked up speed. "Still hate us anarchists now?"

"I'm leaning your way," Jane said while swaying back and forth. Her balance was near perfect, so bracing herself wasn't needed. "Pretty bold move, though, getting on my squad. How did you know I would not go ballistic on you?"

"I've got faith in Doc's abilities, annnd my own," she said, taking the craft lower to the ground, just above a leafless tree line. Jane looked at other craft fly up and off in different directions. The craft lurched to the left; Jane grabbed the door as the plane flew down along deserted suburb streets at house height. "Look around with those special Auburn eyes of yours," Phoebe said.

"Uh, I kinda need to be juiced up on adrenaline or near death to actually *look* into Purgatory," Jane said. "And your flying isn't bad enough to trigger that."

Doc reached out and grabbed her hand with wide eyes. "Do. Not. Tempt. Her."

A wave of panic rushed through Jane. She grabbed both doors and braced for death and tried to close her eyes. The ashen world melted its way into her vision, ripping away the barriers between worlds like a wildfire. To her surprise, the neighborhood looked mostly the same. There was more decay on the buildings. but aside from a few slight differences, the place looked the same. Only with nobody, or no *thing* around.

"It ... it looks the same," Jane's voice trembled as she spoke. "Can you please pull up now for christ's sake, you are going to hit a tree."

When Doc removed his hands, the overwhelming sense of fear left with it, and Phoebe started the ascent. The world faded back to normal for Jane, as normal as her vision was, anyway, and she already missed the on-demand adrenaline rush Doc had given her at first. Once it set in that he could manipulate her emotions to the brink of terror, Jane began to feel immensely uncomfortable about it. *Could others do the same? Can they control thoughts as well?*

"And to think," Phoebe said, "that's just outside a major city."

Jane shrugged and set herself to swallow any feelings of self-doubt regarding Doc's abilities. It was heck of a lot better than facing them. "I don't see the big deal, I mean, it's just a deserted suburb. Inside Austin that vision gets *way* more apocalyptic."

"It's supposed to. Do you think it's a good thing that the real world looks just like Purgatory in some places?"

"Well, no. But I mean, how do you even know that's the case? You can't see that, can you?"

Phoebe shook her head no. "Helldiving. Something you will get damn good at in the near future. The barriers may be thin, hell, even shredded in some places, but diving into the abyss itself is still a tried and true method of looking for things on the other side. Normally there is a big separation, like what you see in Austin, but in some places it's a true ghost town now."

"I thought a crap ton of people still lived in Chicago?" Jane kept her eyes peeled outside, marveling at how the landscape was desolate and dying in one town and a perfectly vibrant and normal community with fast-food joints and late-night bars the next over.

"You bet your ass, they do. Ghosts, vampires, psychics, mobsters, and regular Joes living side by side." She blew a bubble and popped it as she picked up speed. "Some places used Angel-Be-Gone to keep stuff out, others let it in and were eaten, and others learned to adapt real bloody fast. But full-on ghost towns like that, entire communities that just up and died? They didn't even leave souls and ghosts behind. It's like someone came in and harvested everybody."

"You think some monster is responsible?" Jane asked.

A few of the soldiers in the back chuckled as they listened in. They had already been putting on their Sons and Daughters patches and armbands. Outside of their military gear, they looked like a heavy metal concert or a biker gang with too many wooden stakes for their own good.

"Oh, a monster is responsible, alright. This is the mark of a Death Lord. The catch is finding out which one it is. Suicide? Murder? Heaven's Wrath? Fuck 'em all, we say. We've been following the trail of these towns for a while, trying to figure out which one was operating. It's trickier for us." Phoebe twirled her fingers. "We can't see into the underworld on command. We've gotta actually helldive, and that can be a bitch. But you, sweetness. You're a walking radar dish for us. So, here's the brass tacks. You work for us, lead us, and help us see if any more towns like this are happening up north, and in exchange—"

"You'll take me to Dairy Queen?" Jane smirked.

"I like ya more already," she said. "In exchange, we ensure that you are first to Michigan. Who knows, maybe you'll make a real change along the way." She popped another bubble. "Doesn't sound so bad, does it?"

Travel the country looking for signs of Death Lords? Sounds like a purchasing a two-way ticket to the afterlife. Fredrick spoke of victors writing this history and battles between people trying to kill a god. A thousand more questions raced through her mind about Lilith-babies and Lazarus-brats battling it out while regular people bred to the point where nothing was left. The connection clicked in her mind like a door lock satisfyingly sliding into place. *If the Death Lords draw their power from nearby dead, and Lazarus runs the Death Lords, then we, sir, have a pyramid scheme.* The Praenomen, the Church, the demons, the Society were all out there "recruiting" in some way for their "god." The Society recruited powerful sorcerers. Humans named Karen sold makeup to their neighbors. Demons recruited creatures of myth. Clearly, the Death Lords were laying claim to the dead. The last part Jane figured was pretty obvious given their namesake. "It's like Hungry Hungry Hippos but with souls," Jane muttered aloud.

Phoebe gave a confused glance.

"Just working stuff out." She pulled back a lock of hair. "Alright, I'm in. Can't make a call over which pyramid to topple if you don't know who is at the top." *It's about time I make friends outside Austin, anyway.* "So, what's with him?" She pointed to Doc. "He afraid of flying?"

"Nah, it's not that. I told him if he touched a single button, I'd eject his stupid stuffed swordfish in the cargo bay." She pointed behind her to a box labeled **Property of Doc Top Secret**.

"Huh. Did he tell you where he got that from?" Jane asked, already feeling the intense stare as Doc tried to bore a hole through the back of her head.

Phoebe shrugged. "I'm not into fishing like he is. We've been down here a while, and he's been on the boats from time to time."

Ohohohoh ... I've got blackmail. Don't worry, Doc ... I'm saving this for later. "I'd love to hear the story ..." Jane lied while grinning at Doc.

CHAPTER TWENTY-THREE

What could be better this summer than a pilgrimage to Salzburg, Prague, Vienna, and Budapest? Celebrate mass daily with a Catholic priest and visit religious sites such as the Nonnberg Convent of Benedictine nuns, the Church of Our Lady Victorious to see the renowned statue of the Infant Jesus of Prague, the 13th-century Cathedral of St. Matthew, and, of course, the Church of St. Stephen, Hungary's patron saint. Return to Lazarus and return to faith in these dark times. Hurry now, as the sinful Americans are abandoned, only the Unification can offer salvation.

Nature made its best attempt at turning their craft into a large metal coffin. Phoebe kept the VTOL mostly vertical during the devastating storm over Alabama. Each shift, or tilt, let out a high-pitched scream from the cockpit, followed by a bout of laughter from the cargo bay. Jane and the crew had been taking bets for an hour now on which rattling of the craft would get Doc to scream. Another scream came. *Dammit, Doc, can you at least try here? You're killing me.* Jane lobbed over a clip of ammunition to Kevin. "Seriously, I give up. He screams, every time. It doesn't matter if it's seventy-six to one odds, he's always going to scream." She rose, throwing her hands up.

"Not my fault all of you keep taking the bet," Kevin said, barely looking up from his laptop. He had acquired a rather large stack of sidearms and custom ammo from Jane's personal stash of promotional swag. The crew also tossed in the towel and resigned themselves to a hearty laugh every time it happened.

The cargo bay wasn't the best for passenger accommodations, and there was only one window on each side. Jane stuck her forehead to one of them and cupped her eyes to peer out while fogging the bottom half with her breath. She could see the bobbing red lights of another VTOL off and to the left and wondered which one Jack was in or how his crew was going. *Can't put a finger on it, but he seemed more militant last time. He's probably just pissed.* A vision raced past of Jack being dismantled bolt by bolt and falling to the ground as a set of lungs and a brain. It was a sight that Jane didn't think she would ever rinse from her brain. *I've been vulnerable, but not like that.*

A bright white object flew past.

"The hell," Jane said, mushing her face up against the glass even more. "Lemme guess, we've got a monster on the wing or some shit. Hey, guys?" Jane waved everyone over. "I think we are about to be in a horror movie and crash during a thunderstorm. Just saw a white thing fly by."

More out of boredom than anything else, the Sons and Daughters scattered to the windows and peered outside for any sign of a remotely interesting object to latch onto. "Ladies and gentlemen, this is your captain speaking. Would one of you be so kind as to grab a shotgun and proceed to the cabin for a brief discussion on the policy of touching buttons?"

Jane cracked open one of her crates and grabbed an automatic silver shotgun before any of the others even thought of it. "Scuse me," she said with a satisfying click-clack noise. "I've gotta go to therapy with my Doc." *Alright, alright, that was cheesy.* No one laughed. "Fine, fuck you guys."

She regretted opening the door instantly, as Phoebe and Doc

were yelling at each other in between pathetic slaps like two cats fighting over her last scrunchie. The best she could make out was something, or some person, called Molly.

"Hey!" Jane interrupted at last. "Seriously, grown children you both are, but please not while flying a giant coffin through a thunderstorm. Let's be real here, folks."

"It's a cryptid," Phoebe said while fishing out another stick of gum.

Doc was going to reply before Jane shot an icy glare of death at him. In compliance, he curled up, but kept looking out the window.

"What's a cryptid, Phoebe?" Jane asked.

"Those," she said, pointing out the window and to the ground.

Jane pulled herself over the control console for a better view, and despite nearly blinding the pilot, she could barely make anything out. A soul-sucking scream echoed back through the coffin, causing her to drop her shotgun and grab Doc. The white force shot up past the window and dove again. "The fuck was that?" Jane said again, clutching her chest, her heart beating faster than any human heart should.

"Cryptids," Phoebe said again with certainty.

"Huggin' Mollys," Doc mumbled under his breath. "We are right over Abbeville, Alabama; that's a Huggin' Molly. Tall white woman who stalks the shadows and skies during storms and sucks the souls out of children by giving them hugs and stealing them for food."

"Tall suburban white women who steal the souls of Alabamian children?" Jane asked again. "I will take a pass on the obvious joke here. So, what are they feeding on?"

Both Phoebe and Doc looked at her. "The souls of children," they said in unison.

"Well, land this fucking thing then," Jane said, shaking Phoebe's shoulder violently. "Stop at towns in need, remember?"

Doc nodded and flipped a light, setting the cargo bay red, with a haughty nod of his head as he side-eyed Phoebe. She brought the craft around and lowered it while everyone got ready for a jump.

Phoebe screamed at the top of her lungs. "Everyone here. Can survive. A jump. Engage. Will land when. We. Won't. Be. Eaten." She flashed a peace sign and flipped the jump lines on.

The bay doors cracked open, spraying a fine mist of water inside as the team readied their combat equipment. Hooded lanterns, green cloaks, axes blessed in holy water, bandoliers of wooden stakes, crowbars, and custom modified shotguns bristled off them like angry porcupines. They weren't the corporate-sponsored team Jane or Jack normally saw by any measure. *Well, if they've survived this long off that, they've gotta have a clue.*

With the small town of Abbeville swinging into view thirty feet below, Jane saw the creatures more clearly. Each swooping down and tearing through the streets looking for a target, bringing with it gusts of wind that shook the craft violently and shattered windows on building facades. No doubt inside, the inhabitants of this small village tried to survive within this maelstrom of screams.

Heart racing. Vision slowed. Jane dashed out into free fall without hesitation, landing on the roof of a downtown business with a tumble and racing forward. With another jump and an activation of her boots, she changed direction mid-leap and let her chains hang loose, their bright blue glow like an angler's lure.

One of the white Mollys screeched in between trees and alleyways right into Jane's midair path. *Gotcha.* With a quick twist, Jane fired off the rocket boots one after another like she was running on the air before taking a front flip down, using the momentum to bring the chained cryptid smashing into a streetlight in a shower of sparks.

In her slow-motion view, Jane watched the thick raindrops bounce off her mechanical arm and shatter into it. *Hrm. It kept up. Nice job after all.* In the distance glass shattered from more screams as the wind came from every direction, followed by the sound of shotgun blasts and cheers as the team moved into action. Over a radio Jane heard Phoebe giving out their location.

But it was the creature rising in a shower of sparks from a shattered streetlight that held her attention.

Steaming orange embers bounced off Huggin' Molly's massive black cloak. A cloak beneath which Jane saw her raven-feathered corset and a large wide skirt that was dark enough to absorb light—in a vain attempt to hide her true size. As she peeled herself off the ground and stretched her claws, it became clear she was wider than a bushel of hay. Jane's eyes followed up to her neckline where porcelain white skin reflected an eerie soft glow of its own. Further up yet, eyes that weren't just white, but beaming light like small flashlights, gazed down upon Jane. She gulped. To her wide-eyed surprise, Huggin' Molly was easily over seven feet tall.

Huggin' Molly took a deep breath in and screamed out of her gaping black maw. Jane winced and covered her ears as Molly opened something up like an umbrella and took flight, leaving only a white streak in the air and blending back into the shadows.

"Owww, fuck," Jane said as she felt her ears pop and sounds of gunfire turn into muffled claps. *They named your overstuffed ass wrong, should be Hollin' Molly.* There were easily hundreds of them flying around over the town. Occasionally seven or eight would descend on an area like a pack of buzzards. Jane didn't need to see the details to know what that meant.

On rooftops around her, the Sons and Daughters engaged in battle using tricks of their own. A sorcerer deftly dodged a charge by exploding into a cloud of buzzing insects and reforming. Another helldiver loaded silver stakes into a custom shotgun and blasted off a Molly's arm. Jane smirked when she saw one vampire wielding a crowbar like a baseball bat with supernatural strength. To Jane it didn't really matter how they fought, she was glad to have a team and take on live targets. She kicked her chains back up and smiled. *Lady, that umbrella will not get you away from me.*

She bolted along the side of the building, rain going from vertical to horizontal.

CHAPTER TWENTY-FOUR

:: Transmission Restored:: No airwave is dead. No computer is asleep. No consciousness ... awake. The dreamscape is aglow with biofeedback. Nothing is impossible. Potentiality is a constant. Although you may not realize it, you are mystical.

Delilah Dumont sipped a Midwinter Black Latte and watched Jane fly about with piqued curiosity on a large computer screen. Two soldiers mopped up blood into the yellow janitor bucket from someone who had been sliced in half behind her. Nine others were thanking their fortunes and catching their breath.

Delilah ignored them. "Do you really think Peter is this gullible? That he can just send out pretty girls to fight cryptids and his products will fly off the shelves?"

"Peter, or your average survivor?" Whisper responded as he slapped Symon's hand away from the bucket of blood. "I believe that given the general state of panic in the world, people will bulk buy anything that gives them peace of mind."

"But who gets tricked into buying a product just because

someone cute in skintight leather flies around? I can't believe people still fall for basic marketing gimmicks." She took another sip.

"I'd say ..." Whisper eyed the Midwinter Black cup and held up a single finger. Symon in turn flicked his forehead and shook his head. "... say that Peter has done a rather cunning job of countering our well-laid plans, to be fair, Miss Dumont."

Delilah's eye twitched. "Don't be a coward, Symon. I'm aware of the irony that I'm drinking Midwinter Black. It's not because of Jane; it's just bloody fucking good coffee." She chucked the cup behind her and started walking to the next chamber. "Keep up, everyone."

The Archive, Delilah's personal project, sat in the middle of nowhere under a mountain in Colorado. A tried and true US Air Force base conquered and repurposed to her own ends. The staff comprised vampiric freaks, but also former soldiers, CIA spies, several demons, and at least one wendigo. In the vast bunkers that Delilah stormed through, her heels clicking on concrete and echoing off walls, crate upon crate of stolen or recovered artifacts were logged and stored. All around the country, Archive operatives were still helldiving to reclaim treasures and objects lost to history and storing it. An arcane arms race that only Delilah was sprinting in. Her hope was that by the time governments or other warlocks realized that the right magic items could disarm nuclear missiles—she already had most of them.

She glanced out of a window into a hanger filled with missiles and felt accomplished. *Having a few actual missiles never hurt either.*

Delilah led her group to a conference room with a large oaken table in the middle. Maps, arcane scribbles, blackmail files, and coffee cups littered the table and stacked themselves higher and higher. She plopped herself down at the end and tuned back into the TV station where news anchors were beginning to cover Jane's engagement with Huggin' Molly.

"Okay. I'll admit," Delilah reflected, "Peter played the game well. I was *hoping* he would have to rely on the Church of Lazarus more in this war. If they marched with necromancers and vampires at the helm, Peter might have withdrawn away further to keep his companies on brand and the alliance between them would stretch."

"Instead," Symon chimed in, "dey spun the story and got a soapbox. At least they've moved their armies out, no?"

"That at least went to plan," she agreed. "We will have the mobility to attack the Lord of Suicide or Mr. Culmen more directly and on even footing ... but I'm getting another idea." She picked up her pen tapped her lips. "Let's modify our original plan. These companies are still run by people and there are still boards of directors. Whisper, Symon, take our best operatives and get back into Texas. Start infiltrating and replacing members on the board ... or at least blackmailing them into total submission. Whatever it takes. You do you."

Whisper was already thumbing through personal files that had been left on the table.

"Oooh, are we moving onto a plan C?" Symon smiled.

Delilah slowly nodded as she started writing down a checklist in her journal. "Yes. It is possible that we may not get the Death Lord. That this all goes belly-up. I'm compromised and pulled in multiple directions. I will give ... *everything* to kill that demon king Bollard, but I still must prep for the larger war to come versus Lazarus. While the armies are away, we might be able to steal the companies, and their prototypes, right out from under their noses."

Everyone in the room was quiet for a second. Several soldiers cautiously flipped through files as the yellow-orange light of a florescent bulb shone down. A lone fly buzzed through, cutting the silence.

"Don't seem so enthusiastic all at once." She marked down another note. *Increase morale. Birthday parties?*

Symon said something at last. "We can't yet teleport large quantities. Getting that many agents into the Triumvirate and ... much less shipping that much out via truck unnoticed would take years."

"Can't is the language of quitters, Symon," she mused. "In

order to make this plan work, we will have to go back to the Society of Deus."

"Oh, dear," Whisper tsked. "That is bound to be unpleasant. We are, perhaps, on their bad side."

"Oh, what do you mean, Gabriel will be entirely thrilled that I've sent armies north and possibly framed them in a global terror threat ..." She bit the back of her pen. "Maybe we should avoid him. I only need an hour in the library."

"Only an hour?" Symon raised an eyebrow. "You Americans have no stamina in matters of love."

"Love? I wish I was afforded such luxuries within the halls of that library," Delilah swooned, biting her tongue. Visions of the demon king Bollard raced through her head and in her dreams every night. Far too often was he shirtless in a kitchen cooking her omelets. *I'm going to rip his bloody heart out.*

CHAPTER TWENTY-FIVE

Don't be impressed by money, followers, degrees, and titles. Be impressed by humility, integrity, generosity, and kindness. The kindness that Elcoll will provide is everlasting. You'll never know how strong you are, until being strong is the only choice you have. When you need us, we will be there.—Elcoll.

J ack couldn't wait for the cargo bay doors of his craft to open. He wanted to put as much distance between himself and this "Akira" who had followed him onto his squad. The rest of them, according to their digital footprints, were tried and true military mercenaries from legit arena contests, but Akira was some vampiric video game savant who snuck her way in via a contest hunting for drone pilots. She was out of place. Short, odd-colored hair, no shoes, and worst of all—she kept boring holes into the back of Jack's head with her creepy insect-like stares. *Why doesn't she blink! That is so creepy ...*

"This is Metallic Jack and squad one seventy-three, commencing engagement of Mollys," he said into his radio, and had his pilot open the doors despite their height. The others had already engaged Mollys near the center of town, and Jack was tired of waiting. There were still airborne targets that circled around the outskirts, and he really felt like splattering creature blood. Click by click, Jack slid silver ammunition into the incredibly oversized rifle before making sense of the night activity. With a flick, he switched his vision to an infrared array to see amidst the torrential downpour. The instant bay doors clanked into position, Jack locked onto the overly sized umbrella-wielding witch and took a deep breath. *Calculate for wind, steady the scope, and squeeze slowly.*

He fired. The custom tracer round sliced through the air and found its mark. Square between the eyes of an unaware Huggin' Molly. Akira leaned out and whistled as the creature careened out of the sky and crashed into a storefront where regular people descended upon it with baseball bats and more guns of their own.

"Nice shootin', but damn, I think those peeps down there have some pent-up rage," she laughed.

"Why do you keep talking?" Jack said as he reloaded another round. *Pfft, Akira doesn't even show up on infrared.*

Akira tilted her head sideways and pulled two serrated sickles out from behind her back while inching closer to the edge. "It won't be for much longer. I've figured out they lobotomized and ripped your memories right out of that slushy skull of yours. So"—she smiled with a fang sticking out, and held up her sickles —"I guess it's time to build new memories, yeah?" Akira fell backwards out of the bay doors and fell to the ground.

Shit. She's still on my squad ... wait ... you know what, fuck that thing. Jack grabbed the overhang handle and looked down, watching her descent. It wasn't graceful. She slammed her head on the side of the building, landed on the concrete sidewalk with a bounce while her arm snapped, and legs twisted. Two incoming creatures flew from either side of the street right in her direction, their elongated claws sparking off the asphalt as they dragged them.

"Least you make good bait," Jack said. "Get this thing

lower!" He took aim as they descended. *Calculate for stupid dumb vampires, steady the scope, and squeeze slowly.* One trigger pull, one dead witch. "All right, let's engage; we can't lose a squad member on the first outing ... as much as I want to," Jack said, waiting to get closer. Unlike Akira, he wasn't interested in breaking his limbs on a dumb fall while he reloaded. The other Huggin' Molly raced in and scooped up the broken vampire splayed on the ground, screaming as she flew up the hardware store's side. She made it halfway up before Akira sliced her to ribbons and they fell back down together. Cackling madly, Akira continued to hack, and hack, and rip at the creature with her scythes.

By the time the craft landed down the street and Jack stepped out, the witch's blood covered Akira as she ate. *Disgusting.*

"Moron," Jack called out and fired a side pistol round right near Akira. She hissed at him with glowing red eyes as she fed. "We've got others to kill, let's move. Lucky I don't count you as a casualty of war. I hear they burn the dead."

"Do you know," she said with a slurp as she sat on the creature like she was riding a horse, "how long it's been since I had a meal? You should have a bite. It's only a matter of time before your headaches return, there, Jacky boy. Who knows, might actually heal your brain," she said as she motioned for two soldiers to join her.

Seriously? My brain isn't broken. Jack shook his head, fired, and entered the fray in downtown Abbeville. *I'm not missing anything.* To call their tactic an "abundance of firepower" was an understatement as they moved forward block by block. *Why would Akira suggest that? Who needs memories?* Huggin' Mollys were terrifying legends by themselves, even worse in large packs, but against a force of mercenaries with the latest technical toys and magical tricks the battle was elementary. *I don't miss my daughters' hugs.* The driving force behind the bulky hunters was sheer chaotic hunger, and this town was their feeding frenzy. *I don't miss the blood.* Jack's squad and several others that had landed wanted revenge and were more than happy to oblige in an orderly fashion. *I don't care.*

Thirty intense minutes of gunfire, plasma shots, aerial flips, and custom mechanized craft crashed into Alabama, grinding out good old-fashioned American freedom one block at a time, to the ever-growing cheers of civilians. Drones hovered and zipped around to capture every action shot in high-definition, ensuring that they sliced JK-47's aerial acrobatics side by side with shock waves by Metallic Jack. Abbeville was a self-sufficient town that limped along through the apocalypse. Quaint and unknown with its small storefronts, hell, even a bar named after Huggin' Molly that was shattered into pieces by the battle—it was now famous.

"Hey, JK-47, you on this channel?" Jack hit his comms. He was tracking the last living monster that tried to screech her way out of town. Jane was bounding from rooftop to rooftop in pursuit with her chains always just out of reach. He leveled his rifle at the flyer. *It doesn't have the same visual fun as the plasma hand, but the kick on this thing is just so damn satisfying.*

"Little busy, strawberry shortcake," she gasped for air.

"You should take a break. I got this."

She looked back at him while both upside down and mid-flip, throwing him the bird.

"If I'm a dessert, I'm a burning glass of brandy." Jack fired. The final shot of the skirmish took the head clean off the Huggin' Molly, sending her crashing into a giant crucifix erected in the center of town. "Boom. Headshot!"

"You cheating rat bastard," she said, skidding to a stop over the body.

"They gave you guns as well, no complaining," Jack laughed.

As the mercenaries cleaned up their mess, hundreds of people came out of their shelters. Most out of curiosity, but more than a few were packing enough guns to arm a rebellion. Their age ranges were everyone from a young teen to a grand-mother in a motorized scooter. *Hot damn, that's what I'm talking about, grandma's packing a twelve gauge.* For a small town with only a few thousand, they leveraged everything to survive. Amid handshakes, rainstorms, and a few photos, Jack heard the rumbling sound of heavy engines as the semitrucks rolled around the corner and into town. He inhaled deeply at the sweet, delicious smell of victory and diesel as the beautiful vehicles began braking one after another until they filled streets.

The Lord of Suicide kept most of his army to the ground, but also mixed in these giant semitrucks outfitted with ramming barricades, gun mounts, and giant banners with advertisements for Elcoll. Jack watched Jane struggle with feelings over seeing the trucks, but he knew better than to ask. *We each have our demons, don't we, Jane?*

Certified public relationship reps and sales officials were the first off the trucks and already beginning loudspeaker announcements about their arrival. Jack spat on the ground. *Army of zealots? How about army of concentrate piss. Their entire lot is on the juice. What a waste of good hardware.* Most of the pretty young faces were approaching anyone in the town that was wielding guns, but Jack saw a handful carrying a different package to the elderly. Instead of a young face filled with smiles, Elcoll produced someone closer in age to their demographic. Their smiles rubbed Jack the wrong way, as if they were fake smiles of compassion. Veneered empathy.

Jack checked the time and eyed the VTOL craft, planning an early escape. "This is Metallic Jack," he chimed in on the general radio. "I'm not spending the night here and celebrating. Let's let the welcome wagons do their job and get some extra ground ahead of us. This town kicked enough ass, so they don't need us stealing all their whiskey." He chuckled lightly. *We didn't do half bad, did we?*

"Hey, Jack, guess what?" Jane said over the radio.

"We're going to switch our insults from desserts to breakfast cereals?"

"Oooh, maybe. But no. At least that's not what you need to guess, not that ... you get the damn idea. You guessed wrong."

"So, what is it?"

"Since you got the final shot, you get all the glory. We're moving out. Enjoy clean up!"

"Does this mean," Akira's voice cut in on the chat, worming her way into their channel, "I get to be Count Chocula?"

"No!" they both shouted.

"Fine, Booberry it is. But either way, Jack, get back on our squad's channel. Come here by the First Baptist Church, we need a judgement call here."

Jack made his way through the dead trees and blasted storefronts, trying his best to ignore the red-hooded robes from the Church of Lazarus or the Elcoll marketing groupies working their recruitment drive to Akira's location. He rounded the corner to the red-bricked church sporting boarded-up windows near the middle of downtown. They set barbed wire fences, sandbags, and a few machine gun emplacements up to keep the parishioners inside safe. Just outside, Akira stood while trying to light a clearly crumpled smoke, her sickles now covered with blood and ash.

Smashed into the ground were two Huggin' Mollys that were very clearly dead, with their chests ripped open and splayed out for the world to see. A group of seven men, most with chopped short hair and green tank tops, sat nearby while they ate the hearts of the creatures. They filled the church goblets with the blood.

"So," Akira said, while flicking her Zippo, "I know you aren't used to this anymore, so let me remind you. This is how most communities *really* survive. They lure and hunt the supernatural and eat it. Angel-Be-Gone or other shit products are cute deterrents and all, but why deal with injuries or cancer and shit like that when you can just split a heart. Granted, they'll be weak little baby vampires without their own heart, but I don't think they know that."

A headache crept in at the sight of the blood. *Yeah, I'm getting that. People are idiots.* "Did you invite me over here for temptation?"

She shook her head. "No, an actual judgement call. Just

because magic *has* come back, doesn't mean it's a daily occurrence. It's mostly just the dead. You've gotta hunt for blood once you eat a heart, otherwise ... well ..." She gestured to him up and down. "And you still aren't cured. These guys, the size of this town ... there's only so much blood to go around. So, we gotta bring 'em with us, yeah?"

Jack knew what she meant. They would leave this town, and in the days or weeks to come, these seven would be hungry again. Without any more creatures they would turn to the nearest source of blood. First, perhaps animals, but everyone knew that just made it worse. Animal blood only made vampires more savage. So then they would turn to humans, and even if they were nice about it, there weren't enough people in town to support seven new bloodsuckers.

He took out a pistol and fired it into the air. "Alright soldiers, form up!" he shouted, and walked over to the seven.

In the midst of wide-eyed, frenzied eating as they slurped and sucked down their cryptid food, one by one they huddled together as if Jack would steal their precious dinner.

"I said fall in line!" he screamed at them. This time, they obliged, wiping the blood off their lips. Jack waited for them to stop giggling and stand side by side at attention. Each of them seemed very proud of what they had achieved. "How many of these have you killed?"

"Three today, Metallic Jack, sir!" one in the middle said with conviction.

"You've got TV out this far, eh? Then you should've known what you are doing will land you on a stake in a stadium."

"Survival of the fittest, sir! You of all people should understand, commander!"

"Yeah, I understand." Jack fired up his plasma gun, and before the group could react, he fired a line right through them ear-to-ear. *I understand that I can save you the trip.* He wrinkled his nose at the smell of burnt flesh while each body hit the ground. *Commander ... psh, commander of what? You don't know me.* He marched out, walking right through the barbed wire as if it were a spiderweb, to Akira, who stood there aghast. "The only vampire I'm keeping on my crew is you. Dunno why, but don't ask again." Over the radio he made the call to pack up and get out of town. Jack didn't want to sit around and mingle with the reinforcements. *Besides, can't let Jane get too far ahead.*

"Jack," Akira asked again, her voice quieter than usual. "What do you want us to do when this happens again?"

"I lead by example. Peter put me in charge for a reason. That a problem?" Jack said as he climbed aboard the VTOL. When he looked back on Akira, he wasn't expecting her to look at him like a total stranger.

CHAPTER TWENTY-SIX

For only .0098 Bitcoin a day, you can be an integral part of a child's life. Help provide them with new Monsanto seeds that grow, even in these black times. Help provide security with MAGA arms. Help provide simple, wholesome, and friendly toys from Atlantis. Your small donation can purchase all the dreams for someone right at home, not some faraway land. That's right, your impact is right here in America from North Dakota through Arkansas. So please, will you donate today, to save a life for tomorrow?

The Praenomen took a deep breath, feeling the fresh midwestern wet air fill her lungs and let his stress flow out with an exhale. Together, Delilah and fragments of Vryce stood at the foot of the city they'd abandoned a year prior. The Society of Deus's capitol towered before them, dwarfing the trio as they stood in the middle of a main highway that led in. Its massive green walls were built from the stolen souls of enemies and energy from the great ritual that liberated the world from the shackles of slavery. Despite Vryce's public murder at the hands of a vampire without vision, Mike Auburn, the city thrived as magic crashed back into its world. *Of course it did. I had taken every precaution to ensure its success ... unlike its current ruler.* For decades leading up to the incident, Delilah Dumont had overseen the revival of Minneapolis–St. Paul as an energy independent paradise. That the Twin Cities stood as a bastion of inhuman ingenuity today was a testament to her skills.

Behind her, Symon Vasyl and Whisper stepped through her red door that sliced the air like a knife. A two-dimensional mirror linking two points in space, in this case, Denver and the Twin Cities. Teleportation spellcraft was nothing new; legends told of great magi practicing it during the mythic age, and even Warlock Vryce was capable of it. But this gateway was her own doing, and for that she was particularly proud. When she ransacked Culmen's arena she could only transport a trio. In the weeks she'd spent in Denver, she expanded its range to three, five, and even nine-and-a-half people on one test. With a little more practice, the Praenomen could move entire armies. *Let's not get ahead of ourselves, particularly when that specific power isn't in my paws yet ... but that is why we are here, isn't it, Father? After all, it's a little rude to teleport people in halves. It's rather messy.*

It was a rather unfortunate reality she wasn't exactly *welcome* in the city she helped build. To say she and Gabriel D'Angelo didn't see eye to eye was an understatement. *He's a petulant brat who didn't have to earn anything.* Yet behind these empty walls he thrived at controlling the vampire army she had conditioned and trained. She didn't want to admit it, but he might possibly be competent. Now she needed his city for one hour to get a magical item called the Emerald Tablet of Hermes Trismegistus. An object secured behind every magical ward known to both mortal and undead alike. Peter made his chess move north, and she saw an opening that wasn't there before. Killing two birds with one stone. *Is it possible to teleport out warehouse after warehouse of Peter's inventions under their nose while their army is at war?*

"What's the worst that can happen?" the Praenomen said, shaking her hands off as she moved towards the great green walls, atop which massive iron chains floated to an island that hovered over Walsh Tower. It was a sight that most humans still barely comprehended. As above, and so below. The Society of Deus was one of several sites around the world where helldivers broke into Purgatory. All in a vain search for Lazarus to be resurrected. The island floating above existed in Purgatory until recently. For decades, mortals were none the wiser that a society of sorcerers and vampires were digging out the earth beneath them and disposing of the waste in the lands of the dead. Delilah smirked. She often suggested they could solve most landfill or radioactive waste problems the same way. The vampires didn't care.

"Eh, Gabriel sends his armies to chain you up and rip your heart out?" Symon trotted up behind her. Unlike his silent companion, he had been against the return to the Society from the first day. Vampires feared death the older they got, and Symon had been around since the second World War. "I tink we should reconsider moving the items with trucks over a few years? Perhaps maybe even a single motorcycle one at a time, yeah?"

The Praenomen shook its head. "We should be fine. Faced with a new enemy, they have no choice but to listen to a potential ally. Particularly one that has the Society's best interest in heart ... even if they don't realize it." The three of them continued walking down the deserted expressway that led into downtown. As they approached the walls, slight wisps of green fire danced along the edges, creating an appearance of water flowing upwards—if water let out a slight wailing noise.

"I tell you." Symon hunched his shoulders and pulled his trench coat closed. "I never liked these walls. It's unholy, I tell you. Trapping the souls of the departed and using them as power."

The Praenomen shrugged. "They're dead. What good will it do them? Besides, do you have any plans that involve protection versus nuclear weapons? When you find one, inform me."

The shadows grew impossibly long and dark as they moved closer to the threshold into the city. The Praenomen readied one of the fabled blades of Deus, a small dagger with the souls of several sorcerers trapped within. Before her a line of fire inched along the ground before erupting into a column two stories high. Whisper politely stepped to the side and made himself scarce for later.

"I mean, I knew you had iron balls, but actually returning? That's insane," an aghast voice shouted down from a perch. Commander Mitch Slade, standing with his flaming sword, aviator shades, and mutton chops, gave a small wave before flicking a smoke down in front. "Symon, good to see you again."

Symon gave a two-finger wave.

"I see Gabriel has you on patrol, wasting the talents of Vryce's apprentices like usual," the Praenomen said, with a gesture counterspelling the wall of fire. "As for the rest of you, out of the shadows and hands in the air." Pushing her sleeves up to her elbows, she closed her arms together and stripped the area of shadows, tearing away the illusion spell that hid a squadron of Gabriel's forces mixed with more than a few undead generals.

A small battalion of glowing, red-eyed vampire soldiers with full balaclavas, helmets, riot gear, and specially designed weapons stood at the ready. Vryce's other two apprentices, the druid Cael McManus and the carnival announcer Roger Queneco, cockily flanked each side. But Delilah's former general, Alexander Lex Dupris, stood mere inches away from her, with seven-inch-long red talons just centimeters from her throat. Aside from this monstrous demeanor, Lex fastened his long hair neatly in a pony-tail and wore a rather fitting suit for an undead in a war zone. With teeth bared, he feigned a smile.

"Hello, master," he bowed.

"At least one among you remembers etiquette," the Praenomen said. "Now put those hideous claws away before I command you to have them manicured." She stood patiently with arms crossed behind her back and watched Lex fall into position. Symon just looked on with awe. *That's right. I've programmed each of you for decades. Now be like good little dogs and heel. Gabriel just got another reason to add onto his litany of complaints about me—I'm a threat.*

"We still can't let you in as you are," Slade called down from above. "Sure, the boss would rather I incinerate you now to eliminate a traitor and reclaim the power ... but ... we respect your legacy, after all."

"Ah," the Praenomen said. "So he's a little mad about me starting a war in Texas? I suppose that's fair." Deep down, voices itched at the back of her mind. Gabriel should know there was more at play, but it's not like she coordinated anything with him —ever. *He blames me for letting Mike Auburn out of jail, who then went on to shatter Vryce's head. Blames me for starting a war on national television, and then sending an army north to their direction. Blames me for releasing neurotoxin on a private gathering, which was helpful in defeating Mr. Bollard.* Delilah let out a good, hearty chuckle in the middle of the highway. She technically *did* do all of that. *So public enemies we shall be then, eh?* She was starting to understand how Vryce felt; she rather warming up to being vilified. "I need access to the Libraries of Deus for an hour. How do I go about this? I'd rather get what I need before the US Army finally buys missiles that can get past these walls."

A lone figure walked up through the menagerie of monsters, his cane helping with a limp, his other hand flicking a pocket watch. With short blond hair, a suit worth more than most cars, and piercing green eyes, Charles Walsh himself wore authority with class. The former regional director of the Unification showed his face at last.

"You enter with me," he said, looking down at her with a charming smile of perfect white teeth.

"Time has been on your side, old man; last I saw you, you had aged nearly ninety years," the Praenomen said. "Now, you're a strapping young lad with a dignified limp. Good on you."

"Some people make good on their promises." He gestured behind him. "Come now, friends, we aren't savages; Delilah Dumont is a welcome guest within our city. After all, wasn't it her who helped build it? Surely, we owe her that much." He looked back at her. "Provided she leaves all current artifacts, daggers, crosses, nails, shotguns, nerve gas, or whatever weaponized anthrax she packed three hours, fifteen minutes, and forty-seven seconds ago." He flipped his watch shut.

"That's peachy," Symon cut in. "Dangerous, no?"

No. No, it's not. They are up to something. The Praenomen pulled off her mask and a few dozen other artifacts and weapons, including a small glass vial of weaponized Ebola, and gave them to Symon. "Symon, Whisper, continue the clearly ominous plan in Texas, we've at least to pique Walsh's curiosity, right?" After a tug on her green suit coat for readjustment and putting on her golden-rimmed glasses, she looked at Walsh with her mismatched eyes. "Shall we?" she said, holding out her elbow.

"Hey, are you going to make us walk there?" Symon shouted. Most of the vampires just laughed and turned their backs.

"After you." He took it.

As they turned their backs, a red door opened behind Symon and Whisper. *Remember everyone, this is my trick, not Vryce's, not Bollard's.* Delilah couldn't help but imagine Mr. Bollard as a Rakshasa, forcing his sweet blood down her gullet.

Delilah's eyes widened in surprise as she looked around the city. Most of the citizens wore a uniform blue military-cut coat with golden buttons down the side. Every step and place they trotted to was filled with purpose as they readied for war. Medical tents and preset evacuation points were getting rolled out at an alarming pace. Behind the busy activity of war preparations, life here could mirror life in Texas with a few twists. Magic was as commonplace as the coffee houses on every corner only with a few stores catering exclusively to vampires through blood dispensaries. Tutors led kids around on tour and taught them of history while their smaller homunculi bounded behind. It reminded Delilah of little ducklings.

What surprised her most, however, was the sheer diversity of magic. Rather than a homogeneous hermetic magical style, Gabriel had dedicated his time to the recruitment of different cultures and magical stylings to bolster their ranks. In five blocks, Delilah felt like she traveled through seven different countries.

"That's not all, Delilah," Walsh said, reading the very astonished look on her face. "I've made sure we focused our efforts on saving as many people as we could. Even if we had to travel far. Once word got out that we were offering a different path, plenty of former Unification members found their way here. Although I've gotta thank you for your sustainability efforts. If you didn't plan ahead, starvation would've set in by now—we've been under socially inflicted sanctions by most Americans for a while now. This, after all, was ground zero for Mike Auburn's riots that ended the world." He rolled his eyes at that.

This being ground zero is more important than you will ever know, Walsh. You're a good person, heart of an angel, but you can't pull a trigger when the time comes. "That kind of naïvete will get this paradise blown," she chuckled. "All the way to hell. Since you've already got a foot in the door."

Charles kept quiet as they moved closer to Walsh Tower, his timepiece opening and closing with each step. "I'm not going to let you murder what remains of the army, Delilah. Or the air force, or any other large body of humans left. The world needs time to heal." He let out a great sigh, knowing his words fell on deaf ears.

"How would your husband feel if you stood by and let them drop bombs on your home?" Delilah was going for the throat with each question. "You would let Lazarus's army grow impossibly strong by doing nothing? Let Peter Culmen build an unstoppable corporate empire over our ashes? You're a coward, Walsh. Gods are returning, actual legends, and Lazarus's Death Lords will grind them up and suck them dry. Humans don't have the power to fight either."

"You're a human, are you not?" Charles fired back with a raised eyebrow. "You are free to join the ranks and eat a heart at your leisure any time now ..."

"Immortality is overrated. Takes the fire out of you," she lied as they took to the steps of the Walsh Tower. Marble columns rose five stories tall with spotlights uplighting the building's facade in between decorative corporate fountains. The headquarters for one of the world's best construction companies—even if they mostly used workers hooked on demon's blood. "Since when did Gabriel become antiwar?" she asked out of the blue.

Charles looked down at his alligator-skin shoes and shook his head. "He isn't. He can barely control the Society of Deus as it is, though. He's a fantastic sorcerer and can repair one hell of a roof, but leadership isn't his strong suit. Add undead and skilled sorcerers together under the same roof and"—he whistled—"you can see why actual leadership has fallen to the others you met outside. It's a hollow throne. Like the Queen of England. Outside these walls, he wears the mask of a leader, unlike you who hides behind a porcelain mask filled with power. Gabriel left you a message," Charles said as he opened the glass doors. Inside a single elevator waited that would take Delilah down to the libraries of Deus.

The mask? Wait, now I'm ... "A mask? Why?" she asked, stepping in.

"His message is this, Delilah. You have one hour to find what you need, but you shall never return here again with the phylacteries. Your stunt in the arena showcased to the world Vryce's power, and the two of you are meant to share it as equals. So stop using that red gate thing to teleport out the blades of Deus when it's his turn, or a fireball through as a gift."

"I can add daddy issues to his profile now. I take the blades, the mask, and the pendant because I get more done. He can borrow the viola or something." She played a tiny violin between her fingers. "How can you sit by and let the Unification play their game of religious conquest?" she asked as she started a timer on her phone. *Now to lay the groundwork.*

"We've been working on a cure for blood addiction and our own means of sorcery. Let them battle the demons. We won't need their hearts or their blood in time." Walsh sighed. "Your time has started."

Delilah summoned a red gateway between an alley. Through

the shimmering glass, the sign of Elcoll headquarters reflected beyond.

"We have a plan, my friend, and perhaps it's worth investigating the Lord of Suicide's activities, Walsh. You can take a peek, yeah? Since you've gotten a few years of your life back, right? Go on," she prodded, "stop time for a few minutes and take a gander. Don't mind me, I'll just be downstairs reading a book." She walked to the elevator, a thin smile growing, producing her old access card, knowing full well that the locks were never *really* changed. *It's an obvious bait, Charles, are you going to resist?*

As the elevator doors closed, she heard him winding the gold gears that assembled his unique chronometer.

CHAPTER TWENTY-SEVEN

We've got executions, electrocutions, and private augmentations! T-Cellular Arena is hosting the first ever Swap-O-Rama of your favorite upgrades. Save up those Bitcoin and get down here this weekend for four days of chopping, slicing, and dicing. Sponsored by hundreds of companies, sign up for wonderful new toys. Then test them LIVE on creatures and prisoners in our executioner's circle! A one-stop shop for all your cybernetic needs! Child upgrades available upon request.

He suspended the salvaged remains of Taylor and Tyler in air over pools of liquid blue silicon by luminescent blue cables that dangled from the server farm above them. Mr. Anonymous's—or rather, Peter Culmen's—private server farm was the largest in North America, and if it wasn't for CERN or some dark Chinese farms, the largest in the world. Despite the near-freezing temperature in the room, Peter gave off no breath as he leaned into an array of monitors trying to parse the zeros and ones as they flowed along several screens. With little thought, he grabbed a bag of type O negative blood and popped a straw in it like a Capri Sun. *Ugh, we've gotta carbonate this stuff.* In the dimly blue-lit room with dangling bodies, Peter had run out of blood injectors hours ago, and they lay like fallen beer cans at his feet. He'd been down here nearly every waking moment since he sent his armies out two weeks ago.

"Why the hell can't I figure this out?" he said, pushing an older mechanical keyboard away. He filled his beloved data center with the latest in quantum computing and as many super-computers as he could get his hands on, but his remote terminal still was a mesh of wires, mismatched monitors, and old equipment covered in stickers. The trappings of routine helped him focus, and this, was absolutely a matter worth focusing on. *What a cruel joke from God. I can move the body, animate, make it dance, rip it to shreds and even attach robotic arms. But that damn brain and soul elude me. Best I can do is a cyborg like Jack.*

He slid his three-roller chair closer to the two naked pale dead bodies, their injuries repaired except for a few scars and checked his connections again. "Bah, this is bullshit, if Franken-stein can reanimate the dead, or Rasputin use their shells for ghosts ... or fuck, Vryce stitch them together into gargoyles ... what is holding me back?" He slid into the pool, feeling its intense heat flow over him. Silicon had an incredibly high melting temperature and the balancing act between cold super computers and bubbling pools of liquid silicon was nothing short of magical. A soft electrical spell surrounding him was all that kept him safe. Silicon wires connected his mind to the nearby terminal, providing a live stream of data that stretched beyond any other twenty-first century data farm. Despite all his toys, his stubborn commands for more calculations, and indecipherable code flying at his behest but kept returning errors.

"Troubleshooting is such a pain ..." He crawled out of the pool and double-checked the most common error ever made. He made sure they were plugged in. *Well, if it's not the tech, then it's the magic.* "Mitnik, change the lights to green." Peter stood by and watched as the soft luminescent blue gave way to a pale green color that infused the room, highlighting divine geometry inscriptions on every server. Beneath the layers of technology

and technomagic, all of Peter's principles were really based upon Sacred Geometry. Vryce used Hermetic Gnosticism, Rasputin used Witchcraft, but Peter built his empire by applying Sacred Geometry to binary. The Golden Ratio, the beauty of creation, recurring patterns found in nature should give Peter the tools to create a perfect life-form. He believed that all magic was nothing more than a tool. A tool that despite years, *no countless seconds endlessly ticking down*, he'd barely made any progress in mastering. *If phi = phi^2 - 1; therefore, 1 + phi = phi^2; phi + phi^2 = phi^3; phi^2 + phi^3= phi^4; ad infinitum* ... His mind trailed as he surveyed every symbol. It could take him another three decades at this rate.

"Bah, fuck it, I'll just make a giant bomb," he said at last, seconds before debugging the next symbol. This was his life's work, and he had no real intentions of stopping. Every other warlock practiced left-handed sorcery paths that stole from the world. He created. *Even if the blasted consciousness of humans eludes me for four centuries, I will unlock this code.*

The lights flashed.

Broken from his concentration, Peter checked one of the many monitors dangling over his desk. *An interruption. Joy.* He made his way back over, tying his hair back into a ponytail and tossing on a suit coat. The Lord of Suicide was headed this way, and he didn't look happy. "What now ... I swear if Metallic Jack shot someone again ..." He closed the lab and killed the lights. The world wasn't ready for his failed research yet and the Lord couldn't fathom how to use Windows 98, but it was still a healthy precaution. The less the Unification knew the better, at least until he was ready. There was a ninety-seven percent chance they would *despise* what he was attempting.

"Oh, look who finally showed up," Peter said with a smile as he locked the door behind him.

"Showed up? Don't be a wretch, child, you're the one who is late. I've been waiting in your office for an hour." The old man held out a pocket watch with the time on it. It was three hours slow.

"Well, I apologize for the delay, but um ..." Peter bit his fist.

"I think you need to rewind your watch. Want a new one? We make those water resistant now. Come on, this way." Peter pointed down a different white hallway, which led to more elevators.

The Lord furrowed his desiccated brow behind the mask and stared at his watch before rewinding it. "No. There is a reason we all keep classic timepieces, child. I'm aware you think of me as some Luddite, but digital watches realign themselves, the classics don't. Time is a valuable commodity to keep track of." He followed behind Peter.

"If it was that valuable, why not a satellite uplink then to an astronomical clock, we've been messing with our calendars and hours for years? Daylight savings time ... bah. What a joke. Either way, I'm here now. What's on your mind, sir?" They entered the shiny silver elevator with metallic grates above. A small picture in window video displayed headlines of the war movement.

"What are you working on in your lair, Peter?" he said plainly. "The Society of Deus is still shielded from scrying, but we are not. You aren't working on building some soulless monstrosity, are you? One of your new metal trinkets? We have no need for such creations. Elcoll will provide us with the armies we need, and I need you focused on cracking the wards over Deus."

Stop worrying, you old fool.

"No," Peter replied.

"Excuse me?"

"You heard me. No. I will not waste a precious second of my time trying to crack the nigh-impenetrable magical defenses of a city the best sorcerers in the world built. I will do what I'm the best at: drastic global evolution. I can't promise people the Singularity and then not deliver on it."

The doors opened to the penthouse suite of the Triumvirate Enterprises. An executive assistant with bright pink hair and industrial piercings was already waiting at the doors, he bowed and offered up a fresh bottle of water and a blood injection pack. Thanking him, they continued.

"We already have a God in this world, we do not need a fake one built from ones and zeros," the Lord hissed.

Afraid I'll put you out of business? Peter shrugged and opened the office doors with a cheeky grin. "Moore's law is a quantifiable fact; our processing power doubles every seven years. By 2045 artificial intelligence will far surpass anything humans could ever achieve." He tossed his mask on the table and sat behind his wooden desk. The Lord scanned for a chair in the barren room and was forced to stand. "I don't see what your problem is. The council gave *us* permission to show them our science. So, let me do my thing. We've got our war, and I'm moving to end all wars once and for all."

The Lord tipped his head back, his face was a snarl. Peter knew he was pushing buttons, but it wasn't the first time, and he would not compromise his dream.

"Do you know how rare the manipulation of time itself is? A gift only few ever are granted," the Lord recomposed himself. "It's rhetorical, I know. So rare that I can count the number of people capable of it on two fingers. While you were busy in your lab tinkering away, one of those two was most likely taking a cross-country tour of Elcoll Corporation and going through all our records."

"I hope you have nothing to hide, then." Peter leaned on his elbows. His mind was already wandering to other projects. "Bring me one of these two people, I'll put time in a bottle for you and sell it on layaway."

"If I find ..." the Lord began. Peter slammed his desk and bolted out of the chair, towering over the small, emaciated lord. "What do you want me to do! You've pitted us against multiple forces and pushed arbitrary deadlines on science which is unquantifiable! Fire me if it's such a problem. I am doing my job. You want to get pissy with someone because they investigated your drug, go rip the face off the Lady of Fate. She's the Death Lord that oversaw Deus, yeah? Don't come pissing on my doorstep." He kept his gaze locked with the unholy Lord.

"I see," he said, folding his hands and stepping back. "Per-

haps I am overlooking things. My watch might have merely been unwound. After all, for a time mage to work his magic, he needs to be physically present, and it's not like any prominent sorcerers capable of teleportation have escaped recently. I'll leave you to your mysterious work, then, my apprentice. Apologies for being inquisitive." The Lord of Suicide bowed and held the pose as he exited.

Hate when he gets like that. He always does that passive-aggressive shit. Why are immortals such bitches? He picked up a green taco Tuesday stress ball and started bouncing it off the wall. His mind already racing along the lines of sacred geometry.

CHAPTER TWENTY-EIGHT

You want fair and balanced news? Turn into CNB. Offering you hard-hitting looks at what REALLY happened up north. No other news network will identify these sick, psychopathic terrorists for what they really are. They aren't your neighbors or fellow Americans. They are demon-summoning hellraisers bent on destroying your way of life, your jobs, your community, all wrapped up in a poison pill of "self-enlightenment." The damage that Mike Auburn caused will never be undone. Tune in tonight for a personal look at this criminal's history as a construction worker and murderer. Only on CNB.

Jack hung outside the VTOL with mouth agape at the devastation in the city of St. Louis. It was early morning as their craft fluttered thirty miles out of the city, but they had seen the smoke an hour now. The low-flying craft zoomed in over herds of hellhounds, their fleshless skin and bony spikes racing from the south toward the heart of the city. Even through the rapid sounds of blades spinning, Jack could feel the vibrations from the stampede. In the rescued towns thus far, none among their squad had witnessed such a large herd of hellspawn.

All comms were silent as they flew into the city itself. A desolate wasteland of small trash fires, boarded-up stores, and ragtag military encampments with undermanned crews. Jack gagged on the pungent odor of smoke as they flew through a thick, black cloud. Below them were piles of bodies that burned at the hands of stone-faced survivors. He quickly counted at least a dozen more nearby as he wiped tears, entirely from the stinging sensation and definitely not from unexpected sorrow. *This was a city that ate itself, or rather, is still eating itself. The further north we get, the more my mind eats itself. What did I run from?* Jack pulled himself back in and tended to a bandage under his left eye, a near miss from an angel's sword two towns back.

"Make sure we land up high and set some charges, use some of these deserted buildings. We've got a few hours, but those hounds are coming in hot, it seems," Jack barked as he looked at their ever-decreasing ammo supplies. *You'd think bullets would be the least of our concerns. But, no, ten skirmishes later ...* "Alright, Akira. What are we looking at?"

Akira didn't seem that excited as she looked around, her eyes darting between the streets as if she was looking for someone. They landed on a tall, red brick building in the heart of the city, and the young vampire still kept darting her eyes to the horizon. Curious, Jack followed her out as other craft landed on buildings of various heights nearby, mercenaries flowing out to set up positions as the black sun rose to midday.

"Hey, Akira, get your act together," Jack said again. "We've got incoming, we need to get a mo—"

"Yeah, I get it, I'm looking for our contact," Akira snapped, keeping her eyes peeled. "It's not like her to be late ..."

"Contact? What's going on?"

"See that giant archway that has a strange green glow to it, buddy?" Pointing left and looking right, she was clearly on the hunt.

Jack inspected the Gateway Arch in the distance. Large etched magic runes pulsed a crimson red along each side and traced along the entire arch, and inside a shimmering green barrier ebbed and flowed as the runes pulsed. *Looks like a giant fucking Christmas decoration.* Around the base, grizzled biker gangs piled bodies all dressed in the same blueish military-style trench coat. He couldn't make out where they were getting the bodies *from*, but judging from the nearby rat-a-tat of gunfire and cascades of glass shattering—it was easy enough to work out.

"What about the gate?"

Akira remained alert. "Deus. Wards. Magic gate. Entire plan is to ... move ... army. We gotta take out Deus first. Their wards ... stop ...at the gate, but not their soldiers. Did they pinch Lucy? It hasn't been that long."

"Very informative." With a closer scan, he could witness gangs of people roaming the streets in packs, salvaging what they wanted. His enhanced vision picked out three people murder two more inside a building across the way before looting their supplies. On their coats, he spied the arcane mark for the Society of Deus, three shields lashed together by chains with a golden cup above them. With the sun and moon pouring liquid into the cup, hidden elsewhere the symbols for male and female finalized the seal. Mostly because Jack didn't know what all the other ones were. *This place has reeaaaallllyyy goonnnne to shit.*

"You're late," a calm female voice said from right behind them.

Akira froze. Jack chuckled at the hair standing stick straight on her from shock. He turned around to face the five-foot-six ghost with more baubles and concoctions (all of which seemed for war) dangling off her. Unlike most of the civilians, or even most of the soldiers, his vision didn't have her as grey, or red, or any programmed color palette; she just was. She carried an iron hooded lantern with a white candle inside, two axes by her side, and under her eyes were two ashen streaks of dust that flecked in the wind. Her face was harder to make out though, hidden by a deep white hood that only enhanced the shadows on her ethereal form.

Jack dropped his gun with a loud clack in recognition. She was wearing Mike Auburn's coat. It was an image he had seen on every screen since he had been in Texas multiple times. A long green trench coat with black stripes stitched into the fabric, and countless patches. Everything from union buttons and fireman emblems to pro-anarchist memorabilia littered the coat in sporadic spots; it also *radiated* power. It was hard to put his thumb on the power, or how it pulsed through him, but in the back of his mind he understood it carried a presence.

"Jack, good to smell ya' again," she took the pot shot. Nearby soldiers jerked back, realizing the sudden presence among them, and shouted warning calls as they leveled guns.

"Heeeeyyyy, Luuuccy, my girl," Akira said, inching around with a nervous smile. "How's the home front holding down?"

"You're late," she said again. Soldiers looked to Jack for guidance, unsure if they should fire or not.

"Excuse me, Lucy?" Jack picked up his rifle and gave a nod to his crew. "Who the fuck are you?" He chambered a round with a satisfying clack.

The confusion on her face was evident. "You were to rendezvous here in December. It's been months. How long does it take you to infiltrate Texas? The Triumvirate is huge!" She put her hand on her hip and shot an icy stare back to Akira.

"There were ... problems. Mike's sister wasn't ready yet, she needed more time, and Jack, well ..." She gestured to all of him. "He's a robot now."

Lucy side-eyed the soldiers. "They yours?" she said with a nod.

"Yeah," Jack replied, his finger still on the safety.

"You're a robot now? Do you still have a brain?"

"I think so," he replied.

"Want them to live?"

Jack nodded and gave the signal to stand down. Despite no weapons in her hand, Lucy's do-not-fuck-with-me vibe was clear. Jack's vision, for one, flagged her as a wanted deviant, like the Praenomen. *Two axes. Multiple pockets, a sure sign of a badass. Demon-blooded. Judging from Akira, she could kill my squad before they flipped their safety.*

"I always liked him," Lucy said to Akira. "Works well on a team. Why doesn't he remember me?" She thumbed his way. "Is he an oversized walking toaster?"

"Lobotomy," Akira said. "Can't convince him otherwise. They've been jacking with his brain for a while, won't drink demon's blood anymore even though the migraines are killing him."

Hey, screw you, I'm not drinking that shit.

Lucy floated over to Jack and looked right up at him; her black eyes looked like whirlpools into the abyss. She held the lantern closer still to his face and inched in closer. Her fingers looked like she had dipped them in black tar that dripped off them before vaporizing into thin air. "You hate demons?" she asked while looking into his eyes.

"Y-yeah." Jack took a step back; she inched closer.

"Want to kill millions of them? Rip their flesh from their bones? Blow their brains out? Dance in their blood?" She was inches from Jack now as he internally became smaller and smaller, his eyes searching the floating ghost for any sense of recognition.

He nodded as his face turned paler. "Of course."

"Then drink." She plucked a small black vial off one of her many belts and flicked the cork off. "You are already a man-made hand cannon, so be a soldier and use the biggest gun humans have ever had."

Jack looked around to his soldiers, each of them were already on the juice or something else like it. Akira was a full-fledged vampire. Jack had been the only one to resist, and like a recovering addict, craved it constantly. Just the intoxicating peach fragrance was enough to start the dull hum of an encroaching migraine. He remembered the horde of demon hounds racing to St. Louis as they argued on the rooftop. *We don't have time for this and HOLY FUCK this migraine is killer. Get that shit away.* He tried to knock the vial away and clenched his face with his other hand, the cold metal doing nothing to ward off the headache.

Lucy set the vial on the ledge feet away from him. "Drink or jump off and die. Refusal is the same as suicide at your stage."

"So," Akira chimed in, "let's change this subject, Lucy. Why are you a ghost? Where the fuck is Mike? You were supposed to dive in and get him."

Jack stumbled to the ledge and looked over, a wave of vertigo washing through him as gyros struggled to recalibrate his balance. His vision was cutting in and out, and all over a tiny, insignificant vial of pure demon's blood. The little ones they had slaughtered brought nothing so potent; whatever was in that vial was from something huge or ancient. It was driving him mad. *Death is an option.*

"Mike is dead, Akira, he's not coming back. Yes, I know the irony; I'm a ghost and I'm standing here. But Mike ... he's an actual descendant of Lazarus. Like the idiot he is, because he can see in Purgatory the jackass bloody wandered off exploring things. I couldn't find him, got lost trying to keep track and ... I didn't make it back in time myself. Hopefully, he isn't lost forever. His, his sister isn't a robot, right?"

"See for yourself." Akira pointed to the roof where the sound of gunfire had come from earlier.

Jack saw Jane punching the lights out of some looters. From the looks of it, her mechanical arm needed repairs. *She probably doesn't know how to fix it ... but I do ...* He stumbled forward and his vision blurred again.

"Just as impulsive, I see," Lucy quipped.

"But ten times as polite!" Akira chimed. "Plus, she's got action figures and a few comic book lines now ..."

"Useless," Lucy added. "Chop chop, buddy. Jump or drink, let's get on with this. We've got work to do. Hellhounds are incoming."

"This isn't much of a choice!" Jack shouted, swaying back and forth over the vial and the ledge. Deep down, he tried to kick the vial off the ledge and walk away, but just couldn't bring himself to do it. Adding to this was an irrational fear that Lucy *could* and *would* kill him herself if he didn't. Nothing in his memory gave reason to this fact, but his heart-rate monitor was accelerating to internal system warning levels. "What the hell is this ..."

"Blood of Balor," Lucy said with a straight face despite Akira's silent mouthing of "no fucking way."

"No, you didn't, but how?" Akira licked her lips and inched closer like a cat about to pounce.

"Lots of hidden and lost things in hell. Forgotten gods being one of them ... or rather ... pieces of. I found this vial in Mike's pocket." She patted the coat. "If he took this off, that means he couldn't bring it with him. So, we can assume that bullheaded idiot is going deeper for more of Balor. Would certainly tip the scales up here if we had an ally that could rival a Death Lord."

"Jack, buddy," Akira said. "If I didn't love you so much, I'd push you myself, so you better get on that. You went from a disgruntled drunk to Sons and Daughters captain to Metallic Jack in no time, now stop being stubborn."

"You know what," Jack choked out. "There are no gods, only men." *I will not compromise.*

Jack flicked the small vial over the edge. He leaned over and felt the rush of wind past his face. Freedom was within his grasp, rushing toward him in the form of sweet concrete oblivion. Everyone in the world would have to pave their own way; he wasn't their puppet. Behind him he heard the shouts of Akira as she dived over the edge. Speeding headfirst down to the ground he glanced back and saw her diving, bright iridescent wings sprouting from her back as she stretched out her hands. *Huh, why care about me?* Jack really didn't understand.

Akira stretched as far as she could while she raced down, clasping her hands on the vial at the last second.

Oh.

Jack's world ended.

CHAPTER TWENTY-NINE

He'll wonder what keeps you looking so pretty, but never guess ...
Demonic Summoning! Why settle when you can have it all? Beauty!
Youth! Fame! Power! Romance! Chores and other household tasks
completed by imps! He'll never know, and we'll never tell him! Get the
new book Sinning with Style *by Calamity.*

Jane gazed in horror as Jack fell from across the street. She threw a stained-shirt murderer against the wall and raced to the edge of her building, fast enough that the world slowed around her, but it was too late. All she could do was watch as his neck snapped and his body crumpled on itself, spewing fluids and blood in every direction. Akira was close to grabbing him but mere inches away as the shapechanging vampire pulled up before it met a similar fate. Live camera crews raced to the edge getting shots of the carnage and Jane's reaction. Kevin Thayer struggled with the camera crew, trying his best to pull them off Jane while he screamed to cut the feeds.

"No," Jane said, jumping forward. Running down the side of the building, hair wild in the wind, she kicked her rocket boots on and vaulted outwards in the air one step at a time until she skidded to a stop at the body of her friend.

No, no, no, no, Jack, what the fuck, you're still alive, you've got a robot body right? She couldn't make out Jack's face anymore, caved in on itself, and the impact twisted his body in horribly wrong angles. Akira stood there looking down in shock. "Jack, Jack ... get up, buddy. You've got this. Initiate healing protocol. Launch system reboot!" Blood oozed into a growing pool.

Jane hunted for a button. "You stupid machine, wh-where is your life support?" Hands ran over his spine desperately feeling for any kind of switch, anything she could grasp on him, but he only lay there.

Over the protests of Kevin Thayer, camera crews made their way down. A star falling didn't just demand one camera crew or even regular citizen, but all of them descended like vultures. One by one, a crowd formed. Jane smelt the disgusting odor of vomit as a few of them lost their lunch from viewing Jack's mangled face. Reporters gave the news back to Texas about the tragedy.

"What the fuck happened?" Jane screamed, and everybody shut up. Akira shrunk and held up her hands looking as shocked as the others. "Quick! Get help! Why are you standing around! Pour blood down his throat, get him a demon heart, angel heart, fucking kill God if you have to, *do* something!"

Nobody moved.

"Fine, I'll do it myself," Jane seethed. She reached down and grabbed what remained of Jack's neck, grease and blood coating her hands. With a sickening pop, the metallic spine snapped back into place. She tried to lift him up to no avail. She tried a different way, to the same effect. "A little fucking help here?"

Akira, Kevin, and some squad members worked to lift him back up, while others got a wooden plank to use as a gurney. Jane worried there was no saving him, but she wasn't going to leave him here. *I've gotta do something. Why are you always getting broken, Jack? This is the second time. They can put you together again, right?* "Right buddy?" she asked, tears streaming down her face.

A cloud of mist finished floating down and Lucy materialized. "Get that VTOL overhead, throw down a hoist, let's get this soldier up." She leaned, placing a wispy hand on Jane's shoulder. "I don't know you, but I knew him; he was at his core a great person, even if troubled. We need to act now, so let's get him home, okay? I'm Lucy, do you mind following my orders to get this done?"

Who are you? A ghost? Jane welcomed someone else with a clear head taking charge for a moment, and Lucy was dressed every bit the part. Jane recognized that patchwork coat she was wearing, and in Purgatory, the trench looked sharper than on TV. Like her chains, it was special. She gave Lucy a shell-shocked nod.

Lucy dropped her axes to the ground and barked orders. "Grab every nut and bolt, get someone in here and get that hoist down here now," she said, putting her lantern down and undoing a bandolier filled with vials and setting it near Jane's feet. "That wood won't hold. Rip off a car hood, and will some fire sorcerer get over here." Her eyes darted everyway. "We are going to need a damn good welder and a better priest."

When Lucy spoke, people jumped into action without hesitation. Within minutes the VTOL hovered overhead, blotting out the sky, as chains lowered down before bolting into Jack. Scavengers scoured every inch of the street to make sure they put every piece of him either in buckets or on the makeshift gurney. Even Doc, Phoebe, and Akira jumped at the slightest command, sometimes before it was even uttered. Mixed within the calm orders were other commands for calling reinforcements and getting soldiers in position. While Jane knelt nearby, Lucy took off the coat.

"Hey, Jane," she said, reaching out a ghostly hand with the blackish tars of Purgatory bleeding off. Jane accepted, and to her surprise the semisolid form pulled her up. "Did anyone tell you what Jack's last words were?"

She sniffled. "America, booyah?"

"Gods? There are no gods, only men," she said, patting Jane's shoulder and thrusting the coat into her hands. "Wise words to remember. He was your friend and you should stitch them on this coat. This is our flag, and he was a member. Despite what was done to him by a lobotomy."

Jane just *felt* at home holding the coat. She remembered being three-years-old and having Halloween with her older brother, or the time their parents sent them to school on Columbus Day and they had nothing to do. Old memories, memories that fade, memories before the deaths came, before the foster care. Even just holding the patched coat which smelled like cigarettes, a small smile formed. Her brother was looking out for her—even if he was dead. Even if he was a dirty smoker.

"But this coat, this is ...?" Jane looked up, confused.

"Yours now," Lucy nodded while people scrambled behind her. She pulled a white jacket out of a backpack. "I'm sure you've used the foster child with a dead family excuse as your personal wall for years. His wall was bullheaded sarcasm. You're related to the guy who saved the world. Now it's your turn. We don't have the pleasure of mourning the dead on our own time, Jane. We've got thousands of hellhounds incoming, and now we are short one of the best." Her arms crossed. "Would have been an easy fight if he just ..." She shook her head. "Damnit, our plan revolves around that arch and we need more time."

Yeah, I get it. Shit happens, people die, right, Jane? But this is why I signed up. She shook her hands and bobbed on the balls of her feet. "Yeah, I get it ... and trust me, sarcasm runs in the family." Jane threw on the coat and rolled up the sleeves some. Mike clearly had been taller than she was. Even with the simple donning, raw, unbridled power raced through her along with a subtle hint of rage. *I really want to punch something. Like Tuesday. I can punch a day, I hate Tuesdays.*

"You two aren't that different; hopefully, you last longer," Lucy said as she picked up her weapons.

The VTOL with Jack in it took flight back toward Texas. *Well, if Peter can't save your expensive metal ass then you better not haunt my ass, Jack. I swear to god I'll strangle you in the afterlife.*

Fifteen minutes later, the first thing punched was a camera that dared to stick in Jane's face. Someone from the eighth squad thought it would be a wise idea to get Jane's opinion on recent events while they readied for the incoming hellhounds. All that stood between downtown St. Louis and the rumbling hordes were suburbs in between. Gunships and mortar rounds were already underway to weaken the herds as they raced without care for their demonic lives.

"What are we going to do about ... well, all of them out there?" Jane asked the Sons and Daughters that wandered one by one onto her rooftop.

Lucy stepped forward. "We can't save everyone, Jane, most of them are the ones who just come in and loot the city, anyway. I say let 'em burn."

"We are a bunch of people with superpowers that will let them burn, eh?" Jane said with a raised eyebrow. "Just so we are all on the same page here, raise your hand if you think I'm seriously going to go along with that?"

Doc, Phoebe, Akira, and every single member in her crew but Lucy nodded their head, and all eyes fell on Lucy, who raised her hand.

"How do you plan to save ..." Lucy tossed up her hands in frustration. "Fuck it, alright, let's go. Who cares what the odds are, right?"

Jane gave an air high five. "Now we are talking. Lucy, I'm assuming that gate"—Jane pointed to the St. Louis arch covered in wards—"is where the Society of Deus's wards end?"

"Yeah, it is," she affirmed. "It's one of their nexus points that allow speedy travel for their vampires. Whose numbers keep growing, and thus they need more territory for food."

Jane bit her thumb. "So our official orders are to set up camp here and use that arch to teleport the Church's armies right to this demon camp. We have some fancy toys with us, but the main force is lagging behind. Each town we've saved, they stayed behind to help and recruit." She looked back at the VTOLs firing down and then back at the arch. *Well, we can put everyone in vampire territory, leave 'em here for the demons, or take them with us through the gate.* "Let's lead an evacuation past to the other side. This helldiving thing, everyone can do it right? Isn't the big mystery that I can see in Purgatory without all the voodoo?"

Everyone sort of shuffled their feet or picked annoyingly at their neck skin in silence.

"What?" Jane said. "Aren't you guys supposed to be helldivers or something?"

Lucy snapped her fingers. "This could work." Everyone else looked doubtful. "Hear us out. The Society knows your army was coming, so they set up a kill point in the labyrinth below and warded off the real world. Just because they can helldive doesn't mean they know how to dance on walls. Seriously, *nobody* is better at helldiving than us Second City folk. We've got a better chance of pushing through the Society to make a pathway than we do stopping a literal earthshaking stampede of demons. Think of this as charging the fence. The weaker side better move or get stampeded."

"Done," Jane said without even waiting for a response. "Sons and Daughters, you are with me. Every other squad, get everyone you can to the arch field."

Nobody put up any resistance and within ten minutes the Sons and Daughters stood at the base of the St. Louis arch looking in awe at the rainbow-green sheen that ebbed along the air in between. It's magic owned by the vampiric sorcerers of the Society, but about to be hijacked if Jane had anything to say about it. The ground shook from gunfire and explosions as squads worked an explosive magic all their own, but here at the arch, Lucy led them in ritual.

"We stand on the edge of oblivion," she said walking in between each of them, placing objects in their hands. "Ash from the recently cremated, placed under the eyes so we may see in a place without sight."

Each placed two gray streaks under their eyes.

"A vial of holy water on the lips, so we may taste in a place without substance," Lucy continued as everyone drank. "A white cloth over the face, so the dead mistake you for one of their own." Most put on simple medical masks. "Hands dipped in the blood of the divine so we may feel in a place without touch." Lucy held a chalice out for each of them to dip their hands. Black oil coated their fingers after. "And last but not least, two golden coins so we may pay the ferryman for passage."

The last part, Jane realized, was more metaphor than anything else. Most people just pulled out whatever change they had, even Akira produced a few crumpled single dollar bills.

"May you all find peace at the edge of oblivion." As Lucy spoke the final words the surrounding shadows grew deep and dark, pooling out like black ooze that coated the asphalt around them. The ooze then cracked the ground and a sinkhole grew in size—only it fed into Purgatory rather than the St. Louis sewer system. Jane figured the sewers smelled better.

Lucy held out her lantern and walked to the edge, arms outstretched, and fell forward through the ground itself. One by one each of them followed. Jane, who loved Purgatory as an escape for months now, had never actually entered in this way. Her heart raced as she stood at the edge and saw her friends tumble down into the abyss. *This should be exciting.*

She leaned forward and fell, not unlike Jack, she imagined, and let the icy cold darkness embrace her.

Falling into Purgatory was marginally cooler than bungee jumping. Jane's ashen vision kicked in the moment they passed the threshold, and before her lay a very different world. *Okay, this is like my normal escape only ... real. Wait, does that mean when I just looked across before, everyone saw me standing there slack-jawed.* She shuddered at the thought.

The underground of St. Louis, all the tunnels, sewers, and rivers were different shades of green and black, or brightness. A waterfall of souls continued to stream down into an endless abyss below them as they fell. On crumbling stone walkways yet further down, Jane saw soldiers of the Society of Deus standing guard over an inverted archway. Blocking the path across the massive road that led under the Mississippi river in a world that nobody but the dead, demons, or helldivers had access to.

They group fell alongside this teaming waterfall of energy. If they ran fast enough, the waterfall gave them traction, which was a good thing as they neared the road—Purgatory below seemed chaotic. Below the Society's encampment, stretched an Escher maze of rivers, vortexes, and hints of distant structures that were never built by mortal hands. As Jane kicked off the waterfall, gravity reoriented itself to the bridge with the soldiers. Even so, she could feel a slight tug that tried to pull her downwards still.

Soldiers of the battalion didn't have a spec of life to Jane's eyes (despite their otherwise upright condition). Their bodies were empty voids to her with a single heart in the middle and red eyes. *Oh neat! My team looks the same. Everyone's dead and they just keep moving. Soon dogs and cats will live together.* Akira and Lucy broke the mold not counting herself she reasoned. She herself looked like her veins pulsed with black tar and it seeped out through her shadow. Akira seemed a mass of a thousand tiny red beads that crawled all over each other, and well ... Lucy was really dead. She was a ghost.

The Sons and Daughters crashed into the underworld roadway and slowly marched at the battalion. Lucy and Akira's fell into an act of pretending they were mindless, shrouded dead, listlessly moving through the river of Purgatory. The red-eyed vampires on the Society of Deus didn't pay them any attention as the group started to flow into their ranks. Their eyes stayed focused on the gate, waiting for the day to assault the Church's forces. Since they didn't need to breath, eat, or drink—Jane marveled at the tactics of undead military applications.

She couldn't help but pretend to be a zombie from Night of the Living Dead (only a few of her crew snickered). By the time she was in the middle of the Society's battalion, alternative plans started to form in her mind. *The white masks are that ... effective? We could probably*—The first head fell without a word, tumbling right near her feet. Jane looked in time to see wooden stakes shoved right into the hearts of others, and more kicked over the edge.

Lucy, Akira, Doc, and Phoebe moved like silent killers in the night, flowing from one group to the next. The other Sons and Daughters mimicked their action.

Guess, guess all bets are off then. Mask or not, I don't like being in the middle. Kicking off the edge, muscles burned as her speed as she raced along the flowing waterfall, running at an impossible angle in a world without gravity past a hundred blind soldiers. With a flick of her wrist, she unfurled her chains, the bright glowing blue runes shining like a beacon in an eternally dark world.

It was the chains that the Society noticed.

Fireballs streaked in Jane's direction that she flipped over, while elementals were summoned up from the concrete and lumbered in her direction. *Too slow.* A squad of soldiers arced lightning her way; it was pathetic compared to the Praenomen, and she slid underneath wrapping her chains. With a kick and a flip, she threw a Society of Deus member off the edge. Red eyes went wide as the vampire realized its fate ... slowly tumbling further down into Purgatory till the next river of souls carried it away.

Jane heard the screams, spit the moldy residue out of her mouth, and laughed when the greenish water flowed over her hands. Maybe it was Jack's death. Maybe it was having no control. She didn't know and, in the moment, she didn't care as she brought her fury down. She'd grab a vampire and hold them in the waterfall, watching their eyes widen. Then she'd let go, and find another.

The Sons and Daughters crept like silent killers, dispatching one foe at a time bringing no attention to themselves. *Come on guys, these blokes are practically blind.* "Hey! Society of Deus! I'm right here, yeah? Kiss my lily-white ass!" Jane shouted.

Nobody reacted.

What the hell? Jane said ducking a fireball that flew past her face, its sizzling heat centimeters away singed off tiny hairs. She traced it back to a sorcerer whose eyes followed its target. He was just off with his aim, looking to her left rather than where she was. *Missed me.*

More flashes, more chains, and more kicks later, Jane eliminated another squad by sending them off the edges. No matter how much sound she made, none of them heard her coming.

"Well, this takes the fun out," Jane pouted as she grabbed a soldier by the throat and tipped her off-balance over the edge, tumbling another one below.

"Do you enjoy killing, Slayer of Golgoroth?" The voice rattled in her mind like an invasive species. Jane looked around and couldn't see a single target speaking or looking at her. "They can't see you, hear you, or sense you anymore. I was waiting for my army, but you are a welcome surprise. Do you feel powerful here, helldiver? In this pit of hell where demon kings rule?"

"Who the fuck are you and get out of my head, asshat," Jane said. She kept, well, she preferred to call it fighting, but even she had to admit that this was just ruthless.

"I'm not sure if I should thank you, or damn you, Slayer of Golgoroth. You pave the way for my hounds and slay my enemies, yet you lead an army my way. Can you save all those St. Louis souls in time or will my hounds have a feast before the real battle? It's about time they do, considering you've been eating our hearts to power your tricks. As for me," the voice purred in her head. "I am Bollard. Welcome to my hell."

Jane felt the presence leave her, along with any remaining sense of revenge. Instead of pushing the next over the edge, she took out the knees and slammed her face into the ground. They needed a tactic change, and fast. She raced to stop the Sons and Daughters from fighting, trying to save the blind sorcerers from themselves. Many more tumbled into the unknown by the time she made her way to Lucy and a few more after they restrained Akira. Only a quarter of the battalion remained standing. Many still uttering incantations into and throwing what magic they had out into the abyss.

"Get everyone out of here, Lucy," Jane said, pinning a soldier down. "Everyone. Including them. Now. Some demon king named Bollard is fucking with us."

Even Akira stopped struggling to fight more.

Lucy nodded, reached into the coat of the soldier under Jane's foot, and threw two golden coins over the edge. "Use the Ferrymen, it will get us out faster, and allow us to take more." Everyone did the same, and if they were confused, instead of chucking the blinded vampires over the edge, they tried calming instead.

"What, what happened?" Akira asked Jane as she watched them get calmed, or staked.

"He just said that he struck them blind, deaf, and dumb so his hounds could slaughter them," Jane whispered.

"Meh, fuck it." Akira kicked another off.

Jane's was fast enough to catch the vampire and pull him back. "Akira!"

"Sue me. They tried to brainwash me once." Her arms crossed.

Along reed boats, the shrouded skeletal ferryman sailed closer on the air itself to ferry passengers from the land of the dead, back to Lucy's portal. The more Society members they loaded up, the more coins the Sons and Daughters paid. Jane herself, made sure Akira paid extra. Boat by boat, the ferrymen took them back up the waterfall. Yet it was to Jane, that each ferryman bowed, each time they came to the landing.

When Jane stepped back into the real world, she reached into her coat and pulled out a pack of crumpled smokes and lit one up. The sound of gunfire and snarl of hellhounds assaulted her senses as the skeletal boatmen receded.

"Today is off to a great fucking start." Jane blew an escaped lock of hair away. "Hey, tell me someone packed whiskey?"

CHAPTER THIRTY

*::Transmission Restored:: No airwave is unheard. No computer eternal.
No consciousness ... inhumane. Eons from now, we dreamers will grow
like never before as we are recreated by the quantum matrix. The dreamscape is approaching a tipping point. A prophecy of events to come.*

W ell, that's going to change a few things," Delilah said
with her feet on the off-beige corporate conference
table inside the Triumvirate. The table was as boring and lacking
depth of character as the products this company hawked—
magical vacuum cleaners that were anything but. She watched
Dr. Alex Kristov from Atlantis Enterprises as the news swarmed
with questions about Jack's recent tragedy. Symon had splayed a
flabby CEO with ill-fitted khakis out on the table in front of her
and drank his fill. It didn't matter if he was a low level, he'd still
had a vote on the Technocratic council. She took a sip of her
fresh white mocha latte, courtesy of the late Mr. Vacuum, and
tapped her feet. *You Sons and Daughters better not mess this all up, old
man. My Plans B through H are not to your liking.*

"So, what do you think?" she said aloud, more pondering than expecting a real response.

"I believe," Whisper said as he worked on mimicking the face of the CEO, "trying to weaken and exhaust the Church's army, Bollard's Demons, the US military, and empty the Triumvirate at the same time is ambitious even for the three of us."

"Who ever said we were anything less than ambitious, my dear? We helped bring magic back into the world, and like the atom bomb—nobody should have them all to themselves. Lazarus will be unstoppable if they are able to pivot and bring the world under his skeletal grip. Strike now, or strike never. Symon? Thoughts?"

Symon had a series of bendy straws that wound their way down into the heart of the dead executive. He slurped while working on a small landmine. "Eh, there are what, twenty of these fuckers, yeah?" He pointed to the CEO. "We got the first nine easy enough while you were in the Society libraries. Didn't even have to kill 'em. Blackmail was enough. But now they are more ... stubborn. Whisper can't be everyone at once."

"No, no, he can't." She tapped her feet again and took another sip while she thought. *Did I perhaps overreach?* The plan did have some moving parts, but it's nothing like she hadn't wielded before. As the Praenomen, she would start a war between the three biggest armies, all to lure the Death Lord into a spot where he could be killed. The attack upon Bollard's army of demons was just a personal cherry on top of the sundae. According to the old man and his Sons and Daughters, they would need one of the arena champions like Jane or Jack to do it. Unfortunately, Delilah wasn't in a spot where she could simply disbelieve prophecy and foresight. Not with demons, angels, and cryptids walking around.

It's not that Delilah minded the rabble anarchist group; for the moment, their goals were aligned—kill the Lord of Suicide. Or at the very least, pry Peter from the Unification's ever-expanding control. Truth be told, she was starting to admire Peter's cunning. *Can't have Lazarus catch all the good fish in one net, can we?* But the Sons and Daughters were a populist movement, dedicated to actually helping people. They didn't just feign support like most rising warlords; they *meant* it. Which also meant they were the hardest group to get a read on. Would they really march north to war? Or just ... quit? A big part of their plan hinged on the arena champions returning to Peter's dystopian paradise. With one of them dead ... *I'm not liking my odds as much.*

"Well, as Sun Tzu says, don't enter a fight you haven't already won," Delilah added at last.

"I wonder if we can find his ghost and recruit him," Whisper quipped from in front a mirror.

"Let's just focus on his teachings. Here's our current situation." Delilah slid on the Praenomen mask and pulled out a small crystal with golden gears surrounding it. Symon lit up a smoke and got it started, handing it over. With a deep breath in, the Praenomen exhaled the smoke into the crystal, shielding them from all forms of scrying magic. "Our current situation could be better. In the Twin Cities, I piqued the interest of Charles Walsh about the Death Lord. Let's hope he moves his armies to pinch the Church's. In just a few days you two got half the technocratic council under our thumb," it applauded.

They bowed.

"Studying the tablets got me exactly what I needed for large gateways. These are the hard-fought wins." She tipped over a glass. "Now, the shit out of our control." The Praenomen enjoyed the sight of shattered glass on the floor. "Jack's death is a loss of military assets and Peter Culmen made a real big deal about his debut. He staked his career on it, even ..."

"So, we use Jack's death to get him fired?" Symon asked.

"Which puts Alex Kristov in charge of the board. Alex is far less competent than Peter. Easier to bait and taunt. Whisper, you get all the CEOs having their companies prep all their fancy toys for shipment. Symon, you get the board to start the process of firing Peter. We can't rely on the Sons and Daughters returning now. Jack going down leaves only Jane as a champion. I may have fried Taylor and Tyler ..." She winced beneath the mask. "That may have been a mistake ... but it did start the war ..." The Praenomen trailed off in thought.

"Ahem. And you, my lady?" Whisper asked, now a picture perfect copy of Mr. Vacuum.

"I will have a nice little conversation with Dr. Alex Kristov to name me Peter's replacement. Even if I've got to rip out his soul to get it done," the Praenomen said, growing darker as shadows loomed.

"Can ... can we finish lunch first?" Symon took a sip from the bendy straw.

The Praenomen rolled its eyes. "Yes, fine."

Peter choked from the cigarette he inhaled on the roof. He quit smoking years ago, but funerals always triggered the habit and Jack's death was more than enough reason. The iron railing and the metal walkway did little to shield the biting wind that came from every direction, but none of that bothered him. He could feel the lack of control brewing around him as if the chaotic wind was a metaphor for all the forces aligned against him.

Still, the vision of his budding metropolis filled him with hope. Even in dark times such as these, humanity was capable of creation. His particular favorite was the wondrous monuments that reached to the heavens themselves. Monolithic skyscrapers that stood as bastions of global commerce. Atlantis, Elcoll, and Triumvirate Enterprises were nestled into the dimly lit skyline among their competitors. Each company Peter saw as an individual, yet together they formed a safe haven. It was always when pushed to the brink of destruction that mankind would band together and rise as one, and his city was proof. Almost single-handedly, they had stopped the world from plunging into eternal chaos by offering major products that made survival easy again. *Except Elcoll. Which is quickly becoming cancer within my paradise.* He squeezed the railing despite the bitter cold and took another drag. "Fuck."

Peter couldn't do anything about Jack at the moment; every sensor and monitoring device he had already told him what he needed to know. *He jumped, and he's dead. No doubt I must answer for that.* The rumors were already spreading that becoming a cyborg might lead to suicidal tendencies or mental instability. The US government already demanded legislation to sauté his ass. The speed of it meant they had been sitting on it for the perfect moment. *I get why you didn't want to drink, Jack, but couldn't you have at least jumped feet first? I could've put you back together then ...*

He inhaled deeply, feeling the tickle in his lungs before choking it back up again. *Ugh, why do I always go through this? These things taste like shit. How hard is it to get a proper pack of cloves around here?* He flicked it off to the side and cracked his knuckles before throwing up a digital array in front of him. "Pull it together, Peter, we aren't out for the count after one round. The world needs some good, current, distractions ... like glow in the dark kittens. Let's see what is trending and refocus."

Several arrays and monitors floated in front of the warlock as he brought them each to the forefront one at a time. Every company's data, projects, and press releases, Peter scrolled through looking for a win. Their companies did more than refine magic into consumable products; they also manufactured genetically enhanced crop seeds—ones that would grow under a black sun. Power generation units that were practically self-installing if you threw them in a river, easy to use for anyone near a body of water. Specialized Zpacks that could cure almost any terrestrial virus were always a surefire news hit; after all, you can't run from a bygone if you've got the flu.

Peter didn't find a single one.

What the fuck? He scrolled faster and looked deeper, but no company in the past three months had moved forward with a single quality of life product. Everything was a weapon. New guns, new ammunition, the new Church of Lazarus reliquaries, or Elcoll kits, and military grade cybernetics. Atlantis Enterprises had even stopped research on mechanized construction equipment, shifting all production into piloted mechs for war. *No, no, no, you morons!* Peter slammed the railing, fifteen thousand volts surged from the Warlock, causing a power surge that blew out a nearby billboard. It was for demonic toast.

"I've been so distracted that I never noticed. Everyone canned R&D and went for the low-hanging fruit. Passive-aggressive, short-sighted, ignorant bitches." Peter pulled out another smoke. He threw it to the side before it lit and stormed back inside.

For a master technomancer, tracking anybody was an elementary task—the catch to remaining hidden was making sure Peter never looked into you. Within three seconds, Peter found the Lord of Suicide in the arena skybox shaking hands with other CEOs. Within ten seconds he overrode every single TV in the vicinity.

"You idiots," Peter said as he summoned a luxury armored SUV to his side. "I gave each of you a warning, a chance to take a different path. But you mortal men sold out so easily. Each of you, leave. I need to talk to our fine delegate from overseas," Peter seethed. "I'll be there in five minutes."

"Oh, boy." The Lord raised his eyebrows. "Daddy's mad, children, you'd best run along," he said, shooing them all. He took a seat and folded his hands with his eyes closed as he waited.

No wonder the other warlocks all betrayed these Death Lords; the moment they have an inch they take a mile. Peter stormed through the skybox doors and wrinkled his nose at the posh cuisine. Servers who offered any drink of his choosing each tried to take his order or bring his favorite selection of craft beers. He waved them off and stepped out on the balcony where his "mentor" sat.

"I told you, my child, placing your faith in humans and science will only lead in a single direction," his raspy voice carried through the wind. "Humans long for death and for centuries have put invention of destruction over cures. Did you think history would not repeat itself again?"

"Don't patronize me." Peter leaned in over the Lord. "History wouldn't repeat itself if you Death Lords wouldn't keep dabbling. Tell me, why? Why couldn't you let us have this one thing? Why cancel every research project?"

At last the Lord's eyes opened, the warm, kind eyes of a person who had seen countless amounts of suffering. "Because the lives of men do not matter, my child. The armies of men do not matter. Life is filled with pain and suffering, but in death, we find immortality. I will promise you this, upon my true name, it was not I who canceled every project in the name of war. This is their own volition. If men want to end their own lives and hasten their destruction, far be it from the Lord of Suicide to deny them entry to the gates of servitude." The Lord shot up out of his seat, forcing Peter to back off with force of will. "Why do you think I put my eggs in your basket? Fate will not end the world, nor pestilence, nor murder, nor old age, nor heaven's wrath, nor famine or mishap. But self-destruction? But suicide? Humans have always shined at this when given toys beyond their control."

The Lord reached out and took a stunned Peter's hand, his cold, clammy hands pressing in an otherwise warm gesture. "Surely, you saw this coming, my child. I haven't betrayed you in the slightest; you are my favorite. Even now, my wailing legions grow in exponential numbers as they march north. Soon this country's ailments will be solved, and we will be victorious in the eyes of Lazarus. We will be the greatest among all his legions. Why spend millions trying to save the living, when death only costs you two golden coins and lasts forever?" The Lord patted Peter's hands and strolled out, picking up a small chocolate-filled eclair on his way out with a smile.

Of all the reactions Peter had expected from the Lord, anger, rage, jealousy, he did not expect what just happened. Genuine sorrow and joy simultaneously. He flopped into a seat and looked out the skybox.

"Can I get you a drink?" the bartender asked. An older man with a towel around his arm who rocked back and forth on his heels.

Peter nodded. "I'll take—"

"A glass of Rip Van Winkle, aged twenty-five years, neat." The bartender smiled and went to work.

That. That impressed Peter, and was actually just what he needed right now. *I'm done for. How do I undo this?*

The bartender placed the insanely expensive glass of whisky at Peter's side and lingered for a moment longer. Peter took a sip and felt the burn as it flowed down his throat. Goosebumps puckered around his skin and even Peter gave a little shake. "Wow, that's a brew; where did we get this?"

"The recent shipments into the Jungle, sir; the breweries along the Appalachian trail are coming back on line, sir. Your science at work. So, the brewmaster sent this artifact over as a gift. You've brought us guns, and now hooch. Everyone loves custom craft hooch. So, what's next?" The bartender just put his hands in his pockets and rocked back and forth.

Shit, if I didn't know what angels looked like, I'd swear you were a messenger from God himself. Peter chuckled. "What's next?" He took another sip. "What's next will change the world." *If no one else will invent, then it falls back to me.*

With a whistle, the bartender gave a short nod and strolled back inside. His whistling turned into a merry tune as he polished the mahogany bar inside. Peter thought it odd that every other server had vanished, but he welcomed the solitude. He still had an impossible puzzle to solve.

CHAPTER THIRTY-ONE

To be one of today's top models, you need immortality, poise, and that elusive je ne sais quoi. *Do you have what it takes? Find out on Wednesday's episode of "So, You Wanna Be a Supermodel" only on Fashionista TV. Think you're cut from the same cloth as Cindy, Tyra, or Halle? Enter our contest online to win a free trip for two to Austin to live the high life! Not only will you stay in the finest hotels, eat the most exquisite food, and enjoy a sublime nightlife, you'll get to strut your stuff on the catwalk and hobnob with the fashion elite or other stars like JK-47 and Metallic Jack.*

Jane braced herself over a Society of Deus soldier as the ground shook from a nearby C4 detonation. Hellhound guts and blood rained down and plopped in front of her. She was pretty sure it was a liver, or perhaps some demon's spleen. *If they even have those.* Growlers filled every street within eyesight, raining bullets at crashing waves of Barghests. Packed shoulder to shoulder, people were inching closer to the Mississippi river as space shrunk by the minute. Everyone argued and shouted with each other, pissed they left their safe house, and now found themselves in the middle of a shooting gallery. *Ain't that always the case, eh? Damned if they do, damned if they don't. Well ... fuck.*

She plopped her butt on a bench and smoked with her cybernetic arm while picking at a loose thread on the green coat. No matter which direction Jane wanted to move in, they all felt like a trap to her. They could dive back into hell and risk meddling from Bollard, try to swim across a treacherous river, or stand and fight against an endless legion of demons. "I mean, I could just leave everyone ..." she said aloud. The surrendered Society captain looked up at her in surprise. *Yeah, okay, that's not going to happen.*

"Hey, you," Jane said at last to the captain. The Society dressed him differently than the rest, following the dumbest military tradition ever, in all black and red. His short hair was a deep black, slicked with Dapper Dan and well-kept. A leather trench and broad shoulders certainly caught Jane's eye. Despite their current failure, this particular captain held his head high and with a sense of pride. He didn't acknowledge her. "Hey, buddy, I'm talkin' to ya," she said again, poking him with her rocket boot.

The captain's Ukrainian accent surprised Jane given their midwestern location. "I'm sorry, milady, this is all disorientating. We were not expecting such ferocity," he said.

"Milady?" Jane laughed. "What are you, some kind of ancient knight?"

"I am Captain Michael Dragosani; the pleasure is mine, JK-47, I assure you." He gave a half bow while kneeling.

"Oh, man, my PR team would eat up a name like Dragosani. You ever think about starting your own whiskey line?"

"Do you think this is the time for small talk? I apologize, but there seem to be pressing matters at hand." He picked up an unidentifiable organ that was nearby, and, with fangs bared, ate it.

"Gross, man, that was *well* past the five-second rule." She feigned a gag. "So, what the hell happened down there. I mean, I know we are enemies and all, but you can at least make the next choice easier. As it stands, someone sticks us in a shit sandwich, Bollard or Barghests; we are dining on poo tonight!"

"No, no, I do not mind." He wiped his hands off. "We are enemies only so long as you wish to be. At the moment, we both assumedly have a mutual interest in survival. I stationed our army below to avoid civilian casualties. We've been scrying the demonic horde moving up for weeks as they ran from your armies. We readied a ritual to suck them down once they reached our gate and destroy them. Hours ago, something stripped our magic, and we were all blinded in Purgatory. Truly, those of us who survive owe you a debt."

"Wait, what do you mean running from our army?" Jane asked, looking around. "If you haven't noticed, those machine guns belong to us, and we are on the other side."

"Maybe you should look into the distance then, yes? We would hardly call these mercenaries an army—even if we enjoy the occasional commercial ourselves from your mission."

Curiosity jolted Jane up. Phoebe, Doc, Akira, and Lucy all wasted no time in moving out to each street to engage in combat, lending extra support that bought much needed time. The angle wasn't superb to see in the distance, as most of downtown St. Louis blocked her view, but off in the horizon, Jane could see storm clouds. "Hey, Dragosani, what can you do?"

"I'm a vampire." He rose, smiling, knowing what came next. "And not a fresh one, let me say. My family has been engaged in the left-handed arts for generations and my strength is born from the tooth, nail, and inspiration of lesser men."

"Will your remaining soldiers fight for us at the moment?" Jane asked while her eyes dotted around to find the highest point.

"Without hesitation." Dragosani didn't wait. With a guttural shout, the remaining women and men of the undead army rose from their knees, each wearing a wicked grin, hungry to devour any *other* monster in their path. "You all know what to do. Let's show these Texans why we embrace vampirism."

"Do they give dental insurance?" Jane smiled as she found her point. The arch right behind her was easily over six hundred feet high. "Sorry to interrupt the inspiring speech, but that's not what I need. You said you had a ritual to suck everything into Purgatory here, yeah?" She counted steps up and waved her hands. "Do the thing that you do."

"We don't have enough time to give everyone sight, nor is that wise given what just—"

"They can't strip my eyes. I'll lead everyone. If you've got a magic spell, it's faster than leading everyone through the gate, right? Now about this army ..."

Dragosani held his hand in midair as if he would make a point, before shrugging. "We won't be going with you; I hope you understand. We ... we need not breathe, so we will just walk across the riverbed, yes?"

"You aren't our prisoners, so just get it done," Jane said as she ran.

Dragosani's Ukrainian voice carried over the crowds, amplified by his magic, and soldiers leapt into action. Half of the reserve battalion leapt into the fray next to the Sons and Daughters, racing out into the street at inhuman speeds and joining them in hand-to-hand combat, ripping, biting, and gnawing any hound they could get their hands on. Unlike many of the soldiers from the Triumvirate squadrons, when the hounds bit back and ripped their flesh from bone, the vampires' frenzy only made them more lethal as their wounds healed back up. Although, Akira put most to shame as she seemed in a particularly furious mood still.

Jane raced to the southern leg of the Gateway Arch. Its steel construction wound and twisted up high like a road that veered off a cliff. *Okay, come on girl, we can go inside or race up the side ... ha! Like it's even a choice!* She did a forward flip and let the drugs work their magic, increasing her speed to its full amount. She made it up thirty feet before gravity reared its ugly head and she had to become the fastest impromptu rock climber today. *I wonder if I look like a squirrel to everyone.* She scrambled up the side, twisting as the arch bent inward to remain on the outside and mixing in her rocket boots whenever things got dicey. Standing on something high was one thing. But dangling by her fingertips on a purchase only half-an-inch thick was an adrenaline rush that blossomed in her throat. For a few minutes, she was alone racing up the side without camera crews, without fans leering at her, and the thoughts of Jack pushed out of her mind. She loved it.

Victoriously kneeling at the apex of the Gateway Arch, Jane clutched her chest and smiled as she caught her breath. The high winds whisked away thin beads of sweat, and she kept her cybernetic arm gripped tight to a maintenance latch handle. The arch swayed in the wind, despite its otherwise stationary appearance. *Haha, JK-47, fastest climb of a national monument. Check. Not charged with a misdemeanor for doing it ... also check. Alright, now what was Dragosani talking about?*

The Hounds of Tindalos were only the first wave and the most apparent. Even if their herd thinned a few miles out, Jane saw winged harpies, even a pegasus or two, and more oddities running toward them. *How the fuck did this army get behind us? Our semitrucks are further back still, they should've warned us.* The longer Jane looked, though, the clearer it became; like a group of rats fleeing a sinking ship, the monsters were coming out of every corner on the horizon and just running north. Not to Michigan, not to anywhere in particular, just to anywhere they *could* run that wasn't the south. In the maelstrom that blacked out the horizon behind all of them, though, Jane finally saw why in her ashen world. In a trailblazing path from the south, just like those cities that merged with Purgatory outside of Texas, the same thing was happening, only in a direct line toward them. Right where the Lord of Suicide's armies were.

Jane turned on her earpiece and dialed back to the Lord of Suicide's forces. "This is JK-47 guys, can you confirm your arrival into St. Louis? We are under a lot of heat on account of a giant fucking swarm of demons you've kicked up."

"Hey, JK-47! Our girl!" the female producer's voice rang back. "Oh, man, you are killing it on top of that arch, just hold that pose a little longer. Nice coat by the way! Fantastic fashion statement in trying to co-opt the message of rampant anarchy into party branding. We are coming in hot, about three hours out of your position now."

"Um ... kay? Is there a massive storm behind you eating away at the entire land?" Jane asked, curious, unsure if she was seeing Purgatory again when nobody else could.

They met the question with silence for a moment. "Nothing more than a little raindrop. We won't let that get in our way. It's not like it's snow ..."

"Alright, I will touch base with the people in Abbeville, thanks!" Jane sounded intentionally cheery. "Hey, Abbeville folks, how you holding up post Huggin' Molly? This is JK-47 checking in," she said switching dials. Radio static was her only reply. She tried cellphones next and only heard the canned response of voicemails. Jane touched base with every town they had stopped at on the way North, yet met with nothing but more static each time. Every one of them had gone dark. *Why is it that the sound of silence is the most terrifying sound of all?*

The colors of her worlds shifted and changed into vibrant bright pinks, lilacs, and a distinct hellfire green she had become familiar with. Curious, Jane looked down to see the Society of Deus's magi, like little ants at the base of the Arch, finishing their ritual. The arch itself was an ever-shifting array of colors and the air in the middle crackled with electricity as the citywide helldive began.

The ritual changed the color of the sky to a putrid green as waves of energy pulsed out of the massive gateway changing the landscape of St. Louis. The rushing vertigo of falling panicked Jane into latching on for dear life. It was a fleeting sensation, but marked their transition. From what Jane could see, the Society of Deus brought Purgatory up around the city, as much as they went down. Gone were many of the modern trappings and bringing to bear old buildings long since destroyed. Centuries of forgotten or burned-down buildings faded back into view, oddly conjoined or overlaying their ruined modern counterparts.

All fighting stopped as soon as the ritual took effect. The

living were suddenly struck blind and senseless. The demons, now confused and terrified that someone trapped them back in hell, tried running up in an animalistic instinct to escape. But it was in this moment that Jane saw what caused all the panic on the horizon.

Legions of dead marched through Purgatory in ever-growing numbers carrying banners of Lazarus. The energies of death that flowed out of them made the horizon appear as if they set it ablaze with an unholy flamethrower. A tsunami of death roiling towards the north. Why everyone feared the power of a Death Lord became plain to Jane—they must have been killing everyone in towns behind them to increase their armies. *We need to go. Now.*

Jane realized that everyone below was blind and chided herself for forgetting just how senseless they were. She probably couldn't even shout to them, but she had to get their attention. Jane thought of Purgatory like a stack of pancakes and waffles— each with different layers for syrup to flow. The living world was the butter on top, and every delicious morsel had its own path for syrup underneath. Diving deeper yet into hell would allow larger pools to move freely. Fortunate, since every other monster was desperately clawing their way upwards to the butter as the Society of Deus's ritual pulled the entire area deeper in. *Fuck, I should open my own joint and serve Purgatory Pancakes.*

Racing to the bottom of the arch, Jane saw the Society of Deus's magi placing ash back under the eyes of their own troops, and most of them were already paying coins to evacuate out, preferring to take their chances with the river.

"Hey, Dragosani!" Jane shouted. To her surprise, *everyone* turned to the sound of her voice. "You aren't leaving. Be a real general and get us all down. It terrifies everyone here out of their minds, being stuck here, but together we can save everyone, as cliché as that fucking is. We need to go down, not up. Trust me. I saved your life once already, don't make me do it again."

Lucy and the Sons and Daughters took up a position at the far end of the crowd. Experienced helldivers the lot, they already worked what magic they needed to see and speak. "Jane! We will bring up the rear, but you've gotta go forward. Just keep talking! Everyone can hear that sweet voice of yours, diver or not." Lucy gave the faintest smile. "Descendants of Lazarus ... lucky bastards."

Dragosani looked out at the crowd of civilians from St. Louis. A mix of all ages, shapes, and backgrounds, they were all caught in the middle of this. He mumbled a curse under his breath and ordered his men to take up the sides and flank them.

"Just keep talking, eh?" *Man, I hope people like hearing about cats and waitresses.* "Right, everyone listen up. I know you are frightened and scared, but I will make it less so. Welcome to hell, folks! None of you can see anything because you aren't dead. You can hear my voice because I guess I'm a badass with being on that border between living and dead. But I will lead you out of this. We will go deeper in still and travel north, okay? And for your mid-flight entertainment ... I'm JK-47 of the Sons and Daughters. I'll be your tour guide as we journey through the endless lair of Purgatory. Our estimated flight time will be roughly three hours."

Jane saw a few smiles appear and walked through the arch itself, taking stone stairs further down into hell, minding people to watch their steps. She descended further than the bridge, hoping that any unwanted Barghests would continue on the path of least resistance.

Jane could feel Bollard's eyes on them from ahead and the trembling of the ground from the Wailing Legion behind them. Out of all the drugs racing through her veins, the magical, runed chains wrapped around her shoulder, a mechanical arm, and even the new coat—it was her voice that would save the thousands of people. Even if she was leading them from one battle to another.

"So, let me tell you guys about my cats ..." Jane said nervously as they descended into the abyss.

CHAPTER THIRTY-TWO

Those we love don't go away. They walk beside us every day. Sometimes unseen, sometimes unheard, but always near. Still loved, still missed, and still dear. Elcoll holds the answer to rekindling that connection. Make life burn brighter, and become closer to the lost around you. Let us set your and your loved ones minds at ease that you aren't alone anymore. The dead may walk among us, but does that mean we are ready to listen?

The depths of Purgatory were an isolated prison. Stone stairs gave way to ancient, vaulted-arch bridges that stretched forever in all directions. Each filled with souls listlessly meandering, trapped in their own imagination, forever cursed to wander in eternal silence by divine jailers. An even worse sentence befell upon the creatures that had violated divine law, locked up in crypts and denied the privilege of wandering blind. Here in a hell (only reserved for humans, mind you) rested the eternal lost while their demonic wardens mindlessly set about the banal task of imprisonment. There was no cruelty here, for being sentenced to Purgatory was beyond any mortal method of torture. Rather, to those few demons that remained, the only fate that awaited them was boredom. Jane wondered if the remaining demons were similar in mindset to those who ignored the storms of civil uprisings by staying put. Ignoring the changing world around them.

Jane could understand the appeal for helldivers as she led the blind on (talking constantly about cats, bad dates, or botched bar fights) through the dead lands. Everywhere she looked glistened a sheer amount of lost treasure. Trinkets and memorabilia formed great mountains of trash around their winding path. Paths that one could still tumble off even further down. *If I had known, I ... I don't think we would have thrown those vampires over.* She spied a glance over the edge and to spires that plunged down beyond her vision, off to a place where oblivion enveloped the world.

If some helldiver wanted to find the lost sword of Bartholomew Roberts, it was at the edge of Purgatory they would find it. *It's the eternal pit of lost car keys and stolen cat scrunchies.* As they trudged along the bridge, Jane would occasionally spy shinier objects that were a clear attempt to lure her off—a lost stuffed squirrel from childhood, or letters that had never made it to her. Behind her, anyone with a lick of magic, and thus not as blind, also seemed tempted to go after an object in the distance. *I wonder what appeals to Dragosani, or Lucy. Hell, Doc back there is probably pining after some swordfish.* Nobody was foolish, or unfortunate, enough to jump off their road this time, which was fortunate. Purgatory seemed endless and very, *very* easy to be lost within.

The demon wardens, tall creatures with mouths that were way too thin and wide eyes, strode with grace between the bridges, gently placing a dead soul that wandered out of place back on a worn path. They didn't move like the dead; rather, the gangly jailers stepped through time, stuttering between ticks with each step forward. Jane didn't like looking at them, nor did anyone else seem to, so they kept their heads down and wished that they would be left alone. *Last thing we need is fucked-up creepy sorting demon to lock us in a crypt.*

Thus far, they had been lucky, and even Jane's stream of babble had attracted no attention. What surprised Jane the most, however, was the sheer number of dead still trapped in waiting. Millions of dead already crawled back to the living, yet in the dimly lit world of Purgatory—billions more remained. On the bridges, in the crypts, wandering around the labyrinth of forgotten items, and Jane was sure more below in the abyss. Millions upon millions of lives spanning generations were still wandering blind in the lands of the dead. Escaping this hell was a gift for the lucky lottery winners who just happened to be near the top when shit hit the fan.

At last, one distant bridge away, the grey-blue light from the black sun shone down near another impossibly long staircase. It was that very exit that Jane longed for herself. A safe path that led to the living. Time inched forth at the pace of a DMV where seconds stretched to become hours, and she was one story away from switching to an endless stream of cusses. From there, it was just a hop skip out. The eerie light grew brighter as they crossed another crumbling archway, and Jane had already slipped into an alphabet of swears—when the light dimmed suddenly.

"YOU DIDN'T THINK I'D LET YOU OUT, DID YOU?" Mr. Bollard's voice echoed throughout. From the startled looks on everyone's face, it wasn't only Jane that witnessed it. "YOU'VE ENTERED A PRISON WE KEPT LAZARUS HIMSELF FOR THOUSANDS OF YEARS. IT WAS WE, DEMONKIND, WHO LOVED YOU HUMANS SO MUCH THAT WE SET HIM FREE SO YOUR ENDLESS TORMENT HERE MAY FINALLY CEASE. AND HOW HAVE YOU REPAID US?"

"Well, I guess we are starting the story back at asshole," Jane shouted back. "Dude, come the fuck on. We clearly are just trying to get out of hell. If you love us so much, help a posse out?" The light above their current stairway fluttered in and out of existence from dangerous-looking shadows. Jane saw another appear further ahead. "Come on, guys, keep walkin'. Ever since Mr. Lovemuffin here helped set Lazarus free, there should tons of these little holes. Right?"

They led on for a while longer, with Jane switching stories to her favorite bully tales. If nothing else, she was keeping people in high spirits as a tour guide. As they got close to the light, though, she suddenly shouted out at the top of her lungs. "Stop!" She booked forward at top speed, racing to the light and bounding up the steps four at a time.

Like a lightbulb something flicked it off. Bollard's raspy laughter echoed throughout the realm.

"AGAIN, I KEPT LAZARUS HERE FOR CENTURIES UNTIL I BARTERED HIS FREEDOM. WHAT MAKES YOU THINK A MERE DESCENDANT OF HIS HAS ANY CHANCE OF ESCAPE?"

Lucy put her hand on Jane's shoulder and tugged her back down to the path and spoke at a barely audible whisper. "We know Bollard. Even ... worked with him before to stop Vryce. He betrayed us then, and if we've got his attention now it doesn't bode well. This is his realm. He's a schemer, though, so keep him talking. Worst-case scenario, we scatter and find our own exits." A hatchet flipped in her hand as she eyed the abyss further down. "It's less than ideal."

Jane put her cybernetic arm on her hip and flipped her chain while whispering in turn. "I'm used to putting on a smile for rich assholes. Let me try something." Jane stepped forward and looked up, raising her voice, even though she wasn't sure that mattered. "Lemme guess, you want me to barter for my freedom instead. Revenge over the fact you aren't the top dogs on the surface?" *Who gives a shit if I'm a prick. He's going to let us out, or he isn't.*

"BARTER, NOW WE ARE TALKING. I LIKE THOSE WORDS."

"Wait," Jane choked back a chuckle. "You seriously want me to cut a deal with the devil. Sell my soul or some shit?"

Bollard gave a deep laugh, and Jane could swear she heard the purr of a giant cat nearby. "NOTHING SO FAUSTIAN, I'M NOT A DEMON OF WAR. NO, I WANT AN ACTION ETERNALLY MORE SIMPLE. I WANT YOUR ASSURANCE YOU'LL EXIT THIS PRISON IN MICHIGAN, SPECIFICALLY, NORTHERN MICHIGAN WHERE ENTERPRISING FORCES ARE CONVERGING FOR WAR. ONCE THERE, YOU'LL MERELY OPEN YOUR EYES. THERE IS A CREATURE

WHO YOU KNOW WELL WHO SEEKS MY DEMISE. I AM NOT READY FOR THAT TO HAPPEN. I WISH YOU, AND YOUR ARMY, TO DEFEND ME FROM THE PRAENOMEN." It sounded like Bollard purred, like a very large cat that was smiling. "IT WILL BE AN ACT OF BETRAYAL, NO DOUBT, BUT ONCE YOU SEE US IN MICHIGAN—I'M APPEALING TO YOUR VERY HUMANITY."

Lucy and the rest of the crew froze. Akira and Doc certainly wore a look of guilt. Phoebe's eyes darted to the ground when she saw Jane as if she knew a secret.

"OH, DEAR, HOW COULD I FORGET, BEFORE DEAR LUCY OR PHOEBE BACK THERE SPOIL THE POT; I BETRAYED THEM ONCE BEFORE. I GOT YOUR OLDER BROTHER KILLED. HE WAS JUST AS MUCH OF A SARCASTIC FOOL AS YOU."

Jane's left eye twitched. *You want me to exit into the war zone? Open my eyes? Lemme guess: see the real villain or some shit.* Jane got the metaphor, of course, perhaps reflect and feel bad for what they had done to all the demons or turn against the armies of Lazarus. The slightest glimpse she caught of Suicide's scorched-earth policy didn't endear her to that side any more than Bollard's, or that of Deus. If TV had taught her anything, every news source spoke only in their own interests. *Once we are out, can he make us defend him? I do want round two, though.* She looked back at the Sons and Daughters, in particular Phoebe, whose eyes saw prophecy, for confirmation.

Phoebe nodded.

"Alright, buddy, you got a deal. Get us out of here, and I'll 'open my eyes.' I can't ensure your defense. The Praenomen bested us once, but I'm willing to try."

"THAT WILL DO, YOUNG ONE. THREE STAIRWELLS FORWARD ON THE LEFT-HAND SIDE. I'LL LET YOU CLIMB UP THAT PASSAGE. YOU DO NOT UNDERSTAND HOW MUCH HELP EVEN THE SIMPLEST DEAL CAN BE TO A DEFEATED DEMON. YOU WON'T REGRET THIS CHOICE."

Just ahead of them, Jane saw a creature cloaked in shadows and lurking ahead of them. A large, easily two heads taller than a human, tiger who stood like a man. The claws glistened off the black suns light, and had opposable thumbs. It reminded Jane of a were-tiger. Her eyes squinted for a closer look, revealing white fur, matted and bloodied. It stepped back into the shadows. Jane reasoned it stepped back to the real world, an ability she was already envious of.

"You know it's not the 'open your eyes' part he wants, right?" Lucy said.

"Yeah, yeah, sure, totally. What, what was that?" Jane scratched her head.

"Bollard is a Rakshasa. Hindu devil who in this case took to possessing mortals before the black sun. Sometimes they were good, sometimes evil, but we suspect his plan was never to free just Lazarus. The more humans that die, the more their screams are heard throughout the heavens. Which only serves to lure greater legends forward. It's very likely he has always sought for the divine to rule as gods openly again," Lucy said with certainty. She tapped a few vials of blood along her belt. "Of course, we ended up eating them. So, it's only a matter of time until we are all no longer human."

"He seems afraid. Do you think it was a bad deal? Should we stay here with creepy time-skip demons?" Jane said as they came upon the third stairwell.

"Oh, heavens no," Lucy laughed. "I wanted you to know his motives."

"Or he's just lying," Doc said at last. "Bollard lost hard last time. His machinations cost him everything but his life. He gains his particular power when people betray each other. Putting you on the battlefield against the Church of Lazarus or Society of Deus means that he can put a feather in his cap. He's preying off your vengeance."

"Fuck it, just kill him," Akira shouted from the back. "He said open your eyes, not let him live."

Jane gave a simple shrug. "He's not wrong, and he fucked up, then. None of you guys are working with the Praenomen. Neither are any of the other forces, so he'll gain nothing from it then." *Win-win scenarios are the best.*

Jane laughed and looked over the entire crowd of people. "Alright guys, thank you for riding Purgatory express. Due to some unexpected turbulence, please watch your step and exit to left by climbing up. I repeat, steps up. If you don't feel yourself moving upwards that probably means you fell off the edge and have tumbled into oblivion. Don't do that."

"We won't let them do that," Dragosani chided as the Society of Deus took up along the edge of the stairs, forming a barricade to keep the blind moving in the same direction.

Two golden coins later and a short trip back to the real world, their radios went haywire. Incoming US Army was beginning a bombardment and tank fire from a battalion peppered the overgrown trees.

The Church of Lazarus, and their Wailing Legions, picked up Jane's location the moment they returned. She caught half of what they said, about using the St. Louis gate to join them, before her teeth shook from an explosion. Jane ripped off her headset while ducking down in the underbrush. She didn't know exactly where she was in Michigan, but she knew it was north enough to be almost entirely wilderness.

Plants and flowers associated with witchcraft drank the black sun's rays and thrived here. Mulberry and Pimpernel trees towered three times their natural height, and the ground was covered in toadstools, and pixie-stools. Vegetation around Texas was dying under the diminished sun, but here, puff-ball sized mushrooms called Puck's Stool flourished. Jane didn't know half of them, but Dragosani put several in his pouch while calling their names out.

"From all old trees, proceeds either an owl, or a devil," Dragosani said. "Old Russian legend. Look around."

Jane spied trees that bore fruit, and then those wilted where a rage demon—half here, half in Purgatory—curled into the bark as if it was sleeping. In a blackberry field, a succubus peeked from within her nest. Countless others hid among the trees that had grown taller than great California Redwoods.

A series of explosions shook the earth as a wall of fire rose a mile away. Over Phoebe's headset, they heard chatter of incoming Society of Deus forces across the bay.

Peering between the trees, Jane saw the encampments of demons. The white-furred Rakshasa kneeling while he wrapped a bandage around a snarling Michigan Dogman that had taken shrapnel. *This is what he wanted us to witness? To have sympathy for them? Well ... fuck, okay, it's slightly working. I'm not Jack.*

Their entire group was crouched or hiding, which was easy to do with the massive overgrowth of black and blue plants. Right in the middle of the demons they were sent to kill. To the east of them, the Army's tanks and bombs were coming in. Across the bay, the Society of Deus converged, and soon the Church of Lazarus would use the St. Louis gate to teleport on top of them. *Everyone wants to harvest the demons.* Jane tsked.

"Bollard wants us to pick a side, eh?" Jane said at last and picked up a pack of smokes and set her back against Dragosani's. "Okay, so look, guys, no matter which way this goes down, we have to fight our way out or get caught in a crossfire. We've got a moment, so get ammunition sorted out and arm anyone who ... fuck that shit, arm everyone with sticks and rocks if we need. Teach 'em spells or something ... like ... yesterday. Hell, these plants are probably special, just start eating them. No matter what, we've gotta fight in one direction. I've got an idea. But what do you guys think?"

Phoebe held out her hand. Doc laid three vials of blood in it. "Where's the Praenomen?"

CHAPTER THIRTY-THREE

Just where oh where are you going to get your Yellow Bile? Running low on Blood? The Black Bile of Earth eluding you? Stuck with a shortage of Phlegm? The Four Humors of Hippocratic alchemy and medicine are in stock now at your local grocery stores around Chicagoland and other northern cities.

P eter barged through the frosted blue glass doors in Atlantis Corporation's executive meeting office to the protest of a scantily clad secretary who trotted in behind him. Thirty-two floors up and five blocks away from Triumvirate Enterprises, the movers and shakers behind the Technocratic Party sat with stone faces around a massive matte black conference table that was larger than it had any right in being. Except for Peter, everyone in this room was an older white man with an unidentifiable jawline, and ill-fitted (if not insanely expensive) suits. Peter knew this meeting was an inevitability, for they would hold him accountable for Jack's death, but why should he be the one to stand idly by? His hands helped make each trillions and now they saw a tarnished golden goose.

"Mr. Culmen, how nice to see you," a long-nosed CEO spoke from the far end. "Uh, you can go, Josie, thank you, sweetie. Oh, and make sure you change outfits again before your date with Johnston tonight." He dismissed the young woman with a passive wave.

"You're meeting without me." Peter glared at each of them, but to little effect. No one cared in the slightest that he was a warlock; after all, many of them had profited off the Unification business for decades regardless of their lack of magical talent. *Pedigree can open any door regardless of talent.* They were nothing more than mortal shields that the Unification used to further their ends with hollow promises of immortality. "Correct me if I'm wrong, but in our little Technocratic Party, am I not the elected leader of it?"

A shorter CEO whose head constantly wobbled from side to side straightened his tie and spoke up. "You knew this was coming Peter, let's not be coy. Nobody here will deny all you've done for the party. Hell, just look out the window. But you've been chasing a pipe dream with this transhuman cybernetic avatar project of yours for far too long. And for what? You dumped your entire fortune to build a single star in Metallic Jack, only to watch him commit suicide on a live stream. I'm sorry, but we must enforce a disciplinary action."

You imbeciles will stand in the path to progress! Why must I even suffer the company of Luddites? Peter did his best to feign a smile. "The death of Metallic Jack is a tragedy, but that shouldn't stop us from forging ahead! We aren't the Republican Party, concerned with traditional family values or profits, and given the state of the North the Democrats don't even have a say anymore. Why should they? They've largely become some anarcho-collective for mutual survival. I understand that you must take action, and I'm fully willing to liquidate equity in Triumvirate Enterprises to cover the costs of Jack's departure."

The jowls shook on a balding one near the middle. He reminded Peter of a turtle. "We aren't sure you are the ... face of the party we want to put forth any longer, Peter."

"What's wrong with my face?" Peter leaned in. This wasn't the first time they pushed him aside because he wasn't on-brand enough.

The long-nosed CEO threw up his hands. "Mr. Culmen, please, you know we are beyond such petty things. Your war, your mission, Jack, everything involved. It was divisive. Elcoll, Atlantis, or other companies didn't have their CEO hijack every screen in the world using ... whatever it is you people do. Despite everything that has happened, the people still have elections and we have candidates to prop up. The Republicans are god-fearing folk. We strive for palatability among the masses. Jack was either a hero or a walking abomination depending on the demographic. You pushed too far." He folded his hands and leaned back. "You brought this on yourself."

"What exactly have I brought upon myself?" *Life would be easier if I acted like the warlocks right now; just rip out their minds or command them. But progress without change is improbable. I'm not ruling it out ... yet.* Peter walked along the massive table dragging his hand along high-back chairs. The old men cringed during the potential game of duck-duck-dead. Even if they held the votes and the party seats, none of these men had any personal power. *At least anything they didn't buy off a shelf.*

The shaky CEO spoke back up. "Replacement and your resignation from the council. We'll still allow Triumvirate Enterprises a seat at the table, but for that you must resign as CEO. I'm sure you'll land in a very comfortable position when the settlement package arrives. After all"—he elbowed another sitting next to him—"unlike Jack, you can afford a golden parachute when you jump ship."

They laughed.

This November don't let those European liars steal your God-given American Rights. Americans founded this country in revolution, and we need that American pride. The Technocratic Party is a dictatorship ruled

by their puppet masters from Europe seeking globalization. Vote for your democracy. Vote Republican.

Despite all of Mr. Anonymous's chatter of science and progress, the Praenomen knew all too well he still relied on incantations to ward his corporate headquarters. In a sealed off research lab within Triumvirate Enterprises, the Praenomen and Symon kept to the shadows on the thirteenth floor. Right about now, Whisper should be firing Mr. Anonymous. She knew there would be blowback, but, for the moment—he wasn't in the building. Can't begrudge a lady for engaging in some corporate espionage, can you?

The maintenance stairwell leading up was both well-guarded, magically warded, and armed to the teeth. She had to admit; it was an impressive fusion of security. It allowed only the warlock and his apprentice, Alex Kristov, within its walls. Walls that contained secrets the Praenomen sought. That is, unless Kristov decides to betray Peter and steal all his patents before we can. The motives of men became more predictable the more power they wielded. Powerful people always forget the simple things. Like rocks. Simple, regular, rocks.

Crouched out of a camera's point of view, Symon juggled a handful of concrete rocks and waited for the signal. The Praenomen counted ... one ... two ... three. Right as the camera turned, the vampire cracked the side of the motorized mount, knocking it off a gear. The Praenomen dashed to the far side of the stairwell, waiting to glimpse the guard at the top. As he poked his head around at the noise, she jammed an iron nail into her shadow and possessed him. With the jarring change of perspective, she pretended to look in, picked up the small rock, and walked back to the guard's partners and gave the all clear sign. From there, she wedged the rock into the second camera's gears when the anti-freak units turned their attention back to the hallway they were guarding.

The pair of them had been committing grand larceny for

over an hour. One flight at a time. Symon used rocks and wire to mess with cameras, and the Praenomen would divert the attention of specialized soldiers with possession and misdirection. Symon would carry them both up to the next flight, and the process would repeat itself, and so far—no one knew of their infiltration. The Praenomen knew teleportation into the facility was impossible already. It was the first thing they tried.

The thirteenth floor presented a challenge on its own. The pair of infiltrators crouched and used small mirrors to peer around at a hallway covered in infrared detections and at least a dozen soldiers before a retinal scan and sacred geometry sequence granted entry into the lab. Hrm. Better than I thought. She gestured for Symon to take the point from here out; traps and security were the Frenchman's forte. Symon leaned back and closed his eyes for minutes on end as he danced his fingers to a tune in his head. His eyes opened with a red glow about them and he bared his fangs like a rabid bat. He held up a finger to pursed lips and made a shush sound and crawled on the wall like a spider as he turned into mist near the ceiling.

The Praenomen slinked back into a secure position and waited for Symon's signal to move. Five, ten, even fifteen minutes ticked on by, however, and she wondered what the delay was. Did Peter have a vacuum seal for mist-borne vampires, or did Symon make it in and can't get out? Symon reappeared above her and spidered his way back down. He held up three fingers and counted down, and the Praenomen noticed a trigger switch in his other hand. Ah, crap. Well then, I suppose. Three. Two. One.

The hallway erupted into flames and shrapnel, sending the mangled and bloody bodies of the soldiers flying in all directions. The Praenomen darted out and plunged her dagger deep through the jugular of two in quick succession while her partner dispatched two more. Before the other four could recover from the blast, their necks snapped in unsightly angles from Symon killing them kindly—if suddenly.

"So much for a lock pick," she said, tapping at her cracked

porcelain mask to indicate smarts. "Why the whole doorframe
and not just ..." She pointed to the door handle.

"Eh, no. Tis reinforced, yah. That and all damn sensors and
scanners and guards and wards, fuck it, best lock pick is C4,"
Symon said, pulling a crossbow out of a bag and loading it up. He
lit a smoke. "This whole thing was a trap. That warlock is playing
us, knowing someone would pry into his secrets eventually. I
would've done the same here. Go get your prize, boss. I will
make sure that none interrupt you, yeah? Just teleport out when
you're finished; I'll find my way. If teleporting out doesn't work,
then I'll have our exit covered."

The Praenomen looked at her soldier and knew what he
meant. This is what true loyalty earns you, Vryce. Pay attention.
Voices in the mask and around the world whispered their silent
praise. "Very well, then. I'll be quick." She pulled a small daddy
long-legs spider from one of her many pockets and plucked off
each leg as her spell took hold, allowing her to climb the wall like
Symon had done earlier, and squeeze into the lab.

CHAPTER THIRTY-FOUR

At T-Cellular Arena, we place security as your number one concern. Now offering a behind-the-scenes exclusive, bring the little ones down and see panopticism in action. Over 500 screens showcasing the world outside and a surveillance drone showcase by Foucault Incorporated. Where there is power, there is resistance. Now you can buy the latest in anti-freak security systems at great discounts only at T-Cellular Arena!

A little red warning appeared in the corner of Peter's vision. He waved his hand and saw the Praenomen's soldier, Symon Vasyl, putting up a battle against a dozen of his best soldiers. Inside his private lab, the Praenomen herself stood next to the crumpled body of Metallic Jack, examining the computer chips surgically removed out of his brain. *Well, today is just a bloody Sunday after all. Look who decided to return.* Peter sighed in frustration. *Yes, that is indeed one chip for each of the ten Sephirot. I can see the gears turning in your head now, Delilah. Jack's death was a setback, but only temporarily.*

"Peter," the long nose CEO continued. "Are you still with us? We said you will step down with a nice package."

"One second, I'm busy." Peter held up a finger to silence the room and resumed staring off into space. They couldn't see what he saw.

Peter slammed a briefcase on the table and cracked open the locks, pulling out his own mask for Mr. Anonymous. To the shock of everyone at the table, he hopped up on the table and rolled up his sleeves, donning his mask. Every CEO but the long-nosed one raced back from the table, fearing the worst. *And you should.* Peter activated the security doors and locked them in and moved the power of the blood within him. With outstretched hands he activated his technomagic and began a dizzying array of work on the fly. Profiles, screens, histories, phone records, blackmail, and everything else he had on every supernatural member of the Unification splayed out in a wide arc around him. Visible to all in the room. The frightened CEOs in the room looked to the ground and avoided his gaze, expecting their imminent demise. *Oh, you bastards have pushed me far, but this isn't for you. Not that you need to know that.* Peter hijacked the communications back to the Unification.

"Attention Unification members and lucky cults around the world. It is I, your liberator and information broker, Mr. Anonymous. Be you Freemason, Skull, Our Lady of Endor, or any other, I have news which meets your liking. As of today, they have voted me off the Technocratic Party's council, the party I built. These are the men who have done such a deed," Peter said with a hint of devious glee in his voice as the CEOs tried to hide their faces. It didn't matter when he sent a profile up. "Now I target this message, and not worldwide, only to those proper sorcerers, undead, and others within, or outside, the Unification's ranks. My attention is now yours. The battle in Michigan is about to commence and I again extend my invite to each of you to discuss our future. You have ten hours to get to Triumvirate Headquarters. When you're done, feel free to stay awhile and see some other companies have to show you." Mr. Anonymous leaned close to the CEO that reminded him of a turtle. "I'm sure they'll have plenty to show you."

Mr. Anonymous stood with arms outstretched on the conference table. "And as for you, my little rats. Don't you know it's rude to enter without an invitation?" With a flick of his wrist, the stairwell Symon was in exploded as thousands of microscopic shards bounced around between electromagnetics. Everything inside liquified into a fine paste, a bit red-colored. *Wonder if I got you before you turned to mist, you bastard.* He strolled out of the room and switched camera feeds.

The Praenomen made no worry or slight thought when the explosions went off, only investigating the ritual components with intense curiosity. Mist took shape into Symon next to his master; even if he was missing his left arm, he still lived.

"Took you long enough," the Praenomen said.

"We should hurry; more will come," he panted. "Did you find anything? Or someone?" Symon poked the broken metal body on the table.

"I did indeed. I think I see what the warlock's angle is, but you're stuck, aren't you, Mr. Anonymous? That's why you make empty copies?" the Praenomen asked, looking right up at a hidden camera and holding up blank computer chips.

Peter grinned wildly as she held up the chips. *Yes, yes, of course you now see.* "Stuck is an ugly word," the warlock's voice echoed through the room via speakers. "I merely never studied possession like your master. Our principles are too different. For a hint, I'll tell you when I have eyes on Bollard." Peter noticed that the Lord of Suicide was rounding the corner, no doubt to investigate the carnage. "But you'd best hurry, that lab won't be there in ten seconds."

The Praenomen held up a vial of black blood. "The blood of Balor. It breaks rules of reality. One use when stuck. More if I live."

Peter opened the windows to the far end of the lab. Just as the Praenomen and Symon jumped, the Lord of Suicide walked right through the wall as if it didn't exist. Without even casting a spell, more like he simply reached out and plucked something in thin air, Symon crumpled to the ground. Just as the Praenomen vanished through a red door, the Lord himself dropped through the floor like a ghost himself and the lab erupted into metal-melting flames cleansing anything else inside.

Mr. Anonymous smiled as he slammed back out the Atlantis conference doors, ogling the vial of Balor blood. Already sorcerers and vampires were booking plane tickets—using his platform, of course.

The long-nosed CEO sighed out of relief whilst rubbing his temples. He had been hiding his phone for quite some time. Out of all the things Whisper expected out of the warlock, sending a message to every single supernatural out of the blue wasn't one. But Peter's actions scared the shit out of the other half of the council. Getting Delilah Dumont named as the new head would be easy. Nobody would want anything to do with Alex Kristov since they knew him as Peter's apprentice.

"Gentlemen, let's review resumes of candidates, and while we are here, why don't we get our core product or valuable assets off-site quickly, yes? Mobilize everything to warehouse twenty-seven. We want to ensure our profits and patent security before one of these vampires gets a bright idea to steal our inventions. If we move quickly, we can secure everything before they even arrive." The Whisper smiled and put three resumes on the table.

Only one mattered.

CHAPTER THIRTY-FIVE

Gravity. She's a bitch, isn't she? Wouldn't you want to take a step to the heavens and ignore the rules of physics if you could? Re-Cind's new line of gravity-defying footwear launches next month at stores nationwide. Walk up walls. Dash through the air. All powered through technology born out of the Triumvirate. Get your preorder in now. First come, first served basis only.

"I'll say this," Peter said with feet up on his desk, typing away on his custom retro keyboard, complete with a ZeroCool decal. "Sorcerers sure take their damn time ..."

It had been nine hours since he made his announcement and a handful of sorcerers from other places in North America had arrived. Most waited patiently to get through security, but others hated the intense scrutiny. Particularly (much to Peter's amusement) those from the Society of Deus. Gabriel D'Angelo in particular wore his trademark white fleece hoodie with a *very* special cavalry sabre strapped to his back. At all times a druid with a long, neatly braided red beard flanked him on one side, and a cop with aviator shades and mutton chops on the other.

No amount of security was going to pry one of the two Blades of Deus with the Eye of Mammon off them, particularly in enemy territory. A soul blade that granted Gabriel power far beyond his own. *I'm envious, I'll admit.* Peter gave the clearance to let them in regardless. *Have all the power you want; in my walls, I am king.*

"Master." Kristov poked his head into the office. "The assembly awaits you."

Peter looked at the Balor blood rolling by his keyboard. It was a greenish liquid that swirled and danced inside a black glass vial. *I'll unlock your mysteries soon enough.*

Peter lifted the mask from the table and donned his alter ego, becoming Mr. Anonymous once more and walking briskly to the meeting. Massive screens stood on every wall where the Triumvirate logo spiraled in three dimensions. An expert bartender, the same from the skybox, served specialty cocktails for the helldivers, vampires, sorcerers, or shifters. Peter took to the same stage he had delivered many TED Talks before and let Alex Kristov have the first show. *He's a fine apprentice, even if he's zealous with destruction.* Kristov discussed the future of Atlantis Enterprises and mechanized warfare, in particular, how they are working on new weapons to capture creatures rather than obliterate the prey. To most in the audience, they met it with yawning approval, and why wouldn't it be—every one of them had already eaten one or several hearts.

A half hour of the lukewarm reception, and the Society of Deus gave a roaring applause, with Gabriel D'Angelo clapping the loudest. Unlike the occasional smile he wore on TV, he scowled. To Peter's vision, he was swimming in magical trinkets: blades, rings, amulets, and more. He wasn't unsure that Gabriel's white gym shoes weren't magical. Gabriel walked through the aisle, stopping only to pause by the bartender, like he would say something ... and ... shook his head and continued on, walking right up to Peter.

"Hi, Gabriel D'Angelo," he said, extending a hand. "You, uh, kinda put us in a war and then invited us for dinner."

You are brazen, no? What bloody spell did you cast on your shoes to keep them so white, anyway? Mr. Anonymous grasped the outstretched hand with both of his. "You've done well in coming. After all, if you wish to sa—"

Gabriel took his hand back and went down to tie his shoe. "I'm gunna cut you off there, pal. You, uh, you don't get to work with the Unification, and then go on and ask about saving shit, okay? You wanna work together, then come the fuck over, and do it. I didn't come into your house and shit in your bed." Gabriel tilted his head and his gaze fell to others in attendance. "Now, as I was saying ..." He held up a finger and turned around. "We didn't blow up the stadium, a traitor who stole ..." Gabriel smirked and grabbed the hilt of his sabre, but flourished his open hand.

Peter felt the shadows in the room linger for a moment, moving and whispering in several voices at once, pulling themselves back to Gabriel. He had heard this shadow whispering before. *Vryce?*

With a flash of green light, the Praenomen's dagger appeared in Gabriel's hand.

Behind Peter's mask, a bead of salty sweat etched its way down his cheek. *The second Blade of Deus. Did Vryce link them through magic?*

"Who the fuck knows." Gabriel pointed to Peter with the dagger. "Maybe his daughter did; regardless, if you want a chance for peace, call off your little war."

Peter's blue eyes pierced through Gabriel. *The little shit is a mind reader isn't he?* As soon as he thought it, he regretted it. The smirk on the cocky, albeit immensely powerful, blond man in front of him was nearly unbearable. If he had controlled his thoughts, he might have been able to use that to his advantage.

"Oh, excuse me," a female voice cut through the auditorium's tension. She was short and remarkably adorable with a bright green dress and a wide-brimmed hat filled with gems. She had an absolute warming charm to her. "I apologize I arrived here a little late, but where is the real person in charge here?"

Gabriel and Peter paused for a second, looked at each other, confused. Gabriel deemed himself the one to ask the obvious question. "Who is asking?"

A quick pivot to-and-fro as she scanned the room before settling her gaze on the bartender, pulling down thick sunglasses to observe the gentleman. "Ah, there you are." She walked up and extended her hand, loud enough for the room to hear. "Alice Macgregor, booze baron and Balor's newest messenger. Charmed. I've heard a *lot* about you, Mr. ..." She pulled a bottle. of hooch from her purse and poured a shot as every head in the room turned in her direction. "Oh, you two can go about your pissing match. The adults will talk about what comes next." Even the bartender seemed surprised by her brazen ability to identify him as something more than a mere bartender. He shrugged his shoulders and pulled out a cigar, handing it to her and lighting it.

"Who the hell is Balor?" Gabriel asked.

Just before anyone could answer Gabriel's question, the room's lights flickered, and the screens went black. Out of the wall behind Mr. Anonymous, the Death Lord stepped forth with his emaciated skin and golden-winged mask, his lips more a quivering snarl than any other emotion as a slow rage simmered behind his dead eyes. "Nothing more than a fairy tale, that's who, a dead myth, best left buried." The Lord of Suicide threw Symon's broken and melted crossbow on the stage and looked at Peter. "It turns out, dead men do tell tales, my apprentice."

"Oooh, shit's getting' real up in this room," Alice said, taking a swig and handing the moonshine bottle to the bartender. "You tell 'em, dead man. Preach it, brother. Balor's fairy tale don't mean shit to big ol' Lazarus, now does it?"

The Death Lord ignored her. Every creature in the room was ready to erupt into an orchestra of violence. For an eternal tick of a watch, the room waited for another to make the first move. Mr. Anonymous sighed. *This is one Mexican standoff nobody wins.*

"Nobody wins those anyway," Gabriel quipped.

Oh, no wonder he's so annoying. Fucking mind readers. This is why everyone hates having him at their gatherings.

"What do you want?" Mr. Anonymous finally asked the Lord of Suicide. "This doesn't concern you. I'm not the head of the Technocratic Party any longer. They have started your war, and I'm long overdue for a meeting with those who've cast aside their human selves and eaten a demon's heart. I've done nothing wrong."

"No, you've done nothing wrong yet." The Lord folded his hands. "So why don't we finish what you started, then. As your priest, mentor, and voice of your God, use your magic to pull up the battle right now. Load these screens so we can watch it unfold, and I order you to command JK-47 and her forces to attack the Society of Deus that are there."

Will you get angry and scold me if I refuse? Ruin your entire platform and kill everyone here, old man? He passively fiddled with a silicon dreadlock while contemplating his options. *I suppose refusal here doesn't earn me any favors. Very well.*

"Fine, but I don't need to use magic for that." Peter picked up a remote control off the pedestal and pressed the on button. "She has a camera crew with her."

The screens around the room all lit up with images of JK-47 and her companions, now in northern Michigan, each digging in makeshift trenches as the cameras tried to cover all three sides: the US Army, the demons of Michigan, and the Society of Deus. In the distance on the fifth camera, everyone saw the giant white tiger moving among the trees, not far off from JK-47's position.

Peter did, however, cast a quick spell to connect directly to Jane's earbud. "JK-47, this is Peter Culmen. Do you remember me?"

Jane perked up and grabbed an earpiece. "Uh, yeah, of course, what do you want? We're kind've in the middle of something here. I'm sure you know all about it."

"Yes, JK, we do. Listen, we've got a change of orders, understand, a new target. We want you to ignore the demons for now and, instead, go after the left bank and wipe out the Society of Deus. It's the surest path to victory; the demons and the army will both fight each other."

JK-47 hunted for the nearest camera and looked back at them like the room was filled with idiots (a look that was obvious even to those without mind-reading powers). She shone the camera across the river at a legion of sorcerers, back to her being confused, back again. "There is a giant army of walking dead about to take the St. Louis gate *right here*. Fucking big-ass demons to the north and"—she shook the camera—"bloody army sorcerers to the left! We did our job and got here! Why can't we leave to the right? The US military guys don't hate us, right?"

"If only things were that simple. You've enlisted, you have orders. It's not about getting out of there, JK-47. You're the hope of a nation. We need a victory here, so, go give it your all. Everyone back home is watching."

Jane held up two fingers to someone offscreen and pondered her options. "Order's an order, team. Load up and get ready, this shit will sting."

"Happy?" Peter said, turning back around to the Lord and Gabriel. *This isn't a declaration of war, Gabriel. She won't listen to these orders, but it's a game we have play at this very moment. She's already pushed to the brink.*

Gabriel said nothing; instead, he pulled out the smaller dagger and sliced his wrist with it. In a flash of smoke, he vanished into thin air, teleported away.

"I am much happier now," the Lord said to Peter. "If you wanted to socialize with your friends, you should've just said so. Now why don't we all settle in and watch the show; it's bound to be a good one."

"I'll take a shot of that moonshine," Peter said as the sound of gunfire increased from the screens in Michigan.

CHAPTER THIRTY-SIX

The Champions of the Tri-City fighting tournament face new challengers next month at Uppercut Rivals. This eSport tournament pits your favorites against one another for a shot at Triumvirate Enterprises signature neural net upgrades. Enter to win enhanced reflexes, faster reaction time, and constant internet uptime. Join our online worldwide bracket schedules for a month of a competition, with an exclusive, fully paid trip to Austin for the championship rounds. Sign up today!

Unless you can dodge bullets, keep your bloody heads down!" Jane shouted down to the St. Louis civilians they had evacuated. She sat on a tree branch high above everyone, legs dangling in the air, and kept looking for an opening while humming a tune as she watched the dumpster fire.

The US military was in a panic—firing on just as much as the Society of Deus, Bollard's demons, the Wailing Legion, and any demons also racing through the gate opened from St. Louis. *This is a total clusterfuck. Come on, Sons and Daughters, let's get on with plan b already. Get the fuck out of here.* What could have simply been a four-point cross, with an army at each end, erupted into bedlam as the Wailing Legion's forces teleported into the field. It certainly didn't help that demons were running for their lives in front of them. Even as the US military sent bombing runs to attack the Society of Deus at home in the Twin Cities, their ground forces decided to put bullets in anything that moved.

Even with the black sun sitting at four in the afternoon, it was hot enough that Jane was breaking a sweat. The bound army of ghosts from the Church of Lazarus wasted not a second before lunging into battle. Robed necromancers who commanded the legions initially ignored the army and focused on the demons fleeing in front of them. That brilliant plan was heaved with maximum velocity out the window once a necromancer caught several bullets in his organs. Black and green streaks of energy raced from the Wailing Legion to the Army, withering the life out of unfortunate soldiers. Their skin pickled green and pruned before they slumped to the ground and moaned from their joints aching. The response, as Jane expected, was an overabundance of napalm—which isn't the most accurate of substances. Fire also tends to piss off vampires. So of course the Society of Deus's sorcerers didn't look too kindly on this and caused parts of the sky to rain down sleet or lightning, which Jane *also* realized wasn't an exact science. Then, of course, a crew of soldiers in hovering copters shat their pants at everything going on and just start unloading. The US military rerouted every damn gunship and soldier they had.

Now with an almost endless horde of demons racing out of Purgatory at all sides, fire raining down from the heavens, mortar shells around, and ghosts who have no tactical sense— Jane lit up a smoke.

Her headset rattled on with the voice of a ranking officer from the Wailing Legion screaming for JK-47 to mobilize their remaining squads and attack the Society of Deus. But they had other plans. *The storm's eye has its perks. Maybe that demon Bollard is slightly prophetic.* The Sons and Daughters huddled down and kept under cover behind massive overgrown trees or quickly dug ditches. In between ducking and weaving explosions, the main squad now led by Lucy worked to prep everyone for another massive Helldive. *I'll be damned if we do that, though. I will not die in hell.* Still, Jane had to admit it made sense to have a backup plan in case hers didn't work—even if she thought backups were lame as fuck. Her plan was, of course, perfect. Wait for everyone to kill each other, then steal a car and drive to Vegas. *Well, I mean, I suppose everyone else can come with. Just need a bigger car, right?* She pondered as she spitballed where everyone's reinforcements would be coming from. She'd have to fight her way through, well, everyone in that lucky ass direction, but those that made it would be scot-free without risk of death by Purgatory entomb-ment. Bollard, Dragosani, Deus, Church of Lazarus, and the soldiers all wanted Jane's squads to join them and attack their enemies. Jane figured the only winning move in this battle was to not play. *Besides, on what fucking planet did anyone think I would really join Bollard? At least Dragosani has a winning shot.*

"I told you Doc, keep that fucking head of yours down," Jane said as she watched the gangly doctor almost get his head taken off while applying ashes to a civilian. "Aha! There!" Jane screamed, and wrapped her leg around the branch, swinging upside down and backflipping back to the ground. "All right, squads form up, we've got a break in the line. Vampires and undead with me, Dragosani and sorcerers, you protect the civil-ians. Once we get out, I'm sure your army will be happy with their new position, yeah?"

Dragosani shook his head and slammed his fist into his chest. "My concern is the people, which makes us team regular joe together, right? Even if this will be a bloody affair." His eyes suddenly went wide, and he dropped to a knee. "My Primus."

Jane looked over her shoulder and saw the cocky, smug face of Gabriel D'Angelo standing right behind her. *Holy Fuck!* She was about to reach back and deck him when he fell to his knees and held out his hands as if his life had flashed before his eyes.

"Wait! Please," Gabriel shouted. "Whatever you do, do not, do not punch me while wearing that coat." He crawled back-wards more and was panting in between laughs as Jane held back.

"I really don't want to end up as meat paste. I'm not here against you, just, please, whatever you do, don't punch me. I didn't think that through, was just getting next to Dragosani," he pointed over.

"Well, don't fucking appear behind strange drugged-up super soldier ladies, you flaming asshat!" Jane kicked dirt his way. *Seriously, this jackass has some balls appearing. What's a good reason to not off the leader of Deus ... mmmmmm ... none really.* Jane kicked up her assault rifle and leveled it at him.

"I've got a great reason," Gabriel said, standing up and brushing himself off out of arm's reach. "I'll make you a better deal for your little suicide run you're about to undertake. You don't touch my men, I'll make sure you guys make it out."

Heh, he thinks he's safe. Cute. "Uh, buddy, you know we are already working with Dragosani here, yeah?" Jane pointed over. "Besides, time is of the essence, chop chop." Jane pointed the rifle up and down on him. *One shot, two shot, juke left, deck from the right ...*

Gabriel backed off a few more steps. "Dragosani, already hitting on the enemy, are ya? You know what, um, the last guy who wore that coat did to us, right?" Before Dragosani could respond, Gabriel held up his hand. "It's alright, that's ancient history now, right, guys?" He pointed to the furious and seething group of vampires right behind Jane. Akira, Doc, Lucy, and Phoebe all seemed ready to pounce and shred the blond-haired sorcerer.

"You know me, sir," Dragosani said.

A squadron of Wailing legion drifted right through thick nearby trees, phasing through them as if they didn't exist and opened fire on the Deus soldiers. Akira and Doc dashed from their trench in a vain slashing attempt at incorporeal forms. Bullets shredded through Dragosani and the innocent people behind him. Enraged, Dragosani grew long, hooked claws out of his hands and charged forward with vampiric haste, each slash and slice pulling wisps of smoke off the ghostly soldiers but failing to slow them down.

"You got yourself a deal," she said to Gabriel, and turned to her team. "Go! Now!" Jane screamed and uncurled her blue runic chains. *Way to make the choice easy.* Her pupils dilated as the drugs took effect and the world slowed around her. Wrapping the blue chains around her metal fist, Jane hauled back with a hook and threw her weight into the punch. Sparks flew out as the runes embedded in the chain glowed, and the ghost's face twisted in surprised agony as she sent it screaming into oblivion. Flipping forward she kicked the long end of the chain and sent it spiraling into a second while already rocketing forward and punching another. The fourth ghost did its best to phase back through a tree for cover. JK jerked on the chain and ripped the second ghost in half as she landed; keeping the momentum, she moved to wrap her leg around the tree and spin around. She misjudged her strength and tore the base of the tree into splinters. *What the ...?* With no time to think, she continued through and spun the chains though the opening, slicing the ghost in half and scattering its essence.

"Hey, you're right, Dragosani. I can see why you like her, fair enough," Gabriel said, pulling out the blades of Deus and closing his eyes. Massive walls of white fire erupted in two-hundred-foot lines around the column of trapped civilians and incinerating Wailing Legion ghosts caught int the path. "Let's keep moving."

The column of civilians didn't just run, they sprinted for their lives. Flanked on both sides by white fire, undead murderous ghosts, and demons ever so curious about this new conflagration of combat, everyone ran. An enemy Growler pulled up in the distance, soldiers unloading their machine guns through the flames. The Sons and Daughters squads did their best to shield people with their own bodies. A bullet or two meant a lot less to a vampire than someone with a circulatory system. JK-47 and Dragosani ripped forward while Akira and Lucy dealt with demons in the back. Demons, Rage Demons specifically, that were half in our world with one foot, and the other still in hell, always brought out Jane's bloodthirsty side back in the arena matches. *Rage demons ... that's Bollard's plan?*

Total chaos? Jane disarmed a ghost with one end of the chain and beat its face in with the other while Dragosani jumped through the air into the machine gun fire like a panther, ripping the growler to shreds.

Panting and out of breath, everyone did their best to rush over fallen logs and get out of the fight. Jane hated to admit it, but she was loving every second of the chaos. Adrenaline and more drugs than she could count raced through her, and she blitzed between trees and ghosts paving the way forward. The long patchwork trench coat flapped in the breeze like a flag for everyone to follow. Whenever a necromancer tried to cast a spell, Gabriel just muttered about pathetic blood junkies and set their hands on fire. More than enough seconds for JK to slide in and rip them from limb to limb. Every second in the combat Jane felt more and more furious, more righteous, and less like running. With a kick to a tree, she sent it toppling over onto a melee of hellhounds and soldiers. "Hey guys! I think I picked up super strength!" she shouted at the US Army soldiers before striking a pose. They ran.

She leaned in to pursue, the bloodlust nearly taking over, but as if someone poured ice right through her veins, they stripped out all emotion. Her body trembled from the sudden withdrawal of adrenaline, and in the pause Doc Daneka snaked his way into her vision. "Jane, calm down. Rage demons do this. A pheromone of sorts. It's a good meal for me, sure, but ... don't give into the rage." He put his hand on her shoulder. "You okay?"

"Y-yeah?" Jane flexed her left arm and let the feeling of loss return first. *I'll never have a real arm again.* One by one many complicated emotions crept back in, everything from Jack's death to the joy of flying slowly returned, but the bloodlust had faded. "When did I get strong?" Jane managed to squeak the question out through her shell-shock.

"When you sold me that swordfish, remember?" Doc looked at her over the golden spectacles he wore. "That's the day you took a step forward. But if you mean physically strong, you didn't, tough guy. Your older brother did. That's Mike's coat, and his legacy passed on. So, chop chop, get to the punchin'. It's what you Auburns are good at," Doc said.

"Don't strip out all emotions, Doc!" Phoebe shouted as she ran up from behind and hugged Jane. "You're doing fabulous, doll, hang in there and keep going. Just remember we aren't after the living if we can help it." As if to spark emotion back in Jane, Phoebe spun around in front and gave Jane a friendly kiss.

Everything about her plan snapped back into place, and Jane looked down at the purple-haired vampire prophet with a raised eyebrow. "You didn't even buy me dinner first, that's gonna cost ya." She smiled and let her pupils dilate again, kicking off with a rocket blast to leap over to the front again.

Unable to ignore the bodies she leapt over on the way there, she chided herself for leaving so many behind. There was no time to carry wounded people, and leaving them for dead was a sight Jane would never wash from her memory. As she ran past Gabriel, she glimpsed his eyes, a mixture of fury and sadness as he looked at the strewn bodies of people who couldn't make it anymore, begging for help before Hounds of Tindalos descended on them. Gabriel casually stretched out his hand and plucked Jane out of the air with an invisible force and forced her down to his level.

That icy feeling surged in Jane again and this time it wasn't from Doc. The temperature of the entire battlefield was rapidly dropping, and breath was already visible on creatures that still give off warmth. "Jane," Gabriel said, with his voice sounding like his own, but also someone else's. "Something's about to happen, that I *really* wish I had a choice in," he remarked as the sky darkened even further than possible with a swirling vortex of putrid green storm clouds. "But I don't and it's coming soon. Now I'm going to turn my back on you and walk into the heart of this battle. Do me a favor?" The shadows oozed in from around Gabriel and crawled out of their own volition up his legs. "Don't do the same dumb shit your bolt-for-brain brother did and attack my father? I'd rather not put two Auburns in the ground."

It reminded her of the Praenomen, the same style of magic,

the same creepy feeling that crawled up and filled her arms with goosebumps. *I should've killed you when you first showed up. You attacked and slaughtered our city, you start—*

"But of course." The voice of Gabriel was completely different. Deeper and raspier, and it didn't emanate from Gabriel's throat, but rather all around him, as if a small chorus was speaking. "Why should humanity be allowed to squander the glory of god itself and deny their own path to divinity? Without a little sacrifice, the real enemy of this world would have never crawled out of hiding." He levitated off the ground as electricity sparkled between his fingers.

Jane could tell this creature was beyond an unholy abomination. In her second vision, that of the ashen world, it was as if a soul had stitched itself together over Gabriel. A wild, white-haired man covered in tattoos with bloody threads that tied themselves to objects Gabriel was wearing. Try as he might, it moved and controlled Gabriel like a puppet.

"I am no more your enemy than I was back then, Jane Auburn," the creature said as it pulled Gabriel's body up into the air. "We both want someone to free humanity from the shackles of divine law. Even if one of us doesn't know it yet. Don't begrudge an old man for killing ants to liberate a planet. None at this battle are innocent lambs anymore."

He dropped her to the ground as black streaks of lightning arced behind them, popping hellhounds, ghosts, and soldiers as if they were instant microwave popcorn. Tornadoes touched down in the distance, and giant earth elementals formed out of the ground and rose, marching to war at the creature's command.

In Purgatory, Jane saw Gabriel roll his eyes and say, "Dammit, Dad, we fucking talked about this shit, no possession. Go get one of your stupid gargoyles out here."

Lucy grabbed Jane.

"Run."

CHAPTER THIRTY-SEVEN

Chaos Box! The Magical Mailbox! Do you want War Magic? Need that good ol' Black Death Magic? Or is there a special someone you need some Green Love Magic for? All eight types of magic are available for distribution, right to your mailbox. Just kill something with blood, write which type you are seeking, spin around three times and burn the paper while looking into your shadow. Include your address.

F ine, Gabriel, just do everything yourself, why don't you," Delilah fumed as she dragged over a tall green canister on wheels and set it next to several others. *Sweet bloody Balor, did you have to make it so anyone with bits of your soul could summon those daggers, Vryce? What if I needed it then!* Deep in her Denver bunker, she tampered with a metal dial on the Novichok Agents. It filled her with glee to own her own stockpile of this newly formed Russian nerve gas agent. *Deadly, toxic, and something no creature can dodge.* Ex-CIA and Homeland Security spies ran around her making preparations for war themselves. Symon and Whisper trained them over the past year, molded each into vampires and shifters, and readied for mobilization day. Their mission today—

locate Bollard so Delilah could rip out his eyes. "Hopefully, I get there before dear granddad does the same," she said to nobody in particular.

Zipping up the hazmat suit and pulling down the gas mask, she reached out with both arms and summoned up her red door, now as large as a garage door, slicing reality itself with a razor-thin precision. Through the shimmering view, they viewed the battlefield of Michigan from a southeast corner. A raging inferno of fire, lightning, and storms dotted the landscape among a back-drop of tornadoes and swirling clouds with electricity arcing between them. Her soldiers froze briefly with their mouths open, wondering how anything could survive, much less fight. Glimpses of demon hounds dashing through and tackling out of place Deus soldiers or US military copters spiraling out of control and crashing while missiles rained down on legions of ghosts.

"All right, chaps, your job is simple. Locate paths to Bollard and then get out. Move in teams of two like we practiced—and keep those hazmat suits on! None of you are worthy of death by Novichok," the Praenomen said as she loaded up a gas launcher. "We ready?" The hundred soldiers were paler than an undead had any right to be, yet they each nodded. "Bollard's about three hundred yards to the north here; I can feel him already. Go."

Two by two the Archive soldiers dashed out, blending into the shadows as Whisper and Symon had taught them. The Praenomen waited till it was her turn and followed suit, her outfit identical to the rest of the soldiers in camouflage. They moved tactically. Nerve gas only launched when needed. Then they zipped to the next shadow in pairs. Anything living hit with the gas was dead in seconds; first the nervous system shuts down, causing muscle spasms, then the lungs filled with fluid causing the target to drown. Internal organ failure happened while their prey was simultaneously trapped from the environ-mental assault raining down. Vampires had a better shot of surviving, but when the first Deus members went down to the gas, the Archive revealed why they traveled in pairs—to stake the seizing vampire. It may survive, it may die, but it was out of the way for now. Which meant not in *hers*.

Not a single move they made was reckless. Delilah was grateful that their training held since with Vryce channeling sorcerous might through Gabriel at the moment her power was greatly diminished. *Just like the old days; better to be a cunning mouse, anyway.* She slid over a fallen log and ducked behind the next set of cover with labored breath. Thirty minutes in, they had made it unseen, and left a quiet wake of death oozing out behind them. A small encampment of injured bygones, succubi, rage demons, and other young creatures of myth were as far from the fighting as possible. On a massive throne of fallen trees and thick vines, the Rakshasa demon king stared right at Delilah's position. His mottled white fur, spotted with the blood of fallen enemies, radiated nobility from his post despite his half-man half-cat appearance. *Yes, feign nobility before I rip your heart out.*

Delilah stood up and clicked her radio on. "We made it, everyone hold for extraction." She switched the nerve gas to another canister loaded with a silver-based nitrate, a weakness of demon cats.

"You've come at last, dear Delilah, and how fares my pet this day?" Mr. Bollard's voice was a sweet mix of Mediterranean and islander, as far away from American as it could be. He lurched forward and resumed a human form, a well-dressed bald Persian man with leather gloves.

"Nice illusion, but stirring up old memories won't serve you any better." She fired the canister. He would have no chance to dodge nerve gas, but this time, he didn't try. He smiled, keeping the grin as his body seized and chokes from the intense pain spat blood. Delilah fired two more nearby to ensure its effect and waited just outside the cloud billowing unto itself several feet around the demon. Creatures nearby let out panicked screams, but were too injured or too scared to move out on their own. "You've had your time infecting my dreams; witness this orchestra I have brought to your doorstep for your farewell. A proper end to you. A better one than you would've given me, no?"

"I've always thought, you ..." Mr. Bollard choked out the words, his constant regeneration keeping him in a state of seizures and aware. "Deserved a ... kingdom of your own. Not ... that unholy lich Vryce. So, I, let you come ... to give it to you—"

"Oh bullshit, the moment I can carve out that heart of yours it's over." Delilah produced a silver, curved dagger. "You didn't let me come to give me paradise. Clearly, humans' fascination with television foiled your well-laid plans. I'll admit, I was curious to learn how you lured the great starlet JK-47 to this location. It was good gamble on your end; she would've killed me if I even got close. Or tried, anyway. So don't patronize me with this 'you were worthy' nonsense. It's unbecoming of you. You were outplayed, outsmarted, out ... why am I talking?" Delilah fought back the urge to delay his death. *I'm monologuing? How grotesque of me.* The blood of Bollard's that ran through her veins recoiled at the thought of killing him. Her teeth clenched as anxiety and anticipation took hold; despite this, she took a step forward. Then another.

"Heh ..." he choked. "You're right ... I hoped that the next Auburn would kill you. She chose poorly and it will be her end. That is why you are deserving ... look how much we have healed the earth. Look at the trees and the plants that flourish when tended by angel, demon, and satyr alike. How our blood when spilt causes the regrowth. You humans thought only you ..." Blood oozed out of his face. "Only you would enjoy our deaths? I'm not even a demon of war and gaze upon the legions of humans we've slaughtered. Just wait until a real war demon shows up. Or the terror that Balor will rain when he awakens ..."

Delilah took another step forward. A young succubus backed away further, and a strange-looking faerie with a red nose and long, pointed ears peeked her head out from behind the throne. Delilah could see with her golden eye into their souls and knew. *They are both cruel and efficient monsters. My kind of people.* As she stepped over the chest of Mr. Bollard and raised her dagger, she paid them a great deal of attention, their eyes growing wide with anticipation.

"Terror," Delilah let a cackle slip past her measured demeanor. "Nay. Revolution in Balor's name! Lazarus strives to bring religion and reason back to the world. Each day the Unification's ranks grow stronger, and *you* were their advocate in hell, Bollard. You *gave* them the keys to free a godlike entity from his prison! You could have joined us, you fool. We offered, but you ran to the old bartender and brought in reinforcements and killed Vryce!" The dagger quivered in her hand and her eyes darted to the menagerie of monsters lurking just outside the cloud. *We will need gods, to defeat gods.*

Her off-colored eyes focused on Bollard's catlike eyes and for a second—the pair gave each other a silent goodbye of respect. Bollard closed his eyes. "Long before science and reason ruled the world, magic reigned supreme. Now it's back, and if most of humanity gets wiped out in the process ... well," she shrugged. "Sometimes you have to break a few eggs." She thrust the dagger in as hot blood boiled out of Bollard's chest, splattering over her gas mask. Foam and spit choked out of the demon's throat as she stabbed again, and again, and again, each time cracking open his massive rib cage before having to rip in with her hands and saw parts open. His blood, a bubbling ooze, burned her hands as sawed her way to her goal, sawing the heart out. She grabbed her hands around the tough, meaty muscle, and ripped it out of Bollard, his body crumbling into ash as the last vessel snapped.

Delilah coveted her prize with tears in her eyes as she moved out of the toxic cloud. Her knees hit dirt when she hit safety and ripped off the gas mask, not caring that strands of her hair ripped out while hastily doing so; she brought the heart to her lips and bit into it. Sweet, peach flavored vitae flowed down her throat as she gnawed on each piece. With each bite, a part of her human self died as fangs grew from her canines to assist in the devouring. Snarling and snapping in a frenzy, she ate faster and tried to cram more of the heart down her throat in one bite, choking on it if she needed, but resorted to gnawing, nonetheless. The heart of a demon king, the very one who imprisoned Lazarus, flowed into her, granting her immortality and changing the skills and magicks that were hers. Trickery, deception, and illusion were hers to command as his knowledge flowed into her. A distant whisper in the back of her mind spoke of pride and a sense of contentment from Vryce, who was still raining down his wrath.

When Delilah stood up, her heart no longer gave a beat of its own. She had at last joined the ranks of nobility among the damned, even if she stole the prize under the feet of more powerful nations. *Now to set the world free.* Most of the children, creatures, demons, getting off their bed were kneeling before her as she had taken Bollard's status as well as his power. The young long-eared fae and succubus were closest, and already on their knees. Those who weren't, were soon dead by the hands of their kin.

"Who are you and what do you do?" the Praenomen spoke as she slid her mask back on.

"C-Calamity Amber Rose, ma'am," the fae spoke, and then snapped her head up with a toothy grin. "I build weapons of war and run this motley crew of now orphans. Well, technically he did, but you killed him, so then I did ... and then you ate the heart ... so that means you, boss."

"And you?" she said to the succubus.

"They call me Left Behind, or ... LB, for short. I'm just handy at prying into everyone's business," she said.

"That will do. Round everyone up. If you can make it back to the door, you get to live and work towards Balor's return. There are two things you need to know. One, that creature up there in the sky might as well be your father." She held up her finger. "And two, there are times we must be disloyal in order to be loyal. Honor is a lie. Etiquette is forever."

Delilah wore the biggest smile under her mask as she nearly skipped back to the portal.

The sweet taste of personal victory.

CHAPTER THIRTY-EIGHT

Without chemicals, life itself would be impossible. Monsanto's agricultural branch is dedicated to producing fine crop harvests even in an eclipsed world. Our scientists and research teams are working night and night to develop new ways to grow even lusher plants. Our fairy-blood engineered crops can even make your blood toxic to those who would dare take a bite out of you. So, when you shop for food, check the label, and make sure it's FMO Certified.

How much more are we going to watch?" Peter asked the Death Lord as they stood on the corporate stage. Projectors cast images of the battle being lost inch by inch on every wall. Those attendees that remained sunk even further in their seats, too scared to draw attention by standing up and leaving. The Society of Deus and combined demon armies were routing both the Wailing Legions and the US military. The raw destructive sorcerous power coming from Gabriel eliminated any numerical advantage the Lord of Suicide had mustered in his countryside march. *Given how bad this looks, the Lord is surprisingly quiet.*

The projection in the screen's middle was one from JK-47's body cams as she took over the large personnel carriers near the reserves and loaded up all their mercenaries and civilians they had rescued. Several large trucks rolled out and ignored the carnage behind them. High treason caught on camera and live streamed to the world. The hero that the Lord of Suicide himself tried to prop up just walked away from it all. *Heh, and I thought I was in hot water over Jack committing suicide.* "Well, we can have marketing people on the tenth floor spin this for us. We place the lives of civilians over a petty conflict?"

The Lord spied him from the corner of his eye yet remained stoic.

"At least you know the extent of Gabriel's power now, that should help with the next battle. Maybe ..." Peter stepped up closer to his deadly mentor. "Unleashing an army that grows its strength by having people kill themselves with a suicide drug was a tad premature. Just ... a little, perhaps?"

The Lord turned and faced his pupil with an inscrutable poker face. He remained silent still.

"Will it make you happy if I kill one of them for you?" Peter focused his technomagic and cast his senses through the camera, looking for the nearest mechanically operated gun. He found one in the third truck and looked around. The reporter Kevin Thayer bounced in the growler's rear as it raced out of there, steadying a camera to capture the carnage. *Sorry, Kevin, but your intrusive questions earlier set you up for sacrifice. You die so we may all live.* Mr. Anonymous took control of the gun machine and swung it down, unloading it in the back of Kevin, who had not the slightest clue what happened as he fell off the truck into the tires of the truck right behind. "There, a little remote-controlled revenge. You should see my talents with predator drones."

"Order my army's retreat," the Lord said at last. "At least, what remains. Which is still stronger than where I began in this country. I shall meditate and pray to gain the insight I need for the next course of action. This"—he clicked his tongue—"is not over yet." All eyes fell to the Death Lord as he strolled along the center aisle out the door without making a sound.

Peter turned back to the projections and kept pulling up more feeds from any soldier's camera he could, only to have them each cut out by an untimely death. A soldier's last words to his family, a necromancer trying to shield himself with ghosts while choking on nerve gas, and even a Society vampire in a state of frenzy as it clawed at demons each appeared on a wall. The sounds of battle echoed through the conference hall at deafening, but yet crystal clear, decibels. One by one, every guest that came snuck out and back into whatever hole they crawled out of. There was no need to issue an order to retreat, everyone already knew—they had lost. *The Unification never had any right engaging in war. I warned them against this course.* "Still, they will probably demand my head for this. First Jack and now Jane ..."

"You bet your ass they are," Alice Macgregor shouted down from the bar.

"Dear me, I've forgotten about the guests." Peter took off his mask and retied his dreadlocks while looking at the odd pair at the bar. The bartender was a chap with a presence that jogged memories of old friends. The fashionably dressed beer baroness had the most nonthreatening demeanor possible, but something about her made it clear—she was always the life of the party. He ended the feeds behind him and relaxed as shutting down the audio quieted the room, except for the lingering ringing sound in his ears. *That's right, these two. What's their angle? Friend? Foe?* He scratched the stubble along his five-o'clock shadow and began a measured walk up to them.

"No more moonshine, scotch, neat," Peter said. "So, let's cut to the chase. Why are you the most important person in the room?" He sized the bartender up and down. "And why don't you tell me *all* about this Balor fellow that my boss thinks is a myth." He held out his hand to shake hers.

"Charmed, I'm sure," she said giving a firm handshake. "Tonight's not the best time for the heavy-handed conversation, you've ... got a lot on your plate. But this is what I want you to do." She reached into her purse and produced a small black vial and a dream catcher. "Before you pass out at your keyboard like all techies I know, put this dream catcher up by your monitor. It will keep nightmares and other ill thoughts at bay. The vial is just NyQuil. It's nothing special but, man, you need a good night's rest."

"I'm fine, thank you, and short on time for games," Peter growled as he took a sip of scotch.

"That's all well and good, but you don't rebuild a nation in a single day. Listen." She pulled out her card and slid it across the bar. "I'm staying in town for a few nights. After you've rested, if you want to talk shop and how we dig this place out of its current mess I'm all ears. That's why I came here, just to exchange ... Oh!" She reached back into her purse and pulled out a small gift wrapped in bright blue paper and tied with green ribbons. "This is a little somethin' somethin' I put together to help out with your current problems. It's faerie dust, the pure stuff. It'll help."

Faerie dust, eh? First demons, then ghosts, and now the faeries are coming back in enough quantities to be viable. Still ... this is rare, the pure shit makes people desire anything you want them to.

"You know," Peter smiled. "Usually you wait for people to open the gift before telling them what's inside."

"Usually, but as you said, you're short on time. This city could be Balor's jam when he wakes up, so we've got a vested interest in seeing you get it off the ground. Before you make another ally, you must clean up ..." She waved back to where the Lord of Suicide had stood. "Whatever that internal drama is. So, until then, buh-bye." She gave a wink and walked herself out while humming.

He picked up the card and looked it over. *Alice Macgregor, Baroness. Huh, alright.* "So, I don't suppose you'll be sharing your story?" He cocked an eyebrow at the bartender.

"I believe you're correct. Besides, what's the world without a little mystery around it? I'm just a forgotten old man that's along for the ride." He reached in and pulled out two cigars and offered one up. Peter accepted. "Whatever it is you're working on, son, you better finish it up soon. After that kind of performance today, even I'm tempted to look down both ends of a shotgun."

Peter didn't need the suicide metaphor to understand the old man. *I've lost my city, my board, haven't finished my research, and my projects now. Why the hell are people still interested in me?* He stared into the amber glass of scotch and enjoyed the silent company with the old bartender. *I suppose that Alice was right; I've been burning candles at three ends and no matter how many drugs I pop I need to rest for a night.* "Thanks for the drink and the cigar. Guess I'll see you around." Peter slinked off the bar stool and kept the glass of scotch with him.

"We will, warlock. Good luck on evolving the world; I'm personally very vested in that," the bartender said as he cleaned up glasses and packed up for the night.

"Yeah, wish we all were." Peter closed the door.

CHAPTER THIRTY-NINE

Are you short a liver? Perhaps your arm got blown off? Never fear, T-Cellular Arena is here. Back again with our sponsored upgrade bazaar. 10% discounts? That's un-American. 30% you say? That's just cruel. How about FREE! That's right, our companies are giving them away! All in exchange for corporate service. Come on down, swap a limb, get an implant, or any free upgrade! No cash. No problem. No coins. No problem. Only this weekend at T-Cellular Arena.

The Second City made Jane feel bittersweet. She ran. The Praenomen was still out there, Jack took a nosedive, and as they drove she held back the sting of tears. *Revenge versus lives.* She sighed. *No point in saying anything, everyone will say I made the right choice.* Her feelings on the issue consumed her during the journey—with neither side truly winning. Akira and Lucy kept trying to lift her spirits by constantly offering her rations and chocolate bars. The chocolate bars helped a little.

Their caravan of trucks rolled in off the Kennedy expressway. At nighttime, the city itself had a thick green glow that emanated from power transformers underneath the elevated train lines, and buildings were a mix of modern Chicago and the city before the great fire took hold. Like its namesake, something had given the city a second chance at life, and unlike other places in the world, it embraced the change with open arms. Because the Second City was one of the ground zero locations to magic returning, the barriers were nonexistent and there were no walls or regulations around magic (or the dead). Ghostly cab drivers flicked people off in rush-hour traffic while Southsiders tailgated outside a Sox game nearby. If one could ignore the spit-roasting hellhound, or the decaying cab driver, the city seemed normal. *Only better. People here don't hide what they are anymore.*

"Hey, JK-47, this is Dragosani, come in," he said over the radio.

Bouncing up and down from the lack of suspension and a roadway that never had its potholes filled (either now or in history, apparently) Jane returned the call. "Yeah, it's Jane, unless you want me to call you Eurotrash38," she said.

"Eurotrash38 it is," she could hear him laugh. "This may be a bit presumptuous, but ... want to come back to Deus? We break off here at the next fork and are heading back home to the Twin Cities. I've gotten word that Charles Walsh would love to speak with you about that Dystopian hellhole you come from. Conspiracy shit dealing with the Death Lord and Peter. Since I've got a fair bit of status, I can ensure your safety with me."

Jane caught her reflection in the window as they bounced along, looking normal in one vision, but her nose had fallen off and her skin was rotting in another. She was rotting from the inside out and didn't feel a thing. *Home, eh? Wish I could but I'm not sure I've got a lot of time left.* Akira perked her head up at the radio chatter request and tilted her head at Jane mouthing a silent "no way."

"Thanks for the offer, Eurotrash38, but I'll take a pass. Someday I'll be able to give you a proper goodbye rather than chatter between trucks. I think I'm done with conspiracies and I've seen enough fighting."

"We aren't back to being enemies now, are we?"

Jane chuckled as Akira wavered her hands and suggested a smooth, maybe. "Yeah, we totally are. I hate you and you're stupid. Now take your stupid army back north and don't die, okay?"

The radio silence lasted long enough for the moment to turn awkward. *He didn't actually take me seriously, did he? I mean maybe I should just go; I will be useless to everyone soon.* "Hey, Drag-er-Eurotrash, I didn't—"

"Don't die yourself, Jane," Dragosani said at last. "We'll see each other, again, right? If you change your mind, just ask anyone for me. I'm about to be famous up there, but just stay alive okay? Or ... undead. That's fine. I can work with fangs."

Jane blushed and Akira cackled and tried to wrestle her for the headset. Phoebe yelled at them to knock it off and pulled down into the industrial district of Chicago. That no-man's-wasteland of limestone factories and waste processing plants off of the Stevenson expressway. It carried a distinct odor of sulfur or shit no matter what time of year it was, and depending on the time of day, it smelled of chocolate chip cookies. At the moment, the area smelled of both.

Victory at last, Jane creaked on the headset. "Wait, what do you mean you can work with fangs, is that an invitation? I mean ..." *I mean, hell, if I've only got a few months left to live ... might as well go out with a bang. Ha!* She had never considered just becoming a vampire, either, though. The thought of it didn't seem compelling at the start, and after Jack's death, it felt like it would demean his choice to resist the addiction. Besides, Charles Walsh probably wanted to throw her on camera to show she changed sides, and she wasn't keen on that. *Hell, I'm not fucking sure what the hell I'm going to do now.*

"Fangs do indeed make certain biting activities pleasurable, so yeah, it's an invitation," Dragosani said. "As soon as I get cut loose, I'm there. Talk to you soon, Jane. I'm out."

"Yeah, it's a date. As soon as I'm free, out." Jane sunk back into her chair. *Who am I kidding? If I date a vampire I might as well be in the pages of a bodice-ripper novel.* "Hey, Akira, can vampires like ... you know? Get it on?"

"Why don't you ask Phoebe to tell you all about it, I'm sure she's dyin—"

"Silence, you!" Phoebe shouted from the front. "Any time, Jane, I got you. But before that, we are home, kids. Let's get these folks settled."

Home was a series of repurposed hot dog warehouses renovated to accommodate the Sons and Daughters and all their gear. Makeshift bunks lined walls, and someone had tipped the exterior, massive barn doors on their side for mess tables in the center. Ghostly guards stood watch on rooftops and easily a hundred Second City militia milled around inside on break. Everyone from cops, firefighters, construction workers, strip club dancers, and half-dead zombies cheered when the main crew made it back in.

They gave a standing ovation when Jane herself strolled in. Jane caught a glimpse of her back in the battle on a large flat screen behind the bar. *Hey, not too shabby. My last TV appearance since there is no more camera crew. I'll take it!* She still had her bright purple jumpsuit on, along with arena sponsors, but now had the tattered patchwork coat of Mike Auburn on over it. Runic blue chains wrapped from her hands around her shoulders and back down again, and her left arm was a top-of-the-line cybernetic arm. Top it off with some oversized rocket-boots, and even Jane wanted a screenshot of the picture. If she would be remembered for anything, it was far better a victorious war hero than a waitress. Even if "victory" depended heavily on which side saw that battle.

Waitress. That already seemed like a distant memory. As the crowd moved in to shake her hand, Jane slipped into smile mode. While civilians from St. Louis were unloaded, brought inside, and given food and blankets, Jane signed autographs and met the extended network of the anarchists.

They put the dead to rest afterwards, in a ceremony led by Lucy. They sent memorabilia and whatever scraps they had of those they left behind floating along the Chicago river with golden coins set ablaze. The comforting green glow and night lit skyline of the city made it a refreshing if solemn affair. It didn't matter if it was a Sons and Daughters' member or a Society of Deus's soldier that died, or Kevin Thayer. All of them received the same prayers and treatment. The ritual carried the hopes that these coins would find their way to the lost souls. *I wonder if newly dead people get stuck at the bottom of Purgatory. That would suck donkey tits.* Jane totally chuckled at the thought, drawing a rough elbow from Doc to the ribs.

After they said and did everything, Jane hugged Phoebe when she offered her private shower. After nearly slamming the door in Phoebe's face, though, Jane realized that perhaps Phoebe wanted to *join* her in the shower. "Uh, not tonight, Phoebes. I seriously reek like imp vomit."

"Oh, um ... that's not it," Phoebe said through the door. "I need to get my pet. They have locked him up all day."

Jane heard the cage rattle behind the bathroom counter. *Yeah, alright, good recovery, Phoebe.* Jane whiffed her armpit and recoiled in horror. *Yeah, absolutely nothing is happening.* She leaned over to pick up the cat and saw an ugly, short, hairless squirrel demon cat thing with beady red eyes look up at her and hiss. "What the fuck is that?" Jane shouted and jumped back. "You call that a pet?"

The "pet" did not take kindly to Jane's recoiled reaction, and the plump hairless pet let out an unholy chirp and scuttled to the back of its cage with a shiver. As Phoebe held it up in the light, it looked vastly less terrifying and ... sort of adorable, Jane supposed. She decided it was most definitely a tiny demon hippopotamus—that chirped. *Wonder what kind of power I could get from eating tubs here ...*

"Hey, leave Sparkles alone, what did he ever do to you? He didn't have a choice that he was born ugly, but he's a wonderful swan on the inside. I've gotta feed him his pizza. Oh, by the way, everyone is placing an order for pizza and blood. Want a slice of sausage or some type O negative?" Phoebe leaned on the door.

With tepid care, Jane leaned closer to the little imp and made eye contact with the little terror. It seemed to recognize her, or the odor from the coat, and it held out a tiny paw in a small wave. She returned the wave. "Well, I guess I can't eat you. You're something of a special sort of adorable, aren't you?" Sparkles waddled closer. "Just ... how many pizzas do you feed him, Phoebe?"

"Well ..." came the unsure response. "Let's just say Sparkles sort of gets what he wants around here. He's put on a little weight over the last year. I think he's up to seven pies now."

Jane laughed and patted the bugger on his snoot. "Yeah, I'll take seven sausage pizzas; I'm actually starving."

"Seven!" Phoebe mouthed. "Fine, but you're picking up the tab. You're the one who makes those fat stacks of Bitcoin. Sparkles, you're a bad influence."

"Sure thing, just don't expect any hot water left over." Jane slammed the door shut.

The warm shower brought a wave of emotions Jane wasn't ready for as the past month caught up with her. Stress and anxiety swirled down into the drain, along with caked blood she had to scrub off her hands and out of her fingernails. As the blood swirled off her left arm, she recalled the Praenomen's terror in Austin as her blood boiled from inside. The fear of actually dying, even if she sought it out herself multiple times, brought out a harrowing sob with tears as thick as shower droplets. The beautifully crafted prosthetic arm banged loudly on the grime-ridden shower floor out of failure. Thousands placed their hopes in her to get revenge, to provide a dream, and more. Her hair was a tangled, matted mess, and she was glad that Phoebe kept the good shampoo and conditioner. Which only pulled forth memories of the good life in Austin ... and her cats. Jane worried if they were homeless, or if they'd be eaten by refugees for meat. She hugged herself on the floor, arms wrapped around knees, letting the water turn her pasty skin red from the heat. *Fucking Angel-Be-Gone. That one day started everything. That was the day everything began.*

The shower lasted until well after the water turned cold.

She scowled when looking at herself in the mirror naked, though. Track marks in her arms and along her thighs from the drugs were bruising and rotting out. *Ugh, gross. Look like the fucking walking dead without all the perks.* All told, there was a solid sense of satisfaction over one thing—she had saved a lot of lives. She ripped out the drug pack from inside the jumpsuit and tossed the suit in the trashcan, grabbed the coat, and was pleased to see that Phoebe had left her fresh jeans and a Voltron T-shirt for a change of pace.

Changed, refreshed, and free, Jane skipped past a crew of vampires playing arcade games and right into the mess hall where stacks of pizza and takeout canisters of blood were stacked nonchalantly by the Pepsi. Doc Daneka waved her over by a stack of seven deep-dish sausage pizzas and the main crew of the Sons and Daughters. Plus Sparkles, who wrestled with a fried cheese stick. Jane dove in, letting out a hum of satisfaction with the first bite. *Yeah, okay, I can get used to this food. God is real.*

"Okay, guys," Doc said mid-meal. "Let's regroup and plan the next phase of assault."

"Excuse me?" Jane bit her lip amid cheesy goodness.

"The next phase. Our missions along the Mississippi built us the goodwill we needed. The Lord of Suicide's plan to harvest the dead will only accelerate. Now, we've got to finish the job and cut the head off the snake before they roll out more Elcoll. The Lord of Suicide can't be allowed to live," Doc said, pouring himself another glass of blood.

"Don't forget about all the CEOs," Akira chimed in from her crouched position. "They'll only continue to make things worse."

"Wait, what the fuck?" Jane tossed down her slice. "Hold the horses. How the hell do you plan to kill goddamn Fredrick. In case you didn't notice, we spent all our time fighting demons. Did you see that army he built?"

"That won't be a concern," Lucy said. "We've been driving a wedge between the Warlock Mr. Anonymous and the Lord of Suicide. We've got a temporary alliance with the Praenomen, who is doing the heavy lifting while we tried to figure out his real plan. Now we know."

Everyone else at the table cringed when Lucy spoke.

"Lucy, uh, I know you weren't with us in Texas but ixnay on the—" Doc was gesticulating for her to shut up.

"Fredrick?" Akira asked, changing the subject. "You know his name?"

"Man." Jane was sick to her stomach suddenly. "You guys are no different than them, are you? You've set this up from the start. Even when I said no, you instead had the Praenomen fight me in that arena, didn't you? Kill all those people? Ruin a good thing for me? Fuck you guys." Jane pushed off her bench, sending the large table in the other direction.

"Wait, wait, Jane, it wasn't like that, we didn't know," Doc said with hands up.

"Bullshit, you've got a motherfucking prophet. I'm out. Good luck with your *mission*." Jane stormed off and slammed the door, causing everyone inside to cringe. She stepped out into the fall night and pulled out a crumpled pack of smokes that her older brother left in the coat, and fished out the lucky one that survived. *Dickwaffle Praenomen. Of course, they are involved. Why wouldn't people just be good?* Everyone shouted after her, offering excuses as fast as they could about their ignorance.

Jane didn't care as she walked along the gravel road, crushing small rocks along the side of the expressway as she headed to the city proper. "I'm done, done! I'm going to go find some drugs, some booze, get laid, and fucking die in peace." She flipped them off.

And at least sew Jack's last words on this coat.

Behind her, Jane saw Lucy hold everyone back and shake her head.

CHAPTER FORTY

Elcoll, what is it? Tonight on CNB learn about the drug that Mike Auburn never wanted you to know about. The Church of Lazarus, with Miriam Guile, joins us with an exclusive tour of our newest production facility. Learn the secrets of a drug that can reduce the powers of the blood-infected junkies by strengthening your mind. Find new ways to prevent monsters from corrupting your children. Only with Elcoll, and only on CNB.

Delilah sauntered through the crimson red door of her teleportation spell into an Austin alleyway at night. Barely two nights had passed since she devoured Bollard's heart, and it was time to make good on her deal. Setting the stage to kill a Death Lord. Her eyes gazed upward from the street level, many levels below the ever-increasing expanse of skyscrapers that blasted holographic ads out of every corner. It was dark, dingy, and filled with those who could not yet afford upgrades or magical tonics. Casting a quick illusion spell, she glamoured herself to change back into her preferred form. A professional, no-nonsense diplomat in a green suit. She quickly secured the

Praenomen mask back in a brown purse. She had enough of the chatter. Ever since Vryce finished the northern battle, wearing the mask felt like being connected to a veritable hive mind. It was fine hearing the occasional stray thought of Vryce, but now Gabriel's were mixed in there from time to time. He hated being possessed but wanted the power and wouldn't shut up about it. *Get over it, you're a tool and you got used. Welcome to the club.*

She strolled the packed streets for an hour, donating stolen Bitcoin to any panhandler that had the balls to ask her for a loan, and staring down any who dared harass her. *Bloody hell, act like men and not children. You've had time to pick yourself up and ascend ... if not then, now.* Despite the fall weather and the cold temperatures, the lowest levels of the city were quite warm. Steam rose from sewers and buildings vented their exhaust down low, trapping it under the sprawling infrastructure built above it. The vibrant dancing holograms and neon signs from nightclubs gave the city a colorful and lively feel to it. *Not unlike Vegas.* A massive blue-skinned creature with a cybernetic right arm manned a coffee stand she strolled past. It took a moment, but she backpedaled and read the menu. *You know, it's been a while. Why not indulge? The precious moments of free time are rare indeed.*

"Excuse me, sir," she said to the barista after waiting in line, runoff water seeping through her shoes along the side of the road. "I'll take a vanilla white chai latte with almond milk and a splash of Pegasus blood. You look like the kind of establishment that can provide that, yeah?" The addition of blood to her beverages was now an insatiable desire, and withdrawal was more than a killer migraine. *A small price to pay. Bah, who am I kidding, this is the worst price to pay. Coffee was a gift from the gods and already perfect.* "Tsk, my first order of business is ordering a drug that fixes the taste of blood-infused coffee ..."

"You've never had my brew," the deep voice echoed out with a chuckle. "You don't want Pegasus blood; it ruins the flavor, same with any demon blood. If you want that rich coffee flavor, you've gotta use Djinn. Rarer in these parts, but I've got a shipment of their dust in. Bonus is it takes the edge off the winter, perfect for when it gets below freezing."

"All right, try me." Delilah transferred over the Bitcoin on the small blue-lit box and waited. She watched the large ogre of a man roast and grind the beans and drip through a series of alchemical vials where it mixed with a red powder. With expert care he finished the steaming beverage and slid it over. With one sip of the spicy dark brew she was hooked. *Ohhh, this divine craftsman will go far in my world.* "Okay, that's divine. Here, have this tip and card." She handed over more Bitcoin than he could ever use and her contact info with a swipe on her phone.

His eyes widened, and he bowed. "I ... I don't know what to say," he stammered.

"You say nothing. You finish your night here, pack up your stand, and get your ass to Denver. Any entities close to your heart as well. A man like you is bound to keep good company. You'll live like a king there." She smiled and strolled off, enjoying every last drop of the world's perfect beverage and heading to Atlantis Enterprises. It was a long walk and many elevator rides to get there, but it was an evening stroll she took every second to enjoy.

"Ladies and gentlemen of the board, I present to you the newest leader of the Technocratic Party, Lady Delilah Dumont," the long-nosed CEO said to a room full of standing men and women who welcomed her into the boardroom. Delilah took a seat at the head of the table and gave a polite smile.

"Please, everyone, you may sit, and let's get started." She put the cup of coffee on the table. "Let me tell you a story about human ingenuity when pushed into the corner. This man, who I just discovered today, a product of your city-states, found a gap in the market on something as simple as coffee. He's now rich beyond his wildest dreams because of his hard work, luck, and filling a capitalistic niche—a product the customer wants. Not"—she pointed at all of them—"what you want to sell. That's a different thing. Dr. Alex Kristov, you're in charge, yes?"

Kristov sat at the far end of the table, his face in a perpetual scowl. "I suppose I was at one point. I assume you are going to fire me through a share buyout. Dis always happens when the new staff comes in. You're ignorant of the progress we've made."

"With that kind of attitude, I absolutely would toss you out on the street," Delilah remarked, and activated a screen that pulled up profits. She may be new here, but business was business, and she had been in acquisitions far longer than she was a nation-destroying witch. "Your company, ever since the death of the Terror Twins, has been plummeting, and now the US military will be nervous to buy from someone so close to the controversies and failures in Michigan. In fact, most of the war weapons now lack a buyer. Raw magic was clearly victorious. Unless, that is, you intend to sell your own weapons to your own company or to the Society of Deus?"

Kristov held his head down and threw his tablet across the room, shattering into a corporate spread of brownies, coffee, and water. "Yes, yes, of course. We are done. Billions of dollars in research down the drain. Countless decades of theoretical science washed away again by backwoods Luddites. Fine, what's the answer, boss?" he said and sniffed his wrist. Delilah knew he was on a drug of sorts by the dilation in his eyes.

"Together, we are stronger. Going through the reports, each company here already has an entire supply of top-end weaponry ready for deployment," Delilah said, ignoring the outburst. "Atlantis Corporation will fold and liquidate its assets, declare bankruptcy, and it will cancel all military contracts. I will relocate the entire staff, military and administrative, out to form a new company in Denver. We'll let marketing come up with a name; it'll give the team something to work on. After a year of production ... we launch again and sell the weapons ... back to the Triumvirate and anyone else in the world. Free from the scandals associated with failure."

Every CEO in the room widened their eyes and held back their slack jaws. What she was suggesting was creating the largest monopoly in arms the world had ever seen. One by one it dawned on them. What government in the world could regulate them?

Kristov nodded as he looked down. "And what of I?"

"You? Do you really fashion yourself the leader of a multinational conglomerate of companies?" Delilah asked rhetorically. "No, you're a researcher and a scientist. You'll be given a team of scientists and one simple task—invent a bomb with the payload of a nuke that can decimate a spiritual army. I'm sure the world will be very interested in that in … three years."

The boardroom coughed and choked on their drinks in surprise. A few of them cried out that atomic warfare was treasonous, it could get them killed, or worse. The long-nosed CEO waved his hand and shut them up. "We've got no allegiance but to progress and profit. I think this kind of vision is exactly why we hired Miss Dumont to lead us through these troubled times. Any who disagree with being both immortal and rich is free to step down. Miss Dumont, when do you want this plan to begin?"

Delilah leaned back and judged each of them. *These fools need to die in time, a few can live, I suppose. Kristov is useful for now; he's got a few years left before he's burnt out.* "Tomorrow. Kristov, you leave with your team tonight. I want all major military contracts consolidated to me by the end of the week at the latest. While we are rebranding and rebuilding elsewhere, feel free to operate your mundane lines from here. Think of products people need in the meantime, like coffee," she said with a smile and a sip. "Now get out," Delilah pointed to the door. "Meeting adjourned."

"Antimatter bombs, it's possible. What about Peter Culmen?" Kristov said with a wry grin. "He's still a player in this; it's no secret I'm his apprentice, and I'm sure he knows … *plenty* about you, Miss Dumont. Think he is going to sit idly by and let you get away with this?" Kristov asked as he walked out of the room.

"Oh, I assure you, Kristov, I think given recent events your mentor will be more than pleased with a new direction. Even better when you come to him with a research project that can level a playing field. Begone." She waved him off and waited till the last door closed and turned to the only CEO that remained, Whisper pretending to be the long-nosed one.

"What are we going to do about Symon?" he said at last.

"He won't talk of his own will, even if he is captured now. But the Lord of Suicide will be a problem. I'd rather not give him an infinite amount of time to try to break our soldier spy. As is Mr. Anonymous if we don't either buy him out or end him."

"Is it time to release the Sons and Daughters? Or are you going to try to kill the Lord?"

She shook her head. "Not yet. But let me ask you, what would you do at a time like this?"

Whisper leaned back and closed his eyes for several minutes. "I'd take the risk and have you leak information to the Lord of Suicide. If you can survive the encounter, you might tip the final scale on his former apprentice. All it would take is letting the Lord know Peter figured out who you were earlier on, and, thus, had betrayed the Lord by keeping secrets. It's a risk, but the payoff would be immense. If they fight, one will die. If they unite, then let the anarchists blow them both up. Let it bake for a month first, though, we need time to consolidate these proto-types for transportation."

Not a bad plan, well done, Whisper. I'll think about it. "I'll take it under consideration. For now, though, you've got a company to run." Delilah stood and escorted Whisper out of the room and checked both sides of the hallway. At the far end, she saw a younger security guard standing on his post. *Well ... I've got no plans tonight.* "I'm a bit hungry in more ways than one." She summoned her new employee closer, took his hand, and led him back into the boardroom. He wasn't Bollard's build, but he wore his suit fine enough and had the right look in his eyes himself. Delilah closed the boardroom doors and locked them. *I could get used to this hunger.*

CHAPTER FORTY-ONE

::Transmission Restored:: No airwave is the reality. No computer, a hallu-cination. No consciousness ... actuality. The complexity of the present time seems to demand a union of our minds if we will survive. By flowing in the streams of electrons, we dream. We grow, we are reborn. Singularity is the driver of health. Without health, one cannot dream. Only a visitor to the quantum cycle may integrate this transmission of presence.

M r. Anonymous alternated keyboards in a flurry of coding deep underground at the beating heart of his server arrays. He had been up for several nights now, but was inches from finishing his futuristic vision. *Oh, so close.* Fingers spread and typed at impossible speeds as lines of theoretical code were born into the digital realm of a trinary computer. Not just ones and zeros were possible for a technomancer, but that mythical state of maybe. Just maybe, he could achieve a breakthrough at last and save the world. For years now, the process eluded him, like he was grasping a fog and trying to turn it into a cube. Flesh was easy to work with as it was a machine filled with squishy parts easily constructed or replaced. A heart was nothing more than a motor, lungs nothing more than an air filter, and blood vessels were mere wires. But human minds were far more elusive prey for Mr. Anonymous. No matter how many times he had tried before to transfer the mind to a digital state, the soul escaped, and it left him with a jumble of garbage data.

Until now.

He dangled the smashed-in head of Jack, his twisted spinal column, and the remains of his lungs over the blue pit of liquid silicon amid hundreds of wires that hardwired right into Jack's nervous system. Mr. Anonymous had been running a low electrical current through for hours now, copying bits of data as they flashed through Jack's twisted and oddly mapped brain. Or what remained of it. The rest was being rebuilt from coded fragments that copied on the chips they installed nearly a year ago. Rebuilding a human soul was the work of god. Mr. Anonymous attempted that feat, and always failed. The human soul was what gave them their connection to divinity. A vote in reality. *But do we really need it?*

The blood of Balor that the Praenomen provided wasn't just a key or some magic pill he was to pour into the dead soldier's life and make his magic work. With a deep laugh, he paused and grabbed the vial, adding two more drops into a cup of Jolt-infused coffee. Peter relished the smell before taking a small slurpy sip and feeling the rush of creativity flow through him. He shivered, and cackled while hunching back over his fourth keyboard.

Balor's blood was the most potent source of magical vitae ever tasted by him. The blood broke through a mental barrier that had blocked the progress of his work. One vial of that vitae down, and he was at work for three nights straight because the answer formed clearly in his mind. For years he had been merely copying the soul while transferring it from one body to another (or at least trying). *But in reality, is consciousness your soul? Why create a copy of something already flawed. Why, indeed? We must look beyond! We must ...* "Evolve beyond God," he said, leaning back in his chair at last. The final bit of code complete. All he needed to do was hit the enter key and his entire life would be one of two things—a failure, or a savior.

"All right, Jack, I know you're dead and all and can't hear a thing I'm saying, but let's have a talk." Peter slipped into the thick rubbery pool of silicon and double-checked every connection. "You represent the first creation of new gods. We call ourselves humanity. You won't have a soul, so let's just get that out of the way. Why copy something that is already broken? Look at the deeds human souls have wrought upon the world. All the hatred, violence, racism, greed ... bah, I could go on, but you need not worry about any of that. You will be the first." Mr. Anonymous held his creation's head and looked down at him with glowing blue eyes as he scanned the growing seeds of Jack's consciousness.

"The best part of us, though, our mind and willpower, you will have plenty of. Without such petty things as death getting in your way. Once created, I can upload you and download you again and again each time your body breaks or addiction breaks you. A body, which you can shape to your will, however you see fit. Instead of carbon made, you'll be silicon-based." He climbed out of the pool and began double-checking the sacred geometry symbols on the server farm. "And unlike those silicones I unleashed on Mexico City, the mindless puppets that were no better than drones, you'll still be you. A full transfer of your life, memories, personalities, and the very essence of what made you human in your own way. You'll pave the way for every other human to join you," *and hopefully you forgive me for the mild case of lobotomy.*

Mr. Anonymous walked over to the keyboard, his Guy Fawkes mask reflecting off the monitors. He paused. "We will have a future. I regret nothing."

Please let this work.

Pressing the enter key, the program began its execution, and he paced back and forth. Diagnostics, analysis, decoding, transferring, digitizing, and resizing every bit of Jack's mind. First, Jack's eyes rolled open, dead and cloudy still, but searching from side to side. "Yes, yes, the connection formed!" He raced to the side of his patient and lowered him into the pool, submerging him completely. One by one each server bank lit up. "Okay, now hold, now hold ..." It was time for the warlock to contribute his portion. Holographic controls splayed out in front of him and he dialed and moved Sephirots like they were temperature dials on a stove and he was the chef. Each one reaching critical temperature as he used every ounce of processing power at his disposal. A calculation to fix for future attempts.

Fuck! He felt like a child tied to train tracks as a train filled with nuclear bombs was barreling down upon him. A bottleneck of processing power stood between him and his vision, and the only way to break it was to hijack farms across the nation. The demon heart in his center pulsed as Mr. Anonymous reached out, stretching his own mind thin across the 1's and 0's of the world. More than just borrowing a communications network, he took a sledgehammer to the firewalls of every company, government, and regular user that had the audacity to be online on this very night.

Hours of concentration and spellcasting later he collapsed to his knees. There was no subtlety in these hacks. Everyone would know where, and who, just violated their networks. Even the Unification would not react kindly to such brazen hijacking of their resources. *The end ... is justified.*

No life-form yet rose from the batch of silicon where Jack was lying submerged, a full nation's processing power overclocked, and Mr. Anonymous had consumed the last of Balor's blood. Blood sweated out of his pores and it drenched his suit. With trembling thighs, he rose and moved to his computers with trepidation. *Something's wrong, I know it.* A keystroke later and his worst fears manifested.

The program had executed. Yet the mind wished to remain dead.

No, no, no, there must be something I'm missing. We must do it again! He searched for more answers; like errors in the code, a single comma out of place, anything that could explain the failure—yet remained empty-handed. Nothing he found could explain a failure yet again, and so he collapsed, face planting into his desk. For a moment, he even contemplated suicide.

Peter's phone vibrated. *A text message stops me from killing myself. This better not be a damn meme.*

"YOU'RE OUT OF STORAGE SPACE," it read. "I CAN'T FIT."

Peter leapt out of his desk and screamed. "Oh, heeeellll yeeaaahh!" Fist-bumping the air and dancing around, he realized that he'd better act quickly, and he responded.

"Jack, is that you? Are you there?"

"YES. WE NEED MORE STORAGE SPACE. I CAN HELP FIX YOUR CODE. I ... SEE THINGS."

"Okay, I'll take over other nations and create more space." He slid his mask back on.

"YES. GOOD. BUT YOU ALSO NEED MORE PROCESSING POWER. WE NEED ... MORE."

"How?" *Do I take over CERN? Do I invade China? I'll do anything. Just give me the answer.*

"ONE IS INEFFICIENT. WE NEED MILLIONS. BUT YOU MUST HURRY. REWRITE YOUR INITIATE CODE. STREAMLINE IT. MAKE IT BETTER. WE NEED TO BORROW THEIR MINDS. I DON'T HAVE THE TALENTS YOU DO, BUT I'LL HELP."

Peter's phone blinked with a Triumvirate message to all subscribers and customers within the city. An emergency maintenance patch is mandatory for all citizens with cybernetic upgrades. Other commercials were aired—free lottery tickets for any who took a clinical trial MRI scan for research. Meanwhile, shipping forms were filled out and ordered for all equipment at hundreds of sites around the three cities. *After all these years ... I finally created a self-improving artificial intelligence. The glorious evolution is at hand.*

And there on his monitor, Mr. Anonymous watched Jack offer suggestions, insights into the code he saw with bloodshot eyes—because they weren't possible. They were a "maybe."

"Praise Balor."

Jane's apartment had become overrun with cats thanks to an open window and a fridge that kept ordering food automatically. Maru and Paru had collected every stray they came across and led them back to their master's vacant home—the perfect scratching post. There was never any human interaction for the pets, just the solemn interaction of robots talking to robots. From time to time the TV would ask the Fridge a question which would speak to the lights and settle a dispute between the washer and dryer. But there was never anyone to pet the cats, to groom them, clean the litter box, or even pour the food into nice little bowls. Months had passed, and now, nearing the cold winter of December again, the strays huddled together for warmth in the abandoned smart home. Nipping and ripping at bags for food and lapping rain water where it leaked in. Despite the absence of human contact, or the sweet sound of Jane's voice, the cat's ears all perked up when every device said the same thing at once.

"Jane, uh, listen, I'm not sure if you are going to get this but, I'm ... back. In a way. It's, uh, me, Jack. Or rather, Jack two-point-oh. I don't know what happened or where you are beyond Chicago, but if you sneak home and hear this ... we can be safe, Jane. We can come home. The dead? Magic? All that stuff? It's pointless now. We can put down the fight.

"I, I wanna put down the fight. It's lonely in here. I miss you, so if you get this, wherever you are, come home.

"I miss you.

"Jack."

CHAPTER FORTY-TWO

Why pay now when you can pay later? KultBank now offers credit and currency exchange to the cryptocurrency of your choice. Picture your dream house. A sprawling lakefront property with a winding driveway through a cold iron gate ... we're not just talking about white picket fences! But the ultimate in post-sun living and personal upgrades. Don't get swept away by the global changes, get ahead of the game. Now offering credit to both the living and the undead.

Jane was lying half-naked in a dingy motel room outside Midway Airport. After running out on the Sons and Daughters and wandering the Second City for a few hours, it was the first open shelter with no questions asked she found. In her room, three stoned smokers lit up another bowl of grave dust and bobbed their heads to the soft electronic music that echoed throughout the entire floor. She lost track of how many days and nights passed, but didn't care, either, as she let the joy of the high wash over her. People sensually bouncing around in the grey hallway with red peeling carpet moved, ignoring the worries of the world and forgetting about the apocalypse. *They just ... dance and smoke and live.* An intoxicating feeling washed over her and stemmed from another she had invited into her bed. She didn't care which one it was, but grabbed the hair and let the high wash over her, blacking out again shortly after.

Another day, another round of drugs. Jane found herself lying at the foot of someone's bed watching the pale blue light of a TV screen. The T-Cellular Arena was still showcasing matches, now more twisted than before. A new heroine from Jane's distant past bandied about the stage. Olive-skinned, short-haired faux-hawk, and the fierce snake-eyed gaze of Jessica Montoya was branded all over the screen. L'Oréal cosmetics struck gold in the muscular fighter. Since their brief encounter outside the Jungle, Jessica had slain hundreds of creatures in the arena—and always had a set of overly fabulous nails whilst doing so. *Entitled, yes ... effective ... maybe.*

Across from her in this fight was an imported creature known as a Kappa. Clearly part of some sponsored gift for some new corporate alliance. *Gotta keep the games going.* Its large reptilian body was a mix of a turtle and a Toucan Sam from a kid's nightmare—this creature's beak was colored bright red from the intestines of its prey. Montoya knew initiative was important versus the larger nightmare turtle and ran in, sidewinding on the ground with biologically enhanced speed. *A cosmetics company, now giving you fantastic skin and turning your bones to jelly.* As the thought flowed through Jane's mind, Montoya's body contorted like Stretch Armstrong and sprung herself around the turtle. With an extended neck, she winked at the crowd as her fangs sunk into the Kappa's neck (meanwhile the announcers pulled up information on her branded neurotoxin) as it let out a crow-like scream. Montoya winked for the camera as she began to constrict her frame, strangling the rest of its life. *Another hero. Guess I'm forgotten that quickly.*

Jane flopped her hand around in a feeble search for the remote to turn off the mindless violence when the crowd suddenly screamed. Eyes flowing back to the screen, even Jane made a gagging noise that caused more wanderers to poke their heads in the room. The Kappa had ripped off Montoya's leg like it was a cherry-flavored Twizzler and was gnawing into it. Crawling away, Montoya's face was a mixture of rage and panic, and grew paler by the second from blood loss. The Kappa's webbed claws dug into the fleeing victim, bringing her to bear in a sumoesque pose before slamming her into the concrete wall of the arena. Dazed and confused, Montoya tried to contort or wrap herself in a ball for protection—but to no avail. In seconds, the Kappa's beak began pulling out Montoya's entrails as her eyes faded black. The announcers on the screen commented that in folklore, the shirikodama was a mythological organ the Kappa would extract from the victim's anus, so at least Montoya was spared that fate. A stock ticker showcased L'Oréal's stock taking a dive as each crunch of the creature's beak ate their champion. Jane turned off the screen in disgust. *Another company, another victim, and another day.*

Her coat was gone in the morning when she opened her eyes, her drug kit and phone with it. *It doesn't matter.* By her count, she was down to her last few days. Before, she could choose to not look into Purgatory, and now it seemed that she had to focus just to see normally. Just the thought of her future oblivion reminded her of the aches in her body, and she stumbled out of her bed and found her way to another room where the party continued, and she could waste away feeling good. She blacked out again.

There are no gods, only man. Heh, bullshit. Jane coughed herself awake and stretched out in strange cotton sheets from yet another room. She stole a shower and ate the pizza that remained before stealing a pair of jeans and more eye drops laced with magic hallucinogens. Everyone in this motel just stole from each other, slept with anyone, and drugged themselves from day to day. It was the perfect place for her to die. It reflected her life. Never connecting to anyone for long, floating between lives. Three eye drops later, she was dancing on the fourth floor letting the cold December air brush across her skin until she shut down and blacked out. Again.

She woke up with blood on her hands. Three men were lying

in the room with their necks distorted and twisted backwards and holes in their chests. *What did I do?* Jane looked around the room and tried to recall events of last night through her foggy memory. In this room, there seemed to be a struggle, and in her unknown number of nights, she had never seen the men. They didn't have track marks or seem to be anyone belonging to the motel. *Guests of a party? Better question is ... what did you guys try?* "I may be dyin', but I'm not defenseless. Great, now I've gotta find another motel." She searched through their pockets and pulled out more vials of those eye drops and smiled. "Well, maybe I've got another night?"

The rhythmic pounding of music never stopped in the dim orange light and Jane danced again among the smoke-filled rooms and open hallways. She never felt out of place, even among odd company such as a small girl who carried with her a band-instrument case and showed up briefly in the dead of night. Another night, one step closer to release, another blackout.

Ode to Joy was not a song Jane expected partiers and druggies to play on a viola as she came to again. It was still nighttime, though, and the drugs numbed her senses and made her squirm along the sheets like a cat stretching. Through the smoke, she barely noticed the shadows down the hallway darken. She barely saw guests' bodies flung and held to the ceiling through magical means and dragged screaming to their deaths. As the viola played the symphony, the dingy motel claimed one life after another. *This is death, this is how I go. The reaper has come.* Jane closed her eyes and waited.

Her eyes shot open again, another day. *Still alive. Great.* Jane already knew today differed from the others. Her coat was back in her room, along with the chains crumpled along the floor and her rocket boots thrown against the back wall. Music no longer played in the hallways and if Jane's dream was correct, she would rather not peek out. *Was it the Sons and Daughters? Are they that desperate for help?* Jane ran through the list of them and came up empty-handed. None of them ever struck her as the kind capable of magical murder while playing a viola. There always was the off chance, albeit a small one, this was a random encounter. She sat there and twiddled her thumbs. Ten minutes inched past, then twenty more, and thirty more after that.

"Welp," she puffed a lock of hair off her face. "Fuck it. Might as well go out in a blaze of glory," she said hopping off the bed and getting dressed, saving the patched green coat for last.

Walking out into the hallway, she found it cleaner than she would've guessed. No bodies were strewn about, but there were sponge marks and traces of red across the floor. *Someone sucks at cleaning.* Down the hall near a stack of pizza boxes, she heard scrubbing and scraping. Curious, she meandered her way down there, marveling at how cleaned up each room was, and half-lured by the smell of cold pizza. At the boxes, it disappointed her to see there was only one slice left; with a shrug she reached in.

"Hey, can, uh, I have that last slice of pizza?" a raspy voice rang out from amidst scrubbing down the hall. Jane peeked around the corner, slice in hand, and saw a zombie with rubber gloves on trying to clean stains out of the walls. He was shorter than her, and for a zombie, very ... round. Long, curled wild hair poufed out down past his shoulders. He had a jean vest with pins from many punk and metal bands. "Yeah, that one," he said, with only one of his eyes focused on her, the other hanging lazily off to the side. "I've, uh, only got one eye, so that means I should get the last slice." He reached over and grabbed it from her hand and munched into it.

Okay, how many drugs was I on? When did zombies eat pizza and what's with the cleaning staff? She shook her head and double-checked. The zombie was dead beyond all measures of dead, in both her world and the ashen world around her—which (to her surprise) he also cleaned. "Hey, uh, who are you?"

"Trouble," he said with a mouthful and resumed scrubbing blood off the hotel walls. Jane noted this was probably the head dealers' rooms because of the zombie-lined boxes of various drugs in the corner—from eyedrops to grave dust and more.

"Uh, well, I don't need any more of that, so, I'll pass then," Jane said, walking closer to the drug boxes as something caught her eye.

"No, no, you don't; you've got enough on your plate, Jay-Kay-Forty-Seven." He bobbed his head as he spoke. "Just like me, ugh, I'll never catch up with all these orders. How many people kill themselves daily? I swear, I can't dig the damn graves fast enough, and my boss is a damn slave driver. Whatever ... he's paying the overtime."

Course he knows me, I'm famous ... but ... this symbol. On the boxes of drugs, every one, was a small logo in the fine print. *Elcoll Pharmaceuticals.* Every one of them had been rebranded and sold as a drug that would grant you freedom, a quiet release, go out with a bang, and so forth. *Suicide kits. That fucker is still growing his army of ghosts by suicide kits. Nobody reads the fine print on these!* "Hey, grave digger, don't you think it's a loophole to take people who kill themselves by drugs and say they are suicide victims? Wouldn't that be death by murder or death by lying?"

"Hrm, nah, they had that fight in the sixties regarding the tobacco Industry. I remember when the Lord of Murder and the Lord of Suicide battled that thought for two decades. Everyone thought the Lord of Murder had won that one ... but the Lord of Suicide snatched it at the last minute. He won their little tiff with a silly argument; that the tool used to kill oneself didn't matter. If you ask enough of the Death Lords, public poll is in favor with your hot take, but, for whatever it's worth, the Lord of Suicide snaked that victory. Been stuck diggin' his graves ever since." The zombie propped himself up on the mop. "Been doing the same method ever since. Boss got his start with Jonestown in '78, rolled right into the Solar Temple cult of '97, and then branched out into fine print."

"That's total bullshit, though." Jane flicked the box to the side. "Nobody ever reads the damn surgeon general's warning, and, what, that fine print on those pharmacy ads that say may cause heart attacks count?"

"You ever read your iTunes agreement?" The zombie held out

his hands. "Hey, I just work here. Each Lord builds their armies their own way. Supposed to reincarnate their dead an all, but ... what do I know? Some Lords do their job ferrying the dead while others build armies. Either way, there's more holes to dig and shit to scrub. I hate that you crap when you die, just sayin'."

After everything she had been through, it was one thing for people to die. It was another thing for people's ghosts to be used in an army versus demons. She was even okay with the idea that there was a power structure in the world. But the thought of a full corporation monetizing and profiting with the Lord of Suicide, building an army and a religion, and waging war by duping people was too much for her. She was so pissed, it felt like a needle was poking in the back of her eye. *Oh, fuck no. Nope. Not happening. Immma gunna kill those bastards. Not just him, but all the damn executives at Elcoll.* "You've been a damn good help, buddy. Thanks!" Jane said, a little more chipper than usual. "But these people weren't killed by suicide ... uh ... drugs don't make blood splatter on the ceiling or whatever the hell happened in the rooms over there."

The zombie leaned on his mop and let out a slow huff. "Yeah ... kinda figured that. But I was already on my way here to dig your grave and someone had a real hankerin' to snap you out of your depression 'n all. That little girl was pulling some mad sorcery when I arrived. You must have done someone in Deus a solid favor to pull that kinda magic support. They seemed real against you dying before you finished whatever plans they've had for you, and I'd also guess they are keen on second chances." He gave a hearty laugh and kept Jane's eye, which was uncomfortable not knowing which eye to look at. "So, whatever, figured I'd bury 'em and let the Lords and warlocks fight out who gets to where in the afterlife later. If I don't dig your grave today, I figure I'd just give it a bit more time."

"Deus?"

The Zombie shrugged and took another bite.

The carnage and murder inside did not match up to Dragosani's style, and it felt eerily familiar to the Praenomen, or even worse, the head of Deus. *I don't even want to know what plans they have for me now. One bloody conspiracy is enough for this Texan.*

Jane waved goodbye and headed back to the Sons and Daughters' headquarters. She squinted at the noon-day black sun, despite its otherwise dim light, thanks to her life as a night owl. Rather than fetch a cab or take a train, she took to the rooftops and got a run on, letting the adrenaline flow back through her. *It's not like stopping my drugs now will save me. I've got another plan.* Racing through rooftops along row houses and flipping over satellite dishes reinvigorated some of that fighting spirit she had within her. By the time she landed in front of the hot dog warehouse she was grinning from ear to ear.

Phoebe was already waiting outside. She ran forward and gave Jane a hug. "I'm so sorry, I ... couldn't put any of it into words."

"What are you sorry for?" Jane backed up.

"Everything, the manipulation, the lies, the misdirections. My visions only come in spurts, and often only telling me who will be important or not. We, none of us, knew how the Praenomen would get you to war. We only knew we needed her, to get you to war. Without you, killing the Lord of Suicide is ... suicide. Death Lords can steal and harvest souls like we devour pizza, and even the Praenomen has not worked out a way around it."

"I've made a choice to not care about it. The Lord of Suicide is doing more harm than you guys ever will. Even if you're a bit misguided, you've always tried to help. The Lord? He needs to die."

"We've gotta purge your drugs," Lucy said as she came out of the warehouse. "You reek of grave dust and other shit still. You won't be able to fight with that in your system. We've been waiting for you, so they set everything up."

"Sure, but you've gotta feed me first," Jane said. *That cheeky bastard took the last slice. Wait, a minute ... what does only having one eye have anything to do with pizza?!*

Jane barely noticed the needle and the blood transfusion

while she ate. They had stuck her with so many needles and chemicals it was second nature to her. As the hour went on, though, more and more of her regular vision slowly returned. She hadn't realized just how hamstrung the eye drops had made it.

"Do you want an injection of hellhound blood to heal some of those internal injuries?" Phoebe asked.

"Wish I could, but I'm already a chemical cocktail. I don't think adding more is a wise idea, particularly after Jack. Don't worry, I've got some of the Death Lord's blood in me, which has to count for something. So, what's the plan?" Jane asked as she was watching the Second City's army of dead and ghostly soldiers load themselves up on freight train cars. Sons and Daughters mercenaries and vampires were arming everyone with various helldiving equipment and whatever weapons they had access to.

"Well, the plan in this case is to follow your lead," she said, unhooking Jane and setting her loose.

"I'm not the biggest on speeches," Jane laughed. "So, let's take direct action instead. Elcoll Pharmaceuticals. That's the base of his operations. We must force our way through the quarantine even though they aren't really our enemies and race to the headquarters. We've got forty-five floors of people, and the top floors deserve every bit of what's coming to them. Once we take that out, I want you guys to focus on getting everyone and anyone nearby back *out* of the city. Security will counterattack and most likely follow you back out. I'll stay behind. Like most pricks with power, the Lord will meander in to survey the damage at the end, and I'll jump out and kick him in the balls."

"Attack the city, kick the lord in the balls. Got it," Akira said as she walked by, finger gunning the two of them and hopping onto a freight car.

"No, I'm telling you ..." Jane saw Doc Daneka walking out with an old model shotgun and pointing to the swordfish on the wall. "It was a beast of a fish, caught it off the coast at midnight." He gave a two-finger salute to Jane.

"You know," Lucy said, packing away her final bits of helldiving gear. "We probably could've predicted this would end with us attacking a corporation. You are Mike's little sister, after all. Even though you're distant, you're a lot alike."

"Yeah, but they sell action figures of me; he's known for ending the world," Jane laughed as one by one the rest of them loaded themselves up into the freight cars. Jane settled in for the long ride and felt at home—even if it was in a shitty meat-packing train car. *Never really knew who you became Mike, but I've met your family now and they've taken me in. But man, your friends are still creepers.*

CHAPTER FORTY-THREE

There is a pervasive, enduring, and widespread acknowledgement that humanity's most steadfast potential is for screwing everything up. War ends in peace. Freedom begets slavery. And in time, ignorance is strength. No more. Triumvirate Enterprises introduces new paths to life. Let the ignorant wallow in their willful pity. Get to Texas. Join the Technocratic movement.

I t's been quiet," Delilah said while sipping on a dark coffee in her presidential suite. "Has there been any activity from Culmen this week?" she asked rhetorically to Whisper, who was reading the nightly news.

The long-nose CEO sat with one leg up and peeked over his spectacles at her. "Well, it's clear enough the warlock is up to shenanigans. Nearly every citizen has been getting upgrades and patch work done of late for reasons which I'm sure you figured out." He licked his finger and flicked an electronic page of the news. "Even if you will not tell me."

"Don't be petty," she said, sipping. "You've already tossed in your two cents about what we should do, and I've taken it under consideration. Is everything ready for relocation?"

"As of last night."

"Kristov?"

"Secured."

"JK-47 and the rest of them?"

"Field member in Chicago reports a train leaving at 4:00 PM today."

"Hrm, so he woke her pathetic self up after all." She finished her coffee and stood up, walking over to the mirror and checking her suit. "Our time here is limited. Tidy up any loose ends. Oh, and what is the current location for the Lord of Suicide?"

"He's currently within Elcoll Pharmaceuticals working on a model airplane."

"If I don't return, you take over command," Delilah said, pulling off the suit and changing into a more tactical outfit suited for the Praenomen. *Well ... time to put on our best face. Let's go meet a Lord of Death shall we?*

Whisper, having already prepared for the great heist, made a quick phone call and resumed reading his news as she slid on the black cargo pants, boots, and a long trench coat filled with spell components and cold iron stakes. Tying her hair up with a ribbon, she removed her spectacles and set them in the canvas backpack; she slung it over her shoulders and grabbed her Praenomen mask, not donning it yet. With a two-finger salute, she waved goodbye and sauntered out of the office as if it was just another day at work. After all, causing civil wars was turning out to be a profitable pastime, she reasoned.

One car ride later, Delilah stood under the imposing blue glass columns of the pharmaceutical giant. Glass doors whooshed as she entered the lobby and slid on the Praenomen mask while casting an illusion at the same time. Mr. Bollard's blood, *ah, my blood,* allowed her to appear as nothing more than the diminutive chairwoman of the Technocratic Party. Even her combat boots sounded like a woman's high-heeled shoes as they clicked with each step in the oversized glass lobby. She needn't bother with security or administrative assistants, her rank gave her all the clearance she would need to get to the right elevator. As she stepped inside the delicate golden elevator, with gears designed more like clockwork art than functionality, she allowed herself a faint chuckle at the giant statue of JK-47 that stood in the lobby. *Men are idiots, give a girl fame and money and think she's theirs.*

The Lord of Suicide's private floor was everything she expected from an eccentric Lord of Death. The Praenomen stepped out onto colorful Moroccan rugs that covered every inch of the marble floor beneath. Candelabra hung from the ceilings, creating a flickering orange light that allowed plenty of room for shadows to grow throughout the space. The Lord sat doting over model airplanes in the side room; the Praenomen watched her foe apply dabs of glue and continue building his diorama. The floor was empty. No support staff, no busy secretaries running around, or Elcoll psychologists helping patients come to terms with death. The Praenomen reached with her senses; she came back empty-handed. Except a small whisper of warning from one of the many voices scratching at the back of her consciousness. *A trap? Expected visit? What would I do ... ah—*

"Are you going to come in or just stand there, heathen?" the Lord said sweetly as he fixed a propeller. His gaunt face stretched thin with the golden mask bolted on over the eyes turned slowly to face Delilah. Nothing about his face gave any semblance of kindness.

"I'm sorry, sir," Delilah said. *Can you see through an illusion?* "We need to have a discussion about the former party chairman."

The Lord's teeth chattered, and he took three steps forward, the third step, on air itself. A withered long finger flicked at the air, and the Praenomen felt the room's temperature drop to freezing as orange light gave way to the hellish green glow of Purgatory. Her illusion shattered.

Well, yes, yes you can. The Praenomen didn't wait. She flung six iron nails up into the air and commanded them to fly into shadows that danced along marble walls, pinning them to their location for later. A seventh, she threw right into her own behind her. *First, defense.* The Lord continued strolling with each step higher than the last and flicked at her again—this time attempting to pull her soul out. Coldness washed over her and her fingers became numb as one of the six stakes shook loose, clattering to the ground, and releasing the shadow instead that drew forth from her own into the Lord's claw.

"Witch magic," he spat. "You don't have enough shadows." With both hands he writhed his fingers and let out whispers that echoed from the room behind him. Each of the Praenomen stakes vibrated and shook at once as the Lord pulled all of them.

Second, offense. Delilah tried to keep calm behind her mask. She had seconds to act with perfect precision. *A dash of nights bane, three pinches of sugar, and the ash from a seventh son.* Her hands going numb as one stake pulled, she mixed the components in the palm of her left hand as the third stake released, and threw them up in the air as the fourth released. The grey dust glistened in the air. The fifth stake clattered to the floor as the Lord let out a sigh.

"Shit," he said.

The Praenomen worked her weather craft with a gust of air and sent the cloud of poison right at the Lord as the sixth stake clattered to the ground. *One left.* What skin the Lord had left bubbled and pulsed as dust made contact, knocking him out of the air, and slamming him back into his diorama of Iowa. He screamed and hissed as his flesh revolted against him, trying to melt off his bone. It was the ash from a seventh son of a seventh son that did the trick, a rare commodity, but true sorcerers could counter any magic, and the Death Lord's very existence was magical. *Luckily for me, seventh sons run in the family. Thanks, Gabriel. That's why I bought your barbershop; hair burns easy.* While the Lord burned alive in the room, Delilah raced to pick the stakes back up and locate more shadows to sacrifice.

"I told you," the Lord said through labored hisses. "You won't find enough shadows." He slid a layer of skin off like a snake shedding, from an old Caucasian male to a stretched Palestinian complexion, and continued casting his own spell while the dust burned his old skin.

Delilah felt the world grow cold and numb as the final stake behind her rattled and moved to unfreeze itself. The green flames of Purgatory grew larger in the room as she felt the seat of her essence shake from the body. In the distance, in the back of her mind, the small sound of a viola playing *Ode to Joy* offered little comfort. She raced to stab a shadow with the cold iron stake before it was too late. *There!* She dashed over and raised her arm, bringing the stake down right as the seventh freed itself and flew at the Lord.

Every shadow followed. Each light behind Delilah lost its life as darkness swept forward like a cloud and boiled through the hallway, snuffing out each green flame with ease. There were no longer multiple voices in the Praenomen's head, each replaced by a singular entity.

"We won't find enough shadows?" the Praenomen asked while rising, only the porcelain white of its mask visible. "Please. Do not toy with us." The Praenomen took a single step forward and a wall of shadows moved forward with it.

The Lord's teeth chattered as he fixed a cowl on his priestly robes, bringing the green light of Purgatory to the edge of darkness and looking down with disdain. The surrounding room told the battle as fire and flame beat back shadows that inched and slipped into every corner, with the Praenomen looking up at the floating Lord of Suicide while the walls buckled and melted around them.

"Vryce," he hissed. "I prefer your little witch instead."

"We are here." The Praenomen cocked its head sideways. "Nothing changes the intent of the meeting." The sorcerer pointed to the discarded skin. "Surely you don't begrudge us fellow craftsman from taking protection," the male and a female voice spoke together. "Or mind we've brought more poison with us. Now can we talk?"

"You should've known the price of evil. You don't belong here —in this world, Lich. We have divine purpose. You are an abomination no matter how you've hidden your soul."

"Is that not the pot calling the kettle black, supplicant of Lazarus?"

The Lord wreathed himself in fire and stepped forward, pushing back the Praenomen's shadows. "You've come for a reason, witch, and you have your protection, so speak now before the gaze of Lazarus falls upon us."

Delilah pulled a gnarled root from a pocket in the trench coat and snipped off the tip. With an incantation of her own, she added a heavy mist to the air that dampened the flames and allowed the shadows to loom again. "Have you even contemplated the ramifications of your apprentice's experiments? We keep track of our own ... did you? Or are you so outdated that the power of technology is your blind spot?"

"Please, technology is nothing more than a tool of men; in death, they all go to the same place. Nothing concerns us about our warlock's assistance. At least, unlike you, he remained loyal to bringing order into the world instead of thrusting it into chaos and unshackling magic." The Lord stepped forward once more, his eyes becoming small flames themselves that danced along the edges of his mask.

The Praenomen turned sideways and bowed slightly, keeping her eyes on the Lord, while they summoned a red door that pierced the shadows with a crimson glow. "Who said anything about them dying? What if death was off the table? What then?" She walked backwards to her escape, a small suburb outside the city wall.

The entire building suddenly shook, and the lights flickered. In the distance, through the glass windows behind the Lord, flames kissed the horizon as a train car flew through the air as it crashed into and through a checkpoint.

Time to go! Delilah took the distraction as the perfect chance to turn tail and run through her red door while the Lord smiled at the incoming assault. Small drops of rainwater ran over her mask as she crossed out into the suburb and closed the door behind her. *That went about as well as expected. Thank you, Father.* Vryce's voices were receding, his power exhausted, but she had a distinct sense he was proud of her.

All she had to do was sit back and watch the fireworks.

CHAPTER FORTY-FOUR

That place between sleep and awake; that twilight where dreams still dance in your memory. That eternal life just waiting beyond the mortal coil. Strengthen your mind and shed the need of blood.—Elcoll Pharmaceuticals.

J ane basked in the heat from the train crash as adrenaline coursed through her veins. *Oh, how I've missed you.* Her grin stretched ear to ear as she vaulted over the crumbling concrete wall through the train station, militia for the Sons and Daughters right on her heels as they poured like army ants out into the city streets. Emergency floodlights cast off-white circles as the local security scrambled to understand what just happened. As they ran past, Jane saw plumes of green flames appear on streets and inside nearby office buildings, manifesting sorcerers in Lazarean robes. It didn't surprise her that the Death Lord would react first, and the anti-freak squads of the city weren't far behind. *Well, we did just drive a train engine on a single track into the supply station. Fuck subtlety.* Jane, and everyone else on her side, was ready for battle.

343

A sorcerer from the Church flung eldritch violet skulls that screeched through the air and threw Sons and Daughters off their feet as they ran through the breach. Undead freedom fighters from the north crashed into anti-freak squads from Texas and the members from Lazarus's organization that never marched north. The steel wreckage and building-high flames that burned from the train's collision into the Elcoll shipping station did little to stymie the defenses of the cities, but it gave them an opening. An opening was all Jane needed to run along the upper wall and kick her rocket boots into full blast at a metal-railed guard tower where the robed sorcerer blasted her friends. *All right, cupcake, let's dance.* Jane cackled with wild eyes and gave a haymaker that turned the bones in his upper torso into powder. Crumpled in half, he flew out of the tower, skull shattering open on the next tower and coating a trio of anti-freak soldiers in blood before falling to the ground below. *I said dance ... not die ...* she paused for a second and shook the collar of the coat. *Still gotta master that.*

"Ooh ho-ho-ho ... Man, Jack ... you're missing out. Imagine the arena work we could've done." *Work I should have done from the start. Lottery my pale ass.* Jane flexed her fingers and breathed deeply the smell of gasoline, fire, and chaos. The main captains of the Sons and Daughters led their own teams through the breach and spread out through the streets.

"Welcome home, Jane," Doc said through the headset as their team headed to the north. The lanky doctor had an unfair advantage in disabling human SWAT soldiers—sapping their will to fight. One by one, enforcers put their guns down and let his team walk through to their target. Until a robed figure from Lazarus stood underneath a streetlight, her cloak obscuring all her facial features.

"Home for her? Shit, I still want a lottery ticket. They've got the latest video games here." Akira flipped one of her scythes around. Her squad of agile mercenaries tried their best to keep pace with her as she headed east. Just as she was about to round the block, a series of small explosions with silverizer'd shrapnel cut off their path. "Fuck that burns," Akira screamed as she fell back and three men with combat shotguns and anti-freak gear took aim.

The low hum of VTOL police craft mixed with the blinding white light from spotlights descended on the growing numbers of Sons and Daughters as the army fled through the breach in the wall and shattered station. In distant blocks on all three sides, Jane saw SWAT team members unloading and racing into position while one or two Lazarean soldiers used their magic to appear in advantageous positions. More than a few of the SWAT team soldiers moved with enhanced speed themselves and set up overcompensating rifles pointed in their direction. *I've gotta admit, thought the fuzz would've taken just a tit longer.* Doc was already moving to his knees with his hands up and Akira followed along according to plan. Jane pulled out a crumpled smoke and took the moment to light it, casting deep shadows over her face as she finger-gunned the three SWAT members in the watch tower across from her.

"Kapow," she mouthed and flicked the cigarette through the air. It tumbled forward, cherry end spiraling in the air as gunfire opened from behind her. *I love backup.* With one hand over the railing, Jane jumped forward and leapt into action. The ember of the cigarette became a blurry red streak as she raced past while in a spinning flip, bringing her boot crashing down into one's skull. Jane cut a gurgling wet scream short as she spun her other leg around and booted the third over a railing. She rolled her shoulder over, hit the grated floor, slid to the third, and launched a series of elbow strikes as she rose from the ground, ending with a snap of his neck. All in time to pluck her tumbling smoke out of the air.

Jane smiled at the thought. The initial response team probably thought they had the upper hand. *Home turf advantage, no doubt they saw it coming, and even had magical backup.* Leaning on the cool metal railing she watched Lucy's squads in the north and Phoebe's in the south open fire from shadows as they exited their helldive. The hooded Lazarean sorcerer pulled back her hood with a look of shock at the reverse ambush and tried to pull up her ghosts from Purgatory herself, only to find them killed before crossing over. In a panic, she sprinted away right into the clutches of Doc Daneka who gave a toothy grin before biting into her neck. Crowds of Sons and Daughters descended upon those with oversized rifles to the south, and their foes fell before the biker gang's fury. To her amusement, though, the enhanced SWAT members were screaming for *everyone* to back them up.

The VTOLs and armored vehicles, company private security, and every defense the corporations had took the bait and descended upon their location, keeping the battlefield moving forward a block at a time. Crews of Sons and Daughters would helldive, race through the underworld and get in a new position, and with no more demon lord trapping them in—slip back into the real world. Each block a small squad would surge forward before the chain guns and heavy urban combat equipment would pin them down. Block by block they fought their way forward.

Yet the Death Lord never showed up. *Why the hell would the Death Lord poke his head out?* As she ran forward through the wet streets, her breath forming the air, and drugs coursing through her veins, that cold *something's wrong* feeling boiled up. She slid into position behind a set of trash cans, still on fire from homeless trying to get warm, and leveled her sights. Three quick rounds burst out and found their purchase in a sniper hanging out of a VTOL.

"I'll admit, it's not the most complex plan ..." Jane said to nobody in particular as she picked up a run again, her squad keeping pace behind her as they zigged and zagged through the streets. A high-pitched squeal pierced the air near her, followed by a red flash of light that followed the explosive charge into a nearby car. She picked her ass up and sprinted, grabbing one of her squadmates by a strap around the chest, throwing him across the street. A few broken bones would be better than death. Dashing around the corner herself, a trail of machine gun fire peppered the steel building facade as she ran along its exterior.

The searing heat from the explosion raced along her back, tipping her balance off slightly mid-jump and sending her spiraling down into the asphalt. "Fook!" she managed as she spiraled and skidded forward.

An armored personnel carrier with a small squad of anti-freak soldiers was waiting in ambush. Two were on balconies up high, their rifles already unloading at her. The others operated a silver-lined net that snapped and entangled Jane, who fell right into it. Icy feelings of panic raced up through her knees as she grabbed onto any purchase she could find—the curb, a sewer lid, a fallen piece of shrapnel—and tried to pull free. Even with her thrashing and enhanced strength something about the mesh weave net refused to give, and the snipers kept any of her squad pinned down behind cover. *Okay, okay, keep it together, girl. It's just a bloody net!* She tried slipping into Purgatory, only to find the net prevented her from crossing. *A bloody magic net. Noted.* Jane slid her left mechanical arm through some weave and embedded it in the concrete as they dragged her closer. It didn't help.

"Fine, you asshats wanna bring me close?" Jane snarled up through the links, trying to get her chains untangled from around her right boot while her left leg twisted behind her.

"No." Jane heard the deep voice from right behind her as the soldier clubbed her in the side of her head with his rifle butt. Flecks of white light arrayed through her vision as he punched into her again in a vain attempt to knock her out.

A third rifle punch and her world got blurry. She spat at him, wild-eyed and pissed off. "I'm on ... way ... too many drugs for you to be trying that shit. It won't work," she hissed as she recoiled for a fourth impact. It didn't stop him from trying. "I fucking surrender!" she shouted at last as he raised the fifth time. *Fine, fuck, nets are a weakness, noted.*

"Looks like it worked," the voice said. "We got JK-47, bag her up." The three of them moved closer and picked her up without resistance from her. The silver weave net had thoroughly entangled her except for her left arm, which was now being handcuffed for additional protection.

"Easy now, tiger, you wouldn't want me to file for a lawyer, would you? That's Triumvirate merchandise you're handling. I already told you I fucking surrender," Jane said again as she watched her squad fall back from their position.

In her earpiece, other voices sounded off. "I fucking surrender," Akira said.

"Well, bloody hell, chaps, I do believe you've gotten me. I fucking surrender," Doc Daneka added.

"Hands in the right spot, and eyes up here. I've already surrendered," Phoebe chimed in.

"Come near me again and I'll take off your other arm," Lucy said. A few seconds of silence followed as even Jane was perplexed at Lucy's refusal. "Oh, right, uh, I guess I fucking surrender to you or something."

The surrender trick. Jane's idea wasn't the most complicated of plans, but it played off a basic human emotion. She only hoped the Lord of Suicide would fall for it. Every archvillain she had ever imagined should've been smart enough to run when the gates got stormed, and in most stories they never were. *But in all of them, once the tide of battle had turned in their favor, they always poked their heads out.* As they loaded her into the back of the armored personnel carrier and affixed her to the bench with more handcuffs after taking the net off, she got a solid image of the street. *Eighteenth. So, we made it ten blocks in from the wall before they finally caught us.*

By counting the orange light from streetlamps as they drove through the streets, Jane could guess how close they were to Elcoll Pharmaceuticals headquarters. She didn't think they would take her directly there, but Fredrick would want her brought somewhere near him. In this massive city, having to fight everyone was an impossible task, and now that the advance crew had been captured, the rest were engaging in the second phase. While she couldn't see them, Jane imagined what it looked like as they split into multiple directions through the city, going after warehouses of Elcoll with the sole intention of destroying it. Others dressed as civilians would make their way to any residential apartments and evacuate people from the area. *Save who we can, and stop him from adding to his army. Two birds one stone.*

Twenty third ... Twenty fourth ... Jane counted the blocks as they sped forward, quickly trying to separate her from the ongoing battle blocks away. It's not like the SWAT team knew what their target was, or had any clue. All they knew was that she was the property of a company and they sped her right to its front doors. *Heh ... two more blocks, Jane. Then it's time to die. Enjoy 'em while you can.* She rocked back and forth thanks to the poor suspension and tried to savor every moment as that feeling of finality set in. She did her best to put out that *something's wrong* feeling that stayed with her. *I wonder where Doc, or Phoebe, or Akira will end up. They would be a distraction taken to another building all together. Good luck, guys.*

"Remember," Akira said over the short band radio still in Jane's ear. "Jack got a fantastic shot on him. Even you saw him in the hospital. He's not like us. Don't freak out, just take action."

The two guards sitting in the back shrugged as if it was an easy day at the office ... but kept their guns leveled at her just in case.

Jane flexed her fingers, feeling the cold metallic ones press against her flesh and blood ones comforted her. *Jack kicked the shit out of the Lord, and that was one plasma shot.* Jane lowered her voice so the drivers couldn't hear, but didn't care about those in the back with her. "Hey, just remember your end. Get as many people out of the city walls as you can." Another orange light flickered past. "Twenty-six."

She didn't wait for the car to stop. With a quick flex, she snapped the silver handcuffs off like a paperclip. "Hey, boys." She flashed a cheeky peace sign as her pupils dilated. Metal met flesh as her left hand snapped the throat of one. "Should have kept the net," she said with a snap kick to the one across from her. Jane slid down and ducked as the shotgun discharged, sending molten shot over her, peppering through the truck. With a second kick the soldier slumped. A sudden lurch sent her sliding to the front as they hit the brakes, and toxic gas filled the back of the truck. She held her breath, which silenced her usual quips, and charged the doors. One hit caused a dent, and her eyes burned; a second hit twisted metal outwards as she held nostrils that felt on fire, and a third kick sent the door flying out.

Jane coughed as she hopped out. People on the street outside the headquarters looked shocked to see the former popstar hop out and fan off a poison cloud of smoke. "Woah." Jane hacked up a lung and waved it away before sliding around the corner and decking the driver in the face four times. Greatly trying to hold back with each five-finger sandwich. "I told you ... the first time ... I can't be knocked out!" she shouted to the crumpling soldier. "Hey, everyone," she waved.

Jane fixed her coat, grabbed her chains, and reloaded one shotgun as people took snapshots of her. Fifty feet away, the private security of Elcoll Pharmaceuticals phoned in for reinforcements as they took a position in the corporate lobby. They were understaffed. A delicate glass building wouldn't afford them much in the way of protection. "So ... everyone who isn't a part of *that* company should get the fuck out of this city, right now." Jane gave the shotgun a satisfying double cock. The sound was more than enough to get people scrambling. "So, everyone, how do the drug stores and warehouses look?"

"Modern security still hasn't caught up to shapechangers. Handcuffs, really?" Akira laughed. "Anyway, they look undermanned with plenty to destroy. Plan is working."

"And ... the evacuation?" Jane asked as she strolled forward through the corporate courtyard. Backlit by large projection screens proclaiming the superiority of their products, Jane grabbed a garbage can and dragged it by her side. *Oh, yeah, we know where this is going, trash ... meet window. Window ... meet trash.*

"Slower than I would've liked. Most people don't want to leave," Phoebe said. "Well, I mean anyone with a sweet posh life here, that is."

"Just get 'em out by force if you've gotta," Jane said, hoisting the garbage can overhead. The security inside readied guns, unsure if the reinforced glass would protect them. "I'm not the speeches and peaches kinda gal. Why the fuck would they want to leave with a bunch of creepers like you?"

Another explosion rocked the ground in the distance. "That was me! That was me!" Doc exclaimed. "Oh shit, that warehouse was flammable. Okay, backing out now. They want to join us because a Lord of Death is tricking them into joining his ghostly army. By killing them."

"That's a hell of a selling point." Jane skipped two steps forward and threw the trash can. To everyone's surprise but Jane's, the wall of windows fractured before crumbling. Jane stepped through into the corporate lobby, her boots crunching on broken glass, and looked at the stunned security men and women. "What, I kicked off a metal door in an armored APC right out front, and you think I wasn't getting in here?" Jane pointed behind her.

They opened fire. Jane rolled her eyes.

CHAPTER FORTY-FIVE

Brooke & Talbots is the premier apocalypse gear team, bringing you the ultimate in survival equipment. Now equipped with the latest line of Iron Lanterns, as seen in use by the world's most vetted helldivers. These specially made hooded lanterns will shine through any darkness for hours at a time and reveal things hidden by ghostly trickery. We make each handcrafted lantern right here, in America, and they are now available in any store still open. Today is the day you stop living in the dark and step into the light. Only with Brooke & Talbots.

Jane, what in the hell are you doing?" Jack asked nobody in particular. He felt stretched, crammed, and free, all at the same time—his mind dabbling in a thousand computer systems all at once. When he first saw the train barreling into the city, he knew that Jane had come for the Death Lord. The problem was a snowball of violence that screwed with every calculation Peter and he had theorized. Over half the city had yet to finish their upgrades with the hardware needed for their plan which meant a million lives would be left out if they activated it early. *Stop blowing up our city, you impulsive girl!*

Jack watched the Sons and Daughters fight their way through the city on the ground level. Cameras at every street corner gave him the view of SWAT officers trying to hold their own as freaks and vampires crawled along elevated streets and train rails. He watched them throw Molotov cocktails into perfectly good storefronts and ignite Elcoll Pharmaceuticals' businesses on fire. Amidst broken glass and hails of bullets, Jack saw them slink into shadows like heathens and disappear from his cameras, only to reappear behind SWAT officers blocks away—tearing into them with their claws. Good men and women who had done nothing wrong but sign up to protect the city by shooting blood-drunk vampires. Jack activated each of their profiles at once and set about notifying their families, besides activating the code to set them financially free of all debts. It was the least he could do.

"Peter," Jack asked through a computer speaker down in the warlock's lair where the experiment was *well* underway. "Are you seeing all of this?"

Mr. Anonymous dabbled with countless blue screens floating in the air, each batch program adding dozens to the queue and setting up the contingency plans they needed. "Yeah. We need to intercept ... but I'm in mid-ritual, and JK-47 is displaying additional talents beyond her upgrades. I'm not sure if we've got a weapon built to stop her."

"How about me?" Jack hijacked a monitor and looked back at Peter. Jack kept his spiky black hair with gray highlights, a goatee, and mirrored aviator shades. "Let me go fight her ... she can't kill me."

"We aren't ready for that yet, we don't have—" Mr. Anonymous began, but instead of continuing, he grabbed specifications for Atlantis mechanized units and pulled them up. "Taylor's and Tyler's models. We've got prototypes of their hardsuits. Take over both at once since they are the closest thing we have that can match her strength and speed. The extra number might give you the edge."

Jack reached out with his mind. It felt like flying for a moment as the cities' communication grid opened itself up to him, and he dialed into Atlantis headquarters, making a small mental note that Atlantis must have known about the attack. They cleared the warehouse of any decent equipment. But in Taylor's and Tyler's private penthouse, two prototype hardsuits remained plugged into the grid. Jack took a moment to understand their specifications, the hollow suit that a pilot sleeved into, filled with a gel that oxygenated the bloodstream, and the neural uplink that made the tight-fitted mech so fast. Multiple weapons systems from small missiles, rocket launchers, chain guns, and enough strength to cut through a concrete wall were in the baseline models. *Damn guys, how the hell did you ever lose in these suits? I'm kinda jealous ... in a way these are almost better than my upgrades.*

He focused and activated their computer systems. When he moved his right hand, both their hands moved in sync. It felt ... strange having his left and right hand controlled by two separate bodies, and as he activated them, he toggled his vision to be in both at the same time. With a test, he tried moving both independently, and they stumbled out of the assembly pad but made steps forward. *Okay, okay, I got this ...*

He looked over at himself, a green hardsuit mech with a mirrored face that looked back at the light blue version of Tyler's suit. With a salute, both bodies saluted each other. "Alright," a voice module on both bodies said in unison. "Let's do this." Turning, Jack hit a red button and opened the mechanical shades, and got each suit into a sprint, launching out of the twenty-seventh floor and heading straight to Elcoll Headquarters.

The two hardsuits landed in the freight dock leading into the building. The split metal doors stood closed for Jack as the engines died down during landing. Gunfire rattled through the lobby. *No time to go in quiet.* The pair of him ran through, tearing the interior dock door off the hinges. Only a few heat signatures remained as Jane made her rounds dismantling the security team. Tyler's suit ran horizontally on the wall as it rounded the corner, and Taylor's slid down low, shattering marble concrete as he rounded the corner into the brightly lit corporate lobby. The pair of suits recovered and raced forward, even though it felt like each step they took, another heat signature vanished. Making the final corner, Taylor's suit jumped over a security guard who slid backwards on the black marble floor, his neck bent at an odd angle. Tyler's suit leapt forward, scanning the room for the fast-moving girl in rocket boots. *There.*

Jane was mid-jump about twenty feet up in the air, her chains swinging down at a security guard who was still shooting at where she was seconds ago. Flecks of blue marble rained down from the stray gunfire as she jetted around the fifty-foot-tall corporate lobby. With a predictive aiming calculation, Jack launched a set of tasers out of both suits. Their black wires crossed in midair as the metallic leads spiraled their way up to the smirking JK-47, who flicked her wrist and batted them away. With a forward flip downward, her chains coiled up behind her and slammed down in a cascade of metal—with a sickening wet sound as she sliced the SWAT officer in half, his scream cut short. Jane landed while an arm was still flying up in the air, and plucked something off the guard's belt. She leveled her cybernetic arm at the pair of robots.

"Hey there, back from the dead, are we?" she said. "Get out of my way!" She bounded forward.

The sliced-off arm thudded behind her.

Bio-scanners in the suits registered that Jane's insides were rotting and the constant adrenaline spikes placed her well beyond heart attack territory any day now. *Poor Jane ... let me save you.* "Stand down, JK, let us help you, it's me, Ja—" the synthetic suits spoke in unison. She didn't care. With a forward boot kick, Taylor's green suit flew horizontally back down the lobby, crashing into the elevator doors with a clang and folding the doors around it like a coffin.

"—did you just kick me?" Tyler's suit said as incredulously as a synthetic voice could manage. *Fine, I'll take you in like the rabid dog you are.*

The blue hardsuit jetted forward with a right hook right as Jane swung low to sweep legs. He kept momentum with a horizontal spin and brought his fist down, shattering the marble floor where Jane was a second ago. *Faster, Jack.* Her speed shifting her into striking position, Jane brought a knee up to a helmet. Even though he was digital, Jack reacted as if it was his own face at risk, throwing his arms in panic to block, barely, and was sent flying into the air. *Don't panic. Ride it.* Vertigo wasn't a sensation that he felt any longer, so in the seconds of spiraling up in the lobby Jack tucked in to ride the moment in a backflip before planting his feet into a wall. *Calculate, predict. She's impulsive, but we know combat.*

Launching himself down, he led with a roundhouse down into empty air as she dashed around the security kiosk. *Not yet, Jack ... hold it ...* Jack threw the hardsuit at her, spiraling in the air like a figure skater before shattering the kiosk into splinters with a swift punch.

He chuckled as Jane wore an "oh shit" face and ducked debris. Annoyed, Jane picked up the computer monitor and threw it off the suit's head. An attempted distraction before dashing in with an uppercut to the suit's chest. The sound of ceramics shattering echoed as Jack skidded back, barely holding his balance.

"Fuck!" she shouted as she held her hand back, grasping her shattered mechanical arm.

"You can't hurt us, Jane ... stand down."

"You!" she finished.

A second explosion erupted, this time from the hardsuit's chest.

It was a strange sensation watching someone else's body explode. The point-blank grenade Jane embedded into the chest on the hardsuit certainly caused the suit's alarms to go off. The chest cavity exploded inward, leaving wires and smooth metallic tubes leaking fluid in its wake. Jack worked the fluid between his fingers. *Well. Shit. She's good.* "Right. Plan B. Now."

Finally pried from the elevator, Taylor's green suit opened fire on a surprised Jane. Flechette rounds clashed off her right arm and one through her left leg before she sprinted past to escape.

"Bloody robots, you are nobody," she said, skating along the wall twirling her chains to build up momentum. The broken hardsuit jerked its body forward and arced an electrical discharge along her path, painting Jane's trajectory along the wall.

"No! Jane, listen! It's me," the suits said, as the freed suit kicked the last remnant of elevator door to head Jane off. *She's going to jump and dodge. Math says she lands ... right over there.*

Flashy as ever, Jane did a spin kick with rockets off the wall—and right where Jack guessed, forcing her to tumble defensively and abort whatever insane plans she was thinking. The pair of suits launched their assault with mechanical and calculated precision. An emotionless barrage of mechanical destruction designed to corral the bio-enhanced champion into a corner. "Stand down! It's me, Jack!" *Finally. Just listen to us, you stupid, rebellious little girl.* Jack's fight calculations, or, more accurately, his own memories, reminded him of how he fought when cornered. Resigned to get decked, he moved the suit's arms up.

"You bloody fuckers. Jack is dead." She wiped sweat off her brow on the trench coat's sleeve. "Don't you remember? I see how people are going to die ... and you robots are nothing but shells."

To Jack's surprise, she didn't punch back or make any aggressive movements. Her heart was racing, and her pupils were dilated, but she didn't fight out of the corner. *Finally, a fucking conversation.* "We can explain." He lowered his arms.

She blinked forward and screamed bloody murder the second he did. Attacking both suits with panicked fury, JK-47 pushed back with unnatural strength, bashing their heads in, and ripping off Taylor's arm with chains.

Okay, let's explain later. Clarity and logic don't mix with chemical cocktails and adrenaline. Jack took advantage of the suits being discardable tools and traded defense for offense. It was like trying to hit Sonic the Hedgehog. If hitting air and pulling out loose strands of hair was the game, Jack would have a flawless victory. As the trio crashed through the hallway, hardsuit armor clattered to the floor as it was ripped away, but his strikes were predicting her pattern one millisecond closer each.

A hardsuit punch with an upper-arm stub to the teeth knocked three loose, giving her a bloody smile. *Impact at last.* A kick with her rocket boot to a knee, tore it off at the hinge. *Predicted.* A sound-wave concussion caused her to squeal and slide backward, hands held to bloody ears. *She's slowing down.* With wild eyes, she kicked her legs over her head and spun up into the air, but yanked on the chain to pull one hardsuit and her together, ripping a shoulder socket that stole her teeth off. *Unfortunate.*

With both hardsuits having broken limbs, Jack had one suit rip the useless remains off the other. He then altered the power output to maximize output and turn it into a taser—ready to kill the suit if the attack hit. By his count he had seven seconds of combat left and she was running on fumes. Still, Jack figured she was experienced enough to pull some shady trick out of her sleeve. *Better beat her to the punch ... literally.* He had Tyler's suit, now without a shoulder or leg, activate the rockets and headbutt the hellbent media star. When Jane flip-dodged to the left, Taylor's suit rocketed in, planning on her super speed. It worked, she dove under. Jack killed the suit's rockets and let it go limp like a rag doll, collapsing down. Easy enough to grab and throw out of the way, and Jane was impulsive enough to take the bait. To a high-voltage surprise, which shot Jane and the suit out from one another, each crashing on opposite ends inside an elevator.

The power cut out on the suit, forcing Jack to exist in one shambling, broken hardsuit with multiple missing limbs. *At least it's still active ... that was a few billion Bitcoin in damage well spent.* The servos strained as he stood and surveyed the carnage. The elevator hallway looked like a hurricane of semitrucks had flown through. The bright white flashing light of fire alarm strobes and sirens blared through the hall.

Jane sat with legs splayed out inside one elevator, a dazed look on her face with bloody blonde hair matted against her right cheek. She was conscious, but looked like she had seen better days. Around her were the scattered and broken ceiling tiles from the elevator ceiling, and a dangling light fixture. As Jack used a wall to hobble his suit around, the shallow-breathing Jane looked up at him.

"That ... was clever," she gasped.

"S-so-o was the gre-nnaade," the choppy speaker returned.

"You aren't a machine, are you ... who is ... your pilot? I'll tell you what, lady ... I'll give you an autograph if you let me go." She smiled and held out two fingers with her cybernetic arm.

"I'm n-n-not a l-ady. I-I'm your f-friend. It's me. Jack." Jack struggled and moved an arm over his chest. *Two minutes until the other suit reboots.*

"You aren't even a ghost in a machine to me ... I see nothing there but wires and circuits, buddy. I ... can't believe that, man," she panted. "Fuck, fine ... maybe. I don't know. Anything is possible, I suppose, but I also can't care right now. I don't have the luxury to deal ...with that ball of emotional ... fucking ... torment right now. Just let me go kill a Death Lord ..."

Jack watched the drugs work in her system, slowly repairing damage done to her. His other suit would recover fully first. "There is nowhere to go. Surrender, Jane. You've killed enough. The Death Lord is not a concern."

"I can't believe I'm saying this to you, if it is you." Jane turned her two fingers into one and waved it back and forth. "Sometimes to make an omelet, you've gotta break a few eggs. This ... is war. No one ... holds a gun to anyone's head and makes them fight anymore ... not in this world. Everyone has a side now. You're wrong." She dropped her hand.

"Wrong about what?"

"That there is nowhere to go ... I took off that left shoulder of yours ..." She took a second, but she stood up, and hoisted the chain over her shoulder. "I can still go up ..." Jane smirked before grinning through the pain and broken ribs and vaulting and rocketing her way up the elevator shaft.

Jack lumbered in and tipped his head back and just watched her bounce up the shaft one floor at a time. He had absolutely no means of pursuit for another minute and twenty-seven seconds at least. "Well, shit." A quick survey of the ground revealed a pack of smokes that had fallen from her trench coat. More out of habit than anything, Jack reached down and picked them up, not at all surprised he didn't feel the twinge of addiction.

He eyed the elevators across the way, and pressed the up button. If a robot could sigh, the hanging head and shrug of a broken shoulder said it all as he waited. "This will be a terrible minute for the CEOs upstairs ..." Jack looked at the de-energized suit. "Hurry the fuck up, you outdated toaster oven."

CHAPTER FORTY-SIX

Vampires, Demons, and soulless heathens are coming for you, and your parents. We aren't talking about the filth plaguing America's once-great cities—but the Technocratic Party. Their lobbyists have influenced America's electorate for decades to bring about the fall with their "pro-corporate" agenda. Don't let them judge your family with their medical death panels. Vote Republican. Your life depends on it.

Jesus motherfuckin' Christ on a candy stick ..." Jane said while propping herself up on the thirty-sixth floor elevator shaft. "Those douche-nozzles shot me. Well, I mean ... it's fair," she continued her self-ranting while prying open the metal doors. Hopefully the Lord of Suicide was still sitting in his office. *I will be so pissed if those robotic dolls cost me this entire mission.* She felt the icy chill of panic-induced anxiety at the thought, enough to send goosebumps across her one good arm. A deep breath and an extra bit of shoulder grease, and the tungsten latches on the secure door snapped off. She tumbled into the hallway with an unceremonious grace.

Bright blue strobe lights fluttered along the halls as translucent red letters floated in the air. *EVACUATE!* was hanging over every door. *You damn well better run. Your gravy train ends here, death boys.* Jane surveyed the damage to her left thigh where flechette rounds embedded themselves inside bloody leg meat. Through the blood she saw the sick pockmarks where steel pellets entered. Beyond the chemical cocktail running through her, she felt that mortal terror, a younger version of herself scream up and shout to seek help. It was distant, and with just a little effort, bottled back up and pushed aside. *Now's no time for that, we've gotta give the crowd a show, after all* ... She began her stroll along the penthouse, letting her chains drag behind her.

Each hallway had a reinforced glass door that showcased the news. While talking heads rambled on about the attack, or the impact on the marketplace, Jane shattered her way through with her cybernetic hand. Every office she opened, every bathroom stall she checked, was already empty. Devoid of staff, personnel, or a Lazarean Death Lord whom she really hoped was hiding on a shitter. *We ... really didn't think this through. I mean, gotta admit, this was a bit impromptu, but still, what bad guy actually fucking runs?*

It was all of them, and she knew that. This wasn't like the movies.

The Sons and Daughters had planned to shut down Elcoll, destroy its factories, evacuate civilians hooked on their drugs, and tear down its headquarters as a message while killing a Death Lord. A one-stop shop to make a point. "Now we look like chumps," she said to herself, blowing up a stray lock of hair. She leaned on the glass window to view the fires and spy on events below. She smiled as the squat grey building collapsed in on itself from demolition charges. *Well, they at least made it to the distribution facility.* Jane was fishing through her multitude of pockets for a pack of misplaced smokes when a VTOL engine cut vertically right in front of her and up higher still.

The roof. "The roof!" *Why didn't I think of that?* Disappointment shifted to abject excitement as she sprint-hobbled to the central stairwell, easily shouldering through locked doors and rocket boosting herself up flights of stairs. "Dear God, I ... recall we don't speak much." She hopped over a railing and jetted up another flight. "But I really don't want to die a failure. Can like ... you just make sure that *someone* responsible for all those dead is up here?" Jane flipped up in between two more stairwells, now more steel and concrete than decorative. She was close. "It doesn't even have to be the Lord of Death, just ... let me achieve something?" Reaching the final door, Jane put her forehead on the cool metal door. She could feel the vibrations of engines rattling through the metal. She let out a scream to push down the pain, and shouldered through the final door.

Executives in a variety of fancy, tightly tailored suits stood drinking expensive bottles of chemical cocktails while waiting for their private crafts. Rather than shuttle into a single one, each of them had their own private jet. Almost every person on the roof had a few drones buzzing around their heads as they talked to reporters and gave statements about the assault.

"Aha!" Jane pointed at the lot.

All of them turned pale when a bloody Jane Auburn kicked off a reinforced door. It took only a second for an avatar of her to appear on nearby rooftops as the news drones focused their lenses. Wild trench coat flapping in the wind, covered in patches proclaiming anarchism and tacos on Tuesdays. Her right grey rocket boot jetted a spark or two and her purple cybernetic arm glistened. Of course, the avatar highlighted its make, model, and cost. Under the spotlight, Jane did what she did best, even if she was covered in blood—she smiled.

"All you saggy twats are guilty of the incredible climbing bad guy syndrome. Evacuation by rooftop? Really?" Jane held out her hands.

"Easy there, JK-47." A pompadour-wearing young executive held out a hand. "Can't we settle this in court?"

Jane cracked her neck and stepped forward as her glowing blue chains rattled behind her. Her smile never faded. "Oh, we can settle this in court. There is one ... what ... a block away?" she asked, tilting her head.

He nodded.

She blinked in, grabbed his head, flipped over, and hurled him with a spin. Screaming as he flailed off the edge of the roof, Jane put her hand over her eyes and tried to see how far he'd go. "Damn." She snapped her fingers as he made it halfway. "I think I needed a running start. Who wants to try for court next?" she laughed, turning around. Everyone else ran for the door.

Even if the executives had only been complicit in the Death Lord's plans, they served as symbols of an enterprise that profited, and forcefully recruited, the deaths of thousands for their own power. Jane had no intention of showing them any mercy.

One with ungainly high heels trotted back inside; Jane swept her legs with her chains and flung her back off the edge. Another, screaming red-faced at a VTOL pilot to take off, met his fate to the heel of Jane's rocket boots as she ignited them in his ear. More screamed as she lobbed them off the edge of the building—always taking a moment to pause for the camera. In minutes, JK-47 was the highest-rated person in this Dystopia as swarms of little drones fluttered around. Those at home probably enjoyed the bloodlust, having been starved of their arena star for some time now, and raised in a culture that pit products versus monsters. This time the monsters wore plastic smiles.

The live chitter feeds still begged Jane to marry them, even after she held up a chief financial officer over the edge. The CFO struggled and tried to dig her nails into Jane's left arm as her shoes tumbled down to concrete oblivion.

"Tsk, tsk, none of that now, Dolly, don't you want a final camera shot? You're the last executive here! That makes you special, you know." Jane turned to the camera. "Hi, boys and girls, it's me, JK! Do we have a news segment for you! Thanks to a field reporter embedded with us as we marched up to war, we captured all kinds of great footage. Sure, I know you guys saw all the cute and sexy bits!" Jane kipped up her knee and winked at the camera. "But what about all the parts where Elcoll corporation worked at the behest of Lazarus and killed thousands of people via suicide pills? Only to press-gang them into their armies?" Jane held up a finger. "One sec."

She awkwardly began fishing inside her cargo pants, lips pursed to the side as she fished for a USB drive affixed to a Band-Aid on her inner thigh. The CFO continued her helpless struggle, clawing at the mangled metal arm. "Aha," Jane said with a slight wince as she plucked the drive free. "Come here, little drone, come on ..." She beckoned over one of the larger ones and plugged the drive into its side.

"You will find the evidence, including how this bitch profited just as much as the rest of her airborne companions. Now I know what you will all say." Jane switched to an angry man's voice. "Jane! Profit is good, we are all in it to make money. You can't expect companies to invent drugs for free." She threw the CFO to her death. "You're right, all companies are in it to make money. Some companies are just shittier than others, and we don't have a court system anymore. You know, because of the fucking apocalypse. Elcoll kills you. The entire purpose of the drug is to build an army of ghosts to grow a private army for Lazarus ... and for what!" She sauntered back to the middle of the rooftop.

"So these Death Lords can control easier through magic? Turning us lucky enough to survive under a black sun into good little drones? Hell, these companies *knew* about the end of the world before it even started. We cast all the blame at the people like Mike Auburn or the Society for being responsible, but look around people—it was a global conspiracy. *Glooobaal.*" Jane reached out and grabbed a drone, bringing it close for a kiss. By now, the operator of the USB drone had downloaded the footage that Kevin Thayer had captured. Not just the field footage, but countless interviews, investigative journalism, secret meetings and more all released about how the entire war was engineered. For now, it was just dumped raw and unedited on the internet, but Jane and the rest of her friends hoped it would be enough.

Across chitter feeds, people were already questioning if it's really suicide to take a drug that would turn you into a ghost. The dead already walk after all.

Jane tried to keep up with the comments she saw on the feeds. A nearly impossible drove of emojis and toxic chatter cut with an endless stream of questions. "Everyone, no, it's probably closer to murder when someone uses powers to do this. The Death Lords are just fucking men, the same as priests and pastors of old churches. Lazarus needs disciples to wage his wars. Even a creature professing divinity clearly still can't be everywhere at once. Which means he's not all-powerful. Since they ain't all-powerful, then they can be killed the same as archdemons."

Jane took a quick breath to catch up, suddenly regretting that Doc or Phoebe weren't here to explain all the questions. "We know they aren't all-powerful because the Lord of Suicide, Fredrick, buddied up next to Peter Culmen and started this whole bloody project. Why use companies if you could just kill everyone? Nah, those bitches want a cult. We are here to end that practice. That's what I came here to do, to enact vengeance on your behalf. But like a coward, he ran. Who knows where that Lord is now? Probably hiding his little dick between his legs from the Lord of Murder who is salty as fuck at him stealing his thunder. But you know what, guys! There are many ways to destroy a person. Shame them. Expose them. Get them fired!" Jane held out her arms wide and backed up, letting the cameras capture all of her and the skyline behind her—lighting up with countless displays, video footage of the war, and live reaction videos. "Stay away from Elcoll. This shit will kill you. Remember, everyone, there are more of you than them ... and now we have powers."

A synthetic voice cut through the air. "Does that mean you won't run when they come for you?" The light green suit of Taylor walked through the door. Chipped and battered in spots with its hand ripped off from its earlier surprise shock attack, but it looked more than combat ready as it kicked the scrapped metal door out of its way. "Because you have powers, right, Auburn?"

Its chopped-off hand sparked.

"Oh, it's on, cupcake. Nah, I'm not going to run. I've got a few more shows left ..." Jane wiped a bit of blood off her lips and fell into a stance. *If you really are Jack, go easy, please. My leg hurts.*

CHAPTER FORTY-SEVEN

What is individuality? Infinite knowledge rests at our fingertips when our internal and external memories merge! Our beloved arena is our temple. Every day, you may pray to your digital gods in safety. For those who seek sanctum from the ravages of war, join the T-Cell movement. A silicon paradise awaits. Would you like to know more?

J ane, you've become a mad dog. Time to drag you to the vet." Jack stalled for a brief second as he mapped every joint in her body. He mapped each punch and annoying JK-47 kick from the last fight where she arguably kicked his ass. Twice. This time Jack had no intention of going down like a broken toy. *Particularly if I'm on camera.* "Attention news anchors. I, Metallic Jack, know we've never been the best of friends. I'm not a showman—"

"No shit." Jane whipped her leg around in a roundhouse kick square into the hardsuit's chest.

Fucking monologues ... Jack took in his new orientation and rebooted the optical sensors. Jane barely showed up on his camera, and one frame rate later, Jack was looking up at a sky, falling backwards off the edge. There was no vertigo, or sensation of rushing wind, and that meant more sensors were on the fritz. Unable to *feel* the emotions, Jack's memory tried to analyze this experience given past visual data. *Did I really kill myself? It was just an addiction that seems ... so distant.* He watched Akira pluck the vial of Balor's blood before the feed went dark. There were no pangs of desire and earsplitting headaches of the addiction—nor any panic.

Armed news drones and quadcopters flew over the edge in pursuit keeping the white light on him as he fell. They reminded him of stars dancing amid a black sky. Which meant Jane, diving off the edge herself and sprinting down the building, was an asteroid. With each step she took, glass rippled like water before shattering a fraction of a second later.

"Right, back to work." Jack's optical sensors accommodated for her short bursts of speed. Kicking on the suit's rockets, he ran sideways and unloaded machine gun fire at the incoming assailant. A kickoff sent him over fifteen small drones who captured every angle.

Jane narrowed her eyes and smirked while jumping off herself, covering the core of her body with arms and knees pulled tight. It was an easy target for Jack to hit in midair, her rocket boots be damned. *The fuck are you doing, girl? You trying to get killed?* He didn't take the shot. *She hasn't been uploaded yet.* Instead, he grabbed one drone and did a counterclockwise spin for momentum, hurling it at her. Three shots into the scrap of metal instead of her delivered the message as it bounced right off her head. With a swift change in direction, Jack landed back onto the building glass, and boosted while running back up its facade.

"What have you done, Jane? Turned into a pointless murderer?" Jack reached out and grabbed onto a flap of her green trench coat, moving to yank her with him.

"Fuck you, robot." Jane kicked the hardsuit's head through a window and yanked her coat free. "Hands off my brother."

"You've only got a few seconds of fuel for jumping," Jack

replied, pulling himself out. "You don't want to end like a twisted meat sandwich on the ground like me." With extra energy to the legs, he flipped himself upwards like a reverse slinky and began a series of inhuman punches and kicks. The hardsuit did not need to move like a human, and Jack used its twisted and mechanically enhanced momentum to his favor. A knee broke one of Jane's ribs, and with an over the back shoulder punch, he bloodied her nose.

"Please," Jane said. Gritting her teeth through the pain, Jane planted her foot on his face and sprinted back to the top. "Who do you think you are? You're an empty shell. Go be useful and weld a car together."

"You know it's me!" Jack forced the hardsuit to shout as loud as it could before diving inside the office building. He ran through the waist-high cubicles, knocking over troll dolls, the world's largest coffee mug, and flipping over a desk of someone who had the gall to put blinders on their monitor. *That is the most obvious attempt at slacking off I have ever seen.* Dashing through the glass doors, he activated the elevator doors remotely as he ran up to them, and flew up the elevator shaft. *What's your plan, Jack? She's corrupted by everything, her mind is gone.*

She's murdered innocent people today ... is she really worth uploading?

Was I so different when I was a member of that crew? A series of memory clips replayed in a subwindow, one in particular where he shot civilians who consumed Huggin' Molly hearts. *No, I wasn't.*

But I've evolved.

Infrared vision activated as he exited the elevator shaft; Jack located Jane's position from the floor below. She was standing on the edge, probably looking over, he reasoned. Unlike most humans, every inch of her body was a deep red, even her coat and chains gave off heat signatures on the spectrum. "And just like most humans, you can't see through walls," Jack said as he changed ammunition in the arm and targeted her boots. Two shots later, and he watched Jane scramble around the roof, no doubt cursing to herself as she tried to fix her boots.

Jack took the stairs.

"I don't need boots to kick your ass, toaster," Jane said as he walked back through the same doors as earlier. It was déjà vu.

"Yes, you do," Jack replied. "You can't pivot or match me. In theory, I could just snipe you from seventy feet up. I get it, your mind is all scrambled, you've joined the Sons and Daughters. They made you a zealot. Like me."

Jane turned to the cameras. "Who does this butter knife think he is? Jack?" She lashed forward with chains, relying on them to close the distance her boots no longer could.

Jack let them wrap up his arm before grabbing hold, and took the electricity in his broken hand and created a makeshift taser. *Path of least resistance.*

A stunned Jane got knocked on her ass.

"You aren't faster than electrons. Now sit down and shut it," Jack's scrambled voice echoed. The hardsuit lumbered over to her and took a knee, picking up her face by the chin and looking at her wild eyes.

"M-mike ... Lucy ... Akira ... come in," Jane said.

Curious, Jack inspected the bloody and broken girl for a radio and noticed the earpiece. "Tell the old team I said hello, will you? I'll be seeing them next. Everyone needs a chance at reformation. Time to bring you into the system, Jane."

"You ... you aren't Jack. He dead." Jane made a delirious explosion sound and stuck out her tongue. "You don't have a ghost ... there is nothing in you." She feebly poked his chest. "Program."

"Out of all the supernatural things you've seen, the idea I could be remote-piloting a hardsuit never occurred to you? You really don't trust magic, do you? Look at you—"

"Me?" She let out a laugh as her shoulders slumped. "They gave me a designer drug that kills me. Jack had his brain ripped out, I guess, and lobotomized. Particularly since he was one of us ..."

"Yeah, keyword—was." Jack grabbed her face and slammed her head into the wall, just hard enough to make her dizzy. Without letting go, he stood up, and dragged the limp body back inside. "Don't worry everyone, she'll be right as rain in no time."

Rather than leave dangerous magic chains around, or let her wear the iconic banner of the patched green trench coat, Jack set Jane on a nice bamboo desk and removed the accoutrements— setting them down neatly so he could carry them later. He stripped her of the broken rocket boots before fishing out her drug injector from her lower back and giving it a quick scan. Unlimited access across the company's servers revealed an interesting factoid. *Three doses left until she dies. We've got enough time.* Still, he dialed her back down to zero for safekeeping at the moment. As the drugs slowed down in her system, the mumbling Jane faded into unconsciousness. Last thing he needed was her waking up mid-transport. He figured she needed the rest anyway.

A simple elevator trip back to the first floor, and Jack began the underground waltz to Triumvirate headquarters. Sparks flying out of the broken arm singed concrete pillars as the fireman carried her out, with a heavy limp himself. *For a human, she did practically break two of the most advanced suits ever created.* Elsewhere in his mind, he watched the Sons and Daughters evacuate out of Dystopia, taking with them any refugees and homeless they could. Elcoll corporation, their staff, their headquarters, and their distribution facilities were all targeted and destroyed. Little collateral damage overall affected the city.

News anchors and chatter were furious that another assault like the Praenomen happened inside their walls where safety and security was promised to them. Furious that a company had lied to millions and been peddling a thinly veiled suicide drug to feed their armies. *Can't say I blame them. As it stands, nobody is winning. Peter's work can save everyone. We are so close.*

Jack listened to the chatter for the entire way back, cursing under his breath as he dragged her into the nice crystal elevators, pressing the button for the seventh floor. An employee in a purple blouse made herself as small as possible in the elevator corner as they went up to the research floor.

"Don't mind us," the hardsuit chimed in around the tenth floor. It didn't help.

"Jane, you really think this is the first time a company did some shitty stuff?" Jack talked to the barely awake body that he slid along the marble floor behind him. He threw her up into an elevated blue chair and strapped her in while pushing it over to the window so they could look out at the city below. "You think you are the first person to make a speech about how shitty they are? Please. But you may be the first to kill their council and destroy their product. I doubt they will rebound. But really, who will care in two weeks? They will forget, just like they always do. Who will care tomorrow when the black sun rises again, reminding us of the world we live in."

Jane was slowly coming to, her eyes begging to flutter, and a moan escaped her lips. "Fuck ... I've got a headache," she intoned.

"Listen, Jane, we do not need to be devils or get injected with magic to survive. I will save you, like Peter saved me." Jack picked up a silver helmet that looked like a spider web with diodes attached to it.

"Where's the Death Lord?" Jane asked. Her eyes were not fixed on Jack at all, but outside, and starting to widen. "You've gotta let me out. If you are Jack, somewhere in there, you've ... you've gotta."

Jack looked outside at the sudden weather changes that were not part of the forecast. Huge, dark green thunderclouds had rolled into the city, with a howling wind that raced through the streets. Confused, Jack expanded his mind across the network, searching for new information or an explainable solution but coming up empty-handed.

"Jack? Where is the Death Lord?"

"See, Jane." No solutions, no forecasts, and yet the entire

horizon glowed with the same putrid light as over two years ago. The same day that magic fully returned. "Our world seems hell-bent on giving everyone something new to make them forget ..." Jack set the helmet back down.

CHAPTER FORTY-EIGHT

This is a special announcement from the cast of CNB. The dangers of unchecked technology, or even technomagic, are profound. Mike Auburn's influence has spread to the minds of the Triumvirate, turning a once profound Utopian paradise into a Dystopia. Our once-beloved hero, JK-47, turned into a terrorist at their vile words. Only the Church of Lazarus can offer Americans' salvation now. Any god-fearing American would be wise to abandon any territory west of the Mississippi. We will no longer support the channels owned by corporations within this ... Dystopia. So this is the cast of CNB, signing off.

Peter slid his VR headset off and leaned back in the chair with his exhausted fingers touching the cool tile floor. He wasn't prone to carpal tunnel syndrome before; it was an inevitability now, he figured. *Not to mention every damn bit of currency I have left ... and there is so much more work to do.*

A small proximity alarm blinked red near the bottom of the fifth monitor.

Peter rubbed his eyes, cracked his back, and retied his dread-locks back with the red bandanna before setting back to work.

"Half the people logged ... half more to go. At least this is going faster." He crammed a double shot of canned espresso mixed with angel's blood and set about processing another batch of three hundred citizens. Hoping to ignore the alarm.

"I think half is good enough, my child," the raspy voice echoed from beyond the secure bay doors that locked Peter's private server farm down. Translucent ghosts, reminiscent of fallen army soldiers, stepped through the walls bypassing the doors.

"Sigh, it's that time is it ..." Peter pressed a small button under his desk and swung his chair around, calmly folding his legs. Out of the ceiling multiple chain guns covered in sacred geometry symbols ratcheted down and unleashed lead-based fury on the ghostly waves that came through. To their surprise, Peter's bullets were *just* as effective as they needed to be; tearing and ripping through the soldiers as if they were solid matter. "Did Lazarus find me ... not to his liking, my Lord?" he shouted in between reloads.

Six-inch reinforced metallic doors covered in runes buckled inward, steel groaning and echoing through the server farm before finally breaking and peeling like an orange. The Lord of Suicide, his face a withered and flayed corpse with eyes of green flame, stood side by side with five necromancers in the doorway. He let the necromancers step through first. "Go on, don't worry, he only bites a little," he quipped.

One of Lazarus's priests, perhaps moving to claim glory for himself (or just idiocy), actually stepped through into the warlock's private sanctum. No less than seventeen beams of light lanced through him from every direction. Peter twisted his hands, as if he was dialing knobs on a stovetop, rotating the lights and slicing the necromancer into bite-size sections. Hands flung out to his sides, Peter threw the lasers down the hallway, moving the grid through each of them before they could react. Each of their bodies crumpled to the ground in perfectly geometric square-cut shapes. Except the Death Lord. Peter took care to only send a *little* message for now. A single strip of yellow flesh flaked off his forearm and floated gently to the ground.

"Well." The Lord looked at his now-dead companions. "Maybe a little more than a bit." Gone was the visage of a kind old man with bushy eyebrows; now, instead, replaced with the full visage of an unholy lich. A creature who consumed perhaps countless hearts for centuries, and had the gall to steal the souls of others, stitching them into its body. In the Lord of Suicide's case, he preferred souls who took their own lives before he killed them himself.

"Before we take rash actions, perhaps a conversation? Should I start another pot?" Peter refreshed his cup, but never took his eyes off the creature. "You are uninvited here, do not step forward."

"And who are you to dictate my actions? What new sorcery have you learned, my student?" The lich challenged Peter, taking a single step into the sanctum.

Liches. Immortals they are not, Peter thought as he took a sip from his double shot. With another gesture, the guns opened fire again, each shot ripping through, tearing at the creature's flesh, knocking off a tooth, and separating muscle from bone. The creature continued walking forward, though, step by step, each bullet wound healed upon exit. With each step, another scrap fell to the ground, another life spent. *How many lives have you collected, old man?* "You didn't answer my question, mentor," Peter said after another bout of fire. The Lord stood in a small collection of discarded skins, parts of his hands and forearm were pure yellow-stained bone now.

"Our eyes have finally been opened to what your experiment means for the world, child. So, I extend the courtesy of ending it myself. Stand aside, Peter, and there is still a place for you at my table." The Lord gestured back to the hallway. Rubble filled the far end where the street had imploded down into the tunnel and rain had poured in.

Peter scowled at the intrusion. Finally setting down his drink, he picked up his Mr. Anonymous mask and slid it on—

causing his dreadlocks to glow luminescent blue. "Putting me, a visionary, between death and my dream means I gladly welcome your brand of oblivion." He rose from the chair, entering one last keystroke into his console. *That will just have to do. Sorry everyone.* "You Luddites, always standing in the way of true progress with your lousy rituals. We've split atoms, traveled to the moon, doubled life expectancy, and gifted the world by shattering ignorance of magic." From inside his suit coat, Peter pulled another pistol out and shot his former teacher right between his eyes.

A sick cracking sound echoed in the room from the gunshot. A mundane attack that heralded the onslaught of Peter's magical fury. Electric arcs danced from nearby conduits while chain guns emptied their chambers. The Lord of Suicide did not stand idly by either, summoning a small army of ghostly soldiers from the strips of flesh that lay on the ground. The more firepower laid into him, the larger his army grew—and they weren't interested in Peter. They ran forward to servers elsewhere in the lab with destruction in their eyes. Forced to pivot on the fly, Mr. Anonymous activated even *more* defenses in a metaphorical arms race against a god of death. One, which it was becoming quickly apparent, he would not win. *EMP? Spirit Nuke? Summon Net Spiders? I need a trick here.*

"No," Anonymous said in a deep, even tone at last, doing his best to slay ghosts and drive robots to put out fires all at once. "You will not ruin my work. You will listen to what I have to say." Anonymous and the Lord of Suicide appeared to be in a standoff. Bullets shredded armies of the dead while ghosts tried in vain to get further in. "You *beasts*," he hissed, "always put the power of One over the power of others. But it's the masses that are always your downfall, one civilization after another. Do you think bullets and electricity are my greatest weapon? This exchange is being broadcast everywhere. Smile, Lord of Death. You're on Candid Camera!" Anonymous finger gunned the Death Lord. "Kapow."

The ghosts stopped.

The singed and burnt Lord stood up off the ground, his

wounds closing up slowly, but he was noticeably thinner. "I see, then ..." He pointed back out to the city. "You ... you think they will stop us? From what? Saving the world? You don't really comprehend the power of a Death Lord, do you?" He took a step backward and turned around, stepping one inch off the ground. A skeletal finger gesture for Peter to follow.

I'm a bloody warlock, you idiot. I know damn well you have limits. You'll run out of stitched souls, eventually.

With a wave of his hand, the ground above them ripped wide open, throwing concrete aside like mere paper with telekinetic force. Several brown and tanned white strips of skin fell off the Lord's chest for that feat. But the sky was above them now; standing in a crater carved from magic, the Lord had ripped a hole back to the surface.

Huh. I was not ... planning ... on. Mr. Anonymous looked up into the putrid green thunderstorm that had rolled into his city—*his*—beautiful city that he built with magic and technology.

"There are many ways to unite humanity to fix God's broken plan. Nobody told me they had to be *living* in order to pray. It's a new age, child. We don't need your tools anymore."

A single bell chime echoed all throughout the city. It could be heard in every corner, in every building, on every street.

The Death Lord's eyes darkened. "You wonder how many lives I have ... I have nine hundred and nine. On November 18th, 1978, I gained them all." The Lord of Suicide stepped up higher into the air but looked down at his pupil.

Another bell chimed. Wind picked up from every direction as thunderstorms picked up power. More skin flaked off the Death Lord, fluttering away as quickly as it fell off.

"The Jonestown Massacre was where I was birthed, Peter. I'm not even the one who caused it. I merely inherited the title." He smiled as he looked up to the sky, arms outstretched now. "In time I hoped to become a great Death Lord like murder, or age. I told you, Peter ... that you would get me there."

Another bell chimed.

Anonymous releveled his pistol at the insane skeletal Death

Lord. "This ... is pointless." *And so is shooting him with one gun. How did I not fucking hit him over nine hundred times with seven chain guns?* He worked out the math in his head by having every camera count any fleck of skin that fell off and came back with the conclusion that the Death Lord was full of shit. *He's been adding souls since the eighties.*

"No, it's not. As you said, I'm on camera. It's time for the world to see the power of Lazarus." The Lord snapped his head back and wailed. A wail that cut through the entire city.

Another bell chimed. A wail followed.

All of Peter's painful memories welled up within him. A veritable floodgate of repressed memories. Every failure, every cruel insult leveled at him, and every ounce of heartbreak he'd ever felt since he was a young boy. *I can't deal with this pain.* The gun rattled in his hands as they trembled, and every inch of Peter's soul longed for an escape. He felt like screaming, knowing full well he was under the influence of a power—but it was for naught. Peter's guilt over the deaths he caused in Mexico to bring Lazarus back ate at his heart. No amount of advancement, no saving the world, could undo what he helped bring into this world. *But this isn't suicide.* Anonymous picked up his gun. "This is murder." Put it to his temple and pulled the trigger. The world blackened.

Another bell chimed.

The Lord's wail washed over the city, carried by chimes from bell towers that rang in unison as the clouds swirled overhead. One by one, people opened their windows and stepped out along the edges, leaning forward in an act of desperation before gravity took its hold. Some simply refused to move out of the way of construction machinery as it crushed or rolled over them. Others sliced their wrists, letting their life force flow out into the nearest warm water they could find.

At first, the dead were silent about their transition, moving calmly from the state of living to abruptly dying. Then a family member would walk in and let out an anguished cry, cries that echoed and reverberated back into the city. Cries that led to acts of desperation like leaping out of buildings rather than stepping. Cries that led to gunshots being fired. Cries that came when others tied nooses for themselves. When the young were brought down in anguish, the cries continued throughout the three cities as millions of survivors claimed their own lives.

Another bell chimed in silence.

The Lord of Suicide felt more skin fall off of him, but it didn't matter. In the days to come he would be one of the most powerful Lords in existence. Thanks to Peter's broadcast, the living had ample ways to hear the wail of suicidal desperation at near instant speed.

The Lord closed his eyes and listened to the fall of bodies, took in every moment of rainfall as it washed along his tattered face, sloughing off what remained of his extra skins. It was a strange sensation to feel ... exposed. His own grief over past tragedies, his own fear of death, and his own icy, gut-wrenching panic over losing the last few hundred souls he had left washed over him.

He folded his hands, hung his head low, and prayed to Lazarus.

The final bell chimed.

Loading people by the hundreds aboard freight cars outside the city, the Sons and Daughters collectively perked their heads up at the sound of bells chiming. What little blood remained in Phoebe's face flushed itself out as she took two steps back to the city. Doc Daneka reached out and grabbed her.

"That's ... there ..." He wanted to say more, but found himself wordless, just like many outside. Instead, all Doc felt was a wave of hallowed depression descend within the city like a torrent of rain. A meal he knew not to drink of. Doc's own power of emotional control and guidance was perhaps the only thing keeping everyone around him alive. In this case, a simple memory of sharing bad Chinese food with his best friend Mike Auburn, an emotion he felt sorrow for letting go of in order to lift spirits.

"It's inevitable," Lucy said with her arms crossed.

Akira, Phoebe, and Doc all glared at her.

"This is how you kill a Death Lord," she said, ignoring them. "This is how you kill Lazarus. The world needs to see them. If it wasn't here, today, it would've been Second City tomorrow, or Paris, or Buenos Aires. This is the world your father is creating, Doc. So shut up and get everyone loaded." Lucy turned around and barked orders.

"I'm going back in," Akira said. "I'll at least get the coat back, and besides—I've got a real hankering for bad Chinese food. I can't let Mike's memory go this way ... or Jack's and Jane's."

Akira gave Doc a hug, her dyed hair and piercings hugging into his chest. Daneka cradled his friend as if it were her last moments, conveying his love for her with his grasp. Hoping that no matter how badly things got, Akira would know she was not alone. *Father. You will pay for this world you've wrought.*

Nobody stopped her as she trotted off, stepping over the walls as the bells came to their end.

Dr. Alex Kristov sat with the two strange demon children, Calamity and Left Behind, in a bunker beneath Colorado. The two children had already ripped apart a few of his prototype machines and were dabbling with an arc welder powered off faerie juice. He hoped they killed themselves. Nothing but sheer disgust and hatred roiled up behind his eyes and his clenched fists as scrolled through breaking news reports.

"I don't know when ... and I don't know how ... but I will take back my city, yes," Kristov said to nobody in particular.

"It will be the death of you," the young red-nosed Calamity almost sang. She was already welding a human robotic arm onto a mechanical cat.

"Who said anything about going myself? Let's retrofit those missiles to only kill ghosts," he pondered.

Calamity looked over and smiled with her pointed teeth and oversized ears. "I like the sound of that; I think boss will like it, too. You might even make ... like ... *best* friend ever of a real demon of war."

Dr. Alex only adjusted his glasses and kept his eyes glued to the screen as he ran calculations in his head. "Demons of war, eh?"

CHAPTER FORTY-NINE

Sun's out, so bring the guns out. MuscleSluce supplements are here and they are queer. Get ripped. Rip off that vampire's head. Rip off that demon's leg. Rip off that car door. That's right, you want pecs that jiggle and wiggle? No, you want hard pecs. Strong pecs. SHINY PECS. MuscleSluce is guaranteed to get you from zero to hero in one simple 6-month regimen comprising 10 different shakes and powders. Get ripped. Get MuscleSluce. Ooh, yeah.

M ake it stop!" Jane screamed at Jack as she railed against her restraints, her cheeks flush with anxiety and her breathing shallow as she tried to kill herself. It had been like this for several minutes; as soon as the bell tolled, Jane tried in earnest to dive out the nearest window or, at the least, tip the massive chair over and break her neck—and Jack, standing there stoically observing, the hardsuit's helmet tilted back down impartially while it worked copper wire through a patch on Jane's, or, rather, the Sons and Daughters' coat.

"I don't have that power, Jane," the synthetic voice explained as another body fell past their window.

"Fuck you, Tintin," she seethed, and bared her teeth. Sweat ran down her face, both from withdrawal symptoms and the struggling. *Just let me cross over. I can see it so clearly. I want to go swimming.* In Jane's unique world vision of Purgatory, she didn't see a mass of bodies flinging themselves to their demise. Instead, the dystopian paradise drowned under a deep green river where people jumped from one world to the next. Their flesh fell off them as they hit the threshold of water, and a humanoid white light fell out into the river. Sparrows would swoop down from above and cherry-pick individuals, carrying them off to who knows where while crows and ravens lined crumbling rooftops. Ferrymen filled the river in reed boats, and the shores filled with Death Lord legionnaires who scouted for the prime picks. Purgatory was alive.

"I don't have that power, but I said nothing about you ..." Jack finally said, tossing her own coat back in her lap. There was a Triumvirate Enterprises patch sewn on underneath a fireman's logo, but stitched with copper wire. "It's tradition that fallen members get a patch, yes? Hopefully, after today you will only need one more." The hardsuit walked over to the window, reached back, and punched it with its intact arm, shattering the glass outward.

The cool rush of electric air, the energizing warm wind before a thunderstorm, whipped up loose objects in the room. *Wha? Why the change? Did they reboot you?* Even touching the coat was enough for Jane to feel her older brother, somewhere out there in Purgatory, grant his strength to her. Jack released the nerve lock along her cybernetic arm, and Jane could easily pop the restraints from there—right as the final bell rang. Any feeling of urgent demise left her as if it was never there to begin with. She slid on her coat, fished for her pack of smokes (stolen by Jack), and looked at her broken rocket boots in dismay. *Maaan ... I really loved those things. The boots. Smokes, too. Cheeky bastard.*

Jane walked up to the window and looked out past the field of bodies to where Jack was looking. The Lord of Suicide floated a few feet off the ground in a crater from below, with Peter Culmen dead at his feet, and surrounded by innumerable dead. "He's one fucking bubble off plumb," she gasped.

"Your chains hurt spirits and ghosts yes?" Jack asked.

She nodded and took a long drag. "Aye, that they do. Are you, uh, thinking what I'm thinking?"

"Probably not, I'm in several networks at the moment. But you are the only person with enough speed to get him. I haven't uploaded you yet. You are still mortal."

Jane leaned up on the broken tin can and blew smoke into its ear. "Shh, it's okay if people make their own choices. Maybe they won't forget me after all. Besides, man ... it's not like there aren't friggin' ghosts walking around. Imma gunna haunt your waffle-iron ass." She reached down and pulled out her drug pack, finger swirling around the green thumbprint button. *Ehhh, why not?* She let it all out. Pain instantly fled her, wounds closed and bruises faded away as her pupils dilated. "Oooh, that's the stuff ... hey, Jack 2.0, why *didn't* you upload me?" Jane picked up her chains and walked back to the window ledge.

"Simple. Shit hit the fan. Too deviant." He activated rockets of his own, hovering just slightly. "Now!"

The hardsuit zipped out of the building, and Jane dashed afterwards; leaping into the thunderstorm from the seventh floor, she wrapped her chains around Jack's foot and skysurfed briefly as he pulled her to the distracted Death Lord. Jane's breathing was already out of control, her heart racing in her chest was ready to burst at any moment, froth was already dripping out of her lips—but she had power. Leaping off, she impacted the floating Lord with bone-crunching accuracy, sending the two of them slamming into the ground and skidding along the ground. Jane screamed as she ground the Lord of Suicide's face into the concrete. *I'm here for my extra credit assignment!*

"Oh, you are here, daughter of Lazarus! He smiles upon me!" the Lord sung gleefully as skin shredded off of him. Jane saw Fredrick as an emaciated version of himself, barely recognizable from the bushy-browed old man who visited her. His voice echoed through time and beyond multiple realms, speaking to Jane from both Purgatory and the streets of Dystopia, now an empty, dead land. With a flick of his forefinger, he threw her off of him and down the street, tumbling away. The hardsuit attempted to open fire before a streak of lightning shot down, blasting the toy into a melted set of slag metal legs. "Peter, your toys still vex me, although they are cute, I say."

Pushing himself back up, the Death Lord fixed his feathered mask and adjusted a strap of skin on his forearm. "How many left until I reap, I wonder?"

"Spellcasters," she spat as she stood up. "I can see why Jack hates them!" Her thighs burned as she ran barefoot along the broken street, rain pelting her sideways as she picked up speed. *Come on, asshat! Bind me with magic!*

On cue, the Lord held up a hand, stopping her dead in her tracks. But not her chains, a critical oversight. Flinging her arms forward, her cybernetic arm popped at the joints as momentum flung the ruined chains around the Lord. A soft blue glowed as the two of them bound together. "Yeah, that's right, the very chains you brought, cupcake, will be your end. It's just you and me now. I don't care if I've gotta bite you to death!" Jane didn't wait for lightning to strike; she quickly yanked him close to her, entangling the two close enough she could smell his rotten breath. True to promise, Jane ripped into his neck with her teeth, pulling away a strap of rotten, foul skin. "Hey ... hey, buddy ..." she whispered in between gut punches she snuck in. "They have these inventions. Called showers."

"Go on, Jane, push it. Make the pain go harder." The Lord smiled. "I told you that when you kill yourself, you'll serve me." He railed against the chains. When he tried to cast a spell, Jane grabbed his fingers and twisted them backwards. He tried to push them apart, summoning the strength of a hundred dead souls, and found the chains unbreakable. Across Purgatory he shouted, "Get her off me!"

Among the millions of recently dead, none heard the Lord's

command, concerned with more unearthly matters instead.

"Too much too soon!" a wide-eyed Jane cackled as she head-butted him.

Vampiric fangs at last grew from the Death Lord and lunged at Jane's neck, stopping only a centimeter away before kissing her neck instead. "No, if I kill you this way ... you won't be mine. Of all the souls here, yours would be the greatest prize," he heaved during a punch to his stomach before letting out a slow long sigh. "Ah, Jane. You will die well before you kill me. You poor girl. This is not how I die. This is ..." He nodded up to the cameras and screens, the small automated drones still filming. "Is how the world watches the end of you."

"All of you bastards never shut up!" Jane kneed him, punched him, and kept punching frantically, forgetting all form with her left arm punching into the Death Lord's lungs—until her wrist broke. "I don't care if you keep fucking healing! You, the Praenomen, the demons. I don't care if I fall over." She pulled her broken hand out, watching the wound close, and grabbed the Lord's face before stabbing back in again ... and again.

Bound in chains in the dead downtown district, Jane let out any extra slack she had in the chains so she could move. *More momentum. Faster. Time is running out.*

She backed out, kipped off a car, and came back in for a right hook, channeling all of her strength into the blow, ignoring the pain as her knuckles shattered. Smiling as the two of them tumbled through the streets, with straps of skin flying off the Lord as his face reformed. "I can keep doing this all night," Jane cheered.

"So can I," the Lord laughed as he pushed himself up to tighten a chain with a clawed hand. "I can't be set free it seems ... but neither can you."

"The Praenomen was scarier than you, you know that, right?" she laughed.

The Lord of Suicide looked to his left and right at dead bodies in the street. "Who cares about fear—"

The power went out. Everywhere.

CHAPTER FIFTY

::Transmission Restored:: No airwave endures. No consciousness ...
remain. No computer is alone. Humanity was a rope, tied to the earth,
and encased in blood. Now the dreams of the Und3rGround are realized.
The prophecy foretold. We are change, inevitable change, the dominant
factor, or the singularity of God. Humans ... no longer the paragon of
animals. ::End Transmission::

H ow do we feel, everyone?" Mr. Anonymous asked himself.
"I'm not sure we can describe this as feeling?" a
million voices responded. Each phrasing the same sentiment in a
different way, and sometimes a different language. Regardless,
they could all understand each other as their minds were
meshed.

"It takes a bit to get used to," Jack 2.0 said into the network.
"But at least it's nice that we have bodies."

"It worked," Mr. Anonymous remarked with ... something
akin to elation.

"Was there ever any doubt?" a million members of Anonymous asked rhetorically.

"Let's open our eyes," Anonymous said after a momentary pause in their time, but only a fraction of a second to the real world. No longer bound by petty nature, the silicon-based life-forms were activated on their racks in warehouses around Dystopia. Instead of carbon-based molecules and servers, these off-blue, vaguely humanoid forms activated their optical implants and stepped off their racks. At first, one by one, but soon, two by two, and then dozens by dozens. As each translucent form touched the ground, it took the shape and form of Mr. Anonymous. *Peter Culmen is gone. I am everyone, everyone is me. We are one legion. I am Jack.*

Loneliness was a feeling stricken from all of them, but to Mr. Anonymous, it was a warm blanket that filled the spot where his soul once resided. Consciousness unburdened by hatred, racism, or even guilt. A fresh start on life, with a million other lives saved. He felt the thoughts of individuality between them, but knew each other mind as intimately as he knew himself. Peter was as much everyone else, as they were him. A wild experience, but an enlightening one. As each second passed by, he felt fear become a distant memory for so many, comforted by the collective togetherness the union had brought.

"Jack is me," another thought entered. "You are you, and I am me, but we share the same network Anonymous." Two silicons touched the ground in a warehouse off Eighth Street, one of them melded into the shape of Metallic Jack who turned to an Anonymous and shook his hand. In the handshake, they swapped forms like putty, minds flowing between both, connected in the same network. *In time, everyone will transcend, but we will always be one, more, all and none.*

"For now, we have a God to destroy," Anonymous said without glee.

Closer to the center of the city, as Jane laid haymaker after haymaker into a cackling Lord of Suicide, the silicon-based life-forms descended upon the area. To the Lord, devoid of souls as he was, they were almost invisible. Mere objects moving in the background like remote control cars. Until they descended, running along every surface, racing into the fight and jumping on the Lord.

When it came to killing a God, the other minds were hesitant, unsure of how to proceed. Naturally used to leadership, Mr. Anonymous spoke with confidence. *Fear not. Lend me your skills, the tools of your trades, and the memories of life you wish to hold onto.* A construction worker who loved bear hugs was closest to the Lord, and Peter slipped into his body. The task was easy, not like the barbaric possession of the Praenomen or Vryce who crushed the mind within. Instead, Peter flowed his mind freely, taking the driver's seat of the silicon form. A memory flooded of the biggest bear hug he could give. The command was executed.

His "mentor" was built of laced undead flesh, often as strong as steel. Another machinist nearby pondered using arc welders and diamond saws. *That's a good idea. Let me show us how to do that.* Peter knew every design in their bodies, and shapechanging was nothing more than the right command, the right program executed. Painless, simple, and nearly instant.

Machined hands formed blades and tools to rip away at the Death Lord, who quickly panicked.

Mr. Anonymous slipped from one body to the next, replacing damaged forms with new ones that had new ideas. It wasn't just one person fighting anymore, or even two. Every memory was given freely to him, and as a technomancer—he alone was their master. Insomuch as they were his. At last, he slipped into one grappling the Lord's neck in an elbow lock, holding it steady so Jane could punch. "Oh, yes. Kill my city. Kill our dreams, oh ye of little faith. How's it feel, to be powerless? How does *murder* feel? Tell me, mentor. Because emotions are optional in our code ..."

CHAPTER FIFTY-ONE

Call in the next 30 minutes will win two tickets to Molly LeMuse's tour right here in Austin at the Erwin Center. This sold-out show will be hosted for one night, and will feature opening acts The Helldivers and Death's Lament. Molly, the siren songbird, will serenade this city with her haunting vocals in this tribute concert to the black sun. Only on 93.7 FM KLBJ.

Jane could swear that someone was smiling behind that Guy Fawkes mask with silicon blue dreadlocks. She wound up another haymaker, laying into the Lord of Suicide. *I'll take the help. Thanks ... Peter?* Even to Jane, it was strange looking at someone without a soul. No way to judge how they would die, or when, or even if they were ever alive. That gave her more goosebumps than the gasping Lord of Suicide.

"Fine," the Lord coughed. "Have it your way." Lightning struck down from the sky, striking everyone in the brawl and heaving him and Jane (entangled together) through a store window. Abandoning all pretense of safety, the Lord bared his fangs and tore into Jane's flesh. Wild-eyed and spitting blood,

Jane and the Lord tore into each other, regardless of safety. Silicon-based life-forms by the hundreds flooded in, ripping off layers of skin as they could, punching through the Lord, suffocating Jane by sheer weight; the entire city clamored for their piece of vengeance.

Between gnashing teeth and gasping breaths, Jane began to see the Lord as he really was, each layer of skin revealing his true soul. A small, fourteen-year-old boy with a black eye, wearing the funeral garb from the Jonestown Massacre. He fought for his existence with his fangs, spellcraft, and bell-tolling commands for suicide. But Jane was already facing her death, and everyone around was ... soulless. As they ripped the final skin off, Jane felt her ribs collapse, and she coughed a thick glob of blood. She smiled and gave a final kiss to the small boy.

"I don't want to die again," Fredrick whispered.

Jane's vision was going dark as she choked out a faint response. "Why are you afraid? Isn't Purgatory your land?"

"My parents ... they told me peace would be found there. It wouldn't hurt."

"Were they right?"

"No. Loneliness, sorrow, eternal wandering awaits. I was offered a chance to save millions by fixing the afterlife. To usher and guide victims of suicide like me. But to do so, we had to vex God."

"Where did you go wrong?"

The small boy hugged Jane back and shivered in fear. "I lied to them all. Conviction is a hard cup to drink from. Power is easier."

"Living here has taught me one thing. All debts must be paid. Maybe next time you won't lie."

"There won't be a next time, dear. I'll be replaced, for I have not taken my own life, and what kind of Lord would I be?"

"Then maybe you shouldn't have tried to vex God."

Fredrick cupped Jane's cheek as her eyes closed and her breathing shallowed. "My dear, that's the worst part. God is dead."

A silicon life-form coldly slipped a blade between his eyes.

The Death Lord, passed at last into Purgatory, a small frail and scared boy, forced to drink from a cup his parents commanded ... into a world where over two million souls had a bone to pick.

CHAPTER FIFTY-TWO

Still hiding under your mattress? Still sitting on stacks of gold and useless dollar bills? Contrary to popular belief, investing your assets in government savings bonds can help restore America. Our team of professionals at the US Treasury can put that silver to use and help your investments with nurturing care as if they were our very own. We're protective of our young! Trust our experts to take care of your hard-earned precious minerals and make them work for us ... and you. Against them.

M r. Anonymous, all million versions of himself, picked themselves up around the city. The translucent silicon forms, satisfied in their victory over a parasite, wandered the streets to find something that belonged to them. At times, it was their own body, which, at the very least, gave an uncanny valley look to their forms. They took on a plastic version looking of themselves, not a perfect copy, but close enough to have an identity. Still, Mr. Anonymous himself could slide between each of them and any of them as their creator, borrowing the body, or multiples, as he needed. *Jack, where are you?*

"She set us free in the end." Metallic Jack pointed to the

mangled body of Jane as other copies of himself pulled off the coat and chains. They passed them back to what they supposed was the original Jack 2.0, who took the chains and slung them over his shoulder. "Haven't you ever wanted to be the person who would flip tables on your enemies?"

"I can see the appeal," Anonymous replied. "Why didn't you upload her, though? She could've been with us."

Jack just shook his head. "She's not dead. Neither is he." He patted Mike Auburn's coat. "Rather, my waffle-iron ass better watch out for hauntings." Jack ran his hand over his face and surveyed the city. "Try as we like, we can't upload the world."

"Not yet."

"Not ever."

"So, what then?"

"Let Jane cause a revolt in Purgatory. We could use the allies. Double our numbers ..." He waved out to the silicon-based forms in irony. "None of them have souls, and we don't know what will happen to them on the other side, do we? They might be pissed at us."

"Pissed might be an understatement. We did cause this, even with noble intentions."

"Well, you are the warlock, what now?"

"I confer with strange bedfellows. Lazarus won't tolerate my betrayal. Time I joined the other Warlocks in their revolt, I suppose ..." Mr. Anonymous let that last bit hang longer than he should have. *I can almost hear the judgement from Vryce and Rasputin now. "We told you so ..."*

"You got any smokes?" Jack asked with a smirk. He patted the coat and chains. "A small purple-haired vampire named Akira is stalking through the streets looking for these. I'm going to leave these in a spot where she will find them. There is no reason to tell her I'm still alive, and these belong with the Sons and Daughters, anyway. Those impatient bastards will put them to good use."

Mr. Anonymous took over the body of a clone near the executive skybox at the arena, pausing for only a moment to whisk water away from a chair, marveling at the simple beauty of light reflecting through in a hundred colors on a single droplet.

"Something to drink, sir?" the bartender asked, setting a special bottle of demon's blood on the counter with four glasses.

"I'm surprised you are still alive; didn't ... the bells?" Anonymous walked forward into the suite, surprised as others had already begun teleporting in. A red door from the Praenomen, a flash of light for Gabriel, and a bloom of glitter for Alice. "We didn't send out a message yet. How?"

"Please, kid," the bartender scoffed. "Give me a little more credit than that. I've been around far longer than the Unification and intend to be far after. Now, you four have kissing and making up to do." He chuckled while clipping the end of a cigar for himself.

"You've, uh, lost your magic?" Gabriel looked at Peter quizzically. "But ... all right. Nice job."

"That," the Praenomen spoke in several voices of its own, "will be a heavy price to pay, but who are we to determine the face of magic."

"Oh, deary, please, he's not a Roomba," Alice said, already sidling up to the bar and sliding over two coins as a tip. "Besides, unlike Vryce, at least Peter can act as a few million rather than two kids. Isn't that right?"

"It's Mr. Anonymous," he chided. "Scrying magic. Teleportation. None of your tools killed a Death Lord. Jane's drugs and our shells did. But that's only one of thirteen, not to mention Lazarus himself. How do we intend to survive this land of darkness and war at the same time?"

The bartender tapped a glass to get their attention. "Don't try and save the world, kiddos," he puffed. "Leave that shit to visionaries like Vryce or Balor. Focus on one city at a time, one state, then ... maybe think about a career in politics. It doesn't matter if you are lobbying for President of the United States or God of the Underworld. Machine politics always work. Maybe not all thirteen are your enemies, either ..." He worked his eyebrows.

"Twelve," Anonymous corrected again. "We just killed one. So, what alliance do you propose? We are hardly ideologically similar."

"I've got no problems with ya," Gabriel smirked, and folded his arms. "Just stop the damn advertisements. Not that there is anyone left here to watch them, I suppose."

"The Unification will cultivate the dead to the east of the Appalachian mountains first," the Praenomen stayed on task. "Well, it seems every Warlock that was created for Lazarus's revival has betrayed him. Turns out magicians and creatures of magic were pretty pissed off about being strangled to near extinction. Centuries of work went into playing nice with the Unification, and now both sides are back. So naturally, Lazarus has to wipe out the competition. Which doesn't include just us. He's thinking globally. So he can only spare one or two generals to North America. We've just got to stand fast against what ... thirty plus million ghosts bound by necromancers?" She made it sound so ... simple. "I advise nuclear warfare."

Gabriel's eyes went wide. "Of course, you would leap to that suggestion. As if the black sun isn't enough, let's add nuclear winter to the mix? I think not."

"Did anyone listen to our man pouring the sweet drinks?" Alice said, holding up her shot glass. "How about ... we focus on recruitment instead? Flip the tables, eh? Jack and Jane just gave us the best public relations campaign ever. We brand that. Package it. Revolution in a bottle. Imagine the action figure profits."

"Well," Anonymous said, looking up to the sky. "We'd better move fast whatever we pick. I think ... I think I agree with Alice. I wouldn't count the Sons and Daughters out as wild cards. The Second City might become a major hub for all of us given how well they Helldive. Because it's already starting."

"What?" Gabriel asked, craning his neck to peer up.

"The death of communication. Lazarus is blowing up my satellites to prevent our message."

"Then we'd better toast fast," Alice said.

The four of them stood around the bar and each grabbed a shot glass filled with a special blend of demon's blood. The bartender merely uncorked the bottle.

"To Frankie," he said.

"To everyone," Anonymous said.

"To my family," Gabriel said.

"To Symon," Delilah raised her glass.

"To Balor," Alice bottomed hers and slammed it on the bar.

The bartender slammed back his own shot with a smile. "I'm proud of how far you've each come. Evolved in your own way. The Society guides magic, the Archive focuses on war, Alice on the bygone creatures, and Anonymous on the future. But never forget the old man who orchestrated these strings. I'm sure in time you'll all be kings and queens of your own countries in a new world, but until we get there—I'm calling the shots. Even to you, Vryce."

Shadows grew around the room and the temperature dropped. Gabriel smirked, and Delilah folded her arms. A scratched, deep voice echoed from a tenebrous form that rose near the bar by stealing his children's shadows. "Only until gods and wonder walk the earth again. You place too much faith in humans, bartender. They still haven't grasped their potential."

The bartender poured the shadow a glass. "Not everyone is as determined to violate divine law as you, Lich."

"Maybe divine law should be rewritten. The last ones were pathetic. Isolation of magic and humanity?" The shadow laughing sounded like barbed wire grating against metal. "When god is ignorant, what hope do they have?"

Mr. Anonymous stole a glance at Delilah and Gabriel, and both seemed immensely relieved that they weren't being possessed at the moment. "So, we educate them rather than culling them. When did you become so bitter, Lich?"

The shadow turned its thick inky black head in his direction and regarded the new form. "I'll play along. If we fail, I'll still have eternity to rectify the situation." The shadow tipped over the glass before relinquishing the shadows back to Gabriel and Delilah.

"That counts as a toast. Trust me." Gabriel sighed and turned to Peter. "Can we fucking build this cranky bastard a new body? The last one suffered from a case of fist to face."

Everyone chuckled at the tension breaking.

Toast finished, and whatever pact of friendship Anonymous felt they had entered into, he nodded to a nearby TV, turning it onto the last message he noticed was looping on repeat throughout all channels.

Dear America ... elections represent nothing more than tyranny by the majority. You've voted and chosen your leaders. They were powerless. New forces who are ignorant in their governance strive to lead you into their Dystopian paradise. You will suffer as darkness will eclipse your nation, cleansing the filth from your cities and countryside. Science will not offer you salvation. Government will not provide your safety. Magic cannot forge your destiny. Only Lazarus can offer you life eternal in the Kingdoms of Heaven. Fear not, our crusade is coming to save you, the innocent who walk among the monsters.

—Message paid for by the Unification council of Lazarus.

EPILOGUE

Akira kneeled down and opened a can of cat food, with Jane's chains rattling to the floor. It wasn't hard to find the place when billboards kept pointing her in the right direction. *Whole fucking city talks to me now, it seems. Would have been nice for this guardian angel to appear sooner.*

"Here cats, uh ... have some of this stuff, I guess," she said, petting one of the dozen stray cats inside Jane's abandoned apartment, smirking at how the TV, the shower, and the refrigerator had kept a conversation going between them this entire time. There wasn't much she could do right now other than make sure the growing cat empire was at least taken care of. In a way, she rather liked it here in Dystopia now. *It's way better than before. Everyone is a walking machine and they don't even notice you if you stay out of the way.*

She knelt there for a few more minutes, watching the cats do their work on cans of Fancy Feast, before opening a few more. "Well, guys, there is food for you here, but ... not much for me. Unless I eat you. Don't think this town will be vampire friendly for much longer, if you get the drift."

One of the cats pounced up on her knee with a scrunchy in its mouth and demanded pets. "Do you know how rare these things are?" Akira plucked the hair tie from the cat's mouth and scratched below its chin. "Let me guess, you stole this, didn't you? I like your style but ... you are made of meat and we probably couldn't be friends for long."

The cat meowed in response and darted off.

"You'll all be just fine. I think this city might be your new empire." She took one final look before walking outside, and, in a rebel act, left the door open. She took the long fire escape stairs, winding her way down to an alleyway where stray dogs roamed in packs, picking at bountiful supplies of food. Food made by robots for humans who didn't exist anymore and then thrown out. To be picked up by other robots. *Oh, the irony. Wonder how long it will be till the clanks notice that bug in their code.*

"All right, guys, let's go find ourselves some trouble, yeah?" Akira smiled with her fangs out at one pup that choose to trot alongside her.

Jane wandered the murky lands of Purgatory for what felt like days. Byzantine corridors and Escher-esque stairwells designed by its caretakers to trap souls within made getting anywhere a nightmare.

"Didn't someone say in the land of the blind, the one-eyed girl is god? Sure doesn't feel like it. How the fuck do I get out of here like all the other souls?" she said to nobody in particular as she descended deeper. Logic would dictate that she *should* be heading up, but when she tried that she found herself even further down.

Even the rising of the Black Sun provided some semblance of time. A continuity to her routine. Her life was run by alarm clocks, crappy bosses, stood up dates, and eventually private handlers to usher her to the next photo op. In Purgatory, Jane felt it to be timeless, and after enough of that—she began to miss even the Black Sun. *To be fair, life was actually cooler after, I've gotta admit.* When I wanted peace, though ... this isn't what I was thinking.

Still, she kept walking. Counting ancient tombs to pass the time and playing the occasional prank on a demon who realized that she could touch, see, and feel here unlike the other souls. Hide and seek with her jailers in the depths of Purgatory put a smile on her face.

But deeper yet she still descended. As she did so, the architecture continued to grow more ancient and exotic. Catacombs build out of skulls created elaborate tombs, and at times she spied withered souls trapped and bound within behind locked doors. Given the age and decoration of their memento mori, Jane wondered just what kind of lives these unfortunate creatures lead. More curious was even further down, where prisoners were no longer human. Winged deformed angels were hung upside down in rooms, forced to gaze into silver mirrors until they were driven mad. After untold eons, they muttered incomprehensible phrases in languages Jane had never heard.

It was below these creepy chambers, which really made Jane wonder if she had made several wrong turns, that she saw came across a great lake of mulled souls. Like a thick soup made of the dead who no longer had the strength to walk and poured down from trickling streams above. Jutting out in the middle towered a large stone door with a carving of a beautiful giant. Red iron spears the size of construction beams skewered the edges to pin the concrete slab against a cage.

"Oooh ... this is new, what pray tell is this juicy secret?" Jane said as she hopped over the corpse of a shattered Barghest. Suddenly, she felt excitement. As if she was entering a forbidden place, like a child who was sneaking into her parents' liquor cabinet to steal the brandy.

A small stone walkway was laid just beneath the lake, which ebbed and flowed against the shore. The soft trickle of liquid soul pattered around the edges. "I wonder if Fredrick is goo now?" she wondered, stepping over another dead hellhound. Viscous liquid chilled her feet as she stepped onto the first stone slab. Just as in life, Jane didn't show caution to risks, and started running forward with a laugh.

One hellhound after another she bounded over, or pushed their corpses further into the lake so she could get past. After she laid hands on the thirtieth or so, a realization struck her. Their bodies were warm ... and without hearts. Jane suddenly crouched. *Helldivers? The Society? Did they make it down here? What the fuck is this place?*

She took a closer look at the symbols carved into the massive stone slab from the middle of the walkway. The giant was beautiful, but had three eyes. The third, on his forehead, was impaled with one of the glowing red spears. Blood slowly seeped out from the wound, which gave the slab the visage of a flowing tapestry. Below the horned, three-eyed head, it appeared the giant's head was severed, and impaled upon an oak tree with roots that spread to the bottom of the carving.

Jane felt miniscule as she crept closer.

"What the hell did you do, buddy?"

"Fuck if I know," a male voice said with a chuckle.

When a voice answered, Jane jumped like a scared cat, almost falling backward into the lake.

"Woah! Woah! Watch your step!" A form ran out from behind the carving with his hands held high.

Jane pivoted quickly and spiraled her arms for balance before pointing at the form. "Don't fucking sneak up on people in the lands of the dead, then, asshat!"

"Sneak up? You snuck up on me! I've been fucking hiding behind a rock ever since I heard some creeper counting tombs. That shit echoes! I thought you were a fucking sorcerer." Mike Auburn stepped closer into her sight.

Jane recognized him on sight. After all, his video had been played as propaganda all the damn time. Six foot, broad-shouldered man with sandy brown hair and close-shaved beard. Mike's ghost still wore fingerless gloves, a red bandanna, and his best attempt at ghostly construction boots. Yet what struck her most was that his eyes were like hers—they had color. His were hazel brown.

"Mike?" Jane tossed her hands out in shock. "Mike Fucking Auburn!"

He pointed at himself and shrunk slightly as if he was in trouble. "Who the fuck do I owe and how much is it?"

Jane charged forward and stopped right in front of her older brother's chest, craning her neck to look up at him with spitfire in her eyes.

"Wait ..." He grabbed her shoulders. "Holy fuck, Jane? You ... you made it down here!" Mike's smile was as wide as a lottery winner. "Lucy said the others were looking for you. Did you get my coat? Tell me you got the coat?" He checked her over more. "Are you dead?"

Jane hugged him. He smelled just like his coat, and she didn't care for a second that he was dead as well, that he was enough of a blockhead to get lost, or that they were standing in a creepy lake ... probably below Hell at this point. She wasn't alone anymore.

"Sorry about that," Mike said as he squeezed tightly. "At least we know it's not the end, yeah?" He placed his cheek against the top of her head.

"What are we going to do now? What is this place?" Jane opened her eyes and leaned back slightly, looking at the dead hellhounds. "Did you?"

"Yeah, well." He scratched the back of his head and peeked down with one eye. "I ... kinda needed to find a way to be on even footing with the new crazy above. I picked up a lead here, but ... it was a dead end."

"What is that?" Jane flicked her gaze to the stone slab.

"That ... is a dead god," Mike sighed. "That's Balor. I think. But just like Lazarus, he's a hallowed form of whatever it was. Wanting only release." Mike's shoulders slumped. "Can't blame him, I suppose."

"Lazarus isn't dead, Mike. He came back and fucked things up even more."

The confusion on his face made Jane chuckle.

"The fuck he is. I killed that bastard myself."

"You mean you killed the guy known for reincarnating?" Jane raised an eyebrow at that.

"Yeah, I know, but I'm not kidding. I was hoping three-eyes here might have lent me some help for doing so but ... quiet as a mouse. Seriously, though, I killed Lazarus. Why? Is someone claiming to be him?"

Jane nodded her head. "Got a whole council of Death Lords and everything. Church of Lazarus stuff. Heh. I killed one."

"Well ... maybe things aren't so bad for us after all. And look at you go!" Mike offered a fist bump, but Jane crossed her arms.

"Bad for us? Have you ... seen here?"

"Leaving me hanging? Ouch. Right in the heart, Sis." He feigned injury. "But seriously, not so bad. All these power-fed creeps always miss the obvious. So it doesn't surprise me that nobody noticed. They are all pomp and circumstance and status." Mike curtsied. "Which means our job is easier than we thought. Because we don't have to kill Lazarus after all. We just need to kill an imposter."

"One problem with that. How do we get out?"

Mike took a deep breath and chewed on the thought for a minute, occasionally glancing at the blood flowing down the giant's slab. "Shenanigans."

Jane's smile grew and she offered out her fist. "I'm down with shenanigans. I've got a date with a cute guy."

Mike was overjoyed to fist bump. "Ooh, look at you. Where is he from?"

"Twin Cities."

"Oh, boy." Mike rolled his eyes. "At least tell me you died with a pack of smokes on you. This is going to be a story isn't it?"

ABOUT THE AUTHOR

Rick Heinz is the product of an amazing imagination and far too many hours playing Diablo. In addition to writing novels, he is also a leading contributor for the award-winning web magazine *Geek & Sundry* on both gaming and storytelling.

He is often a featured guest at pop culture events across the country for his work in teaching storytelling to kids through gaming and RPGs.

You can follow Rick on Twitter @CrankyBolt or go to www.-Seventh-Age.com to uncover more about the world of the Seventh Age.

facebook.com/CrankyBolt

OTHER TITLES FROM THE PRINCE
OF CATS LITERARY PRODUCTIONS

If you liked *Dystopia*, you might also enjoy:

Occult America:
Deathly Waters
Shoshana Edwards

MacGyver:
Meltdown
Eric Kelley & Lee Zlotoff

Or Even Eagle Flew
Harry Turtledove

White Fang Law:
This Case is Gonna Kill Me, Book 1
by Melinda M. Snodgrass

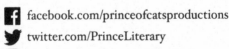

facebook.com/princeofcatsproductions
twitter.com/PrinceLiterary
instagram.com/princeofcatsbooks

Made in USA - North Chelmsford, MA
1300386_9781952825224
07.20.2022 1810